OUTLAW'S KISS

Mason twisted in the saddle, grabbed a handful of curls from the back of Amelia's head, and pulled her to him. He leaned forward, his intentions writ plain upon his face. He was going to kiss her.

She was too surprised to move. She ought to stop him, she knew. But the curiosity bubbling inside her made that nigh impossible. Excitement jolted through her and her whole body felt atremble, almost as though she were about to faint.

Dear heaven, she couldn't swoon now. She'd miss her first real kiss.

She had plenty of time to stop him—and none of the will required to do it. Slowly, he brought his mouth to hers. His lips touched hers, and then her mind went blank. His grip gentled in her hair, his hand spanning the back of her head as softly . . . so very softly . . . he touched his lips to hers. Her heart seemed to stop beating for an instant, stilled by the warmth of his mouth, the sensuous glide of his lips, the power of his arms cradling her.

Breathless, half-protesting, Amelia fluttered her hands. Her seeking fingertips caught and held his shirt, and though she knew she ought to push him away, instead she found herself winding the fabric round until it pulled taut against the warmth of the outlaw's chest beneath. Her knuckles skimmed the hard contours of his chest, sought and found the place where his heart beat wild and fast.

She closed her eyes, wanting to moan, wanting to cry out at the feelings that welled within her. So this was what it was to be desired, to be wanted, cherished . . .

* * *

Advance praise for Lisa Plumley's *Outlaw:*
"A delightful, totally pleasing romp through the Old West. A great read."

"OUTLAW is a true gem

BOOK YOUR PLACE ON OUR WEBSITE AND MAKE THE READING CONNECTION!

We've created a customized website just for our very special readers, where you can get the inside scoop on everything that's going on with Zebra, Pinnacle and Kensington books.

When you come online, you'll have the exciting opportunity to:

- View covers of upcoming books
- Read sample chapters
- Learn about our future publishing schedule (listed by publication month *and author*)
- Find out when your favorite authors will be visiting a city near you
- Search for and order backlist books from our online catalog
- Check out author bios and background information
- Send e-mail to your favorite authors
- Meet the Kensington staff online
- Join us in weekly chats with authors, readers and other guests
- Get writing guidelines
- AND MUCH MORE!

**Visit our website at
http://www.zebrabooks.com**

OUTLAW

Lisa Plumley

Zebra Books
Kensington Publishing Corp.
http://www.zebrabooks.com

To Mary and Larry Plumley,
with love and thanks for your encouragement,
and to John,
who captured my heart
and made everything more fun.

ZEBRA BOOKS are published by

Kensington Publishing Corp.
850 Third Avenue
New York, NY 10022

Zebra and the Z logo Reg. U.S. Pat. & TM Off.

First Printing: February, 1999
10 9 8 7 6 5 4 3 2 1

Printed in the United States of America

One

April, 1879
Near Gila Bend, Arizona Territory

"You say you're guaranteed to please?"

Amelia O'Malley blinked at her questioner as their stage-coach rolled deeper into the wilds of the Arizona Territory. He appeared harmless enough—an elderly gentleman passenger dressed in a gray-checked cutaway suit, tie, and small, rolled-brim hat. He was seated so closely across from her their knees nearly touched.

"P-pardon me?"

"Guaranteed to please, that's what you said," he repeated, raising an eyebrow. The grizzled, dusty-clothed miner reclining beside him shifted his attention to Amelia, too, his interest apparently caught by their conversation. She felt her face heat.

"Well, now," she began, loudly enough to be heard over the clattering stagecoach wheels and jingling harnesses, "I—"

He elbowed the miner. "How 'bout that, Horace? The lady's guar-ran-teed."

They both gazed at her with interested, narrow-eyed expressions. The gray-haired man licked his lips.

"The books, sir, are guaranteed," Amelia explained rapidly, smoothing her palm over the leather-bound volume in her lap. "As I said before. Every publication issued by J. G. O'Malley and Sons is beautifully printed on toned paper and illustrated with several engravings. This volume of p-poetry, for instance—"

"Don't need no poetry out here." The miner spat a wet brown stream of tobacco juice out the stagecoach window, and it was borne away by the hot, dusty wind. Although it was nearly sunset, the air felt only a few degrees cooler than it had at midday. "Now a guaranteed, sure-to-please woman, I could use me one of them."

The two men laughed, both of them fixing Amelia with a look that made her grateful for the presence of the two remaining stagecoach passengers. Why hadn't Jacob warned her there might be rude and dangerous men out West?

Simply deliver the books, he'd told her. *There's nothing to it—just a long stagecoach ride between Yuma and Tucson, then a few deliveries in town.* And Amelia, unable to say no and eager for the chance to prove to her father and brothers she really could help with the family business, had agreed.

For the sake of her mission, she fixed a polite, professional smile on her face, although the last thing she felt like doing was smiling.

"For as little as fifty-nine cents, any one of you can own the immortal words of Keats or Milton," she said, addressing the passengers as a group. It was hard to keep her voice from quavering. The men laughed harder.

Amelia frowned. She was only supposed to deliver the books that Jacob had taken orders for on his last turn through the Arizona Territory, but she couldn't resist trying to take new orders of her own. She imagined the surprise and pleasure on her father's face when she returned home to Michigan with a full order book, and redoubled her efforts.

"For a little more, you can indulge in a cloth and gilt bound volume of Mark Twain's stories and essays—"

"How much to *indulge* in a kiss?" asked the elderly passenger, leering. The miner guffawed, jabbing him in the ribs.

Amelia could scarcely believe this man, who was probably somebody's beloved grandfather, was asking such a question. Beneath his whiskers, his smirk revealed straight teeth and thin red lips. The lout puckered them, making kissing sounds.

"Oh!" She whisked the book from her lap and thrust it into her J. G. O'Malley & Sons satchel, then snapped the locks closed with quivering fingers. "Sir, my . . . I—I am *not* for sale!"

The stagecoach lurched, swaying from side to side and picking up speed. The motion echoed the sick feeling in Amelia's stomach as she contemplated a hundred more miles in the close company of men like these. She must have been insane to even have begun such a mission.

She might have expected as much, as a woman engaged in trade, traveling unaccompanied. But Amelia had hoped such things might be different in the West than they were back in the States—after all, in Wyoming Territory, women had been allowed to vote for ten years already. Surely, she'd hoped, Westerners would be more progressive.

The miner eyed Amelia's curled blond hair and fashionable pink polonaise dress. "All women's for sale," he said. "One way or t'other."

"I can assure you, sir, that I am not!"

Amelia cast a beseeching glance at the dark-clothed, bespectacled banker seated to her right. He stared stone-faced out the canvas-curtained opposite window, shutting out everyone, but he'd have to be deaf not to hear what was happening. Why didn't he speak up? Why didn't he act to protect her?

Her eyes met those of the banker's pale-eyed young wife, seated directly across from him. That lady offered a slight, fleeting smile of commiseration, then wedged herself further into the corner, completely crushing her traveling gown. Amelia was on her own.

The notion terrified her.

Perhaps she could go sit up front with the stagecoach driver, she thought suddenly. Surely a man like that would protect her?

"Come, now," said the elderly man suddenly. "There's no need for this book agent ruse, Miss O'Malley. We're all mature folk here."

He leaned forward, sending the overpowering scent of liberally applied Bay Rum hair tonic washing over her. Before she could guess what he intended, he snatched Amelia's bulging J. G. O'Malley & Sons rubber cloth satchel from beneath her seat.

"Only a lady of a *certain sort* is compelled to work for a living," he said, struggling to pry open the satchel's sturdy gold-colored lock. "I'll wager there's not a single book in here, other than the one cheap volume you showed us."

Amelia grabbed for her satchel. It, along with the second identical case tucked beneath her seat, represented more than a hundred dollars worth of book sales for her family's company. It also contained her order book and all of her traveling money. If she lost that satchel, she might as well never return home, her father would disown her for certain.

She missed. "Please, that satchel belongs to the J. G. O'Malley and Sons book company. You can't—"

"Yer playing us for fools," interrupted the miner, scowling at Amelia as he rummaged in his pockets for something. An instant later he pulled out a wicked-looking knife. The blade gleamed in a shaft of golden-orange light from the setting Arizona Territory sun as he tested its sharpness with his thumb.

Amelia moaned, fervently wishing herself safely back at the Briarwood Young Ladies' Seminary—where her father and brothers all believed her to be. Only Jacob knew her true whereabouts, and he was busy eloping with Melissa Chancellor, her closest friend from the seminary.

"Please, I'm only trying to do my job," she said, gripping the smooth russet leather seat beneath her with both hands to steady herself. Her palms squeaked across it, too damp to offer much purchase.

"I believe we know what line of enterprise you're in," said the elderly man, pausing in his struggles with the satchel long enough to leer at Amelia. His gaze dipped and centered itself on the lace-trimmed neckline of her new traveling gown. "Ain't that right, Horace?"

The miner's bushy eyebrows furrowed in concentration as he peered at the satchel's lock. Briefly he glanced at Amelia. She fought the urge to yank her perfectly respectable bodice higher.

"No, you're wr-wrong," she stammered. "I—"

With a savage thrust, the miner rammed the tip of his knife blade into the lock. Amelia jumped. What kind of men were these, to ravage her poor satchel so viciously? Wiggling his knife fiercely back and forth, the man worked at the lock.

Amelia stifled another moan. At least he hadn't meant to use that knife on her. Then, realizing they'd probably destroy the books if they managed to pick the lock open, she lunged for the satchel again. Her fingers brushed the black rubber cloth, caught hold of the handle . . .

The stagecoach heaved and came abruptly to a stop. Hatboxes, assorted baggage, and the banker's wife all fell to the floor. So did Amelia; she found herself inelegantly on her hands and knees, staring at the elderly man's shoes. Dust swirled, filling her nose with a dry, ticklish itch. She sneezed mightily— right on his laced-up brown oxfords.

Above her, the miner abandoned the lock and stuck his head out the stagecoach window. Taking advantage of the distraction, Amelia reached around his denim-clad leg and snatched her satchel from the elderly man's lap. Luckily, the mean old lecher was too engrossed in what was transpiring outside the window to notice. She got warily to her feet, hugging her bag tight against her chest.

The miner looked over his shoulder. "We're bein' robbed!"

he said, the wad of tobacco in his lip waggling with the words. He spat, then looked out the window again.

"Robbed!" The banker's wife clutched both pale hands to her bosom and gave a little moan of fear. Her husband glanced heavenward, his lips moving silently.

Amelia gasped, nearly dropping her satchel with shock. *Robbed?* Her heart racing, she lurched toward the other window. The canvas curtain slapped her nose. She leaned back just in time to miss another stinging blow. The canvas, unrolled from its mooring, flapped noisily in the breeze. She couldn't see a thing past it.

"Oh, for pity's sake," she muttered, shoving her satchel toward the banker. "Would you hold this please?"

Before the words had left her mouth, Amelia had rerolled the stiff black canvas. Her trembling fingers made fastening it considerably more difficult, but finally she managed it. She stuck her head out the window.

"What's happening?" wailed the banker's wife. "Can you see anything?"

Amelia's breath caught. Near the driver, just to the rear of the horses, stood a man dressed entirely in black. His rifle was aimed directly at the driver as he shouted something to him.

"Don't be tiresome," prodded the banker from the depths of the stagecoach. "Miss O'Malley, what do you see?"

She ducked her head toward her shoulder and spoke rapidly. "We are being robbed."

The banker's wife burst into tears. Amelia pulled her head back inside and wrapped her arms around the woman's bony, lace-enshrouded shoulders. "There, there," she murmured, giving her a little pat. "I'm sure everything will be fine. All any road agent wants is the strong box, and the driver's probably handing it down right now. Don't you worry a bit."

The woman wailed louder. "They'll k-k-kill us!" she cried,

sniffling. Her head bobbed wetly against Amelia's neck. "Ohhhh!"

"Shhh," Amelia soothed, patting harder. She glared at the banker, who still hadn't moved to comfort his wife. He clutched Amelia's satchel, looking terrified himself. Were there no good, brave men in the West?

"There's only one robber," she said to the woman, trying to sound comforting, "and he'll do no such thing, I'm sure of it."

She wished her stomach were sure of it, too; Amelia's insides somersaulted with fear, despite her brave words. If she were to die on a lonely Arizona Territory road, who would tell her family? They might wonder forever what had happened to her. Why, oh why, had she agreed to deliver Jacob's book orders?

The woman raised her red, puffy face to Amelia's. "H-how can you be so s-s-sure?"

Despite her tears, she looked a little calmer. For that, Amelia was glad. Being the person somebody turned to for help was a new, unexpected experience for her. It made her feel surprisingly brave herself. She drew in a deep, courage-enhancing breath.

"Because it's the poet bandit out there," she explained, dabbing at the young lady's watery eyes with the soft corner of her lace shawl. "Haven't you heard of him?"

Mutely, the banker's wife shook her head.

"Well, I have," Amelia rushed to assure her. "I've read all about the poet bandit in the periodicals—publishing is my business, remember?"

Delivering book orders for her father's company hardly constituted a future in publishing, but Amelia figured it couldn't hurt to embroider the truth a bit. It was for a good cause, after all.

"The poet bandit is strictly a gentleman. He won't hurt us, really he won't. He's never hurt anyone, in all his stagecoach robberies."

The banker snorted. Just beyond him, the miner dragged the elderly man up by his shirt and shoved him toward the window.

"Look, he's comin' this way!"

The banker's wife shrieked.

"Now you've done it," said the banker, waving his plump finger in Amelia's face as though she'd brought the whole thing on them herself.

"Save yourselves!" yelled the elderly man. Amelia watched in astonishment as he wrenched his gold pocket watch from its chain and flung it out the window. His billfold was next, followed by a pocketful of coins.

"Give him everything you've got!" he cried, whirling away from the window. Rushing forward, he plucked the dangling pearl earrings right from the ears of the banker's wife. Her screams of pain became one continuous, ear-splitting cry as he tossed them outside.

"It's our only hope!" said the banker, his gaze roving over Amelia—looking for valuables, she presumed. She clapped her hands over her earlobes, protecting her new gold, flower-shaped earrings.

"The poet bandit doesn't care about that!" she protested. "He only takes the contents of the strong box, not personal belongings. He—"

No one was listening to her. The banker's wife pulled a folded wad of money from her bodice and flung it toward the window, then, shaking, went to work removing her jewelry.

The banker gaped at the satchel on his lap. He leaned backward, eyeing it as though the bag were a rattlesnake ready to strike.

"I'm not dying to protect your books," he shouted, raising her satchel in both hands. Amelia rushed forward, too late, as he hurled it out of the coach with all his strength.

"Nooo!" She hung out the window set into the stagecoach door, her fingers biting hard into its frame, and watched in horror as her satchel thudded to the ground. Dust billowed around it, stirred by the impact. She clapped a hand over her mouth, hardly able to breathe. Everything was in that bag—her money, her order book, and most of the J. G. O'Malley & Sons books to be delivered. Without it, Amelia's chance to prove herself in her father's eyes was gone too.

"Yeah, I ain't dying for nobody," cried the miner from some-place behind her. An instant later, her second satchel followed the first, sailing past only a few inches from Amelia's head. Hearing it land on the ground outside the stagecoach was like hearing the door close on her future. Jacob would likely lose his job because of her, and now he had a wife, Amelia's best and closest friend, to support.

"Nooo!" Amelia screamed again, twisting the handle of the stagecoach door. The door swung open and she swung with it, her toes dangling above the ground. It was too high to jump; she'd probably break an ankle. Frantically, Amelia stretched backward.

The toes of her new high-laced balmoral shoes scraped the thin iron coach steps, then settled atop them. She scrambled down, mindless of modesty as her gown and petticoats billowed upward in the warm breeze. Her gaze fastened on her satchels. She could retrieve them both and be back inside the stagecoach within seconds, she knew it.

The stagecoach drove away almost before Amelia's feet touched the ground. Her heart, already racing, thundered in her chest. *They were leaving her!* Whirling around, she opened her mouth to yell for the driver to stop and choked on a huge mouth-ful of dust instead.

Sputtering and coughing, she ran after the stagecoach. It out-distanced her easily; the driver laid his whip on the horses like the devil was after him. Before long, the lash of the whip faded into the hillside, along with the racket of the coach wheels and the horses' hooves. She stopped, panting, in the middle of the rutted, narrow road. Her sturdy boned corset dug painfully into her ribs with every breath.

She was alone. Amelia hugged herself, looking around at the quickly darkening countryside. There was no sign of the poet bandit; evidently he'd vanished as quickly and noiselessly as he'd appeared. In fact, Amelia realized, there was no sign of civilization at all. Nothing. A wave of frustration washed over her. What had the driver been thinking, to just drive off and leave her like that, in such danger?

Obviously, he hadn't known she'd stepped out of the stagecoach. When the driver realized his mistake, surely he'd turn right around and come back to get her.

Wouldn't he?

Yes, Amelia told herself. Everything will be all right.

She made herself start walking back toward her J. G. O'Malley & Sons satchels. Every step sounded loud; every scrape of her shoes across the sandy soil wound her nerves tighter. What if the poet bandit was still out there? Humming quietly between her clenched teeth, she glanced over her shoulder, then kept walking.

It occurred to her that they might not be back to get her for a long time. A very long time. Amelia quit humming. Standing beside her satchels, she watched the last of the daylight fade as the sun sank beyond the jagged, tumbledown mountains in the distance. What was she going to do?

Meet the stagecoach partway, she decided. She had to try. First she scooped up the money and jewelry the other passengers had thrown onto the dusty road so she could return it to them later, then opened one of her satchels and dropped everything inside, feeling a little pang of righteousness despite herself. She'd been right—the poet bandit *hadn't* wanted anyone's money.

Unfortunately, that was small comfort now. Lifting a satchel in each hand, Amelia breathed deeply and set off. Even if she didn't catch up with the stagecoach right away, she was bound to run into a town or a stage stop a few miles down the road.

Anything was better than simply standing there, waiting for fate to take its course with her.

If she were back home, or even at Briarwood Young Ladies' Seminary, nothing like this would've ever happened to her, Amelia thought, staring out at the unfamiliar landscape as she trudged along. Nothing ever happened in Big Pike Lake, Michigan—especially to her. Her father and brothers simply wouldn't stand for it.

In Big Pike Lake, trees lined the streets—big maples and oaks, not the scrubby bushes that passed for trees in the West. And the streets were paved roads, not bumpy dirt trails that would almost certainly ruin her shoes before she caught up with the stagecoach. Amelia tightened her grip on the worn ivory handles of her satchels. Feeling sorry for herself wouldn't help anyone. Still, she couldn't help but wish—

A sound in the underbrush caught her attention. A wild animal? Or maybe an Indian? She'd read all about the dangers of the West in the dime novels sold by J. G. O'Malley & Sons. Was she about to come face-to-face with one of them herself?

Amelia steadied her pace, darting a quick glance toward the sound. She couldn't see anything there. Slowing, she turned her head toward it to take a closer look, and promptly walked into a hole in the road.

Her foot remained in the hole, but the rest of her just kept going. With a shriek, Amelia tried to break her fall with her hands; her satchels flew from her grasp and skidded away. She landed on her hands and knees in the dirt, her palms stinging.

Hoisting herself onto her backside, she raised her hands and gingerly brushed away a few sharp pebbles. It was too dark to tell how badly she'd scraped her palms in her fall, so Amelia turned her attention to her hurt ankle instead. Tears burned in her eyes, blurring her view, making her ankle look huge and wobbly. She didn't see how things could possibly get any worse.

"Come with me."

The words came from just behind her; Amelia jerked her head upward, her heart hammering. She could barely see the man standing there, because his clothes were so dark. She had a brief impression of masculine height, strength, and danger— and then she had no more time to look. He grabbed her arm with strong leather-gloved fingers and hauled her to her feet, nearly in one swift motion.

Two

Amelia's body collided with his. She shrieked, her pulse racing madly. It felt as though she couldn't possibly get enough air to keep breathing. A second later, her ankle refused to support her weight. It buckled beneath her, sending pain up through her calf. She clutched at the man for support—he was the poet bandit, he had to be; she was ninety-nine percent certain of that—and tried not to cry.

"My—my ankle's hurt," she whispered, forcing the words past her dry throat. Still clutching the sleeve of his dark duster coat, Amelia dared to look up at him. She saw only a shadowed face beneath his flat-brimmed black hat, and a brief flash of whisker-stubbled jaw before she ducked her head again.

Her belly flip-flopped with excitement. She was being rescued by the poet bandit! It was just like a dime novel she'd read once—*The Amazing True Adventures of Miss Beadle in the Villainous West*. She could hardly wait to tell Melissa and Jacob all about it.

"I—I don't think I can walk far," she admitted, feeling breathless.

Perhaps he'd carry her down the road to the next stage stop! The poet bandit was a gentleman, she knew that from reading the periodicals. Embellishing the scene, Amelia imagined herself being carried into town in the courageous poet bandit's arms, saw the astonished townspeople surrounding her. She'd be a heroine!

"Hell," the outlaw muttered.

The deep, rumbling sound of his voice sent a thrilling shiver through her. He smelled like sagebrush and tobacco and dark smoky leather, like a real man of the Wild West. This was undoubtedly the most exciting event of her life. He slipped his arm around her waist to hold her upright, then started walking.

When she got to Tucson, the townspeople would want to know all about her ordeal, of course. "How brave you've been!" they'd say. Why, she'd be the toast of the town for weeks, quite likely. Maybe they'd even write about her in the newspaper. Everyone would want to buy a J. G. O'Malley & Sons book!

This could only help her mission. She'd return home triumphant, and . . .

. . . And the poet bandit was not carrying her down the road in the direction the stagecoach had gone, Amelia realized. He was leading her off the road into the desert beyond.

She was being abducted, not rescued. Screaming for all she was worth and squirming against him, Amelia thought wildly that if she had one of her satchels, she could wallop him with it to make him let her go. And then what? a part of her prodded; she could barely walk. Besides, both her satchels were still on the ground beside the hole she'd tripped over. She yelled louder.

His free hand clamped over the lower half of her face. "Quiet," he commanded.

"Let me go," she tried to say, but all that emerged was "Mmmph." With his big gloved hand smothering her, it was impossible to speak. Panicked, she couldn't breathe either, until she remembered to close her mouth and breathe in through her nose. In, out, in, out; Amelia let herself be led across the uneven ground toward whatever destination he had in mind for her.

Behind an outcropping of rock some distance from the road

he finally lowered her onto a cold hunk of boulder. Her ankle forgotten, Amelia looked up at him.

He was definitely the poet bandit. Most certainly so. He was dressed all in black—at least she thought he was, it was too dark to be certain—and even his hat was dark. He must have removed the black bandanna he wore to hide his face, but with the exception of that one detail, he looked exactly like the artists' drawings she'd seen.

"Stay here," he said, then vanished into the darkness again.

Now that she'd glimpsed his true nature, the last thing Amelia meant to do was wait for him to come back. In the dark, without the security of the stagecoach and her fellow passengers nearby, the poet bandit was considerably less romantic than the periodicals had led her to believe. He was downright scary.

The poet bandit might be a gentleman, but he was still an outlaw. Whatever gentlemanly impulses she'd attributed to him had been proved wrong the instant he'd taken her from the road. Amelia wasn't sure what he meant to do with her, but she didn't intend to stay where he'd left her and find out.

Leaving her J. G. O'Malley & Sons satchels behind was surely better than whatever fate the outlaw had planned for her. Even her father would agree her life was worth more than the books and money they contained. She hoped.

Amelia pushed herself away from the boulder she was sitting on and stood up slowly. She listened; the only sounds were the chirping of insects and her own raspy, fear-filled breathing. What a fool she'd been to imagine an outlaw might rescue her!

Gathering her courage and putting as little weight on her hurt ankle as possible, Amelia headed for the nearest pile of boulders. All she had to do was get far enough away to hide.

Her progress was slow. Her ankle hurt too much to walk on it, so she hopped a few steps on her good leg, listened to make sure no one was coming, then hopped a little farther. Her breath came faster, sounding unnaturally loud in the stillness. It was harder than she'd have imagined to hop quietly.

Eventually Amelia made it behind the boulders she'd chosen. Her plan was to hide behind them until the poet bandit left, then go back to the road and wait for the stagecoach driver to return for her. Putting her palms against the cold stone face of the rock, Amelia crouched down and listened.

Her J. G. O'Malley & Sons satchels landed with twin thuds on the ground beside her.

"Comfortable?" asked a masculine voice.

She nearly jumped out of her skin. She didn't need to turn around to know who it was; the poet bandit's deep bass voice was familiar to her already. Besides, who else could it be? He'd found her easily. She hadn't even heard him approach. Amelia caught hold of a chunk of boulder for balance and straightened awkwardly. Her knees felt too wobbly to support her.

"How did you know I was here?"

His teeth were a flash of white in the moonlight. "You couldn't have gotten far."

Amelia's pulse leaped. Her whole body trembled. Hoping the outlaw couldn't tell, she tilted her head upward and looked him in the eye.

Her body shook harder, and dizziness swamped her, making her feel faint. Oh, please, Lord, I can't swoon now, Amelia silently begged. She then ducked her head again.

"I'd like to go back to the road, p-please. The coach will be returning for me at any minute."

"No, it won't." His tone was final. And chilling.

He reached out, caught hold of her wrist, and dragged her to him. Tucking one arm behind her knees, he lifted Amelia into his arms. She caught a whiff of tobacco, felt the strength of him as he hoisted her upward against his chest. It was like being held against a wall of solid stone—warm, solid, impassive stone. He grabbed her satchels, then started to walk. Useless as the effort probably was, Amelia wriggled in his arms, trying to free herself.

She succeeded. He dropped her onto the ground with bone-jarring quickness and stood over her, looking down.

"Don't fight me."

Amelia nodded, growing more frightened by the second. This wasn't the romantic bandit of her dime novels and periodicals. This was a flesh-and-blood man—a very big man—and he looked dangerous.

He pulled her up again, but this time he didn't carry her. He kept his arm around her waist and half-dragged her with him, carrying both her satchels in his other hand. Her hip bumped against his as they walked; her new dress dragged across his boots, blown by the wind, dangerously close to being trod upon. His arm tightened, nearly encircling her waist as he hauled Amelia over the rocky, uneven ground. She wondered if he could feel her trembling.

His hand rested warm against her ribs, his big gloved fingers curled intimately just beneath her bosom. The rough leather rubbed faintly against the bodice of her dress. Amelia tried to stand straighter. He won't hurt me, she told herself. He won't hurt me. It became a litany in her mind. She tried to remember everything she'd ever read about stagecoach robbers in general and the poet bandit in particular. It wasn't as reassuring as she'd hoped.

They hadn't gone very far before they came to his horse. The animal's reins were tethered to what looked like a scraggly bush, and its saddle, silhouetted by the rising moon, rose up some ways above Amelia's head. She took an automatic step backward.

Her captor's hand on the small of her back stopped her. His breath teased the nape of her neck. He gave her a little push forward. "Get on. I'll ride behind you."

He hefted one of her satchels and began lashing it to the

saddle, then the other. His action made his intentions all too plain—he meant to take Amelia with him. She couldn't begin to imagine why.

"Why?" she cried. "What are you going to do with me? You can have all my money"—the words came faster and faster, the more panicked she felt—"just leave me my books. I've got to get back to the—"

"Get on."

"Please! I—"

He stared down at her from his much greater height, making Amelia feel, for once in her life, petite and delicate. She was too afraid to savor the novelty. His mouth tightened, straight and unsmiling.

"I could put you on myself," he said. His expression told her she wouldn't enjoy the experience.

"No, no—see? I'm getting on right now," she babbled, scared nearly witless as the outlaw moved toward her.

With some help, Amelia managed to put one foot into the stirrup and pull herself upward. The bandit boosted her up from behind. Before she could protest, her bottom landed painfully in the saddle. Amelia clutched the pommel with both hands to keep from falling, her gown hiked humiliatingly to her knees. Her stockinged legs dangled gracelessly down both sides of the horse's hairy body.

It was just the opportunity she needed.

"Yah!" she shouted, pressing her legs against the horse to urge it toward the road—and safety. Instead the stupid animal sidestepped, ducked its massive head, and snorted. Frantic, Amelia screamed louder and slapped her hand down on the horse's neck. It didn't move.

An instant later, the poet bandit swung up, a solid, silent presence in the saddle behind her. His arms wrapped around hers, but before they could encircle her Amelia leaned down, groping for the reins. She felt herself slide lower, out of control and unbalanced by her haste to get away.

The outlaw caught her just before she toppled headlong into the underbrush. Then he pulled her back tight against him and set the horse into motion.

He said nothing. They rode at a pace that terrified Amelia, straight into a wind that had turned so cold tears streamed from her eyes. She was too scared to let go of the pommel and wipe them away. They passed swiftly between ever-thickening clumps of bushes, over rocky hills that threatened to send the horse skidding dangerously backward. Gradually she realized they were traveling upward, probably into the foothills.

She remembered watching the mountains from the stage-coach window, remembered watching from the road as the sun sank behind those scrub brush-covered slabs of granite. They weren't what she'd expected to find in the Arizona Territory, a place she'd imagined as nothing but sand dunes and cactus.

Neither was the poet bandit.

His arms felt tight around her, but his attention was all for the ride. His chin pressed close against her temple, the outlaw leaned forward in the saddle, guiding the horse across a moonlit path Amelia couldn't discern. Silently he pressed his muscular thighs into the horse's sides, turning their mount in a new direction.

The steady clomping of the horse's hooves quickened as they rode faster down the new path. Wind whistled past her ears, making them ring. Amelia clung to the pommel as the outlaw's stubble-covered jaw scraped across her skin, leaving a prickle of warmth behind. She wanted to ask him again where they were going, but she didn't dare.

She wasn't sure how much time had passed before they stopped. Amelia sat numbly atop the horse, her fingers seemingly frozen to the pommel, as the poet bandit dismounted. The saddle leather creaked, relieved of his weight as he jumped lightly to the ground and held up his arms for her. Amelia wasn't at all sure she could move. It felt twice as cold, sitting atop the horse alone.

A flicker of hope came to life inside her. Moving slowly, she unwrapped her stiff fingers from the pommel and leaned forward. All she had to do was grab the reins and—

"Get down here."

His hand closed around her forearm, yanking Amelia sideways. He'd guessed what she'd been thinking. Despair washed over her as the bandit hauled her from the saddle. Being rescued by the poet bandit would have been one thing—being abducted by him was something else entirely. How would she ever get away?

As soon as the toes of Amelia's balmorals touched the ground, the outlaw released her. Her legs refused to hold her. With a startled cry, Amelia reached out wildly, caught hold of her escort's sleeve, and righted herself. He didn't even sway. His face impassive, the outlaw worked to loosen the knot holding one of her satchels to the saddle. Straightening gingerly, Amelia looked around.

They were in a clearing, bordered on two sides by red-brown rock and shielded by more of the bushes she'd noticed earlier. Wind swept through their meager-leafed branches, tossing them in the moonlight. Behind her, the rest of the mountain rose in heaps of boulders, looking as though the whole thing might tumble straight down if she so much as sneezed. It was too dark to see much more.

She was standing in the outlaw's hideout, Amelia supposed. The place looked as desolate as she felt.

The rough-woven texture of the poet bandit's duster sleeve against her fingertips reminded Amelia she was still clutching a fistful of it. With dignity, she released him, then headed for the rock she'd seen. The outlaw let her go. Why wouldn't he? Amelia thought, sensing the sting of helpless tears behind her eyes. She couldn't get far in the dark, in the mountains, without a mount.

Her knees felt approximately as solid as marmalade as Amelia limped toward the sheltered space near the middle of the rocks. She sank to the sandy ground, glad not to be riding anymore and unmindful of the damage to the bustle of her dress. She was sure it was crushed beyond repair already. Across the clearing, the outlaw dropped one of her J. G. O'Malley & Sons satchels to the ground. It landed with a crackle atop the dried undergrowth. The horse shifted and snorted as the bandit went to work on the second bag.

She didn't know what to do. Why had he taken her with him? Amelia wanted to believe he was the gentleman bandit the newspapers portrayed him to be. She wanted to believe that when it was light enough to travel he'd take her to Tucson, where she could deliver her book orders as planned. Reality was the gun in his belt, the coldness she'd seen in his eyes, and the masculine strength that enabled him to do whatever he wanted with her.

She looked up. His back was to Amelia; she watched as he unsaddled the horse, his actions smooth and assured, then set the saddle and blanket aside next to her satchels. He ran his hands over the horse's neck, rubbed it down with the cloth he held, and checked its hooves for stones. His voice carried across the clearing as he talked to the animal, too low for Amelia to make out the words—and more soothing than her peace of mind allowed her to admit.

When he'd finished, he walked wordlessly toward Amelia's resting place with a bundle of branches and set about laying a fire. She heard him strike a match, smelled the acrid odor of phosphorus just before the fire crackled into life. A few feet away, the outlaw crouched low beside it, his face hidden by his hat. Then, in the light of the flames he looked up at her for the first time since dragging her from his horse.

His gaze dipped over her, taking in her hair, face, and new pink polonaise dress in turn. She had the uncomfortable feeling he was measuring her, but whatever his reaction, it was indecipherable from his expression. Amelia stiffened, pressing her back tighter against the chilly, jagged boulder behind her.

"P-people will be looking for me, you know," she blurted out, unable to stop herself.

The bandit nodded, slowly. He looked so unconcerned that she added, "They're probably looking for me right now."

He rose and walked nearer, stopping where the hem of her dress lay across the ground. His big boots very nearly touched the ruffled white lace edge. He was closer than she wanted, but with the boulder at her back Amelia couldn't move away. She twisted her hands in her lap. He towered over her, stealing her breath.

"I'm not going to hurt you," he said.

Goose bumps spread along her arms at the low, rumbling sound of his voice. She didn't feel reassured.

"Let me see your ankle."

Amelia yanked both feet back beneath her skirts and shook her head. His suggestion was scandalous. With another quick, menacing grin the outlaw knelt on the ground, closed both hands around her calf, and easily lifted her injured ankle onto his lap.

After the cold ride and the even colder ground she was sitting on, his body was shockingly warm. He'd removed his gloves, and his hands felt hot, callused, and strong. Amelia tried to pull her leg away, but he held fast. His hands slid over her dark cotton stockings down toward her ankle, probing gently.

"Tell me your name," he said.

Her pulse raced like a frightened rabbit's. His thumb found the hollow behind her ankle bone and stroked over it.

"Tell me your name."

She pressed her lips together. Since he didn't look up to see it, though, her gesture of defiance was wasted.

"Amelia O'Malley," she finally replied. Each syllable came out grudgingly, like slivers chipped from the icy boulder at her back. Without even a nod to indicate he'd heard her, he pressed his thumbs downward and continued his examination. Amelia had a fleeting, but extremely satisfying, image of herself kicking him in the chin. As though he'd somehow guessed her thoughts, the outlaw's fingers tightened.

She squealed. "Ouch! That hurts."

He released her ankle. "I don't think it's broken."

He sounded oddly hoarse. Amelia said nothing as she whipped her foot beneath her skirt again with lightning speed. Truly, a broken ankle would be the least of her troubles right now.

She expected him to move away, but the outlaw remained exactly where he was, silhouetted by the campfire behind him.

"You made it worse trying to run from me."

He pinned her with a look that said exactly how stupid he thought running away from him was.

"I was hardly running. I had to hop most of the way."

He turned his head, almost as though he were hiding a smile. Impossible, Amelia decided.

"I need to go back to the road," she felt brave enough to say. "I have urgent business to attend to."

The outlaw quirked an eyebrow. She thought of her father learning the Arizona Territory book orders had never been de-livered—and who was at fault. Her.

"You must take me back!"

She'd already failed at the usual feminine pursuits. Amelia had honored her family with neither marriage nor children, and likely never would. If she failed at this mission, too, her father's low opinion of her would be confirmed. She *needed* to deliver those books. She pushed out her lower lip and glared at the man standing in her way, her fear of him momentarily forgotten.

The outlaw shook his head. "You're in no position to give orders, lady."

His tone chilled her. Maddeningly, he stood without another word and went to the fire. He took something from his shirt pocket and turned it in his hands, but it was too dark for Amelia to see what it was.

The silence lengthened. Amelia's temporary bravado fled. Every bird beating its wings above the spindly-branched bushes, every rustle beyond the bright circle of the campfire made her jump. She'd gone too far. She guessed the outlaw was deciding what to do with her, and the thought made her shiver.

He lifted a burning twig from the fire. Amelia watched the glowing tip of it move closer to the bandit's face, burnishing his features with firelight. For a handsome man—and he undoubtedly was that, she realized—he still seemed every inch the outlaw.

The twig burned low, and the outlaw tossed it back into the fire in an arc of reddish light. The smoky scent of tobacco reached her, borne on a breath of cold wind. It had been so warm until sunset.

She lifted her head and called out to him. "If you take me back, I won't tell a soul who you are," Amelia promised.

The outlaw gazed at her, his expression inscrutable. "You don't know who I am."

Amelia hugged her knees to her chest, her conviction wavering. Some road agents were known to be ruthless killers—was he one of them, or was he the gentlemanly poet bandit after all?

He hardly appeared a gentleman now. The firelight glinted off the gun he wore at his hip, and the shadows turned his profile hard and uncompromising. There was no way around it. She'd been a fool to step off that stagecoach, and now she was paying the price.

"Here."

Just as she glanced up, the outlaw lifted his arm and something sailed through the air in her direction. She cupped her hands to catch it and was rewarded with what looked like two pieces of flat tree bark.

"There's water in the canteen," he offered. With a motion of his boot-clad foot, he indicated a round, leather-strapped container on the ground beside the fire.

Amelia looked at the canteen, then at what he'd given her. It had the texture of old cracked shoe leather. She took a hesitant sniff. Dried salted beef. She had read about it in *Tales of a Mountain Man in the West,* but she'd certainly never thought to find herself presented with some.

"Thank you," she called out. The bandit tossed his cigarette into the flames and began to eat. Emboldened by his example, she licked at one of her pieces. It tasted of salt and gamey meat.

"You'd be warmer by the fire."

Her spirits rose. His concern was heartening. A ruthless desperado wouldn't have cared if she froze to death, Amelia told herself. Perhaps her companion only looked mean, for the sake of his reputation. She got to her feet, still clutching the beef strips in one hand, and half-limped toward the fire.

It was blessedly warm, at least on the side of her that faced it. The flames crackled, sending an occasional spark popping into the sky. She managed to bite off a piece of the beef, but it was devilishly hard to chew. She glanced over at him.

He was watching her. Amelia looked away, chewing madly, trying to keep splinters of the tough meat from poking out of the corners of her mouth. She swallowed, then glanced at him again.

At some point, he'd taken off his hat. The outlaw seemed different without it; a shade less frightening, maybe. His hair looked dark and untidy, his face clean-shaven except for a faint shadow of beard. His eyes, dark like his collar-length hair, glittered at her across the campfire.

Amelia gasped and quickly recalled her earlier estimation:

his expression looked ominous as ever. Wordlessly, he picked up the canteen and handed it to her, then walked away, pulling a whiskey flask from his coat pocket as he went.

The canteen smelled of horse. Amelia was just thirsty enough not to care. She wrinkled her nose, unscrewed the cap, and took a sip. It tasted warm, but good. After a furtive glance to make sure she wasn't being watched, she tipped back her head and gulped some more.

A few minutes later he reached over her head to take back the canteen. Surprised at his unexpected reappearance, she choked on a mouthful of warm water; it dribbled in a most unladylike fashion down her chin and soaked into the bodice of her dress.

"I didn't hear you come back," Amelia managed to croak, swiping a hand at her mouth. Her eyes darted to the stoppered whiskey flask in his hand. She couldn't tell if he'd drunk any of it.

"Obviously."

The outlaw's gaze fastened on the place where her sodden pink bodice clung tight to her skin. She couldn't decipher his expression, but it made a blush warm her cheeks all the same.

Chagrined, Amelia looked away and plucked ineffectually at her clothes. The water seeped beneath the fabric to wet her chemise as well. She couldn't believe she'd blushed at his gaze. She was all of twenty-one years old and a spinster; surely she had no cause to simper and blush at a man's scrutiny.

His eyes met hers. "There's no fresh water nearby," he explained in a voice suddenly turned huskier than before. "That's all there is."

"Oh." She nodded. "Oh, I'm sorry." Her head bobbled like a marionette. Amelia made herself stop and looked up at the night sky instead, pretending great interest in the stars.

He put his hand on her arm and turned her around. She had to look up to see his face. Something in the outlaw's eyes, some gentling of his expression, drew her closer. She waited breath-lessly for him to speak.

"I can't take you back," he said.

She could only stare at him for a second, absorbing his words. He wasn't taking her back? "I . . . I'm sure if you just take me back to the road, then—"

"No. I've lost too much time already."

"Well, you could leave me here, and I'll—"

"And you'll do what?" he interrupted meanly. "Why the hell do you think I went back for you in the first place, lady?"

He glared down at her, bigger, taller, stronger than she was. The firelight shadowed his face, making him seem twice as menacing as before.

"I don't know," Amelia whispered. Judging by the look on his face, whatever the reason, it was fearsome. He turned away, and she followed him toward the lone mesquite tree where the horse was tethered, stumbling over the rocks and clumps of cactus. Dear heaven, in terrain like this, a person could step on an innocent-looking pile of rocks and wind up skidding halfway down the mountainside in no time!

By the time she reached him again, Amelia was breathing hard. The outlaw, obviously finished with their discussion, set aside one of her J. G. O'Malley & Sons satchels and picked up his bedroll.

"I've only got one blanket. We'll have to share it."

"No!" Things were going from bad to worse.

"We're riding out at sunrise tomorrow, and we both need some sleep first."

"I can't go with you! I—I can't sleep with you! It wouldn't be right. Please, I—"

"Suit yourself," he replied, not looking at her as he headed back toward the fire.

Amelia would have sworn the temperature dropped at least ten degrees at that moment. The wind swished through the mesquite branches and raised goose bumps on her arms. The horse nickered behind her. The crackling warmth of the fire reached brightly into the air. Beyond it, the poet bandit spread a blanket on the ground, apparently engrossed in the task at hand.

He left her with no other choice. It was, Amelia decided, the perfect opportunity to make her escape.

Three

Still wearing his boots and doing his best to ignore the woman, who was busy muttering to herself across the campsite, Mason Kincaid stretched out on the old striped woolen blanket that had been his bed for the past month. It was worn thin in spots and smelled vaguely like horse sweat, but a cushion of cleared sand beneath made it comfortable enough. A wanted man could hardly complain about these conditions.

Mason reached his arms overhead and folded them beneath his neck, waiting for the muscles in his back and shoulders to unknot themselves. Above him the night sky stretched wide, veiled in clouds that hid the moon. When he breathed, the spring-cold air held no hint of rain, though, and Mason was glad.

Dry weather would make it that much easier to track down the Sharpe brothers in the morning. If he made an early start, he might even catch up with the lazy sons of bitches while they were still snoring in their bedrolls at one of the stage stops nearby.

Catch up with them and reclaim all they'd stolen from him.

He might have had them already if not for Amelia O'Malley. Hell! Mason didn't know what had possessed him to double back and pick her up by the side of the road. He'd been a half-mile away when he'd heard her screaming after that stagecoach driver like a scalded cat. He'd gone back for her without thinking, knowing the driver wouldn't return. Knowing she couldn't survive alone.

He wondered why she'd gotten out of the stagecoach in the first place. Maybe she was touched in the head. Maybe all those fussy blond curls in her hair were wound too tight; they'd addled her brains. Whatever the reason, he was stuck with her, at least for a while.

She was pretty enough, if a man liked his women all decked out in geegaws like a fancy cake. Mason didn't. And for a little woman, she'd looked plump as a stuffed sofa in that ruffly pink dress she had on. He'd wager Amelia O'Malley had more than bustle to thank for a backside like hers. No, she wasn't the kind of woman he liked at all, he told himself.

And if he'd noticed the way the spilled canteen water made her dress cling a little tighter on top, if he was wondering what she'd look like with her prissy-looking blond hair undone, well . . . He was a man. A man noticing a woman like that was only natural.

Mason pulled the blanket higher and rolled over, willing himself to sleep. He needed it, wanted it . . . and knew just as plainly that tonight he wasn't going to get it. Again. He might as well pack up and head after the Sharpes, he decided; make up for the time he'd lost going after Amelia O'Malley. Even better, he'd pack her up and take her down to Gila Bend before she started screaming again. If he wasn't going to sleep he'd have plenty of time to do it.

He sat up, raked his fingers through his hair, and looked toward the stand of creosote bushes where she'd been pouting over sharing the blanket. Then he looked near the rocks, the horse, and beside the fire. She was gone.

Awww, hell. Mason grabbed his hat and went to look for Miss Fancy Pants.

Her trail wasn't hard to spot. Only a loco bear crashing through the creosote, paloverde trees, and clumps of burr sage would've left a clearer sign. Except a loco bear didn't wear fancy pink dresses. A few yards from the campsite, Mason plucked a wisp of white lace from a stand of cholla and rubbed the fabric between his fingertips. It was soft, soft like a lady's skin . . . soft like Ellen used to be, in his memories.

Frowning, he ducked beneath a branch and went on. He didn't want to think about Ellen, about home, about his life . . . before. The damned Sharpe brothers had made sure none of it would be left to return to.

Amelia O'Malley's trail ended at the top of a boulder-strewn ridge. Mason paused beside a one-armed saguaro, peering into the darkness. Below him, the ridge sloped into a pitch-dark valley; the undergrowth was crushed, leading downward, but he doubted Miss Amelia would've taken that way—at least not intentionally.

To his left, a copse of mesquites leaned, whistling in the wind. On his right, the rocky face of the mountain rose up, boulder piled upon boulder. It wasn't as solid as it looked, Mason knew; irregular caves and sheltering overhangs dotted the mountainside. Miss Hoity-Toity could be hiding in any one of them.

The woman brought nothing but trouble. It would serve her right if he just left her out there—in one of those caves or down in the valley below. Mason sighed and gauged the slope of the ridge again. If she'd fallen down there, it wouldn't do a damn bit of good for him to go after her.

Unless she'd gotten stuck halfway down.

Unless she was hurt at the bottom.

Hell. Shaking his head at what he was about to do, Mason headed for the ridge, turned his back to the night sky, and started to climb down. He'd only climbed a few steps before he realized it was a lot steeper than it looked. No sooner had the realization come to him than a root gave way beneath his foot, sending him skidding down the ridge on his knees.

Mason grabbed with both hands. He'd be damned if he'd

break his own neck chasing after a blasted fancy woman with more curly hair than sense. His fingernails scraped the dirt, seeking purchase. Nothing to catch hold of. Grunting, he landed on his belly and slid another few feet before his fingers touched something solid.

Another root. Great. Mason decided to take his chances, and grabbed it. This one held.

Spitting dirt and pebbles, he inched his way to a more stable position. He glanced over his shoulder at the valley below, wishing he'd brought a rope. Who would've thought little Miss Corkscrew Curls would get so far?

" 'Aaaaamazing Grace, how sweeeeeeet the sound . . .' "

The melody floated across the ridge, echoing faintly in the mountains beyond. A hymn? He was hearing things. Mason cocked his head and listened again.

" 'A wretch like meeeee . . .' "

Amelia O'Malley. It had to be. What other woman would be loony enough to sing hymns—even quiet, quavery ones—on the middle of a mountainside? The sound grew tear-choked and mournful, like a cat wailing after its mate. A sick cat. Mason gritted his teeth and climbed in the direction of the wail. It was his first stroke of luck all day.

Running away from the poet bandit was a mistake. Amelia O'Malley was plumb certain of that now. She'd thought she could find the trail they'd followed and go back to the road by herself, then catch the next passing stage. It hadn't seemed all that complicated when the outlaw guided the horse up the mountainside. Instead she'd gotten herself lost.

Amelia rested her chin on her upraised knees and sighed. Perhaps the animal had a better sense of direction than she did. In any case, she wasn't moving another inch until daybreak. Maybe then she'd be able to spot the trail.

At least she'd managed to salvage both of her J. G. O'Malley

& Sons satchels. She could still deliver the book orders to Tucson, and maybe even gather a few new ones. She'd make her father proud of her if it took her last breath to accomplish it.

But that was in the future. Now, wedged securely in her hiding place between two cold, filthy boulders, Amelia thought longingly of hot chocolate, a steaming bath, and a bed with fluffy blankets and feather pillows. Instead she'd made a meal of stringy dried beef and a bed out of sticky, jabbing mesquite branches.

Even the foliage was dangerous in the Arizona Territory.

She was sure her poor derriere must be perforated by now—the things had tiny thorns that poked right through her new pink dress. It was ruined for certain, ruined after only one wearing. She didn't even want to consider the condition of her balmorals, after scrabbling for the past half-hour amongst the rocks and cacti that made up the mountainside.

Even so, sitting atop mesquite branches was better than just plopping onto the bare ground. Amelia shuddered to think what kinds of *things* lived and crawled and slithered in the dark. Every once in a while, she heard a telltale scuttling—the movements of a desert mouse, perhaps, or a snake. Dear Lord, maybe even a coyote.

Maybe all three.

Scooting deeper into the crevice she'd found, Amelia sucked in a big breath and began singing again. As long as she was singing, she couldn't hear the mysterious screeches and cries amongst the peculiar stringy-leafed trees just beyond her hiding place. As long as she was singing, Amelia felt a little less lonely. And there was no situation that a good song couldn't improve—at least that's what Miss Fitzsimmons always told the Briarwood ladies. At the moment, Amelia was just desperate enough to try it.

Hugging herself for warmth, she took up her song again.

" 'I ooooonce was lost,' " she warbled softly, " 'but now am found . . .' "

"Got that right," growled a masculine voice from somewhere above her. A big hand shot down between the boulders and clamped onto her shoulder. Amelia screamed.

And kept on screaming.

The hand's owner pulled hard. *Another outlaw?* The mountain must be a blessed den of thieves, she thought crazily. She wriggled backward, then slapped both hands on the boulders beside her for balance. Ughh, they were dusty . . . and then, slimy. With an involuntary grimace, she whisked her hands away. He pulled her the rest of the way out of the crevice.

Amelia screamed louder, flailing her arms in a wild attempt to escape. He pinned them to her sides and dragged her back against him, then covered her mouth with his palm. It tasted gritty with dirt, and smelled of tobacco. At her back, his chest felt every bit as solid as the boulders had; so did the bunched-up muscles in his upper arms as he tightened his hold on her.

"Quit your caterwauling. You'll have every lawman within fifty miles on us."

The poet bandit. She'd have recognized his low-pitched, grouchy voice anyplace. Amelia stilled, trying not to sag with defeat. He'd found her—again. And found her easily, too.

A powerful wave of homesickness washed over her. Why was this happening to her, of all people? Despite her yearnings for adventure, now that she was faced with it, Amelia found herself less like the brave heroine of one of her dime novels and more like a person who belonged safe at home, in the quiet brick house she shared with her family when she wasn't at Briarwood.

Amelia just wanted to go home. She wanted to go back to Big Pike Lake, Michigan—back to civilization. Even her four older brothers' incessant watching over her, their teasing and their insistence on driving her places in their dashing spider phaeton carriages seemed wonderfully homey, now that she was without them, and . . . and what was that the poet bandit had said?

She tugged at his hand. Amazingly, he took it away from her mouth.

"Lawman?" Amelia croaked. "Did you say lawman?" She turned to face him, her gaze taking in the poet bandit's powerful physique, his unsmiling, rugged face, and the gun strapped to his hip. "Are they after you right now?"

Don't be daft, she told herself, of course the law is after him. A person only has to look at him to know he's dangerous. He'd abducted her, for heaven's sakes.

His mouth turned up at the corners in an expression somewhere between a smile and a sneer. "I'm a wanted man," he said simply. "That's why we've got to keep moving."

Amelia stepped backward. "Well, I—I knew that," she warbled, fear and nervousness combining to loosen her tongue. "I just thought they'd given up on catching you, that's all, with you being so famous for your poetry and such. You have to admit, that kind of thing does sell newspapers."

This last was her brother Denton's oft-expressed opinion, but Amelia felt justified in claiming it, under the circumstances.

The bandit gave her a funny look.

"Haven't I mentioned it?" she asked. "I thought for certain I had. Oh, well." Amelia drew a deep breath and then chattered on about how she'd recognized him back at the stagecoach.

"I've read all about you in the periodicals," she added helpfully, thinking it couldn't possibly hurt to butter him up a little. She'd never met a man who didn't appreciate a kind word about his work. Amelia raised her hands as though spanning the width of a newspaper headline. "The famous poet bandit."

He scowled. Amelia's hopes for kinder treatment fled, replaced with a fresh shiver of fear. What could have happened to turn him into a desperado like the poet bandit, anyway?

"I'm not who you think I am," he said, giving her a dark, wholly incomprehensible smile.

It had the disturbing effect of making her insides feel like warm, melted jelly, something Amelia had never in a million years expected to experience in the company of a desperado. To be fair, she had to admit he was a fine-looking man, if a little unschooled in the social graces. A *lady* bandit would probably find him downright irresistible.

He wrapped his fingers around her wrist. "We're going back to camp," he announced. Then he proceeded to pull her, stumbling with weariness and befuddlement and the effort of juggling her satchels, along behind him.

"You must be the poet bandit," she insisted, feeling vaguely combative and too exhausted to care if she angered him. What else could the outlaw do to her? He'd made it all too clear that escaping him was nearly impossible. What was the harm in finding out a little more about her captor?

"I'm *certain* you're the poet bandit."

He trudged on, ignoring her.

She cleared her throat and asked, a little more loudly, "Who are you, then?"

He stopped, causing Amelia to bump smack into his black canvas duster coat. She stepped backward and tried to raise her hand to rub her nose, but his strong, warm fingers held her fast. The outlaw faced her, holding Amelia's wrist between their bodies where the chill night air couldn't penetrate.

His eyes met hers. "It's better if you don't know," he said.

His deep, rumbling voice wound its way inside her, raising goose bumps along her arms. Why was he being so mysterious? They trekked a little farther, leaving Amelia to mull it over. Of course he couldn't just come right out and admit to being a famous outlaw; he hadn't evaded capture this long by telling folks who he really was.

Deciding it would be wise to play along with him if that was what he wanted, Amelia addressed her next question to his broad back. "What shall I call you, then?"

She waited. Typically, he remained silent. His shoulders were vague outlines in the scattered moonlight, as he marched tirelessly ahead. She hoped he knew where they were going, because she was well and truly lost now.

"Mr. Bandit?" she proposed. "The Black Bandit? Outlaw—?"

"Don't you ever shut up?"

Amelia stopped talking. She decided he was probably lost, too, and didn't want to admit it. It felt as though they'd been walking through the stunted trees and bushes, over the rocky, ankle-twisting ground, for hours. He showed no signs of slowing down, either.

"Er, Mr. . . . Bandit?" Amelia panted. They'd traveled, by her best reckoning, at least two miles. "Could we stop for a minute, please?"

He scowled over his shoulder at her. In the faint moonlight she saw that his jaw and cheeks were smudged black with dirt. "No."

"But my ankle hurts. Remember? From the hole in the road?"

He trudged on. A little ways from that surprising ridge Amelia had slid down on her way to her crevice, he suddenly stopped. His offhanded wave toward a pile of boulders was the closest he was likely to come to issuing an invitation to rest.

"Thank you." She plopped onto them, her dignity mostly gone, and gingerly pressed her ankle with her fingertip. It felt swollen. It looked fat, sticking up out of the top of her dusty shoe. Amelia sighed and pulled her skirt over her shoe tips. If the other ladies at Briarwood could see her now, they'd laugh their heads off. They always teased her about her plump ankles, and now her ankle was twice as big as usual.

Beside her, her no-name abductor glared at the ridge. She couldn't see what the old hunk of rocks could've done to bother him so much. Doing her best to ignore him, Amelia sniffled and sang, very quietly, " 'Aaamazing Grace, how sweet the sound . . .' "

"Do you have to make noise all the time?"

His growled inquiry, along with the murderous look in his eyes, stopped her instantly. Amelia snapped her mouth closed. He was just like her brothers; they always complained about her singing, too.

The outlaw bent, scooped something shiny from the ground, and pocketed it before she could see what it was. At the moment, she was too indignant to care.

"I like to sing," Amelia said. "It makes me feel better."

"It makes me feel like gagging you."

"Humph."

"You haven't quit talking, singing, or humming since I found you. Come on," he said, reaching for her wrist and hauling Amelia to her feet, "if you've got punch enough to sing, you can walk the rest of the way to camp."

It didn't take much longer to get there. After another few minutes of walking, they reached the clearing. Near the rocks, the bandit's horse nickered a welcome. In the center, the campfire smoldered; the poet bandit released her, then ambled over to tend it. Amelia hobbled to the blanket and sank onto it.

Ahhh, it was blissful to rest her ankle. She lay back, rolled herself in the tattered, horsey-smelling blanket, and felt grateful for its meager warmth after the time she'd spent in that chilly crevice and then hiking through the woods. Craning her neck, Amelia watched the bandit coax the fire higher.

Her eyes drifted closed. Above her, the wind whispered through the trees and an owl hooted, but Amelia felt surprisingly snug—and much too safe for her own peace of mind—now that the bandit was nearby. Why should that be? It was ridiculous to feel safe around an outlaw, she thought as she drifted asleep.

* * *

Sometime later, something hard nudged her ribs. She muttered and squirmed away from it. It nudged her again, then something tickled her ear. Amelia swatted it away, but it came back. She was about to open her eyes to investigate when a masculine voice whispered in her ear, "Rise and shine, Curly Girl."

The poet bandit. Amelia cracked open her eyes to see him crouched beside her; his black twill pants legs wavered in the breeze just a few inches from her nose, giving her an up-close and personal view of his legs. She turned her head a little, bringing his hard-muscled thighs into view. There his pants stretched tight, with creases leading up to . . . his gun belt.

Feeling her cheeks redden, Amelia pushed herself up on her elbows. He smirked at her.

"Mornin'."

She looked around, breathing deeply of the brisk, dew-damp desert air. "It's not morning," she told him, yawning. "It's still half-dark out."

Amelia closed her eyes and flopped onto the blanket again. Rudely, the bandit wrenched her upward, using her elbow for leverage.

"Ouch!" She rubbed her elbow, glaring at him from beneath her limp curled bangs. The man obviously had no notion of proper behavior—his was barbaric.

"It's morning enough for me," the outlaw told her. "We're heading out."

At his words, Amelia peered around the camp. He was serious. He'd already snuffed out the fire, packed up everything but the bedroll, and saddled the horse.

"Don't you ever sleep?" she blurted out.

His eyes darkened. "Are you getting up, or do I have to take you out of there myself and sling you over my horse again?"

She rolled out of the blanket and hastily kicked it toward

him. "Here's your stupid blanket," she muttered as she got up. "I'm coming."

Amelia swabbed her tongue around in her mouth, wishing for a toothbrush. Hers, still packed inside her baggage aboard the stagecoach, had probably made it all the way to Maricopa Wells by now. Briefly, she considered asking to borrow the bandit's toothbrush—his breath was nice and clean, she'd noticed while he'd loomed over her—then decided against it. He'd probably make her crawl over to get it out of his pack, or something equally mean.

"Here."

He lofted the canteen toward her. She caught it between her arms and stomach with an unladylike grunt and stalked into a stand of nearby bushes where she could have some privacy. Through their screen of branches studded with tiny yellow flowers, Amelia was surprised to notice the outlaw was invisible to her. She hoped she was equally hidden from his view.

Unfortunately, she couldn't dismiss his voice as easily.

"Hurry up," he called after her.

Amelia's throat tightened. She blinked rapidly, hardly able to see as she unscrewed the canteen's cap so she'd have water to wash her face with.

What did you expect, she chided herself, *breakfast in bed?* She was a captive, with no say at all in how her abductor treated her. She was lucky he hadn't ravished her while she slept—or abandoned her, which somehow frightened her even more.

Feeling grumpy, Amelia crouched down, tipping the canteen toward her open palm. An instant before the water sloshed from the canteen, she recalled the bandit's words. *There's no fresh water nearby. That's all there is.*

Her lips tightened. She was in the West now, Amelia decided. She'd just have to learn to adapt to Western ways. Instead of splashing her face with a whole handful of water, she wet her petticoat hem—her underclothes, at least, were still somewhat clean—and scrubbed her face with it. Then she swished some water in her mouth, attended to her personal needs, hastily repinned her hair, and marched into the clearing again.

"Took you long enough," the outlaw remarked.

Amelia heaved the canteen at him. It landed a good yard away from his boot-clad feet, sending up a little puff of reddish dust.

He scooped up the canteen. When he straightened, amazingly, he was smiling at her. "You always so pert in the morning?"

Dear Lord in heaven, he was one of those people who awakened cheerfully.

"If I'm so much trouble, Mr. . . . Mr. Whatever-your-name-is," Amelia replied, hands on her hips, "why don't you just take me back where you found me?"

Something in his expression softened. His brown eyes met hers. For an instant, she thought she saw compassion there. Just as quickly, it was replaced with a look of plain determination.

"I've got no time to take you back. I've got somebody to meet, and a lot's depending on it."

It was a veritable speech coming from him. He turned his back to her and headed for the other side of the clearing, returning a moment later leading the horse.

Amelia sighed and gave up. She could tell when she was licked; her father got that same look on his face every time she asked him to let her join J. G. O'Malley & Sons. A man, having chosen a path, would rather die than change his mind, however unreasonable it made him seem. If the outlaw wouldn't take her back, she'd just have to bide her time and hope for another, better opportunity to escape.

The outlaw mounted, then helped her up into the saddle.

"You could at least tell me your name," Amelia muttered as she settled in behind him. Tentatively, she wrapped her arms around his waist.

They sat that way for a moment, the horse shifting and blowing beneath them, anxious to be off. Still the outlaw made no move to spur the animal forward. What was the matter? She stared at the thick brown hair waving beneath his hat brim, wishing it was his face that greeted her, instead of the back of his head. At least then she might have had a chance at guessing his thoughts.

Finally he glanced over his shoulder at her. This close, Amelia could see the faint shadow of his beard and the twitch of a tiny muscle in his jaw.

"My name is Mason," he said. "You can call me Mason." Then he set the horse in motion.

Four

Mason didn't know what had possessed him to tell Miss Twirly Curls his real name. All her infernal singing and chattering must have done something to his brain. He eased slightly in the saddle, the leather creaking beneath his thighs, and sneaked a look at her.

She smiled. Smugly. I knew you'd tell me, her expression said.

Well, hell. Mason turned around, half his brain feeling bamboozled by feminine wiles and the other half struggling to think about something besides how good it felt to be held by a woman—any woman—again. As they rode east toward the foothills, he tried to concentrate on the trail ahead of them, instead of on the rhythmic bouncing of her breasts against his back. It was damn near impossible. He sighed.

Her arms tightened around his waist. "My full name is Amelia Josephine O'Malley," she said, sounding magnanimous, "but you can call me Amelia."

"The hell I will."

"What?"

Mason guided the horse slowly down the craggy trail. The poor animal would be useless for anything but a long, clover-munching rest in a field after this, thanks to the extra weight it was carrying. They'd have to stop someplace and find another mount, else he'd never catch up with the damned Sharpe brothers.

Squinting against an orange shaft of light from the rising sun, Mason tried to ignore the tapping of Amelia Josephine O'Malley's foot against his calf.

"Why can't you call me Amelia?" she asked again.

"Doesn't suit you," he said.

She stiffened behind him, wary but curious. "Why not?"

"Haven't given it much thought."

"Well, what would suit me, then?"

She wiggled in the saddle, trying to peer at his face. The movement made her breasts jounce double-time against his back. Mason tried to think about something else—like why he was grateful for his saddle's low cantle, which kept Miss Fancy Pants from getting any closer to him on the bottom than she already was on top.

She tossed her head, and the flowery smell of whatever she used on her hair filled his nostrils. Mason breathed deeply.

"Chatterbox," he suggested, frowning as he slid closer to the pommel. It didn't help, because she moved forward right along with him. He wondered if Miss Amelia feared he'd drop her into the sagebrush if she didn't maintain a death grip on him all the time.

The idea had a certain appeal. It would undoubtedly make tracking the Sharpe brothers easier if he didn't have a woman along for the ride. She'd delayed him too long already. The last thing he wanted was someone who needed taking care of.

She made a disgruntled sound. "Chatterbox? That's hardly charitable, Mr. Mason."

"Just Mason. And outlaws aren't supposed to be charitable."

She was silent for a moment. "You don't seem like an outlaw in the daytime," she remarked. "Even your black clothes don't appear as fearsome as they did. Are they an affectation, or do they serve another purpose, too—like hiding? I suppose it must be difficult to evade—"

"I'm not hiding."

"You seem to be hiding. That was your hideout back there, wasn't it?"

Mason ground his teeth. "If I don't seem much like an outlaw to you now," he said, keeping his voice purposely low and menacing, "it's because you haven't given me a reason to act like one. Yet."

Her hands went slack. Good. Maybe he'd scared her into being quiet.

It lasted all of five minutes.

"Are you planning to rob another stagecoach today?" Amelia asked.

They'd reached the upper foothills. Here the paloverde and mesquite trees grew farther apart, and cholla and saguaro took their places. Hazy in the distance, the Maricopa Mountains foretold the western approach to Maricopa Wells. Between them wound the Gila Trail, the road leading to the Sharpes, if he were lucky.

"I didn't rob the stagecoach yesterday," Mason told her.

"Of course you did," she protested, wrapping her hands around his middle again as she warmed to her subject. His muscles tightened, all his attention centered on the good feeling of her arms holding him. Briefly Mason closed his eyes, savoring it.

"I saw you holding a gun on the driver," she said. "The poor man looked scared to death."

His eyes opened. The poor man had been the first to draw iron, but Mason doubted it would change her mind if she knew that.

"I was looking for someone," he said, wanting, needing her to hold him tighter, to press against him and . . .

"You didn't find them?"

"No."

"Who were you looking for? Was it"—she paused, humming slightly, tapping his calf again as she considered her question—"your wife?"

Ellen. She was lost to him now.

"No."

Mason leaned forward, forcing Amelia's arms to loosen. Blond, sweet-smelling temptation like her he didn't need.

"You're not married, then?" she asked, her hands resting lightly around his middle. "If you don't mind so personal a question, I mean. The periodicals I've read seem divided on the issue. Some say you have a family, in hiding, and you've resorted to thievery to support them. Others say you're a modern-day Robin Hood, stealing from the big stagecoach lines and giving the money to unfortunates."

Her notion that he was the infamous poet bandit had resurfaced. Mason grinned, glad she couldn't see his face. He hadn't set out to impersonate a known outlaw, but Miss Hoity-Toity had no need to know the truth.

"What do you think?"

She sighed. "I think it's romantic, either way."

He laughed. "Where are you from? Are you sure you're old enough to be out on your own?"

"I'm from Big Pike Lake, Michigan, if you must know," she told him, accompanying her statement with an indignant sniff. "And I'm plenty old enough to be on my own—I'll be twenty-two next month."

"That explains it."

"Explains what?" Amelia leaned sideways to look at his face, nearly toppling them both out of the saddle with her sudden movement. She clenched a handful of his shirt to steady herself, and said, "If you're insinuating that I'm ignorant about life in the West, Mr. Mason—"

"Just Mason." Next, she'd have him tipping his hat, he

thought sourly. The woman was dead-set on formality for some reason.

"—then you're wrong."

The measure of pride he heard in her voice made Mason smile, despite himself.

"I'll have you know I read all about the West in my novels before I came here. This is my territory, for the time being, at least."

"Your territory?"

"I'm a book agent with J. G. O'Malley and Sons," she said, pride resonating in her voice. "Covering the entire United States and every one of its territories with the finest volumes and periodicals of all sorts—"

She went on at length about gilded spines and classic literature, barely pausing for breath. Her talk had the sound of a well-practiced spiel. Mason could almost believe Curly Girl really was engaged in commerce. Finally, she stopped.

"It's not a woman's place to conduct business," he said flatly, turning the horse westward.

He examined the gullies and rock piles they passed, looking for a sheltered place to stop and make camp. It wasn't a woman's place to conduct business, but it was *definitely* a woman's place to cook. As long as he had a woman along, Mason figured he might as well make use of her. The least he deserved for rescuing her was a good, woman-cooked meal.

"It's my place, Mr. Mason, I assure you!" she said. "I'll have you know, I'm a very good book agent."

"If it takes this much talking to folks, I don't doubt it."

"Whatever do you mean by that?"

"Just that you're an exceptional fine talker," Mason said, grinning. "Folks probably buy books just to shut you up."

"What?"

Amelia shifted behind him, inadvertently rubbing her breasts against his back. He wouldn't have believed so much heat could travel through so many layers of dress, duster coat, and shirt.

"Never mind," Mason said, trying to think of something besides how soft, how warm, how . . . tempting the woman behind him was.

"This J. G. O'Malley—is he your husband?"

If he was, he ought to be shot for letting her traipse across the Territory alone. A woman like her wasn't equipped for more than tea parties and gossip. Navigating the forty-mile desert between Gila Bend and Maricopa Wells took more than mouthiness, two bags of books, and a lacy dress. Men had died crossing that stretch—women, too.

"He's my father."

Mason waited to hear the rest of her explanation. None came. He couldn't believe she wasn't saying more. When he wanted her to quit jawing, she never would. "And . . . ?"

"And he's expecting me to make a number of deliveries in Tucson," she said, sounding exasperated. "That's why I have to get back to the road. I have to catch another stagecoach. I have to—"

"No." His hands tightened on the reins. He could take her to the next town, but not back to the road. "Your book deliveries will have to wait."

Amelia gasped, her fingernails digging into his ribs. "My books! You didn't leave my satchels back in the mountains, did you? All my books are in them."

Mason thought of the twin rubber cloth satchels he'd strapped to the horse's flanks like two ten-pound saddlebags. Yet another burden the poor beast shouldn't have had to bear.

"I brought them," he said. "Thought they'd make good kindling."

Another gasp. She lowered her voice. "You wouldn't dare."

He let his silence speak for itself.

"You're barbaric," Amelia muttered, leaning back in the saddle again. "Barbaric."

"Maybe so," Mason agreed. He rolled his shoulders to ease the kinks out of his muscles and gazed across the land, scanning the territory for movements that didn't belong there—movements that might betray the presence of an enemy. A lawman. The posse that was surely after him by now.

The Sharpes.

It was second nature for him to be cautious; he was a wanted man. All the same, he felt doubly so today, with Miss Curly Girl mounted behind him.

"Definitely so," she insisted.

"I reckon a woman likes a man like that," he told her, rubbing his stubble-covered jaw. *"Barbaric."*

Her reply was preceded by an indelicate snort. "That's what you think, Mr. Mason. I'll have you know, I prefer a gentleman—someone who knows how to treat a lady properly."

Mason could almost see her freckled, pert nose hoisted in the air. If she could have, he had little doubt Amelia O'Malley would've flounced away from him with her frilly, impractical pink skirts flying.

"I know how to give a lady what she wants," he couldn't resist saying, punctuating the words with a wicked grin she couldn't see and Mason couldn't hold back. *"And* how to do it properly."

Amelia sniffed. "That, Mr. Mason, remains to be seen."

It was a challenge Mason could hardly let pass uncontested.

Five

"Just Mason," growled the outlaw, and then he twisted in the saddle, grabbed a handful of curls from the back of Amelia's head, and pulled her to him. He leaned forward, his intentions writ plain upon his face. He was going to kiss her.

She was too surprised to move. She ought to stop him, Amelia knew. But the curiosity bubbling inside her made that nigh impossible. Her heart started pounding, setting a pace that would surely kill her if it kept up for long.

Mason's lips quirked upward, very nearly smiling, and excitement jolted through her. Her whole body felt atremble, almost as though she were about to faint.

Oh, dear heaven, she couldn't swoon now. She'd miss her first real kiss.

She had plenty of time to stop him—and none of the will required to do it. It felt an eternity that Mason held her there, watching her, his eyes dark with an emotion she couldn't begin to guess. Slowly he brought his mouth to hers. She heard herself give a little squeak, seconds before his lips touched hers, and then her mind went blank.

His grip gentled in her hair, his hand spanning the back of her head as softly . . . so very softly . . . he touched his lips to hers. Her heart seemed to stop beating for an instant, stilled by the warmth of his mouth, the sensuous glide of his lips, the power of his arms cradling her.

If Mason had meant to prove he was barbaric, he was failing, failing. His touch couldn't have been more tender. He brought her closer, his fingertips rubbing warmly against her scalp, and nibbled gently at her lower lip.

Breathless, half-protesting, Amelia fluttered her hands. Her seeking fingertips caught and held his shirt, and though she knew she ought to push him away, instead she found herself winding the fabric round until it pulled taut against the warmth of the outlaw's chest beneath. Her knuckles skimmed the hard contours of his chest, sought and found the place where his heart beat wild and fast.

She closed her eyes, wanting to moan, wanting to cry out at the feelings that welled within her. So this was what it was to be desired, to be wanted, cherished . . .

Mason's fingers roamed lower, stroking the fine hairs beneath the chignon twisted at the nape of her neck. She tipped her head back, feeling hot sunlight spill onto her eyelids and across her cheeks. The horse shifted beneath them, then settled; it could have ridden away with them both, for all Amelia cared at that moment.

Her lips parted, and coolness washed over her as Mason shadowed her from the sun. His mouth brushed across hers, making her yearn to pull him closer.

"Sweet . . . so sweet," he whispered.

She opened her eyes, gazing at him in wonder. *Sweet . . . sweet.* The endearment, so heartfelt, warmed her more strongly than the sunshine slanting over them both. No one had ever suggested she was anything but an unfortunate mistake, a girl born into a family of men.

Amelia sighed. Carefully, bravely, she raised her trembling hand to his face, cradled the hard line of his jaw in her palm. She stroked her thumb across the rugged angle of his cheekbone. His color was high, blooming across his cheeks like a fever. Oh, he wanted her, wanted her just as she was, and the knowledge sent Amelia's spirits soaring.

Closing his eyes, Mason tilted his face into her palm, rubbing against her skin. "Mmmm," he breathed, "so soft . . ."

His whiskers prickled, making her twice as aware of the differences between them, of the masculine strength and sureness of him. The appealing roughness of his features, the breadth of his chest and shoulders, the muscular hardness of his arms—all intrigued her, made Amelia yearn to discover what secrets could be shared between men and women, for this was a man she held. A man—and an outlaw.

An outlaw who'd abducted her.

An outlaw who'd thoughtlessly dragged her over a mountain and partway across the desert.

An outlaw who'd already admitted he didn't plan to let her go.

Amelia released him, feeling breathless and uncertain. Did he care even a little for her, or was this what it meant to be ravished? And she—she was enjoying it! She found herself staring at his mouth, and tore her gaze away. Was she wanton, to desire a man she'd only just met?

But what if he'd told her the right of it yesterday? What if the stagecoach never *would* have returned for her? She might have died alone on that distant road already, if not for Mason.

He raised his gaze to hers, and the tenderness she saw there made Amelia catch her breath. No man had ever looked at her that way before. It doubled her confusion. "Mason, I . . ."

"Shhh, I won't hurt you, Amy." His hands slid to the middle of her back, pressing her closer; his eyelids lowered as his gaze swept to her lips, then held. She quivered as a tiny, forbidden thrill raced up her spine. He wanted to kiss her again, she could tell.

Heaven help her, she wanted him to do it.

She held her breath as he brought his mouth nearer . . .

nearer. His hands flattened against her back, holding her close against the warmth of his body. Her bosom pressed tight against his arm and chest, her breasts aching at the contact, yearning for something she couldn't name. Amelia's eyes closed, all her attention centered on the moment when their lips would meet.

She waited, sensing his face only inches from her own, chilled by the shadow he cast over her—and warmed all over by the spell he'd somehow woven. Blindly, she cupped her hand around Mason's neck, urging him without words to come to her.

He didn't yield an inch. Surprised, Amelia opened her eyes to see Mason exactly where she'd expected him—close enough to feel her breath on his cheek. But his attention had shifted someplace else, she realized. His expression was faraway. As she watched, he cocked his head slightly, as though listening.

"Mason! I—" She hadn't the faintest notion what to say to him. Heat rose in her cheeks, her heart still pounding wildly from what had passed between them. Had he lost interest in her already? Was it only she who felt the attraction between them? Or maybe her kisses were lacking, that he'd stopped right amidst one and not even missed it?

Shamefaced, she whipped her hand from his neck. Mason caught hold of her wrist, his gaze shifting instantly to her.

"Listen," he commanded.

Her gaze locked with his. Amelia tried to focus her attention on whatever he'd heard. Bird cries . . . something skittering across the desert floor nearby . . . then, faintly, a rhythmic beating. Drums?

"A stagecoach," Mason said, releasing her wrist. His eyes gleamed—with passion? Or a desperado's anticipation of the chase? He turned in the saddle. "I'll help you dismount."

"No! Why?"

Heedless, he all but flung her from behind the saddle, forcing her to hold on to him for dear life as she descended to the ground. She landed beside the horse, still clutching his hard-muscled forearm with both hands.

"Why, Mason? Tell me!"

"Stay here," he said, taking up the reins in his free hand, making ready to leave. She had little doubt he'd ride off with her dragging behind the horse, if that was what it took.

"No! Where are you going?" Amelia cried. Panic made her voice shrill, but she couldn't help it. The horse pranced forward, sensing its master's mood. Both man and beast wanted to be away—now. Its trampling hooves came too close; she released Mason's arm.

Far away on the leftmost horizon, a rising cloud of dust foretold the stagecoach's progress. The team's thundering hooves sounded louder now, faintly overlaid with the clank of the harness metal.

"You're going to rob that stagecoach!" Horrified, she backed away from Mason. "You can't! Not now, not with me here to—"

"I won't be gone long."

He pulled a black bandanna from his duster pocket and tied it at the back of his head, concealing his face. Amelia suppressed a shiver. She'd been wrong earlier—he did look fearsome, even in the daytime.

"Stay here." The horse danced beneath him, despite Mason's hold on the reins. "I mean it."

He spurred the horse into motion, riding toward the dust cloud in the distance.

Amelia stared after him, hardly able to believe her eyes. Thoughts of their kiss fled, chased by a tangle of emotions she didn't want to feel. He'd left her so easily, but what else could come of trusting an outlaw? She was a fool to believe he might behave decently toward her.

Might begin to care for you, a voice within her whispered.

She clenched her fist within the dirty pink folds of her skirt, filled with frustration. He'd seemed less an outlaw before, only a man—a man who could set her atremble with the gentleness of his touch. Now Mason rode with no thought of her, to perform an action Amelia knew—*knew*—was wrong.

He could be hurt. Caught. *Killed*.

She cried out, imagining Mason fallen to the ground, wounded, surrounded by vengeful stage passengers. She shouldn't care for a man who'd abducted her, shouldn't worry over a desperado's safety. But still, somehow, she did. Pacing, Amelia shook her skirt free of a spiny, pincushion-like cactus and stared again toward the stagecoach. He won't get hurt, she told herself. No one would dare fire upon the poet bandit.

It was small comfort. She remembered the fear of her fellow stagecoach passengers, the lecherous old man and the miner and the banker, and knew any one of them might have taken aim at the outlaw if given an opportunity. They simply hadn't had one. The bandit had remained at the head of the coach, dealing only with the driver.

The driver. A driver who could bear her safely away from the outlaw, a driver who could take her to Tucson to deliver her books! Amelia squinted into the distance, trying to gauge how far it was to the road the coach traveled over.

Less than half a mile. Surely near enough to hobble to. Near enough to escape to.

If it made her a traitor to Mason, so be it. What did fidelity mean to an outlaw? This was what she could expect from him— to be seduced and abandoned. He didn't care for her. And she had to make her own way somehow, take care of herself somehow, else she'd never survive, let alone fulfill her mission.

She'd sworn to deliver every last one of those J. G. O'Malley & Sons book orders, and that was what Amelia meant to do. Her father and brothers would know she was capable . . . worthy of respect and even love. Never mind that her heart clenched at the thought of confronting Mason to do it. If proving her

worth meant interrupting a stagecoach robbery first, that was
exactly what she'd do.

Panting from her awkward race across the desert, Amelia
skidded to a stop when she saw Mason's chestnut-colored mare
picketed behind a cluster of bushes a short distance from the
road. The bushes' disjointed-looking branches drooped in wide
circles to the ground below, each yellow-blooming length growing just closely enough to its neighbor to conceal the horse from
the stagecoach beyond.

Her J. G. O'Malley & Sons satchels were still strapped to
the saddle, exactly where Mason had lashed them on. Their
metal bindings winked at her in the sunlight. She had to retrieve
them before going on, else she'd never succeed. Crooning softly,
Amelia approached the horse.

"Hello there, girl," she called soothingly, easing closer. The
horse raised its head and looked at her through its placid, dark
eyes, still chewing a mouthful of feathery leaves stripped from
the nearest of the bushes.

"Shhh, that's right," she said. Almost there. "Easy now. I just
want my satchels back, that's all."

The horse's ears pricked forward at the sound of her voice.
An instant later, Amelia touched the saddle, then the horse's
muzzle. She rubbed it softly. "Good horse. Steady now. I'm
just going to untie these satchels—"

Easing sideways, she laid a hand atop the knot fastening the
first satchel. The animal didn't move, so Amelia felt encouraged
enough to scoot all the way over to the knot.

Could horses be loyal to their owners? She sincerely hoped
not; one whinny would likely give away her presence and her
plan alike. Frowning, she peered closely at the thick, complicated knot and bit back a cry of frustration. It looked nigh impossible to untie.

In the distance, Mason called out to the stagecoach driver—

probably a command to throw down the strong box, Amelia supposed. Although she couldn't make out the words, the fearsome tone of his voice carried clearly to her hiding place. How much time did she have? She shuddered to imagine what the consequences might be if the outlaw discovered her trying to escape again.

She had to succeed, had to be away on the stage before Mason returned. But not without her satchels.

Trying to bolster her courage anew, Amelia surveyed the knot. It was probably as easy to untie as a shoelace, she told herself. She only had to find the correct piece of rope to pull, and the rest would come free. With that thought in mind, she caught hold of a likely-looking dangling section and tugged.

Nothing happened. Blowing her bangs upward to clear her vision, she straightened her stance and tried again. Digging her fingers into the knot, Amelia pulled hard. The rope slid! It budged mere fractions of an inch, but it was progress, all the same. Working with both hands, she just managed to loosen the center of the knot.

Encouraged, she gripped the topmost hank of rope and tugged with all her strength. Just as it came untied, the horse shifted—and so did her satchel. Its weight pulled the rope against itself, making the twisted fibers hiss and rasp against each other as the knot finally slithered free.

Heavy with books, her satchel plopped to the ground in a flurry of dust, landing halfway atop the sagging picket rope. The horse skittered backward as the sudden weight drew the tether taut. Her satchel snapped free like an arrow released from a bow. Success! Amelia scooped up her satchel and rounded the horse. Only one more knot to go.

From the direction of the stagecoach, feminine wails sounded, mixed with a rumbling undercurrent of men's voices. Frightened passengers, Amelia supposed. Something about the sound of them sent a shiver of foreboding fluttering through her stomach.

Frightened, cornered animals were dangerous. Were people the same way?

She couldn't think about that now. Doing her best to ignore her churning stomach, she scanned the outlaw's saddle, looking for the knot fastening her second satchel to it.

There wouldn't be much time before Mason returned. She had to get on that stage, now, before it was too late. Her jaw clenched with determination, Amelia examined the knot.

Thank heavens, it appeared similar to the one she'd already untied. Dropping her first satchel, she set to work undoing it, trying not to steal glances toward the stagecoach as she worked. What was happening? Was Mason all right?

The rough woven rope abraded her fingers—she could almost feel her knuckles and fingertips reddening from constant contact with it—but only two broken fingernails later, she'd untied it. She bent to scoop the heavy black case into her arms, then picked up the other one. Hefting them both, Amelia headed toward the road. Toward rescue.

She hadn't gone three steps into the open desert before the horse whinnied.

It sounded loud as a gunshot in the silence surrounding her. Surely a sound like that would attract the outlaw's attention. Frantic, her feet seemingly glued to the desert soil, Amelia glanced about for a hiding place. A few feet away, she spotted a tall, spiny cactus, and all but dove behind it.

The plant's branches—what they were called on a cactus, she didn't know—reached for the sky like two thick green arms, high above her head. The spiky plant's base squatted atop the thirsty desert soil, looking barely wide enough to conceal her. Dropping her satchels, Amelia crouched behind it anyway, afraid to breathe.

When nothing happened, she dared to lean carefully around the inches-long needles protruding from the cactus and peer toward the stagecoach.

It was just as she'd hoped—a red-lacquered passenger stage, pulled by three pairs of horses. Wooden boxes and luggage were piled atop its metal-framed top and almost spilled from the boot. Inside, there were only a few wailing passengers, most of them hanging from the windows to see what was happening, just as Amelia's fellow passengers had done. She almost sighed with relief at the sight of it. Civilization! Safety, only steps away.

And there, only steps away himself, stood Mason. His rifle, like the driver's, rested with deceptive casualness over his shoulder. He spoke quietly with the driver, but Amelia couldn't make out the words. Both looked intent on their conversation—too intent to notice her. For a moment longer she watched him, some sense of foreboding prickling down her spine.

Why should that be? Amelia wondered, rubbing her arms for warmth against a sudden chill. Mason was an outlaw engaged in dangerous work. He'd probably robbed a hundred stagecoaches just like this one, and lived to tell about it. Surely there was no cause for her to worry about his safety.

Especially with her own safe rescue parked just a few steps away. Breathing deeply, Amelia hoisted her satchels and hobbled for the stage.

Six

"They were on your stage, then?" Mason asked the driver, hardly able to credit what the old man had told him only moments before. "You're sure?"

"Yessiree." Hooking both his thumbs into a cracked leather cavalryman's belt small enough around to fit Miss Curly Top's waist, the driver squinted into the sun, deepening the creases in his leathery skin. " 'Bout two days ago, maybe three. Dunno for sure." He spat into the gritty road between their feet and glanced at Mason. "Been lookin' for 'em long?"

Mason nodded. "Too long," he said, yanking his black bandanna from his face. He didn't need it now. The breeze swirled in cooling currents against his newly exposed skin as he shoved the square of cloth into his duster pocket. No point antagonizing the man who'd given him the first piece of useful information he'd had in seven days' time.

The Sharpe brothers *had* passed this way. He'd begun to wonder if he'd misjudged them somehow, if he'd lost the trail—and his last chance for redemption along with it.

"The boy was with them?" he asked the driver. "Small, dark-haired boy about this high?" He raised his hand to hip height, and a shaft of longing seared through him at the memory of all he'd lost. First Ellen, and now—if he failed again—their son, too. Ben. For an instant, he closed his eyes, beating back the need to hold his child—his blood, his life—and see him safe.

"Yep," the driver said. "Damned ruffian 'bout sent my passengers screaming 'cross the desert with his antics. Them three with him had their hands full, I'll tell you."

Mason smiled. "That's my boy."

"*Your* boy?" The driver looked startled for a second, then nodded as though he'd known the right of it all along. "Such a hell-raiser I ain't never seen." Looking over Mason's black outlaw clothes, full gun belt, and rifle, he added, "And no wonder, with a sire like you, sir."

Mason tipped his hat. "I'll leave you to be on your way," he said, too relieved at what he'd learned to waste time wondering if the words had been an insult or not. He'd wager not—not if the old man's gap-toothed grin was anything to judge by. "Thank you."

He turned away amidst the driver's goodbyes, his step lighter than at any time since he'd left his homestead on the Gila with the sheriff on his trail. Mason only had a few days' gain on the lawman following him. But lawman or no, barring disaster or capture, in a few days' time he'd see his son returned to him.

And by the first sunrise after, he'd see the men who'd taken Ben repaid for their part in the thieving, else know no rest until he had.

The Sharpes had taken his boy to Tucson, only two or three days' ride southeast. Even with Miss Twirly Curls along for the ride, Mason could reach the former territorial capital in that much time.

Behind him, the harnesses holding the stagecoach's team of horses jangled, stirred by the animals' movements, Mason supposed, as the driver climbed into his high-set seat. Glancing backward, he just glimpsed the hollow-cheeked old man take up the reins again. Mason raised his hand in a solemn farewell. He owed the man much, not the least of which was thanks. He was one of the few drivers who hadn't pulled iron to claim an outlaw's head for bounty at his approach.

The driver returned the gesture, then pulled his team into line. At the same instant, a blurry flash of pink caught Mason's eye. Something darted from behind a gnarled saguaro, then crashed through the rocks toward the stagecoach. For one confused moment, he thought it was a bizarrely dressed Indian laying siege to the stagecoach—until he saw the blond hair.

Amelia.

Escaping.

He'd barely registered that fact before a high-pitched whinny called his gaze toward the sheltering stand of creosote bushes where he'd tethered his horse. A rustle of leaves, a scrape of iron across stone, and then his horse shot across the desert at a dead run. The iron picket post, dug from the ground somehow and useless to hold the animal, banged loudly along in the mare's wake, doing a fine job of scaring the hell out of his horse.

Mason didn't know how, but he'd lay odds Amelia Josephine O'Malley was involved.

Damn.

He wavered an instant, trying to decide if he should go after his horse or follow and find out what she was up to. A glance backward showed him Amelia's long, stocking-clad legs as she scrambled onto the stagecoach, her gaudy pink dress swinging wildly in the breeze. She barely made it aboard the metal steps before the stage began rolling forward.

A woman he could do without right now, Mason decided, a horse, he couldn't. An unmounted man in the desert this far from water was as good as dead. His decision made, he slung his rifle over his shoulder and ran toward the panicked mare.

Something blasted behind him, then heat whizzed past his rifle arm. Shotgun fire. One of the passengers must have found his courage renewed by the outlaw's retreat. Another shot came, too wild to strike anything, but too close to ignore. Mason dropped to the dirt, landing hard on his shoulder. Rolling onto his belly, he grabbed for his rifle strap and swung the weapon around.

A woman's scream pierced the air, shrill enough to cut through the dust clouds billowing behind the stagecoach.

Amelia.

"Stop!" she yelled, her voice garbled but undeniably snooty enough to belong to no one else. "Stop shooting!"

Mason squinted past the scrub brush littering the ground and over a pile of broken rock, looking in the direction his horse had gone. He could just make out the animal as it rounded a low mesa and trotted in a wide arc toward the road. Its tail streamed behind it in the breeze, a beautiful display of animal grace—except for the iron picket still clunking along behind it.

If the shooter on the stage would pack up his weapon for a minute, Mason knew he'd be able to catch his horse and get the hell out of there.

Instead, another shot came. His hat blew backward and his heart whipped into double-time rhythm as he realized how close the bullet had come to making his son an orphan.

Mason flattened himself into the prickly soil and leveled his rifle again. He didn't want to open fire on a stage full of innocent passengers, but if this went on much longer he'd be left with no choice.

"What are you *doing?*" screamed Amelia. The sound of her voice could've split logs in winter. Mason lifted his head just high enough to see the whole carriage sway as the driver yanked his teams to a stop. In the middle of the vehicle, Mason spotted little Miss Twirly Curls . . . wrestling with an armed man nearly twice her size.

"You've probably killed him!" she cried, both hands clamped onto the man's shotgun. They tugged it back and forth between them, like children playing a particularly vicious game of tug-of-war. Cursing, the shooter suddenly heaved his weapon, slinging Amelia hard onto another passenger's lap.

"Thieving desperado deserved it!" came the snarled reply.

Mason had to agree. From their point of view, he was a known outlaw—the infamous poet bandit. Taking advantage of the opportunity their argument afforded him, Mason shouldered his rifle again and began creeping away from the road. If he could only get to his horse, he could . . .

"There he is!" yelled another passenger. "He's gettin' away!"

Mason moved faster, only inches away from a sheltering mesquite. In the distance, his horse still ran like a creature of the wild, despite its heavy pack saddle. He had a feeling he'd never catch it now.

"Don't shoot!" came Amelia's imperious, high-pitched command. Feet plunked down the Concord's steps and across the rocky soil, and then the steps were drowned out by the passengers' shouted arguments inside the stage. Hell. Mason halted midstride, a sense of foreboding overtaking him. He wasn't clear of this yet.

"Oh, Mason!"

He straightened warily, reluctantly. An instant later, Amelia O'Malley barreled into him, all arms and legs and messy perfumed hair. The impact of her soft, small body sent him swaying as he absorbed the force of her lunge into his arms. Her forehead bashed into his chin.

"I thought you were dead!" she gasped, her voice muffled against his chest. Her nose pushed into his collarbone, making a warm spot just above his shirt.

Mason's eyes watered, set off by the stinging impact of her forehead against his chin. The woman's skull must be made of solid rock. He wanted to rub away the hurt, but her head was in the way. At least the damned shooting had stopped. He blew a strand of curly blond hair from his lips.

"You should've stayed on the stage," he said.

"I couldn't! You were hurt."

He set her away from him, trying to look severe. "I'm not hurt."

Undaunted, she latched onto his upper arms the moment he released her. Her fingernails dug through his coat and shirt-sleeves as she leaned back to examine him. Her gaze, openly and irritatingly skeptical, roved clear over his body.

"But I saw you fall down! Oh, Mason . . . I—"

He winced. "I was ducking gunfire," he said, glancing behind her at the still-halted stagecoach. A group of male passengers had disembarked, and they were headed straight for him and Amelia.

"—I thought you were shot or wounded or in trouble," she went on, oblivious to the trouble gathering right behind him as she probed his shoulder, his chest, and then his arm for injuries. Apparently unsatisfied, she rose on tiptoes to press her hand against his jaw, turning his head for a closer inspection. "I had to save you."

Mason scowled and captured her wrist, stopping her. "Trouble?" he interrupted. "You're worried that I'm in trouble?" Hell, she was responsible for a good portion of his troubles her-self.

Her hand began to tremble within his grasp. Amelia's blue eyes darkened with concern beneath her tangle of curly bangs. "Well, well, yes, I—"

Of course I was worried, her expression said.

"You should've stayed on the stage," he said again. "You've got no idea the kind of trouble I'm in." He looked past Amelia's shoulder into the faces of the advancing stagecoach passengers. A hanging crowd if ever he'd seen one.

His gaze shifted back to her. She looked perplexed; beneath their dusting of smudged black dirt, her eyebrows dipped lower and her mouth pulled into an oval of confusion.

Mason gave her a nasty, mean-tempered smile. If not for Miss Fancy Pants, he'd already be on his way to Tucson by now to reclaim his son. Instead, he was about to face a roadside lynch mob.

Worse, he could've been rid of her, too, and gotten to Ben twice as quickly. If only she'd stayed on the stagecoach. Why in the hell had she run to a man she believed was an outlaw?

His original estimation had been correct, Mason decided. She was addled somehow. Any woman with a lick of sense would've abandoned him the first chance she got.

Frowning, he shoved Amelia behind him, shielding her with his body as the crowd came nearer. "Curly Top," he said, "welcome to my necktie party."

"Goodness, I thought they'd kill him for certain," said the plump little woman seated to the left of Amelia on the stagecoach. She fussed with the dainty wrist strap of her beaded reticule and eyed Amelia again. "Honestly, we couldn't very well let the menfolk do *that,* now could we?"

"Oh, no!" cried the woman on Amelia's right, a dowager with piled-high, fancy hair and a righteous expression. The three of them jounced together as the stagecoach passed over a particularly bumpy spot in the road, then righted themselves again. On the vehicle's opposite bench, all four men in their party sat crammed like sardines with their arms crossed tight over their chests. All, that is, save one man.

The opposing camps glared at each other across the space dividing them.

"A nasty, distasteful business," opined the plump lady, dabbing delicately at her nose with an embroidered handkerchief. The linen square appeared to have seen much hard use.

"Deserved to hang," muttered the man who'd been shooting at Mason. He was, Amelia had learned, the dowager's husband.

"Yeah," agreed another man with a hard look at the outlaw.

"Why, that would have been cold-blooded murder!" cried the

dowager, her nostrils flaring slightly. "Isn't that right, Miss O'Malley?"

Her tone dared Amelia to disagree. Even knowing if she did speak out, it would likely ease the dissension that made the air feel heavy and hard to breathe, Amelia nodded instead. With the help of these women—and the stagecoach driver's inexplicable assistance—she'd persuaded the male passengers not to strike down the outlaw where he stood. No amount of peaceful coexistence was worth a man's life.

With Amelia's allegiance duly confirmed on the side of womankind, the other ladies carried on their discussion in lively, gossiping tones. Amelia was too sick at heart to join in. Her concern for Mason had gotten the better of her, had compelled her to run off the stagecoach to help him—and now look at the fix they were in.

Alive but madder than she'd ever seen him, the outlaw emanated hostility from the seat directly opposite her. He was the only man with his arms uncrossed, but that wasn't his posture by choice.

He was bound hand-to-foot in anything the male passengers had been able to dredge up. A hank of rope secured his wrists in front of him, and a leather bridle twined securely around his booted ankles. More rope, combined with two pairs of red suspenders and a length of chain, strapped his arms to his sides with a series of horizontal bindings. Even for a man with Mason's strength, it would be impossible to break free of so many restraints.

If not for the gentleman's necktie stuffed partway in his mouth and tied at the back of his head, she felt sure Mason would've given her a piece of his mind long before now.

"I'm sorry," she mouthed silently to him. She'd really only meant to help. When she'd seen him fall into the cactus-strewn dirt, every bit of common sense she possessed had fled.

He glared at her over the paisley-printed necktie that kept him from speaking. Then he . . . growled.

"Goodness!" shrieked the lady beside Amelia. "He is barbaric, isn't he?"

Barbaric. Amelia recalled accusing him of the same thing—and the memory of his answering kiss made her cheeks flush hotly.

"I—I'm just glad we were able to persuade the gentlemen here to let justice take its course," she said, choked with the mixture of remembered excitement and embarrassment that flooded her.

Trying her best to ignore the predatory gleam in Mason's eye—obviously he remembered the private moment they'd shared, too—Amelia added, "I'm certain everything will be set right once we reach Tucson."

And once they did reach Tucson, Amelia thought, turning her mind toward a safer topic, she had a wealth of work to do. She'd already reserved a room at one of the town's finest hotels. From there she planned to tour the city, delivering J. G. O'Malley & Sons book orders and taking as many new ones as she could secure before it was time to return to the States. After she and Mason went their separate ways, she'd have to put this whole unfortunate incident straight out of her mind and get started.

It's not a woman's place to conduct business. Mason had said that to her only this morning, his words an uncanny echo of her father's business philosophy. Perhaps they believed that, Amelia mused, gazing unseeing out the stagecoach window. Or perhaps it was her abilities they doubted.

After all, her father and brothers routinely did business with women—widows, mostly—running their husbands' shops. Amelia refused to believe the only females possessed of ambition and business acumen were those whose husbands had gone on to their heavenly rewards. What possible advantage could widowhood confer? And yet they were allowed to engage in trade unmolested.

Only one explanation seemed possible. Her father believed her incompetent, untrustworthy . . . lacking, somehow.

She'd prove him wrong, Amelia vowed. She stared at the satchels beneath her feet, but in her mind's eye it was her father's face she saw. To see his face alight with fatherly pride had been her goal for as long as she could remember. Finally, finally, she had the means to make her hopes a reality.

Determined despite the troubles she found herself in now, Amelia grabbed the handle of the heaviest satchel and hefted it onto her lap. She'd refresh her knowledge of the book orders to be delivered, and be that much more prepared when she reached Tucson.

The satchel locks appeared intact, even after the harsh treatment they'd received over the past few days. One was a bit scraped from the miner's attempts to pry it open, but otherwise secure. Trying to cheer herself with a quietly hummed tune, Amelia slipped her finger inside the neckline of her dress, feeling for the thin gold chain on which she'd strung the key to the locked satchels for safekeeping.

It wasn't there.

Frowning, Amelia pushed her forefinger a bit lower. Perhaps it had slid aside—the chain and key were always there. She'd chosen that hiding place specifically for its security. A sense of alarm tightened her stomach, and she ran her finger quickly to the other side of her neck. The key wasn't there.

The next note of her tune died in her throat. How would she deliver her book orders if she couldn't unlock her J. G. O'Malley & Sons satchels? How would she pay for food and her room at the Palace Hotel, with all her money locked away? A burgeoning sense of despair tightened her throat as she glanced down at the filthy pink rag that passed for her pink polonaise dress. How would she even change clothes? She could hardly represent her father's company dressed like this!

A questioning noise from Mason's direction made her look up. He'd been watching her. His eyebrows lifted, but beneath their overly innocent arch, Amelia recognized a familiar gleam. It was the same light that filled her brothers' eyes whenever she'd fallen unwarily into one of their pranks. Instinctively, she straightened against the back of the leather-upholstered bench, looking around her as she tried in vain to spot the joke.

"Mmm-mmm?" came Mason's rumbled inquiry.

She paused, having spotted nothing. "What? What are you trying to say?"

His reply was a nod toward her satchel. Could he possibly know where the key was?

"Do you know what I'm looking for?" she asked him, desperation pushing the question from her lips in spite of the disapproving stares of her fellow passengers. This was no time for pranks or propriety. She had to have that key.

Mason made another indistinguishable sound.

"Can you tell me where it is?" she asked, leaning toward him. He remained silent, but above the gag his dark eyes twinkled at her, warm with amusement. She'd have appreciated it more, had she not been the subject of his good humor.

"Do you really think it's safe to speak with him, Miss O'Malley?" asked the plump lady to her left. "He appears quite dangerous to me."

He did to Amelia, too. Without his hat, the outlaw's thick coffee-colored hair stuck up in aggressive little shafts, and his jaw looked bristly with beard stubble. His broad, muscular body dwarfed those of the men seated beside him. They'd removed his rifle and gun belt, but rather than mellowing his demeanor, the weapons' absence only made Mason's natural strength seem twice as prominent. He looked like he could take apart a man with his bare hands—and enjoy the diversion.

"He . . . he won't hurt me," Amelia said. Her fingers fairly itched to remove the gag and hear what the outlaw had to say, but she didn't dare. Doubtless she'd have a bigger earful than she'd bargained for.

More importantly, she still hoped to keep their fellow passengers from realizing they were together. What if they believed she was the poet bandit's accomplice and locked her in jail, too?

"Wave your arms," she begged Mason. "Maybe I can guess."

Muffled masculine laughter came from behind the gag.

Amelia felt like shrieking aloud in frustration. Tapping her fingernails against her smooth rubber cloth satchel, she narrowed her eyes at Mason and considered her options. He couldn't speak unless she ungagged him, but she doubted the other passengers would allow that. And he refused to cooperate by giving her visual clues. Perhaps she could search his person for the key! He was helpless. How would he stop her?

She lowered her satchel to the floor, her heartbeat coming faster as she rose to her feet. The stupefied stares of the other passengers made her knees feel wobbly as she crossed the small distance to the outlaw's seat. She stopped when her skirts brushed his knees. Sucking in a deep breath to bolster her courage, she shifted her concentration wholly onto Mason.

"This is your last chance," she told him, wishing her voice sounded stronger, surer, than it did. Bracing her arms on the seat back behind him, Amelia leaned slightly over him in an attempt to keep their conversation private. "If you know what I want," she said slowly, "please give it to me. Now."

She wouldn't have thought it possible, but behind the gag, Mason's grin grew wider. His gaze dropped to her wilted pink bodice and lower, an intimate sweep that somehow made her feel hot and cold at once. She should have been insulted, Amelia knew, but somehow she didn't have the will to manage it.

His eyes met hers again. The playfulness that had filled his gaze before vanished, replaced with a hunger so intense it swept through her like a physical force. Barely leashed, it called to some part of her Amelia had never recognized before. Her breath left her. Mesmerized, she swayed almost imperceptibly closer.

"Mason?" she whispered.

"Good heavens, Miss O'Malley!" cried the dowager, startling Amelia so badly that she nearly toppled into Mason's lap.

"Get away from that man," the older woman commanded. "What on earth is he supposed to give you?"

"Well," she stammered, at a loss to explain, "I, ahhh . . ."

"I think she's in cahoots with him," interrupted the dowager's husband, the same weasel-faced man who'd been shooting at Mason. He leveled his shifty-eyed, suspicious gaze on Amelia. "Ain't that right, missy?"

"No! I—" Her face turned, automatically, toward the outlaw. He gave her a hard look, his brown eyes burning with some message she couldn't decipher. What was he trying to tell her?

"I'm no outlaw," she cried, turning to address her likeliest allies—the women. "My . . . my stagecoach left me at the road-side by mistake, that's all, and I, I . . ." Her voice trailed away. They didn't believe her, Amelia could tell. She tried another approach. "I didn't even know him before yesterday!"

"Yesterday?" asked the dowager.

"Please, I only want to get to Tucson and get on with my business," Amelia said.

"Business?" echoed the plump lady, raising her eyebrows.

Not again, Amelia thought in despair, remembering her earlier stagecoach companions' reactions to her status as a J. G. O'Malley & Sons book agent. If that episode had taught her anything, it was that a stagecoach was not the place for business discussions.

She adopted her most genteel manner, lowering her head modestly as she grasped two handfuls of her beleaguered pink polonaise dress. Good upbringing will always show, her father said. His conviction was about to be put to the test. Raising her skirts slightly, Amelia dipped into a brief curtsy.

"Truly," she asked, "do I look as though I'd cavort with a common criminal?"

Choked laughter came from the men's side of the stagecoach.

It was silenced with one icy glance from the dowager. Still seated, she raised her chin and, despite the fact that her head came only as high as Amelia's waist, somehow succeeded in looking down her nose at her. *"Cavort,* Miss O'Malley?"

For an instant, she couldn't fathom what was wrong. When it came to her, Amelia clapped her hand over her mouth. Unfortunately, she was too late in recalling what she'd said.

"Conspire! I meant, conspire—not cavort." A hot blush climbed her cheeks. "I—"

"I think we've heard all we need to," said Mr. Dowager.

"This has certainly enlivened our travels," remarked the man beside him. "It'll make quite the feature in my newspaper this week."

"Your newspaper?" squeaked Amelia. She imagined her name emblazoned on whatever Western periodical he spoke of, and a wave of nausea overtook her. Dear heaven, please let this news remain here, she prayed. If word of a scandal such as this reached her father back in the States, he'd disown her for certain.

"Yes," the man said, examining her from above his dark handlebar mustache. "John Clum, *Arizona Citizen,* at your service, ma'am."

"Oh, no."

The plump lady examined Amelia with new interest. "Imagine," she breathed out, "a lady bandit!" Not unkindly, she patted Amelia's hand.

Blindly, Amelia sank into her seat again.

"Everything will be fine, dear," the lady said soothingly. "I understand the justice of the peace in Tucson has a kind heart toward females."

Amelia did not feel comforted. Glancing toward Mason for reassurance, she spotted the one thing that had the ability to make her feel worse than she already did. Winking at her from a gap in the outlaw's shirt, a tiny bit of gold glinted against Mason's bare chest. The chain was barely visible amidst the tawny hair curling against his skin, but the item responsible for setting off the whole embarrassing misunderstanding could be seen plainly.

Her satchel key.

With a teasing lift of his eyebrows, Mason grinned behind the gag. "Mmm-mmm?"

Seven

"I can't believe they locked me in here with you!" Amelia cried, tossing Mason an accusing glance.

He sighed, leaning as far from her as the chilly crisscrossed iron bars at his back would allow, watching as she paced yet again across the length of their shared cell.

They'd made it as far as Maricopa Wells, about eighty miles northwest of Tucson. Once there, their former stagecoach companions had decided to rid themselves of the troublemakers in their midst. The stationmaster had been only too happy to lock up him and Amelia both, in return for the full bounty he expected to receive.

"It's not so bad," Mason said, eyeing their cramped adobe cell.

His attempt to offer comfort earned him a dose of rolled-eyed exasperation from Miss Fancy Pants.

"For a prison," she shot back. "I don't belong here."

Two days in their new accommodations had only ripened Amelia's sense of outrage at being mistaken for his . . . consort. Unfortunately, Mason was her sole target until the law saw fit to move them to the jailhouse in Tucson.

He shrugged. "You're the one who jumped off that stagecoach to go after me. You should've gotten away from me when you still could. I reckon you implicated yourself."

He ran his fingers along the iron bars above his head, stretching the kinks from his back. "Besides, it's not a prison, it's a stage station."

Amelia crossed her arms over her chest. Her gaze followed his fingers' path. "It's got cell bars."

"You'd want cell bars, too, if you were holding a pair of outlaws."

She cocked her head and raised her eyebrows. Mason felt just ornery enough to ignore her unspoken complaint.

"I've seen worse," he finished blithely, folding his arms and propping them behind his head for support. The flat metal cell bars were wearing permanent dents into his skull. He had to figure out a way to get out of there—and soon.

"You've seen worse? When?" she asked. "I thought the poet bandit had never been caught."

Mason hesitated. "I told you—I'm not who you think I am."

"Then who are you?" Amelia's eyes narrowed. "Is your name even Mason?"

"I can't tell you any more now." He couldn't risk it, not with so much still at stake. What if she revealed who he really was? In the Territory, hanging was too good for a man accused of murder.

The sheriff's wanted posters might have reached this far north by now; it was only a matter of time before he was recognized. He'd deal with that when it happened. But Mason would be damned before handing over his name to a woman he couldn't trust.

He might as well slide the noose over his head himself as confide in a female.

"It's better if you don't know," he told her.

"Humph." She straightened and flounced away from him. "You're just mad because I'm your only captive who ever escaped," she announced, examining her fingernails with a seeming utter lack of interest in his reply.

"Captive?"

"That's right, captive. Prisoner, hostage . . ."

"I know what the word means."

She smiled, fleetingly. "Call it what you like," she told him with a carefree flutter of her fingers. "I escaped through cunning and bravery, just like the heroine of a novel—"

Mason tried to suppress a burst of laughter and failed.

"—and it hurts your masculine pride to admit it."

"I admit nothing."

Except that Amelia was right about one thing: the Maricopa Wells stage station was very much like a jail. The place was as well fortified as a presidio, with thick outside walls that squatted squarely around the inner buildings. Those adobe walls served as well to keep prisoners in as they did to keep hostile Indians out. Even if he managed to get out of the damned cell, there'd still be the walls to overcome.

"Ha!" Amelia beamed triumphantly, as though his silence meant he agreed with her. Pacing again, she amused herself with some addle-headed talk about his masculine pride. All of a sudden, though, Mason didn't have the gumption to spar with her.

With a change of horses—and luck in stealing a mount to begin with—the Maricopa Wells station was only two days' ride north of Tucson. But it seemed a hundred times as far.

Not knowing where the Sharpes had taken his son had been bad enough. Knowing where Ben was and being wholly unable to go to him was worse. He had to find a way to get out.

"And anyway, I'm no outlaw. It's as plain as that," Amelia muttered, abandoning her attack on his manhood for a fresh tour of their cell and a loudly hummed hymn.

Mason would swear the woman knew nothing but church music. If they ever got out, he was sorely tempted to teach her a saloon song or two. If folks had to be subjected to her constant prattling, at least they deserved some variety.

She traveled past both metal cots, kicking up puffs of dirt

beneath her high-laced shoes as she went. Theirs were rudimentary accommodations, at best, designed for temporarily holding hostile Apache prisoners or road agents like they were assumed to be.

Amelia had been allowed a bath and a change into a borrowed blue-checked dress, but he'd been unshackled only for meals. His wrists were already rubbed raw from the bindings.

"And I'm not an outlaw's consort, either!" Amelia added, darting a glance at him from beneath her bangs.

"I told them that," Mason said, shrugging. Keeping his back to the bars, he stretched his legs along the hard metal cot. "They didn't believe me."

"Of course not!" She whirled on him, the ruffled edge of her dress swinging fast as the change in her mood. "I don't know why I ever believed you, either," she went on, her mouth suddenly wobbling with suppressed tears. "I thought you were a gentleman. I—-I thought you'd never hurt anyone in your robberies, so why was that man shooting at you? I trusted you, and now, now . . ."

With a faint cry she pressed her knuckles to her lips and turned away from him, leaving her words unfinished. A moment later, faint sniffling reached him from her corner of their cell. Her shoulders quivered beneath her too-large borrowed dress.

Mason couldn't keep up. One minute she was arguing with him like a drunk staring down the neck of his last whiskey bottle, and the next she was blubbering like a little girl. He didn't know how to help her, and he hated it.

"That kind of trusting can get you into trouble, Amelia."

She turned back, her eyes large and luminous in the meager daylight that fought its way through the bars of their cell's single window.

"You mean trusting *you* can get me into trouble."

Silence filled the space between them.

Did he? Mason thought of Ellen's trust in him, thought of

his failure to reclaim his son, and couldn't reply. One look at Amelia's straight-backed, defensive stance told him more than her words ever could. She'd already lost whatever belief in him she'd found. Now she feared him, too, feared the reprisal her words would earn her.

Shaking off the doubt those words aroused, Mason said the only thing he could think of that might protect her from greater hurt later. "Trust me? I never said I was anything but an outlaw," he replied harshly. "Forget what I am at your peril."

She raised her head, tears turning her eyes a brighter blue. "How could I forget," she asked, "when we're locked up together in . . . in *here?*"

Her outflung arm took in their cell's rough adobe walls, packed-earth floor, and crude black iron bars. Her fist balled against her skirt, marking an uneven beat. "I—I just never imagined—"

She was scared, he realized with some amazement. In the time he'd known her, Amelia had seemed snooty, bossy, sometimes foolish—and foolhardy—but never scared. Until now.

"Come here." Mason swung his legs from the cot, making a place for her, then levered himself into a sitting position. He nodded toward the place beside him.

"No."

Amelia shook her head, appeared to reconsider, then crossed her arms beneath her breasts decisively. The motion pushed her breasts higher and closer together, rounding them beneath her borrowed dress in a way Mason couldn't help but notice. He tried to focus on something else, and failed.

"No!" she said again, raising her chin slightly. "Why would I want comfort from you anyway? It's your fault I'm here in the first place."

Biting back the harsh reply that rose to his lips, he gentled his tone instead. "If not for me, you wouldn't know what that kind of comfort was like."

She started to reply, then snapped her mouth closed.

"Come here, Amy," he said softly. "We're not enemies."

Suddenly, the air felt charged around him. All at once, the most important thing in the world was that she come to him. He could protect her, dammit! She was a frightened woman and he was a man, a man who could take care of her until they got free. He only needed a chance to show her. Mason tamped down his impatience, waiting as Amelia made her decision.

She moved a step closer. Warily, she glanced up at him from beneath her eyelashes. He saw a tremor pass through her, quick as lightning in a summer storm, and knew she was deciding on more than a place to rest. Anticipation quickened his heartbeat. He raised his hand to reassure her—and the chains binding him clanked quietly against the metal cot.

Mason closed his eyes against the anger that surged through him. Helpless! He was helpless as hell here, no good to himself or Amelia . . . or his child. Was Ben still in Tucson with the Sharpe brothers, or had they moved on already?

He sensed warmth just in front of him, and opened his eyes. Amelia stood there, only inches away. Her hand, so much smaller and paler than his own, reached toward his shoulder as though to comfort him. But when she saw Mason watching, she whipped her hand back to her side.

"Why didn't you give me my key?"

He blinked. "What?"

"My key. The key to my satchel. I know you have it."

At its mention, he felt the small weight of it settled on the chain against his chest. "I couldn't."

Come closer, he thought. Trust me.

At the realization of his thoughts, Mason leaned backward, stricken. Why should he want Amelia to trust him, when he'd failed so many others in the past?

He didn't.

"Why not?"

The key. Grinning without humor, he raised his bound arms. "I meant, I couldn't give it to you—not like this."

Her gaze fell to his wrists. With a poorly stifled cry, she caught his raw, reddened wrists and cradled them gently in her palms. The heat and scent of her skin flowed over him, soothing him, warming him in ways Mason was sure she'd never intended.

She couldn't know how her touch affected him, couldn't know how long it had been since he'd known a woman's care. And he shouldn't want it. He knew better, had every reason to distrust it, and yet . . . the warmth of her skin against his felt too good to refuse.

"Oh, Mason!" Amelia whispered. "I didn't know." She slipped her thumb beneath the binding, lifting it away from his skin for a closer look.

For a moment he was content to simply let himself watch her, taking in the smooth, straight line of her nose, the delicate arch of her eyebrows, the graceful curve of her temple and cheek. For once, she was too absorbed in what she was doing to scrutinize Mason's every move. He could watch her freely, and did.

Her hair looked soft as chick's down, curving in ringlets to her shoulders. Without her fancy, fussy pink dress, Mason realized, Amelia looked younger than before. Fresher. Prettier.

He longed to trace the freckles that dusted the top of her nose and cheeks, to cup her face in his hands and smooth away the worry that made her look so solemn. He could scarce believe it. A woman like her, worried over someone like him?

It was more than he deserved.

If he'd been a man for sighs and regrets, Mason would have said Amelia O'Malley was his penance; that after losing Ellen, there was nothing more for him to hope for. But thoughts like that were for poets—or poet bandits—and he was neither one.

Oh, Twirly Curls believed he was, and Mason meant to let

her go right on believing it. For now, it was safer than revealing who he really was.

By the time the lie wasn't needed—by the time he regained what the Sharpe brothers had stolen from him—Amy would be gone from his life.

"They can't do this to you," she said, still staring at the chains that bound him. A tear gathered at the corner of her eye and traveled down her cheek. A moment later Mason felt it fall onto his bare wrist, warm and wet and almost faint enough to believe he'd only imagined it. Just like he'd imagined a woman could care for him again, after all he'd done.

He wrenched his hands away, wincing as the motion made the bindings rub against his abraded flesh. "It doesn't matter."

"But I—"

"I found your key," he said, overriding her protests, "on the mountain that night, and held it for safekeeping. I meant to give it to you before."

"Mason, you're hurt! I—"

"I can't give it to you now," Mason went on doggedly. That wasn't gratitude he felt at her concern for him, it wasn't. The last damn thing he needed was another woman depending on him. Yet he'd called her to him. He didn't know what the hell he wanted anymore, not since Amelia had sung her way into his life and turned it upside down.

"But you can take it." He lifted his chin, giving her free access to his neck and chest so she could lift away the gold chain and key. "It's yours."

Amelia stared, first at his wrists and then at his neck. Her fingers flexed, her gaze flew to his. "I'm putting a stop to this."

Turning away, she stepped to the cell bars and rapped sharply on them. "Guard!"

She yanked her hand away. "Ouch!" Sucking her bruised knuckles, Amelia looked around for something else to strike the bars with. There was nothing.

"Amelia—"

"Guard!" she tried again, louder this time, ignoring Mason's protest. Her spine straightened, regal as a queen's, as she waited for the lone man who'd been assigned their watch to appear.

Finally he did, entering the room on legs that seemed too long for his body, carrying a rifle over his shoulder. His hair fell in filthy reddish waves to his shoulders, half-covering his gaunt, hairless face. Mason doubted the boy had ever wielded a razor in his life, much less a firearm.

It was his final humiliation. They'd set a gawky boy to watch over him. Mason wished he could sink straight into the warm brown adobe brick. Either that, or pound the daylights out of the damned insolent upstart. Right this minute, the boy stood grinning at Amelia like a half-wit, lacking only for his tongue to hang out a little farther to complete his resemblance to a mongrel dog after a bone.

"Ma'am?" The boy's Adam's apple bobbled as he swallowed hard. His gaze seemed glued to Amelia's bosom. He talked straight to it. "What can I do for you, Miss . . . uh, Miss Bandit, ma'am?"

Mason ground his teeth, fighting the urge to cuff their guard.

"I'll thank you, *boy,* to address me as Miss O'Malley."

Amelia's voice could've frozen them both to the spot. Mason sat up straighter, eyeing her with renewed respect. Amelia might not know a *mesa* from a mountain, but maybe—just maybe— he'd underestimated her other useful qualities.

"S-sorry, Miss O'Malley, ma'am. Ma'am." The boy thrust his head forward, then down, in an awkward attempt at a bow. "I—"

"That will do." Amelia's fingers shook—whether from nervousness or anger or some other emotion, Mason didn't know. As though to hide that fact, she pressed her palms together, fingertips splayed in a thoughtful pose. The boy quit bobbing, and she rewarded him with a faint smile.

"You must never address your superiors so familiarly," she admonished. *His superiors?* A statement like that took more grit than Mason had given Twirly Curls credit for.

"It's impolite," she was saying now. "Furthermore—"

"I know," the boy interrupted, staring at the ground as he spoke. "The schoolmarm always used to tell us that at school. But—"

"Address me directly, and look at me as you speak," Amelia instructed sharply, moving nearer to the cell bars. Obediently, the boy raised his head.

"Sorry, Miss O'Malley."

Mason's mouth dropped open. If Amelia kept on the way she was, she'd have the boy locking himself into their cell next.

It wasn't a bad idea.

"This man requires medical attention," said Amelia, stepping back a few paces to indicate Mason. She straightened her stance and looked down her nose at the boy. "Release his bindings at once, and then bring a physician."

The boy shook his head. "We don't have no physi-physi—no doctor here at the station, ma'am. I mean, Miss O'Malley, ma'am," he added quickly. "And I can't release him. He's an outlaw, ma'am! The stationmaster would like to have my hide if I unlocked that cell."

He backed away, gripping his rifle tighter. The stock slid across his palm with a squeak, and the weapon's barrel wavered in the air above his shoulder. He was nervous. Scared of a woman's scolding.

Mason frowned. This wasn't just any boy they'd set to guard him—this was a boy too young to shave, too inexperienced to handle his gun properly, and too afraid to stand up to a female prisoner. Mason would wager he had no more than seventeen years in him, if that.

Perfect.

"Then bring me some clean water and cloths," Amelia

snapped. "I'll not stand by while this man is mistreated. Do you comprehend me . . . ?"

"Uh, Jody," the boy supplied, glancing quickly toward the door. Afraid he'd be discovered talking with the prisoners? Watching out for the stationmaster?

"Perhaps I should speak with the stationmaster instead," Amelia said, patience worn thin evident in her voice.

The boy turned toward her, a guilty flush coloring his pock-marked cheeks. "Uh, everybody's in the *zaguán,* eatin' dinner. 'Cluding the stationmaster. I—"

"Snap to it, boy!" she commanded, sounding for all the world like a mean old schoolmarm about to rap his knuckles with her ruler. "Every second you delay, this man is suffering."

"But—"

She sighed. "Then bring me the stationmaster. Interrupt his meal, I don't care. Whatever you decide, be quick about it."

The boy wavered, visibly torn. A moment later, he threw up his hands and stomped off, muttering something beneath his breath. As soon as he'd left the room, Amelia turned to Mason. Her eyes looked bright, and her hands still trembled, but her face was well and truly lit with a proud, lopsided smile.

"Don't worry," she told him quietly. "He'll be back with everything I asked for, you'll see. I'll take care of you, Mason."

Mason leaned back. *She'd* take care of *him?* He felt like shuddering at the notion. First a child to guard him, then a woman to take care of him? He had to get out of that cell before he was reduced to being spoon-fed like a damned infant.

"What if he brings the stationmaster instead?" he asked her.

"He won't."

She whirled away before he could see her expression, leaving Mason more irritable than before. He was escaping from that cell no matter what he had to do to accomplish it.

Within minutes the boy returned, clutching a bundle of white cloths against his chest and a worn key ring in his fist. He stopped at their cell door, beating the keys against his thigh. "You sure 'bout this, ma'am? Uh, Miss O'Malley? That's a dangerous outlaw in there with you."

Mason bared his teeth. The boy retreated a pace, jangling the keys faster.

"Of course," Amelia snapped, assuming her schoolmarm's demeanor like a clean-starched coat. "This man hasn't harmed me, now has he? He needs medical care, and I intend to see that he receives it." She paused. "Or are you the sort of person who'd leave another to suffer needlessly?"

Her tone suggested such a man belonged in the pits of hell— or at least in the Arizona Territory in the summertime without a canteen of water. Mason suppressed a grin. The boy didn't.

"No, ma'am." The keys shook as he brought them close and unlocked the cell door. It creaked forward into the room, leaving their guard waiting nervously in the opening.

Mason tried to look less threatening. Maybe a smile? He gritted his teeth.

The boy's mouth dropped open. He didn't move an inch.

"What's the—" Amelia glanced from the boy to Mason. "Oh, for heaven's sake! Come in here, boy, and make it quick."

"He—he's—I think he's growling at me, Miss O'Malley," the boy protested with a sideways glance at Mason. "I don't think—"

"He's in pain," Amelia explained, laying her hand on the boy's forearm to draw him forward. "That's why we must help him."

At her touch, the boy's mouth went slack. Gazing at her adoringly, he obediently followed her into the cell. When he got within a foot of Mason's cot, though, his wits returned.

"I dunno about this," he protested, squinting suspiciously down at the cot where Mason waited, tense beneath his shackles.

"He won't hurt you," she assured him. "I can't treat him if you don't unlock the bindings."

The boy's head raised sharply. "I ain't scared of him, ma'am. It's you I'm worried about, Miss O'Malley."

Mason rolled his eyes.

Amelia patted the boy's sleeve. "I'm sure you'll watch over me admirably, Jody."

The boy pushed his chest forward. "Yes, ma'am!"

Mason held up his wrists. A moment later the boy had unlocked the bindings, then stepped back toward the cell door. Cool air rushed over Mason's wounds, making them sting. He knew an instant of gratitude, followed swiftly by regret at what he was about to do.

Rising from the cot, he grabbed Amelia. He glimpsed her face, pale and surprised, before he turned her around and hauled her back against his chest.

"Mason! What are you—?"

"Shut up." Using his left arm to hold her tight in front of him, Mason raised his other arm and wrapped his fingers around her throat.

"You—" he nodded roughly toward the guard—"get out of my way."

The boy looked rooted to the spot.

"Are you insane?" Amelia struggled against him, jabbing her elbow painfully into his belly. "I was trying to help you! I—"

Mason tightened his fingers against her throat, just hard enough to make her quit talking. "I said, move!" he growled at the boy.

"Uh-uh—" The boy glanced around wildly, his hands clenching and unclenching at his sides. His fingers flexed only inches from the rifle slung over his shoulder. As though just then remembering he carried it, the boy's head snapped downward toward the weapon.

"I could break her neck right now," Mason said softly.

A smothered cry came from Amelia. He was glad she

couldn't speak. Mason didn't want to know what this desperate act would cost him.

Abandoning all thoughts of his rifle, the guard sidled aside, his gaze fastened on Amelia. Mason passed though the doorway, keeping Amelia in front of him like a shield. He'd guessed correctly. A boy like that wouldn't endanger a woman—and he wouldn't have the first notion how to save her.

"Get inside," he told the guard, nodding toward their open cell door.

"Uh-uh . . ." The boy swallowed hard, frowning indecisively toward Amelia and then Mason.

"And give me your rifle, too."

Resigned, the boy swung his weapon, stock-first, toward Mason. He shuffled inside the small cell. "Station master's gonna have my hide for this," he muttered. "He was wanting that reward."

His mournful, worried gaze shifted to Amelia again. "I—I'm sorry about this, ma'am."

A garbled reply came from Amelia. Mason slammed the cell door shut and locked it, then glared through the bars at the boy.

"Never trust a woman," he told him.

Keeping one eye on their guard, Mason paused beside the squat wooden table outside their cell. He scooped up his own rifle and left the guard's weapon out of reach, pocketed his pistol, and shoved his ammunition belt toward Amelia. She slumped beneath its weight, then straightened, clutching it tight against her middle.

"Mason, please—"

His fingers tightened until nothing remained of her protest but a faint, strangled plea.

"No."

He reached the doorway and glanced outside, squinting at the bright light after two day's captivity. The yard looked all but deserted. With luck, the stables would be the same.

Still holding Amelia, Mason squinted over his shoulder at the guard. "You know what I'm wanted for?" he asked.

Trembling, the boy swallowed hard. He nodded. "We—we got the wire from Gila Bend this morning," he said.

Damn. The sheriff had wasted no time—the Sharpe brothers' lie had taken root and spread faster than Mason had expected. Doubtless word of his latest escape would fly quickly, too. He had to hurry.

"Not stage robbery," Mason said, backing up with Amelia held tight.

"No." The boy retreated into the cell corner. "M-murder," he stammered. "Murdering a woman."

Amelia cried out, her body fairly vibrating with fear against his chest and legs. Now she knew what he was accused of. That knowledge would cost him her trust and more, but nothing could be more important than reclaiming his son.

Mason squeezed his arm closer around her waist, struggling to ignore the part of him that urged him to release her. He stroked Amelia's neck, feeling her pulse beat wild beneath his fingertips.

"If anyone follows me," he told the guard. "I'll kill her."

Another cry from Amelia. Mason couldn't listen. Tightening his fingers again to keep her from crying out for help, he stepped into the sunshine and turned his face south, toward Tucson.

I'm coming, Ben, he thought. Hang on.

Eight

Amelia had a confused impression of cloud-strewn blue sky, muddy adobe walls, and hot air swirling around them before Mason shoved her up against the outer wall of the building they'd just left. The back of her head thudded into the wall, then her whole body pitched forward. Mason's ammunition belt dropped from her hands.

He caught it before it hit the ground. Still holding it, he pressed his hand into her belly and loomed over her. Amelia's breath left her. Dimly, she registered the bite of the prickly textured adobe through her clothes and the uneven dirt beneath her feet before Mason's body squashed her harder into the wall. It felt as though he wanted to push her straight through the wall back into the cell on the other side.

"Be still," he commanded, his gaze sweeping down to hold hers. Desperation darkened his eyes and straightened his mouth into an unforgiving line.

Before she could do so much as nod, the sounds of footsteps reached her, coming from just beyond the shadowed coolness of the building they leaned against. Only a faint scuffling against the soil, they seemed loud in the stage station's noontime stillness. Closer, slowing . . . then faster. Finally the sounds faded. Amelia sagged; whether with relief or despair, she couldn't tell.

How could she have misjudged Mason so sorely? How had

she believed he wouldn't hurt her? His hard, callused palm against her throat proved that belief wrong beyond a doubt. Worse, she'd brought it all upon herself by tricking the guard into releasing him. Stupid, stupid . . .

She had to find a way to make Mason leave her behind. Anything else was foolhardy. Even prison would surely be preferable to being abducted by an escaped outlaw—an escaped outlaw *murderer.*

Mason, a murderer? Amelia's mind recoiled at the thought, but still their guard's fear-filled admission of Mason's crime echoed in her mind. Was it true? Had he really killed a woman?

Her knees quaked. If not for his arm holding her up, she felt sure she'd have fainted clean away already. No wonder he hadn't wanted to admit who he really was!

His chin brushed against the top of her head as he looked around the station, probably seeking the best escape route. She couldn't tell for certain what he was looking at, because his shoulder pinned her to the wall, making it impossible to see much beyond him. Amelia tried to remember what she'd seen of the stage station when they'd been brought in, but all she could recall were high, thick walls and a cluster of long, windowless adobe buildings.

Would anyone come to her aid if she screamed? All she needed was for Mason to loosen his hold on her throat just a little bit, and then . . .

"This way."

He grabbed her arm and dragged her through the dusty square toward one of the buildings. Just outside it stood several buckboards, a canvas-covered wagon with a yoke of oxen, and a single deserted Wells Fargo stagecoach. The passengers were probably all inside for the noon meal, along with the stage station's hands. Mason couldn't have timed his escape better if he'd planned it.

Or maybe he had—and used her to accomplish it.

He peered into each conveyance as they passed, then doubled back toward the canvas-covered wagon. When they stopped at its rear, he tossed his rifle and ammunition belt through the drawstring-tightened opening in the canvas.

"Get in," he said, taking his hand from her throat to motion toward the steps at the wagon's rear. He gave her a little shove forward.

Too surprised to move at first, Amelia hesitated at the back of the wagon. He'd released her! Her throat felt sore, and a bump was probably growing on the back of her head, but she was free. She started trembling harder. Should she run, or simply yell for help?

Run.

She turned, drew a big breath past her burning throat—and Mason caught her. Grabbing her around the waist, he growled and hefted her into the air. Amelia shrieked. A second later, she tumbled into the back of the wagon amidst barrels and blankets and farm tools.

She could only lie there, stunned and staring, as he climbed in after her. Only the haziest light penetrated the thick canvas, but Mason's fearsome expression was plain even through the gloom. His lips curled back, baring his teeth, and his eyebrows angled sharply downward. His fists clenched, closing over empty air, but Amelia would've bet every last book in her J. G. O'Malley & Sons satchels that he wished it was her neck laid bare between his hands. She whimpered.

"Another sound from you," he warned in a harsh whisper, "and it's the last one you make."

She scooted backward, burrowing deeper into the things piled beneath her in her haste to get away from him. He didn't pursue her, though. With one last, snarling look, Mason turned away from her and started rummaging through the things that filled the wagon bed.

"I'm getting out of here," he said as he cast aside a patchwork quilt and a barrel of something that rattled when it moved. "And you're going to help."

Help? Help him, and then likely be killed for her trouble? Amelia started to say so aloud, but a look from him silenced her. Suddenly Mason seemed twice as violent as he ever had. He'd probably break her arm just for fun if she disagreed with him. And this was the man she'd let kiss her, only a few short days ago!

Her father and brothers were right: Amelia Josephine O'Malley did *not* belong in the West, not in any capacity and certainly not as a book agent. She didn't even have the first idea where her book satchels were.

Mason thrust a limp bit of calico toward her. "Put this on."

Automatically, she took it. Beside her, Mason strapped on his gun belt while she examined the thing he'd given her. She turned it over in her hands.

A sunbonnet?

"But why would I—?"

"Just do it." He lifted his pistol to the shaft of light shining in through the opening in the canvas, opened the barrel, and peered inside. Pushing some bullets from his gun belt into his palm, Mason started to load the ammunition.

When she hesitated, he snapped the loaded chamber closed and leveled the weapon at her. "I said, put it on."

"All right!" With trembling fingers, Amelia raised the worn sunbonnet over her head and smoothed it over her hair. She ran her fingers down the bonnet's strings, trying to gather them into a knot beneath her chin. Her hands refused to cooperate. Clumsily, she dropped the strings and had to start over again.

Swearing, Mason holstered his gun, then pushed her fingers aside and grabbed the ties himself. Amelia hardly dared breathe while he drew them taut, tugging the bonnet all the way onto her head. Frowning, he pulled the bonnet's sides toward her cheeks, then took up the strings again.

Suddenly, he stopped, his gaze centered on her bare neck. The bonnet strings dangled from his still fingers, their soft frayed fabric ends brushing against her skin just above the bodice of her dress. Amelia felt one of them touch the hollow of her throat. Then, guided by his hands, it slid upward over the place that ached most from the bruising pressure of Mason's fingers.

His knuckles caressed her throat, his touch soft as a warm breeze. "Swollen," he whispered, his voice turned thick . . . with sadness?

Their eyes met, just for a moment. In the dark depths of his she saw regret, and compassion . . . and an overriding sense of desperation unlike anything she'd ever experienced. Whatever was driving Mason, it was something that mattered intensely to him, something he'd risk his life and soul to find. And in that moment Amelia knew, beyond all doubt, that he couldn't have murdered anyone. How could he, when simply bruising a woman caused him such pain?

Mason closed his eyes briefly, ending their contact as though it had never begun. When he opened them again, his gaze was level and sure.

"I'm sorry, Amy," he said.

"Mason, I—"

"There was no other way."

I understand, she wanted to say; I forgive you. But the sound of masculine voices and shuffling footsteps outside cut short her words. Shaking his head to warn her into silence, Mason swiftly gathered up the bonnet strings again and tied them in a snug bow beneath her chin. That done, he laid his hand on her upper arm.

"Get up there," he told her, indicating the front of the wagon with a curt motion of his head. Through the wider canvas opening there, Amelia just glimpsed the brown-haired heads and bulky bodies of the oxen team. They shifted restlessly in their traces, waiting for the wagon's owner to return and set them on their journey again.

"Up . . . there?" Amelia shook her head, resisting the slight pressure of Mason's hand against the small of her back.

"Keep your bonnet pulled forward to hide your face and drive straight out of here," he said. "If they see me, we'll never make it. You have to do it."

"No! No, Mason. I've never driven a team of oxen! I've never even driven a wagon before," Amelia protested in a frantic whisper. At the thought her heart beat faster, making her feel half-swoony. "I can't do it! My brothers wouldn't even let me drive their phaetons, and they were half the size of this. I—"

He caught her chin in his hand and turned her to face him.

"You can do it."

Mutely, Amelia shook her head. She'd kill them both! If those two beasts took it into their animal heads to run away with the wagon, she'd never, never be able to stop them. Didn't Mason understand that? Wide-eyed, she stared back at him.

He met her gaze unflinchingly. Mason understood what he was asking of her, and he meant to get it. Tenderly he brushed his thumb along her jaw, a silent demand that she listen—and accede to him.

"Please," he said. "I need your help."

A masculine voice rang out from the other side of the canvas, then more voices joined his. It sounded as though they came from one direction—the stage station, most likely. The afternoon meal must be finished.

She clenched her fists, meeting Mason's gaze again. "If I kill us both with this fool plan of yours," she whispered, "don't say I didn't warn you."

Mason's smile flashed at her, briefly lighting all the murky depths of the wagon. "If you do kill the pair of us, I doubt I'll have much to say about it from six feet under."

"I can't believe you'd joke about this!"

"Just go. Past these walls and a few miles south, and we're safe. I'll take over from there."

"All right." If he'd take over later, she could find the courage to get them started.

It took less time than Amelia expected to climb through the jumbled supplies piled inside the wagon bed, then lower herself onto the plank seat supplied for the driver. There, sunshine beat relentlessly, hard enough to have turned the seat gray and splintered. The heat, combined with a good dose of plain, bullheaded fear, made perspiration trickle between Amelia's shoulder blades, dampening the back of her borrowed dress.

Tugging her sunbonnet forward, she examined the wagon's fittings as nonchalantly as she was able. No one would guess she didn't belong with the rig, she vowed, at least not from her demeanor.

Something nudged her side. "Put these on."

Amelia glanced down to see Mason's hand tuck something between her elbow and waist, where she could grab it easily. A pair of men's leather work gloves. She pulled out the stiff, mud-splotched gloves and put them on, grateful for the extra layer of protection and camouflage. Having the correct accouterments could only make her disguise more believable, she reasoned.

"It's not a garden party!" Mason hissed from behind her. "Get moving."

She realized she'd been staring at the gloves while she contemplated their escape plan, and stopped. Lowering her head, Amelia listened to the rest of Mason's instructions. Doubtless he was better equipped to deal with such things as subterfuge and jailbreaks than she was.

"The traces are right there," he whispered to the small of her back. "Unwrap them from the foot brake, then slowly lower the lever."

Sounds drifted nearer—men and horses milling near the wagon, then passing it by; men and a few women speaking to each other in both English and exotically melodic Spanish. From the corner of her eye, Amelia spied passengers climbing into the red-lacquered stagecoach to her left. Their movements stirred up a cloud of dust that reminded her of exactly how different this Arizona Territory landscape was from her home.

If she was ever to return there again, see her father and brothers again, she had to take action now. They had to move soon, else be discovered and lose their chance to escape.

With a quick prayer for courage, Amelia bit her lip and carefully unwrapped the long braided-leather traces from the brake lever. As though sensing her presence, the oxen stepped forward, snorting eagerly.

"Ahhh!" Teetering atop her hard plank seat, she just managed to regain control of the animals. She couldn't contain the smile that burst forth from her lips. She'd done it! She'd kept them from running willy-nilly into the desert! Maybe she and Mason could make it after all.

Some folks were going to be very unhappy when they finished eating and found their wagon missing. But that couldn't be helped now. She'd just have to think about that later. Amelia arranged the traces in her gloved palms.

"Mason, I'm ready."

"Good work, Amelia," came his voice from behind her.

Mason's hand smoothed across her back, then settled lightly against her left hip. "Very good. Now just release the brake with your foot and let up a little on the traces. The oxen will take care of the rest."

"Easy for you to say," Amelia muttered over her shoulder. She wished mightily that he was the one driving. But there was nothing to be done about that now, either. With one final swipe at her damp forehead and a forceful tug on her sunbonnet, she propped her foot atop the brake.

Sunlight glinted from something on the seat just below her

right elbow. Hesitating, Amelia looked down. It was the barrel
of Mason's rifle. She gasped.

"What do you need that thing for?"

Impatience added steel to Mason's voice. "For as long as it
takes to get us out of here," he replied. "Now drive."

At least the weapon wasn't aimed at her. Taking comfort in
that fact, she kicked down the brake lever. The wagon lurched
forward, its iron-clad wheels creaking over stones and ruts in
the stage station's yard.

Ahead of them, the tan adobe walls of Maricopa Wells station
stood tall against the brilliant blue sky. Keeping her gaze fastened on them, Amelia gave the oxen their head. They plodded
forward, scattering chickens beneath their slowly advancing
hooves.

Apparently, even unreined oxen were pitifully slow. She felt
like screaming with frustration.

"Can't they go any faster?" Amelia hissed toward Mason.

"This is it," came his laconic reply.

Any second now, she'd be recognized as the impostor she
was and dragged from the wagon, she felt sure of it. Her fingers
tightened on the traces. Ahead, the opened gate promised freedom from an outlaw's fate—and a chance to quit driving the
wagon. Maybe she could hurry the oxen a bit, despite Mason's
pessimistic opinion of the animals' capabilities.

What was it the driver called to oxen to make them go faster?
Searching her memory for the times she'd seen local farmers
driving into the market place back home in Big Pike Lake,
finally Amelia remembered something.

She jerked the traces. "Haw!"

Both beasts turned to the left and plodded on. Darn! That,
wasn't it.

She straightened her sunbonnet, getting ready to try something else. Glancing forward again, Amelia realized the oxen's
new path was taking them—and the wagon—smack into what

appeared to be a wash house. Panicked, she tugged fruitlessly on the traces. The animals didn't even slow. Now they felt like hurrying!

A cluster of dark-haired Mexican women glanced up from their washing. Their eyes widened as they realized Amelia and the oxen weren't stopping.

"Ahh—ahh! What do I do?" she whispered frantically to Mason. But she couldn't wait for him to reply—they were almost upon the women. A few more oxen-sized steps, and they'd smash right into the wash house.

"Whoa! Stop! Stop!"

The oxen kept going, just as though she hadn't spoken.

Mason was saying something, but Amelia couldn't hear him over the cries of the washerwomen. Suddenly, an idea occurred to her.

"Haw!"

The oxen turned left again, narrowly missing the wash house.

"I'm so sorry!" Amelia called; then she remembered she was supposed to be in disguise and ducked her head again. When she looked up from between her hunched shoulders, she realized they were headed back in the direction they'd come from.

"No! No!" she cried. "I mean, haw!"

They turned, their movement spewing choking dust from beneath the wagon wheels, and headed straight for the nearest wall. "Haw!" Amelia yelled.

Mason jabbed her, none too gently, in the backside. "When you're finished driving us in circles," he said into her ear, "can we get the hell out of here?"

"I'm trying!"

Slapping the oxen with the traces, Amelia succeeded in getting the animals to speed up just enough. Hallelujah! They were facing the open gate again.

In the stage-station yard below her, several faces turned upward as she passed. Most wore wide, indulgent smiles. Look at the lady drive in circles, they seemed to be saying. Have you ever seen such a thing?

Amelia's heart sank. She couldn't have made their escape from Maricopa Wells more conspicuous if she'd set out to do it apurpose. Keeping her attention fixed on the open gate, she gritted her teeth and did her best to ignore the onlookers.

The stagecoach's fast teams of horses came abreast of her wagon, then the coach itself rolled along beside her. From within came the sound of amused male voices, calling to her.

"Don't them animals know how to walk straight?" yelled one. "How'd ya get this far, immigrant?"

Amelia stared straight ahead. Blessedly, the stagecoach's horses picked up speed before any more catcalls reached her, and the vehicle passed through the open gate. Only a few more yards, and they'd be past it, too.

A station hand, swarthy skinned and well armed, stepped from the shadows of the adobe wall, directly into her path. Amelia gaped at him, trying hard not to beat the oxen into running faster. To do so—even if it worked—would only jeopardize their getaway plan. The man raised his hand, signaling her to stop the wagon.

Nine

"What do I do? What do I do?" Amelia whispered to Mason from the corner of her mouth. Her stomach turned over with nervousness. Had their former guard alerted the station hands to their escape? Were they about to be recaptured?

"Go along with him—for now," Mason muttered back.

Something cool slid further along Amelia's hip, then settled partway across the plank seat beside her. Mason's rifle. With the outlaw himself at the business end of the weapon, ready to fire, she was sure. Her heartbeat, already frantic, soared.

"Hold up there a minute, ma'am," called the station hand.

"M-me?" Amelia croaked. She swallowed, vainly trying to moisten her parched throat.

He nodded, walking nearer. The shotgun propped casually against his shoulder was all she could see.

"Uh, ah . . . gee!" she called hoarsely to the oxen. The animals slowly turned to the right, and kept going.

Oh, dear heaven. Not again!

She waved her hand holding the traces, trying desperately to think up the command to make the oxen stop. Haw meant left, and gee must mean right, so . . .

"Ho," rumbled the station hand. Just as though he were Paul Bunyon himself, the animals heard his command and stopped in their tracks. Reaching out, the man seized the lead animal's harness.

Here it was, Amelia thought. Capture. What had Mason been thinking, to put her in charge of their escape? After all, *he'd* caught her every time except the last.

Mason's rifle inched forward. Behind her, she sensed his awareness of their precarious situation, his taut control—and his utter willingness to sacrifice anything to reach his goal.

"Looked like you needed some help," remarked the station hand in heavily Spanish-accented speech, squinting upward at her. He doffed his battered *sombrero,* then grinned. He appeared to be settling in for a nice, friendly conversation—at least if his smile and openhanded stance could be believed. Amelia wasn't sure it could.

"Thank him and get moving," Mason whispered, nudging her from behind.

"Th-thank you," she managed to say. Still holding the traces, she slapped her gloved palms onto her thighs, trying to make her legs quit trembling.

"Nice day, ain't it?" asked the station hand.

Mason groaned. She felt the exhalation of his breath against her bare elbow. Too afraid to speak, she nodded and sat straighter. Loosely she clasped the traces, and kept staring straight ahead. Perhaps he'd think her simply standoffish, and allow her to pass.

But what if the station hand recognized her as the outlaw's consort? Worse, what if he already had, and was only toying with her until he was ready to spring the trap closed?

"Pretty little *mariquita* like you needs a man's help in territory like this," the station hand went on.

Why, he was making a pass at her! Amazed, Amelia peeped at him from beneath the broad, flat floral edge of her sunbonnet. At this sign of feminine encouragement, he spat into the dirt and grinned again.

"That's a fine rig, too," he said, examining her newly stolen Conestoga wagon.

Privately, Amelia gave thanks for the thick canvas cover that hid Mason from his scrutiny. Publicly, she gave the station hand a wan acknowledging smile.

Mason's rifle edged forward. "Move!" he hissed, the sound low and for her ears alone.

"I could be persuaded to help you out, ma'am," proposed the station hand, "seeing as how you don't have any menfolk with you to—"

"No!" Amelia cried hastily. Had Mason's rifle moved even closer? She pictured his finger on the trigger, ready to shoot their way out of the Maricopa Wells compound if necessary, and renewed panic tightened her stomach. "No, but thank you very much for offering."

The station hand released the lead ox and walked closer. Again he eyed her stolen wagon covetously—and this time, he included her figure in his smirking perusal. "You should think about it, *mariquita*. A man like me could be a big help to a woman alone—"

"I—I've got a man!" What? she asked herself desperately. Now what?

The station hand frowned. He was nearly upon her—she was close enough to see the bulge of chewing tobacco that distended his lower lip.

"Amelia . . ." whispered Mason.

Think, *think,* Amelia commanded herself. Nothing came to mind except plain, blind fear of being captured and hung as an outlaw.

"Move right on my signal," Mason instructed grimly. "Then run like hell."

He was going to shoot! She had to do something.

"I don't see nobody with you," said the station hand. He set one big, booted foot atop the wagon's edge, preparing to climb onto the plank seat beside her.

"It's my husband. He's . . . he's got influenza!" she cried.

"He's horribly sick, nearly dead back there," she added, nodding toward the covered part of the wagon. "The rest of our party's already died from it," she elaborated.

"Enough," gritted Mason, silencing her.

"Ah, *sí.*"

The station hand dropped from the wagon as though scalded, his face a mask of revulsion. In the West, far from most doctors and hospitals, he'd obviously learned to fear illness. Especially virulent, contagious illness.

"Sorry to bother you, ma'am. You'd best be on your way."

He slapped the oxen, sending them from the station nearly at a run. It was all Amelia could do to hang on. She bounced on the hard plank seat, her feet braced against the wagon for support, and felt like applauding herself for her quick thinking. Influenza! And he'd believed her, too. Despite everything, a smile spread across her face.

The desert flashed by in tones of gold, brown, and muted green; dust churned from the animals' massive hooves, making her breath taste gritty and her eyes hurt. She squinted against it, determined to get as far away from Maricopa Wells as possible.

Miles passed rapidly. Before very long, Mason shifted behind her, then his hand came forward and grabbed the front edge of her seat. A moment later, his other hand followed the first. Amelia could feel the muscles in his arms bunch and strain, then he climbed onto the seat with a grunt of exertion. She didn't dare look at him and risk overturning the wagon—or worse.

His hands closed over her contraband leather work gloves. Gently, Mason pried the traces from her grasp. Relieved of the responsibility of driving, Amelia gripped the thick edge of the seat and watched him do it instead.

Mason drove with assurance, like a man well accustomed to handling a team of draft animals, a ten-foot wagon, and the rutted Territory roads. He'd been skilled with his horse, too. The same horse, she recalled, wincing, she'd made run away on the day of their capture.

As far as she knew, he'd lost all his possessions—save those on his back—that day. Yet not a single word of recrimination had passed his lips, not in the whole time they'd spent locked up at Maricopa Wells. To look at him now, she'd almost believe Mason didn't care how much he'd lost as long as he regained whatever it was he sought so desperately.

But what was it?

Mason scanned the countryside surrounding them, then guided the oxen away from the road toward a low, cactus-dotted hill nearby. He settled the traces loosely in his hands and rested his elbows on his thighs. Finally, as though sensing her gaze upon him, he turned his face toward Amelia.

His appearance had changed since she'd met him. Then, his expression had seemed inscrutable to her, his demeanor wild and frightening. Now, she recognized the pleasure in the faint upward tilt of his lips, the fierce gladness to be free in the brightness of his eyes. And she was glad to have helped make it happen.

Two days spent in their makeshift jail cell had given Mason the beginnings of a soft brown beard. He'd lost his hat, too—his hair blew wild in the wind, tossed back starkly from his face. Seeing it, something loosened within Amelia. She experienced a sense of carelessness, of revelry, such as she'd never known. They were free. Free! And she'd helped bring it about.

She untied her sunbonnet and flung it into the wind.

"What's the matter with you?" Mason asked, staring over his shoulder toward the spot where her sunbonnet had vanished.

Grinning at him, Amelia set to work removing her hairpins. One by one, she pitched them from her fingers toward the desert beyond.

Mason frowned. "You've gone daft," he announced, aiming another sideways look at her.

She aimed a hairpin at the top of his head, and missed. Luckily, she still had more ammunition holding the thick chignon at the back of her head.

They reached the hill, their destination. His face grim, Mason steered the wagon into a sheltered gully behind it. Here, desert bushes grew close together in the powerful sunshine, and birds chattered and flitted amongst them. Clouds high in the sky divided the light into shafts of shadow and gold. Amelia aimed her last hairpin toward a pincushionlike cactus as they passed through a shadowed spot, then started unwinding her hair.

"Stop that," Mason ordered.

"No." She dug her fingers into her scalp and shook her hair free, unmindful of the tangles that would surely result. The wind lifted the wavy blond strands of her hair like caressing hands. Ringlets streamed behind Amelia's head, across her lips, into her eyes, and she couldn't stop the smile that rose to her lips at Mason's astonished expression.

"Amelia—"

He must be worried, to address her by her given name.

"We made it!" she cried, launching herself at him. He caught her with a muffled exclamation, and she wrapped her arms around his neck. "We made it, we made it!"

She felt like laughing aloud. Beneath her, Mason squirmed. He transferred the traces to a single hand and called for the oxen to stop. Slowly, the wagon quit jouncing. They both lurched forward. Amelia buried her face in the warm crook of his neck and held on.

Mason grabbed her arms and set her away from him with a suspicious scowl. "What's wrong with you?"

"Are we safe here?"

He cocked his head. "For now," he admitted. "We're a ways from the road, and hidden behind that hill."

Leaning forward, Mason set the brake and wrapped the traces around it. Dust motes flickered in a shaft of light shining on the lever, and without the clamor of the wagon and team's movement surrounding them, everything seemed hushed in their hiding place.

Nevertheless Mason frowned, clearly preparing another argument. "I don't think anybody followed us, but—"

"But we're safe!" For once, Amelia was the one to interrupt him. "Safe because of *me!*" She tucked a hank of errant hair behind her ear, feeling as though her chest might well explode with her sense of pride.

"I was so scared back there, Mason. I thought we were going to be captured at any moment. Do you know, my knees still haven't quit knocking?" He scowled, still not understanding, she guessed. "I've never been more afraid in my life, but I—"

"But you did it." He crossed his arms over his chest, gazing at her with an odd mixture of tolerance and confusion.

"Yes!" She threw herself toward him again. This time, her target was his waist. She wrapped her arms as tight around his middle as she was able, and squeezed. Mason's hands, hovering someplace over her head, settled lightly on her shoulders.

"See? I told you I'd take care of you," she said against his chest. His shirt felt soft and warm against her cheek, heated by the strong male body beneath it. "Remember? Back at the jail, I told you I'd take care of you."

She stroked his back, feeling the muscles there flex and smooth beneath her palm. His hands slid from her shoulders, moving hesitantly toward her waist. If she'd ever wondered how a man might hold a woman gone loony, now she knew. Mason seemed almost afraid to touch her, lest the craziness was catching.

Amelia sighed, too buoyed by her recent success to let his suspicions that she was addled bring her spirits low.

"You know," she confessed, touching her fingertip to one of his carved-horn shirt buttons, then another, "I've never taken care of anybody before."

Mason grunted. She figured it was a sign of agreement and

went on. "I never even thought I could. I'll admit it—you're the first person I've ever rescued. But who knows what I'm capable of?"

If she could pull off a jailbreak and rescue a desperado, surely she could manage to track down her J. G. O'Malley & Sons satchels and deliver her book orders to Tucson. Why, it would be simple compared with what she'd already accomplished today! She'd never felt more confident in her life.

His hands stilled. "You—rescued *me?*"

"Well, yes," Amelia replied.

Mason shook his head above her. His reaction wasn't really all that surprising—what sort of man would just come right out and admit a woman had rescued him? None, in her experience. Her father and brothers never would have, not in a million years. Still, after all she'd been through, Amelia didn't think her contribution ought to be ignored.

"Twice!" she added.

His chest rumbled with laughter. Indignant, she pushed away from him and lifted her chin to explain. "Yes, don't you remember? The first time I saved you was when that horrible man was shooting at you from the stagecoach—"

"Mmm-hmm," he replied noncommittally, raising his eyebrows as he waited for her to recount the second instance of her rescuing him.

His open skepticism was galling.

"And the second time was when I drove us out of the stage station," she went on.

"Mmm-hmm."

He sounded for all the world like one of her book customers listening to her sales talk. Bored. He turned on the seat beside her, lifting his leg and then lowering it on the other side so he straddled the wood. His hands rested open on his thighs. She was right in the open vee of his legs.

"Thereby saving us!" Amelia finished, her gaze straying to

his thighs. Feeling her cheeks flush, she looked upward again. "You can't deny it."

"Ahhh," he murmured, nodding. He captured a wavering strand of her hair, and smoothed it gently over her shoulder. "I see what you mean."

Suddenly, she had the distinct impression Mason wasn't listening to her at all. Unsmiling, he delved both his hands into her unbound hair, stroking his fingers against her scalp. His eyes closed, affording her an excellent opportunity to observe him, without his knowledge, as much as she wanted.

Or to restate her case for having rescued him.

Except she didn't want to. His hands moved in her hair, gently tugging the long strands, smoothing them away from her face and stealing her will to assert her claim at the same time. The breeze, cooler now, lifted the ends of her hair in counterpoint, wrapping blond strands around Mason's hands. He captured them, smiling.

"Even your hair's willful," he murmured, smoothing the strands in place again.

Willful. The word called to some hidden, devilish place inside Amelia, secretly thrilling her. Today, now, she did feel willful. Willful and brave and exhilarated. Together they'd risked everything to escape . . . and won.

Mason's thumbs stroked across her temples, igniting warmth that followed his touch over her ears and down to the sensitive skin just behind her earlobes. How did he manage to impart so much sensation with a simple touch? It was all Amelia could do not to sway toward him, lulled by the mesmerizing feel of his hands.

He flicked each tiny lobe, teasing them with the faint pressure of his fingertips. She shivered in response, a nonsensical reaction if ever she'd had one, but Amelia lacked the will to consider it further. He stroked her again, and goose bumps prickled over her bare arms, startling her.

Her breath caught and held. Hearing it, Mason smiled faintly, then circled her earlobes with his fingertips once more. Pleasure followed his touch, spiking clear to her toes.

"Thank you, Amy," he whispered, repeating the small caress. "Thank you for helping me."

He should have sounded humble, admitting she'd saved him. She should have rejoiced in the acknowledgment, having only moments before argued to gain it. But neither of those things were true. Mason's words had the sound of a wish, not a concession. And somehow the touch of his hands made Amelia feel anything but argumentative.

"I want to help you more," she told him, the idea growing and taking shape within her even as she spoke it aloud. "I want to help you find—"

"No one can help me," he broke in, shaking his head against her automatic protest. His fingertip traced the curve of her ear, making her eyelids flutter closed and all other thoughts flee. "No more than your touch helps me now. You're so . . . my God, so sweet, Amy. Mmmm, so . . . good."

His words ended on a groan, and his fingers grew taut in her hair. Alarmed, she looked up at him. Was she causing him pain somehow, despite all he'd said?

"Mason?" Bravely, Amelia dared to touch his cheek, then sweep her hand deeper into the thick softness of his dark hair. His head tilted partway back, exposing the straight, solid line of his throat. He swallowed hard, like a man mustering courage for a battle—or a man surrendering to the inevitable.

"Am I hurting you?"

With a choked exclamation, Mason closed the small distance between them. His hand covered hers, big and callused, blunt-fingered and strong.

"Hurting me?" His face neared hers, and his eyes opened. "Only as much as it hurts to know what I'll never have, Amelia. Only that."

His eyes glittered, savage with need and something akin to regret. At the emotions she glimpsed in their depths, Amelia knew a nearly overpowering urge to run. Run as fast, and as far, as she could. Whatever was happening between them here would change her, was already changing her. It felt unknown, and exciting. It felt inescapable.

"Run, Amy," he said roughly, his voice an uncanny echo to her thoughts. His hands raised to the sides of her neck, his fingers caressing circles within the wispy hairs at her nape. "Run, or send me away." His gaze roamed over her, touching her face, her neck, her eyes . . . her lips. "I'll go if you ask."

"Oh, Mason . . ." Her belly tightened, feeling as though a thousand butterflies were trapped inside. She became aware of her heartbeat, thudding with painful slowness against her breast.

"I . . . I can't," she said, kneading his hair in her hand. Its spiky length prickled between her fingers. She wanted to close her eyes, to scream, to drag him closer. The warning in his expression stopped her.

"You don't know what you're saying," he murmured, but he believed her well enough to wrap his arm around her waist and pull her closer.

Inexplicably, tears stung her eyes. Why tears, why now? Her emotions seemed all jumbled-together, yet jubilant. Mason's hand flattened hard against her spine as though he felt it too, as though he could barely keep from crushing her to him.

"I—I know this feels right," she said, biting back a moan as his upper arm brushed against the side of her breast, sending a renewed jolt of pleasure through her. He shouldn't be touching her this way; it was scandalous, she knew. And she didn't care.

"Ahhh, Amelia. Just because it feels good doesn't make it right."

"It doesn't make it wrong, either," she insisted. How could something that made her feel so cherished, so valued, be wrong? She refused to believe it.

Mason's intense, brown-eyed gaze swept over her face, taking in her features as though they were the most mesmerizing he'd ever seen.

"Pretty . . ." he murmured, and the single word made her heart race faster. He smiled, and her heart turned over.

". . . but willful. I was right about you," he said, stroking her cheek. "You're a danger to a man like me."

His approving look made the damning words into a compliment. The pressure of his thighs capturing hers made them into a lie. This was all his doing—not hers. Amelia couldn't have resisted him if she'd wanted to. He made her blood feel heated clear to boiling.

His knee rubbed against her hip; the ball of his thumb brushed over her lower lip. "I think your madness is catching," Mason said. "I can't stop touching you."

Amelia quivered. "If this is madness, I've got it, too," she whispered. "Oh, Mason—what are you doing to me? I've never felt anything like this, not even when you kissed me!"

Around them the wind's momentum increased, swirling her skirts and her hair, its turbulence echoing the wildness of her feelings. The air suddenly became heavy, moist with impending rain.

Wordlessly Mason smiled and leaned forward. She felt his beard soft against her jaw, then the warmth of his mouth took his hand's place at her earlobe.

"I feel it, too," he said, his lips moving against the soft outer arch of her ear. "It's *your* doing, Amy."

She gasped as the tip of his tongue tickled her ear, then retreated. He moaned, low in his throat, and the sound vibrated against her neck. "I suppose next you'll want a reward. And I won't be able to say no."

The sun slipped behind a cloud, sending shadows and a deepening coolness around them. Compared with the wind, Mason's body felt twice as hot beside her. The fresh scent of rainfall nearby mixed with the pungency of sagebrush and soil. Dimly, Amelia realized a storm was gathering.

"Re- . . . reward?" she whispered, not caring at that moment if the wind rushed down and swept them up where they sat, if only Mason would stay with her.

"For rescuing me."

Mason kissed her earlobe, then the curve of her jaw. Pleasure swept from the places his lips touched, swirling in a hot current that made her clench fistfuls of his shirt for support. Dizziness threatened to swamp her, but it was sweet, so sweet.

"What you did took courage"—he trailed more kisses along her jaw, nearer and nearer to her lips—"more courage than I gave you credit for."

Amelia shook her head. "I drove the oxen in circles, I almost k-killed the washer women, and that station hand nearly c-caught us," she protested.

Oh, but his lips felt good! It was hard to speak with him kissing her throat like that. Her voice sounded breathless and husky, even to her own ears. "I—I was scared the whole time."

Mason's hands flattened along her cheeks, tilting her face upward. "The fear is what makes it courageous."

His mouth covered hers, sending a shudder of pleasure through her. His lips slid along hers, warm and inviting, and it suddenly seemed as though every ounce of sensation in her body was centered in the union of their mouths. Breathlessly, Amelia curved her hand along Mason's neck and held on. His need, his urgency, buffeted her . . . and thrilled her.

Courageous . . . She'd never done anything more courageous than return Mason's kiss. Tentatively she touched her lips to his again. His low groan was her reward. His arms tightened around her, holding her ever closer, crushing her breasts against his chest.

Her senses reeled with the leathery, musky scent of man, with the vibrant feel of his hard-muscled body beneath her fingertips.

Gently his tongue stroked hers, softly and then with mounting intensity as they became caught up in the kiss.

So this was what all the fuss was about, Amelia thought disjointedly. No wonder poets wrote of true love; no wonder people were said to die of a broken heart. At that moment, she understood everything. One taste of this could never, never be enough. Despite everything that separated them, at that moment she knew the truth.

She was falling in love with Mason.

Smiling, filled with wonder at the realization, Amelia eased him down to meet her again. He closed his eyes and trembled beneath her palms. His kiss was giddy pleasure she knew she'd never get her fill of. Bliss.

Mason's hands moved to her waist, cradling her. His thumbs caressed her, skimming lightly over her ribs, arousing more sensation there. His knuckles grazed the underside of her bosom, and beneath her dress and chemise Amelia's nipples puckered with thrilling sensitivity. Her plain borrowed chemise suddenly seemed two sizes too small.

He smiled at her, and the tenderness in his gaze was nearly her undoing. She had to tell him how she felt.

"Mason, I think I'm falling in lo—"

A raindrop plopped onto her head; another landed on her cheek, followed quickly by a third.

"What?" She raised her open palms skyward, frowning, momentarily distracted from her declaration by the surprise of rain on a mostly sunny afternoon.

Another fat drop fell onto her bare collarbone and traveled downward toward the neckline of her dress. Mason followed its progress with his fingertip, a rakish grin lighting his face. Amelia felt his warm, callused fingertip trace a wet trail an inch below her blue-checked neckline, and nearly forgot what she'd been about to tell him.

She stopped his finger and held it tight in her fist. How else to tell him such important news? If he kept on the way he was, she wouldn't have a thought in her head aside from the wicked ones already there.

She took a deep breath. "Mason, I lo—"

More rain fell, harder now, battering the wagon's canvas cover. Suddenly, it became a downpour. Amelia could barely see for the rainwater coming down on them. The sky had darkened so much that the hillside looked muddy and indistinct beside the wagon.

She swiped at her eyes, then, without thinking, tried to shake the water from her fingers. Mason laughed.

"You won't be able to shake your hands dry in this," he said, shielding his head from the downpour. Somewhere nearby thunder boomed, followed by a bright white flash of lightning. He grabbed her hand, nodding toward the covered rear of the wagon. "Go back there. We've got to get to higher ground."

"But—"

"Go." Typically, he didn't give her a chance to explain. A final nod toward the wagon bed, then Mason bent to unwind the traces and get the oxen in motion.

Her declaration would have to wait for a better time. Sighing, Amelia climbed obediently behind the driver's bench into the wagon bed. The wagon lurched forward a few inches, headed around the incline beside them. Rain pattered on the canvas cover, gaining intensity with each passing minute.

Just as she'd almost cleared a place to sit amidst the supplies, the wagon slid backward, pitching her hard onto a barrel. The wind seemed to change direction, sending new torrents of rain into the wagon.

This wasn't one of the gentle spring showers Amelia was used to back home in the States. This was a full-fledged storm—and the middle of a gully was probably the worst place for them to be.

Mason swore, flinging rainwater backward from his sodden

shirt as he worked the traces, trying to urge the animals forward again. At this pace, they'd end up farther down the hill than they'd begun.

"Are Arizona Territory storms always like this?" Amelia shouted from beneath the canvas.

"Yes," he called back through gritted teeth.

Water sloshed against the wagon wheels, splattering muddy liquid onto the bench beside him. She stared at the gritty brown spots it left behind, beginning to feel afraid for the first time. What if the gully filled with rainwater? What if it just kept on raining?

"Let me help," she said, shouting to be heard over the increased noise of the rain.

"No! Get back."

He rose and wrapped the traces around the mud-splashed bench, leaving as much slack in the lines as he could without letting them droop behind the animals. Turning, Mason leaned into the covered part of the wagon, bracing both big hands on the edge. Water dripped from his hair, his nose, his chin . . . every stitch of clothing he had on had been soaked in mere minutes.

He grabbed her arm, moving his face close to hers. Between the gloom beneath the canvas and the darkening, storm-clouded sky, Amelia could barely see him.

"I'm going out to lead them up the hill," he said, breathing heavily from the exertion of controlling the oxen. "Stay here and hang on."

"No! Mason, you can't—"

But he was already gone.

Ten

Outside the wagon stinging rain drove hard at Mason, drenching his clothes, his hair, his face. His shirt and pants stuck to his skin, but somehow water still managed to drip beneath his collar and run cold down his spine.

Stream tendrils curled from his body and were whipped away instantly. The wind buffeted the rain in wet gray sheets, making it damn near impossible to see where he was going. Swearing, he ducked his head and pushed onward against it. At least the rain might wipe out their tracks, making it harder for anyone from Maricopa Wells to follow their trail.

Just ahead, the oxen kept their heads low, too. Their huge bulky bodies dripped rainwater into the fast-growing puddles beneath their hooves. When he reached them, the sharp smell of wet animal hair was almost enough to make him retch. Ignoring it, Mason grabbed the end of the wooden yoke nearest him and urged the oxen forward.

They moved a few feet, their hooves slipping in the thick brown mud. They snorted and blew, straining to pull the wagon around the side of the hill to higher ground. The *arroyo* they'd stopped beside was the worst possible place to be in a storm like this one. If the rain kept up like it was, he knew, the dry stream bed would fill and overflow with lightning speed. Men and animals had been killed trying to cross the deceptively shallow-looking water. Mason didn't intend Curly Top and himself to be among them.

He squinted through the rain toward the *arroyo,* only a few feet ahead. Already dirty brown water rushed past, swirling with dead mesquite branches and tumbleweeds. The parched desert ground couldn't absorb the onslaught; the water level rose even as they neared it. Hoping the wagon bed—whoever it belonged to—was watertight and the oxen were strong enough, he pressed forward. He had to cross now, else wait behind it until the storm had passed and risk being trapped there.

He reached the swift-flowing water and waded in. Even though he'd expected it, the force of its icy current took his breath away. The team pulled mightily, muscles working in unison. Giving thanks for dumb strong beasts, Mason gritted his teeth and started forward beside them.

His feet sunk ankle-deep in *arroyo*-bottom muck; it sucked at his boots as he slogged forward. The filthy water seethed and eddied, nearly knee-high, trying to drag him downstream with the current. The first pair of wagon wheels rolled into the water, making the wagon slump and sink. The oxen faltered, stopped by the dead weight of the partly stuck wagon.

"Hah!" Mason screamed, desperate for them to move. Move to the other side, dammit! Slowly, they pulled the wagon over the *arroyo.* The wheels slurped free of the muck and spewed water as they rolled faster.

The rain drove harder, making the whole world sound liquid. It beat against the canvas wagon cover like Indian war drums and pattered through the thin-leafed plants nearby. He should've anticipated a monsoon rain, should've made accommodations for it.

It wasn't his brain that had been making decisions for them, Mason knew, and cursed himself for it. He'd put his woman and himself both in danger, and risked not finding his son, to boot.

Regret ate at his gut. Was he doomed to endanger everyone around him?

His feet hit the stream bank. Slipping, grabbing the yoke for balance, Mason climbed up the edge. They were going to make it. The rear wagon wheels struck the muddy bank, slid, then jerked forward. Their iron cladding was obliterated by muck; more mud churned beneath as they spun, seeking purchase.

He swiped the water from his eyes and looked toward Amelia. He had to let her know everything would be all right. Peering through the rain toward the front of the wagon, Mason scanned the front and both sides.

Amy wasn't there.

She had to be. With a parting slap on the nearest ox's shoulder, he left them to haul the wagon higher on the *arroyo* bank and turned back. Still nothing. Had she climbed farther into the back of the wagon? With the sun disappeared behind the swollen black clouds, it was hard to see within.

A flash of movement just downstream caught his eye. A garbled sound got his feet working before Mason was sure what he was running to.

Amy. Floundering in the midst of the rushing *arroyo,* trying to get to her feet. She was a blur amidst the rainfall. Her arms windmilled against the storm, lashing into the flowing water as she tried to catch her balance. Mason remembered the mud sucking him hard into the stream bed, and ran faster.

His foot struck a wet prickly pear cactus. He fell to his knees, felt the long sharp spines pierce his soaked pants clean through to his right knee and thigh, and pushed himself upward again. The spines worked deeper into his flesh as he ran, hot needles sending pain through his leg. Another abortive cry came from Amelia, only a wagon's-length away now.

He spied her, on her knees in the water. What in the hell was she doing out in the *arroyo* when he'd told her to stay in the wagon? Her unbound hair was plastered to her head and neck, her face white beneath a smudged coating of mud. Rain beat upon her, making her next cry sound choked. Coughing, she lunged toward a passing tree branch—and missed.

"Mason!" she cried. "Mason!"

His heart seized, like a fist in his chest. He knew she hadn't seen him yet, hadn't even looked his way, yet Amy had called for him to help her. *Believed* he could help her.

Something else swirled past, a dark lumpy shape in the water. She surged toward it, lugged it closer . . . and screamed. Hysterically, she beat at the water, trying to make whatever it was flow downstream. Unbalanced by the effort, she flailed sideways. The current knocked her shoulder-first into the water.

Mason reached the water's edge just as Amelia came up sputtering. The thing she'd grabbed—a dead coyote, he saw now—flowed over a half-submerged clump of barrel cactus and disappeared.

"Amy!" he yelled, cupping his hands around his mouth to make his voice carry farther. "Amy, hang on!"

Her face turned unerringly toward him. She gaped as though he were a vision standing there, too much to hope for. Rainwater ran into her mouth and down her neck, making her gag. Coughing, she tried to shout his name.

The water flowed chest-high around her as she struggled uselessly to free herself from the muddy *arroyo* bottom. Between the weight of her sodden layers of skirts, the vicious speed of the current, and the boot-sucking muck, she was well and truly caught. Her fate would be the same as the coyote's if he didn't reach her in time. The thought made his blood run cold.

"I'm coming!" Mason yelled again, plunging into the water as fast as he could move.

The temperature had plummeted; he shivered at the feel of the icy water against his calves and knew how bone-cold Amelia must be, submerged in it. Kicking water aside with violent strides, finally Mason reached her.

"Mason!" She lurched toward him, both arms flung wide. Her fingers clenched, searching for something, anything to grab onto. Her teeth clattered uncontrollably from the chill.

He caught her beneath her arms and lifted her upward, yelling with the effort of dragging her free from the mud and murky water. Her wet, shivering body slammed into his. Sobbing, she wrapped her arms around his neck.

Beneath his spread fingers Amy's shoulder blades poked sharp and shuddery through her dress. She was more delicately made than he'd known. She gasped for air, her shoulders heaving, holding onto Mason as though he were the only solid thing in a world turned liquid and treacherous. The rain pelted them both, wrapping them in a cold cloak of mist. The storm showed no sign of letting up.

The tightness in Mason's chest eased as he held her. He'd gotten to her in time; she was going to be all right. He looked down at her mud-splattered, pale face squashed fearfully against his chest, and hard on the heels of that small relief came white-hot anger. What in the hell had she been thinking, to get out of the wagon and put herself in danger? She could've been killed. It was pure dead luck he'd looked back for Amelia when he had, and spotted her in the *arroyo*.

"Let's get you back to the wagon," he said gruffly, swinging his arm behind her knees to lift her against his chest. He felt ornery, conflicted as a new preacher in a whorehouse—and a sight more relieved Amy was safe than he wanted to be.

His irritation must have shown, because she cried out when he hauled her upward, splashing water in a wide arc all around them, then turned toward the *arroyo* bank.

"I'm sorry!" she said. "I—"

"Don't."

Scowling, Mason reached higher ground. Their clothes streamed water onto the marshy soil, but the sound was lost amidst the water filling the puddles underfoot and trickling from the rocks and low-country bushes nearby. Still he carried her, straight toward the now-motionless wagon. At its head, the nearest ox watched their approach, lowing mournfully.

In his arms, Amy coughed. Stubbornly, she went on explaining herself. "I only wanted to help you," she yelled hoarsely over the sounds of the storm. She panted between the words, doubtless worn out from her struggles. "I found an apple in the—"

"Shut up," Mason gritted. There wasn't an explanation he wanted to hear for nearly losing her. He ducked his head, trying to shield her from the downpour.

Her hands tightened at the back of his neck—with frustration, he guessed, and didn't give a damn. Amelia could damn well stew in frustration for all he cared.

His arms burned with fatigue by the time Mason stopped beside the rear of the wagon. His time on the run—and everything that had gone before—had weakened him. If he hadn't been sure of it before, he was now. When had everything started changing?

"I found an apple in the wagon," Amy went on, tilting her chin at a dog-determined angle, "and decided to help you lure the oxen up the hillside with it." She panted, weary from her struggles. "I didn't know the water would be like that—"

"Stay out of the *arroyos,* full or not."

Mason raised her higher and shoved her toward the opening in the canvas. Wisely—for a change—she grabbed the slippery, water-darkened edges and levered herself inside. Her skirts slapped on the edge, sending a shower of droplets onto his head.

Swearing, Mason climbed in after her. The sudden cessation of rain pouring on his head, the added comfort of a dry place to sit, and the fact that the wind had quit howling in his ears did little to improve his disposition.

"Take off your clothes," he barked. He grabbed a folded red

and white patchwork quilt from an opened crate and threw it toward her with barely a glance. "Then put this on."

"But—"

"Do it."

She pressed her lips tight together and started unbuttoning the front of her dress The clattering of her teeth grew louder. Mason turned away and rummaged through the crate he'd taken the quilt from, looking for food or dry clothes for either of them. There wasn't much room to ignore the woman undressing behind him in a four-foot-wide wagon, but he did his best to give her some privacy.

Amy's small sounds of frustration rose above the pattering of the rain. Frowning, mad enough to smash something—everything—Mason glared at her.

"My—my hands are too shaky," she whispered, futilely trying to slip one of her tiny pearl dress buttons through the buttonhole in her bodice.

Her hands shook like mesquite leaves in the wind. She'd managed to get the first few buttons undone, but in the time it had taken her Twirly Curls should've been able to shuck every stitch she had on.

"Hell," Mason muttered, grabbing for her. He caught hold of the front of her dress, twisted the loosened fabric in his fist, and roughly dragged her to him. Dammit, having her with him was nothing but trouble. He should've already been to Tucson to get Ben from the Sharpes.

Would have been if not for Amelia.

Her face crumpled slowly, her lower lip wobbling. She clasped her hands together behind her like a little girl, trying to blink back the tears pooling in her eyes.

"Don't go getting weepy on me," he warned her, rapidly unbuttoning her dress. It proved difficult work with his big workman's hands. It had been a long time since he'd undressed a woman, even under circumstances as unromantic as this.

Amy swallowed hard and nodded. "I just . . . thank you for saving me, Mason. I knew you' d c-come for me."

She sniffed, looking at him with wide-eyed puppy dog gratitude that grated on Mason like nothing else could have. He ripped the two halves of her dress apart, scattering buttons willy-nilly.

"Don't depend on me!" he roared, wrenching her dress down her arms to take it off. Fury made his hands shake. Hadn't he already told her what he was? Hadn't she heard what he'd been accused of? "Don't wait for me to save you, and don't thank me for it either, goddammit!"

Stepping back a pace, he bunched her dress into a ball and hurled it into the wagon's corner. It slapped into a tin water bucket, knocked it from its hook, and slid down the canvas. Mason rounded on Amy, ready to tell her exactly how addle-headed her behavior had been. Ready to tell her how it had put both of them in danger.

Ready to tell her how he'd risked forfeiting his son to drag her from a flooded *arroyo*.

The horrified look on her face stopped him where he stood. Only half-dressed, Amy fell to her knees at his feet, her fingers tentatively stretched toward his knee.

"What happened to you?" she whispered. She cupped her hands in the air around the cactus spines poking through his pants as though afraid to touch them. "What is this?"

Her forehead creased with worry. She reached for a spine, about to pinch it between her fingers.

"Don't."

She looked up at him questioningly, still shivering with cold, although Mason doubted she was aware of it. He picked up the quilt she'd abandoned and draped it over her shoulders.

"They're prickly pear spines—"

"Pear?" Her confusion showed in the way she stared at the cluster of needlelike spines embedded near his knee and thigh.

"Cactus," he explained. "They're worked in pretty deep. You can't just pluck one out like taking a needle from a pincushion."

"Dear God, Mason!" Her fingers fluttered around the spines. "Are they poisonous?" Rising, Amelia touched his arm and tried to ease him back onto a nearby barrel. "You'd better sit down."

He threw off her hand, all but snarling at her. What gave her the right to fuss over him like a . . . like a wife? He could take care of himself. He sure as hell didn't need a woman to do it.

"I'll be fine."

Amy stared at him, her teeth still clattering faintly. Although she clenched the blanket in front of her breasts with one hand, it had slipped partway from her shoulders, revealing bare skin and lacy chemise straps. Mason stared at them, thrown backward by the image to a time when feminine fripperies like fancy underclothes and hair combs, and a sweet-smelling woman, had been his to savor. Ellen. Like Amy, she'd trusted him.

And come to regret it.

He frowned. "Take off the rest of those wet clothes," he told her, unbuttoning his own shirt.

"I—"

"I won't look at you, if that's what you're worried about."

Mason stretched apart the sides of his shirt, sliding it from his shoulders. Her eyes grew wide. Then, apparently realizing she'd been staring at his bare chest—and embarrassed at being found out—Amelia lifted her chin.

"I *think*," she said pointedly, "that if we hang these things up, they might dry by morning."

Her hands bumped and moved beneath the blanket as she removed her underclothes. Mason looked toward the front of the wagon, trying not to imagine what she looked like without them.

"That's all I was going to say." Her gaze darted toward the cactus spines protruding from his leg, then moved to his face.

"If you want to suffer, that's up to you," Amy added. "I guess I forgot how stupidly stubborn men can be when they're hurt."

Moving with exaggerated dignity, she draped her lacy white underthings to dry, from a long iron hook set in one of the wagon top's curved braces. Pointedly ignoring him, she leaned over a barrel and searched through it. Quietly at first, and then more loudly, she began singing a hymn.

Hell. He could ignore her, too—and would, Mason vowed. His eyes narrowed. He could even ignore her damned impertinent backside waving in the air at him, however fetching it looked curving beneath the quilt. Savagely, he started unbuttoning his pants.

His body had begun warming within the shelter of the wagon, and the spines buried in his thigh started burning anew. Irritatingly proving Miss Twirly Curls partly right, Mason felt like he'd be damned and hung to dry before admitting it. *Stubborn men.* How many men did she know, anyway?

His fingers paused midbutton. "What the hell do you know about how men behave when they're hurt?" he asked.

Her backside wiggled over the barrel as she reached for something. Mason was in half a mind to believe she was doing it just to provoke him. Her singing stopped.

"I do have a father and three brothers," she told him, her voice muffled. She sounded aggravatingly reasonable. Part of him realized that Amelia O'Malley was easier to deal with when she wasn't feeling plumb certain about something.

Perversely, the rest of him wondered where her concern for him had vanished to.

She emerged with an apple in her fist. She took a bite of it, started chewing, and nearly choked when she saw his hands working at his pants buttons.

The most instinctive part of him relished her reaction. Despite the rising blush on her cheeks—or hell, maybe even because of it—Mason kept right on unbuttoning. He started sliding his pants down, and both her apple-packed cheeks bulged with shock.

"We'll have to share the quilt, too," he pointed out. "We can't start a fire in the wagon bed, and everything outside's drenched. All we've got is body heat."

Eleven

Amy swallowed hastily. She whipped sideways, still clutching her partly eaten apple. The sweet, tangy scent of it made Mason's mouth water.

"Oh, no, we don't!" she cried, digging around in the supplies filling every square inch of the wagon bed.

Whoever they'd stolen it from hadn't been very organized—but he'd been well prepared.

Amy pulled another quilt from someplace within the pile and threw it toward him. "I found this while I was looking for the apples for the oxen."

Her aim wasn't very good, but Mason figured her imitation of his earlier hotheaded blanket toss was dead on. Another half-foot to the left and the heavy quilt would've walloped him in the head. She stared at him, looking aggrieved at her poor aim, then crunched into her apple again.

His belly rumbled. "Are there more of those?"

Amy looked at the apple as though it had magically appeared in her hand. "These?" she asked innocently.

Scowling back at her, Mason wrapped the blanket around his shoulders. Blessed warmth started gathering beneath it, except for below his waist. Until he wrenched loose the cactus spines, he couldn't take off his wet pants.

"Yes, those."

"There's a whole barrel full." She gave an offhand wave toward the front of the wagon. "Plus cornmeal, clothes, water, whiskey, and a whole lot of bullets. Help yourself."

"We picked a well-equipped wagon to steal."

Teetering a bit, Amy kicked aside some pots and sat down on the floor, then pulled the quilt closer around her.

"You stole the wagon. I just drove it." She started laughing, choked on her apple again, and tossed the apple core out the rear of the wagon. She slapped her knees with laughter. She wiped a tear from the corner of her eye.

She'd gone hysterical on him.

Mason felt like bolting from the wagon and taking his chances with the storm. Anything but stay here with this woman—this woman who couldn't take a walk without getting stuck in a pile of boulders, who couldn't take a stagecoach ride without stirring up trouble, who couldn't get by in the Territory without help.

Without his help.

Away from the Eastern life she was used to, Amelia O'Malley was in so far over her head she was a danger to everybody around her. Now, Mason feared, she was finally beginning to understand that.

She coughed, finally bringing her laughter under control. "I'm sorry, Mason. I'm just not used to all this, that's all. I'll do better in the future, I promise."

He shook his head. "You've got no future," he said. "When we get to Tucson, I'm putting you on the first stage to Yuma. You can catch a train back East to Big Trout Pond from there."

"Big Pike Lake," she replied automatically, the ghost of a smile on her face at his misuse of her hometown's name. She hugged the quilt closer, like she'd finally begun to get warm and wanted to savor it.

Slowly, her eyes widened. "No! I can't go back!" she cried, her head wrenching toward him as she realized what he'd said.

"I have satchels to find, books to deliver, work to be done. I can't—"

"You don't belong here," Mason said bluntly, "and I have people to meet. Important business to take care of." *A child to recover,* but he couldn't tell her that.

"I'll do better! I won't get into any more trouble, I won't!" Amy swore.

Her eyes brightened hopefully. Mason felt like groaning at whatever harebrained scheme she was likely hatching in that curly blond head.

"In fact," she said quickly, "I'll help you. It's the least I can do. I'll help you find whatever you're looking for. You're a wanted man, and it'll be hard for you to get around in Tucson. I can—"

"You're wanted, too."

Mason turned, heading for the driver's seat. The tools were bound to be stored there. Between a good set of pliers and a good horn of the whiskey Amelia had mentioned, he'd have the prickly pear spines out in no time.

He'd regained some measure of control, and it felt good. Amy could complain all she wanted to—they had to go their separate ways in Tucson. It was the only right thing to do.

"Oh, drat. That's right. We're both wanted," she said, starting to hum her hymn again.

Evidently, church music got Amelia's brain working, Mason thought sourly. She paused.

"Then we'll just have to stick together, I guess," she announced, sounding pleased with herself. "You'll be helping me just by getting me to Tucson safely, and I'll help you after we get there. I know about cities."

Mason doubted it. If she knew about cities like she knew about Arizona Territory—from dime novels, if her conversations aboard the Maricopa Wells stagecoach could be believed—they were both in trouble.

He unearthed a pair of long-handled pliers from the box of tools near the driver's bench, pulled them out, then tested their grip by opening and closing them. Satisfied, Mason headed back toward the barrel he'd been seated on earlier.

"It's best if we're not together any longer than we have to be," he told her, settling onto the barrel.

Amy snuggled deeper into her quilt. "I owe you my life, Mason. You saved me! I can't just get on a stage and forget all that."

"Yes, you can." Grimacing, he examined the spines in his leg. Holding his pants taut with one hand, he set the pliers around one of the spines embedded just below his knee and pulled.

A pinpoint of fire slid through his skin, making sweat break out on his forehead. He raised the pliers, peering at the long, needlelike spine. It was tipped with blood on one end. Taking it from the pliers' grip, he set to work on the rest of the spines. Pulling out each of those one by one was going to be a sonofabitch.

Four spines later, his vision swam and his leg felt like a pincushion for six-inch ladies' hat pins. "Where did you say the whiskey was?" he asked.

Amy stared, transfixed, at the spine he'd just pulled out. Her mouth opened slightly, but no sound emerged.

He frowned. "Maybe you ought to have a plug, too, Amelia."

She found her voice, but her gaze remained fixed on the quivering spines still stuck in his leg. "I never imbibe anything stronger than wine," she told him. Her eyes met his. "Are you sure that's all right to do? What if your leg turns septic or something?"

"Never mind. I'll get it myself." Mason set the pliers on a crate beside him, then rose. He remembered seeing the whiskey bottle someplace near the tool box . . .

"I'm sorry you hurt yourself," Amy said in a small voice behind him. "You did it coming to get me, didn't you?"

"Doesn't matter."

He found the bottle and raised it to the meager daylight that still forced its way through the rainstorm. The liquor inside sloshed faintly. Still more than half-full.

"It does matter!" Amy insisted. "Not every man would jump into a flooded river like that, just to save a woman he barely knew. You risked yourself for me."

Her voice sounded far away, as though it came from underwater. Only half-listening, Mason rubbed his thumbs over the smooth glass bottle in his hands. How long since he'd tasted whiskey? A week after Ellen's death? Two? It had made him numb enough not to fight when the Sharpes had arrived from the East. Numb enough not to argue when they'd made their damned accusations.

It had made him too numb to stop them from taking Ben away.

Damn. He rolled the bottle between his palms, trying not to remember. After a long while, he realized he was staring at it. With unsteady fingers Mason uncorked the whiskey, then rolled the cork between his thumb and forefinger.

He raised the bottle and inhaled the tangy smell of the liquor. The crooked finger of a soiled dove inviting him upstairs couldn't have beckoned him more. Just one drink, he told himself, studying the bottle. Just a slug or two to dull the pain, and then he'd get the rest of those prickly pear spines out.

It wouldn't be like it was before. He wouldn't let it numb him again.

Amelia was still talking, but he couldn't listen. Staring into the distance, his back to her, Mason raised the whiskey. One pull of liquor couldn't hurt. A man was entitled to that much— even a man who'd done the things Mason had. The warm glass neck of the bottle fit his lips like a forgotten lover, promising relief . . . promising he'd forget. He only had to tilt his head back, let the whiskey burn down his throat . . .

And prove that Ellen meant nothing. That Ben meant nothing.

Swearing, Mason wrenched the bottle downward. His damned fingers shook as he corked it again with a final, savage twist, then raised his arm to hurl the whiskey into the deepening shadows beyond the covered wagon. Better to be rid of the temptation once and for all.

He stretched his arm back, preparing to throw, his mind filled with images of his life before.

"Mason?"

Amy's arms wrapped around him from behind, bringing the warmth of the quilt with her. The red and white pattern flowed over both of them, enfolding them together. Slowly, he lowered the whiskey bottle.

"You're a good man," she said, hugging him tightly. "I don't need to know your name to know that. I can see it. I can feel it." She wrapped her arms around his middle and hugged him closer. "I don't care what you've done, what they say you've done."

He couldn't speak, couldn't move for the sense of gratitude her words aroused. He couldn't remember the last time kindness like that had touched him. The last time anyone had believed in him.

But it had been a long time.

"I don't need to know your name to know a man like you could never be an outlaw," she went on, her voice low. "You just saved my life! How—"

"My name's Kincaid," Mason told her.

Her hands stilled. "What?"

"Mason Kincaid." He turned, encircling her waist in his arms, and lifted her high against him. He wanted to crush her to him, to keep her with him, to prove to Amy he could keep her safe.

To prove it to himself.

"My real name is Mason Kincaid."

Her smile was a benediction. The warmth of it went straight to his soul. He needed nothing else to know, once and for all, that he had to send her away.

He eased Amy down his body and set her on a barrel beside him. "I escaped from the lawman who came to arrest me a little more than a week ago, and I've been on the run ever since."

"But—"

"Let me finish." Damn, but his chest ached with something he couldn't name. Mason made himself say the words that she needed to hear, but it had never been harder to push them past his lips. Stiffly, he went on: "He came for me because I was accused two days before that of murdering my wife."

God, but the words still choked him. Mason moved away from her, leaving Amelia on the barrel alone.

Leaving him alone again, too.

"I knew he was coming for me, and I left before he got there," Mason said. He looked down at her. "I *am* an outlaw—whatever you believe."

Amy touched his arm. "But they're wrong. They have to be! I don't believe you could do such a thing. You've saved me again and again, and I—"

"Because I don't want another damned murder charge hanging on my head!" Mason shouted. She flinched, driven backward by the sudden intensity of his anger. He tried to gentle his voice, and failed. "I've got nothing else to lose—except what's waiting for me in Tucson. Don't stand in my way."

Clenching her fists, Amy stepped closer to him. She raised her head and looked him in the eye. "Every time I escaped from you," she said, her voice shuddering with emotion, "you came after me."

"I already told you, I—"

"No. This time, you let *me* finish." She caught hold of his

hand and squeezed hard. "And every time, I kept thinking you'd recaptured me."

Mason wrenched his hand away, scowling. He couldn't shake loose her grip on his heart as easily. Amelia had picked a hell of a time to turn determined on him.

"You should have gotten the hell away from me while you still could," he said.

As though he'd never spoken, never moved, Amy followed him.

"And every time I was wrong," she said. Holding the quilt up with one hand, she slipped her other hand from beneath it and tunneled under his blanket instead. He felt her hand smooth warmth across his chest. It came to rest directly over his heart.

"Don't you see?" she asked, looking up at him with tears shimmering in her eyes. "All those times, you weren't capturing me."

How had his attempts to scare her away from him backfired so quickly, so completely? He didn't want this, didn't want anyone else depending on him. Mason tried to sound mean, tried to sound like it cost him nothing to say, "I wasn't?"

"No."

A tear spilled onto her cheek. He had to fight the urge to caress it away.

"You were *rescuing* me," she said.

"Amy—"

"And I'm going to rescue you in return."

Twelve

Falling in love with Mason had been a fluke. By the time Amelia had woken up, bruised and half-exhausted from a night spent sleeping amidst a wagon bed of supplies, she felt fairly certain she was starting to get over it already. She had to be. Otherwise, she didn't know how she was going to deal with a man who pulled her to him with one hand and pushed her away with the other. At the same time.

By all indications, he wanted nothing whatsoever to do with her this morning. Mason had wakened her before sunrise, rumbling something in that mean outlaw's voice of his about not lolling around like sitting ducks. Then he'd taken himself off to the swollen stream with a bucket of clean water and a straight-edge razor to shave with, leaving her alone to fend for herself.

Amelia didn't understand him—or herself, for that matter. Mason Kincaid was the wrong kind of man for her to care about. He was wholly unsuitable. Yet he'd held her as though he couldn't get enough of her, kissed her in a way that still made her lips tingle when she remembered it.

How could that be? How was it possible that she, who'd had no trouble resisting improper advances from the few young men who'd approached her in the past, found herself longing for yet another kiss from Mason—even at this very moment?

She brushed her fingertips across her lips, remembering. Looking toward the nearby ridge where Mason sat, she spotted his lithe, powerful body silhouetted by the rising sun, his arm propped with deceptive casualness on his bent knee as he scanned the countryside for signs they'd been pursued from Maricopa Wells. Shafts of orange and gold sunlight burnished his body and hid his expression at the same time. She'd never known anyone more enigmatic. Mason protected her at every turn, even while seeming aggrieved by her very presence.

He was a puzzle, Amelia decided. A puzzle she didn't even have all the pieces to. She meant to figure him out, though. Soon. In the meantime, she intended to get to Tucson safely, to retrieve her J. G. O'Malley & Sons satchels, and to deliver those book orders.

And sometime along the way, she intended for Mason to kiss her again. Exactly the way he had before. Maybe then she could satisfy her curiosity once and for all, and be done with mooning over an outlaw.

Sighing, Amelia crouched beside the campfire he'd made for her outside their stolen wagon and checked the breakfast she was cooking inside their stolen cast-iron spider. The cornmeal flapjacks sizzled beside thick strips of bacon, sending the aromas of toasted corn and smoked meat wafting upward. Thank heaven the rain had stopped late last night, giving the ground time to dry out somewhat. The warmth of their small fire was bliss.

Standing, stretching, Amelia tried to work the kinks out of her back before heading toward the covered wagon. Last night she'd been grateful for its shelter, however illegally gained. This morning, her conscience poked at her constantly, trying to make itself heard.

Stealing that wagon was probably a hanging offense. Things hadn't been bad enough, Amelia thought wryly as she rummaged inside the wagon bed. She and Mason had felt compelled to commit a mortal sin on top of it.

Telling herself they'd find a way to set it right somehow,

Amelia pulled out the coffee beans and grinder she'd found. She carried them back to the fire, turned out the first batch of flapjacks onto a tin plate, then poured more batter into the spider. Maybe she'd eat the first batch herself, and not even wait for Mason to return, she thought rebelliously. What was the point in propriety when a lady found herself stuck in the middle of the desert?

Mason's shadow fell over her just as Amelia poured the green coffee beans into a fresh skillet to roast them. Shaking them back and forth in the pan, she nodded toward the plate of flapjacks without looking at him.

"You can have the first batch," she said, feeling unreasonably like smoothing her wrinkled dress and primping to gain his favor. She tamped down the urge. Had she no pride left? "The coffee will be done in a little while."

The campfire flames licked higher, burning her hand. Yelling, Amelia let go of the skillet. It fell sideways into the fire, scattering coffee beans in every direction.

"Blast!" she cried, standing and kicking at the wayward skillet in frustration. Now Mason probably thought she was as useless at cooking as she'd proved to be at everything else in this godforsaken Territory. "Goldanged stupid skillet."

She kicked it again, and only succeeded in stubbing her toe on the hard cast iron. Tears prickled behind her eyes, making her even madder.

"Let me make the coffee, before you catch yourself on fire," Mason said.

She refused to look at him. As a man who didn't even want to be around her, Mason didn't deserve the satisfaction of an acknowledgment. Still she felt him grinning at her, and the knowledge irked her beyond reason.

This was like the worst girlhood crush on a boy she'd ever suffered—only magnified a hundred times, because there was no escaping Mason. At least for now, they were stuck together.

Not that it mattered. They'd probably be hunted down by a posse and hung as thieves before she convinced him to satisfy her curiosity about the kiss.

"I know how to make coffee," Mason persisted.

"No. I can do it," Amelia gritted out, wadding her skirt around the skillet handle to pull it from the fire. This time, she was successful. Dropping it onto the ground to cool, she turned to Mason with her hands on her hips.

"You might as well eat. There's nothing wrong with the flap-jacks or bacon."

He raised his eyebrows.

Was he trying to provoke her apurpose?

She'd ignore him, Amelia vowed. Humming, scooping her hand into the container of coffee beans again, she pulled out a handful and poured them carefully into the skillet. She held it over the fire, farther away this time, and shook it with a trium-phant look toward Mason.

"I happen to be a very good cook," she announced. Her ex-pression, she felt sure, fairly dared him to disagree.

"I'm sure you are," he agreed, sounding utterly unconvinced. She might have announced she was a circus performer and earned as much credibility. He pierced the sizzling bacon with his fork, examining each slice as he transferred it to his plate.

By the time he'd scrutinized the fifth piece, Amelia couldn't contain herself any longer.

"Exactly what do you expect to find?" she asked.

Propping his plate on his knee, Mason looked up at her. "It looks browner than I expected," he said, shrugging. "I thought maybe you'd fried up some jerky."

"Even I know better than that." She flipped two cornmeal flapjacks onto a plate for herself, then added one of the few remaining strips of bacon. She glanced at him again. "It's just crispy. I like crispy bacon."

"It's burned."

"It's good." To prove her point, Amelia picked up a piece and bit into it. The bacon crunched in her mouth, salty and crispy and exactly the way she liked it. Still munching, she pierced a second piece and added it to her plate, too.

"Burned." Mason peered suspiciously at his bacon, frowning as though she'd cooked some specially for her and he'd gotten only the dregs.

Seeing him in full daylight, Amelia was taken aback at his appearance. Although he looked somewhat more respectable now that he was clean-shaven, Mason seemed . . . weary. Dark circles cast shadows beneath his eyes, and without their usual brown beard-stubble, his cheeks looked a bit sunken. Suddenly, crispy bacon or not, she wanted him to eat his fill.

"I'll cook some more bacon if you want," she offered, setting her plate down to pour more batter onto the blistering cast-iron surface of the spider. That done, Amelia maneuvered the cooled, roasted coffee beans into the top of the grinder and replaced the lid.

Cranking the handle, she added, "You look as though you could use the fortification."

Mason choked on a bite of meat. Reaching around him, Amelia slapped his back helpfully.

"Quit that!" he muttered once he'd quit coughing. He cast her a dark look, then turned his attention toward his flapjacks.

Fine. Whatever got him to eat, Amelia reasoned. She poured the coffee grounds into the pot, filled it with water, and hung it over the fire. Slapping her palms together, she surveyed her campsite with satisfaction. She'd turned it quite homey, between the warmth of the fire and the good smells of flapjacks, bacon—and soon—coffee perking.

She picked up her plate and settled herself on a rock opposite Mason. With not a few surreptitious glances in his direction—did he like the food or not?—she cut a bite of flapjack with the edge of her fork and ate it.

Before long, Mason's plate was nearly empty. He took more from the spider, poured himself some coffee into a tin cup, and ate more. Finally, he paused for breath. He pointed his fork toward the overturned crate Amelia had set up beside the campfire to hold the bowl of flapjack batter and the uncooked bacon strips.

"What I can't figure out," he said, "is what the creosote branches are for. Did you season the flapjacks with them?"

"They're a centerpiece." Hurt, Amelia glanced at the tin cup filled with bush branches she'd set on one edge of the crate. "Don't you think the flowers are pretty?"

They were the best she'd been able to find—the narrow-leafed branches of some desert bush, with tiny yellow blossoms on them. The wet ones did carry a somewhat pungent aroma, but it wasn't as though she could just run down to the green-grocer's for flowers. What did he expect?

Mason grunted, but as he lowered his head to concentrate on his meal again, Amelia plainly spotted the smile on his face.

"What's so funny?" she demanded. "You don't like flowers?"

"I—"

"But I don't suppose you would," she went on before he could finish. Waving her arm, she ended up slamming her plate onto the rock beside her, feeling piqued. "You don't like anything. You don't like the flowers"—she raised her index finger—"or the bacon." Another finger went up. "You haven't said a word about the flapjacks, so I suppose they don't meet your standards either."

Her ring finger joined the first two, enumerating his many dislikes. Mason started to say something else, but Amelia cut him off. "And you obviously don't like me, either, so—"

Suddenly, Mason's hand clapped over her mouth. Muffled, she stared up at him in shock. At some point during her speech, he'd leaned right over her without her even noticing it. Now his chest loomed directly in her line of vision, giving her an excellent—if unwanted—view of his tawny skin and muscular torso through the opened vee of his wrinkly shirt.

She couldn't help but notice what a fine-looking man Mason Kincaid was, outlaw or not. Memories of how he'd looked taking off his wet shirt in the wagon last night edged into her mind.

"If you'd let a man get a word in edgewise," he said, "you might like what you'd hear."

Amelia nodded, unable to manage more with his hand over her mouth. He took it away, scowling.

"In case you didn't notice," Mason pointed out as he returned to the rock he'd been using for a seat, "I just ate a good half-dozen of your flapjacks, and all the rest of your damned burned bacon. If that doesn't pass for liking the food, I don't know what does."

"Oh." It was a compliment, Amelia realized. He liked her cooking. But what about the rest? If she asked, would Mason reveal how he felt about her, too?

"You're right," she said, trying to appear conciliatory. "I guess that does prove you like the food."

He nodded and said nothing more.

The man understood instinctively how to vex her.

She held back a sigh. "You like the food and . . . ?"

"And what?"

He had to be vexing her apurpose. Perhaps it was the male version of being coy in the hope of promoting a flirtation. Amelia hadn't much experience in that arena.

Deciding she might as well play along, she prompted, "And you also like . . . ?"

He brightened and gave her a wide, openhearted grin. Encouraged, Amelia waited for him to speak. Any moment now, Mason would say something kind and romantic and heroic, like the men in her dime novels.

"I like the creosote branches, too," he admitted. "In spite of the smell. Puts a nice lady's touch on things."

She stared at him. Mason's grin, if anything, only got wider.

"Quit fishing, Amelia. I already said I liked the food—I'm not the kind of man to go on about it all morning." He stood, pushing himself upright with his hands on his thighs. "Besides, we've got work to be done."

"What kind of work? Did somebody follow us?"

Panic sent Amelia to her feet, too. Craning her neck, she tried to see beyond Mason and around the hill, back toward Maricopa Wells. Was that only a cloud she saw low in the sky? Or was it dust kicked up from the hooves of a mounted posse's horses as they pursued the outlaws?

"Nobody's following us. My guess is, the wagon's owner is blind drunk, passed out someplace at the station, and hasn't realized his rig is missing yet."

"But there are a woman's things in the wagon," Amelia protested. "What about her?"

"Maybe they're both holed up someplace."

She put her hands on her hips. "Oh, Mason—really. I just can't imagine a lady imbibing so heavily that she—"

"I didn't mean they were holed up drinking," he said, heading for the wagon. He climbed inside the back, emerging headfirst a moment later to untie the thick drawstring cinching the canvas together.

"Well, what did you . . . ?" Amelia started to ask, following him. A peculiar reddening of Mason's cheeks made the words stick in her throat. Why, he was blushing!

"Ahhh," she murmured, feeling her own cheeks heat. He meant the wagon owners had holed up someplace to be intimate.

The notion reminded her of the night she and Mason had just spent together, sleeping only a few feet apart from each other. Wearing not a stitch aside from quilts. Shivering, she tried to concentrate on what Mason was doing rather than the intriguing images in her head, and failed.

He ducked his head and went on loosening the drawstrings "I see you take my meaning, then," he said.

"I, ahhh . . ." An idea struck her. "No, I don't," she lied. After all, any subject that could cause an outlaw to blush was one capable of piquing her interest.

"And I've been curious about this very thing lately," Amelia said, digging the toe of her shoe into the soil rather than raise her eyes to Mason. He spread the canvas opening wider apart, for all appearances barely listening to her.

Trying to sound nonchalant, if unworldly, she went on: "Perhaps you could instruct me in the nature of—"

"And anyway, the rain washed away our wagon tracks and the hill hides us from the road, so—" Mason's voice faltered, his hand tightening abruptly on the canvas edge. His gaze locked with hers. *"What did you say?"*

Amelia's boldness deserted her. Her throat tightened, making it hard to speak. "Well, you're a worldly man. At—at least if our kiss was anything to go by," she said, "and I'm curious to know about . . . that is, perhaps you could instruct me in—"

"No," he said flatly.

His eyes narrowed. Roughly he tied off the drawstring, then jumped down from the wagon. He landed right next to her—tall, broad-shouldered, and inexplicably angry.

If she'd wanted him to pay attention to her, surely she'd accomplished that goal with room to spare.

"I should think you'd be flattered," Amelia said. "I've never asked a man to kiss me before. You're the first."

"I'm honored."

His tone said he was anything but.

His gaze dropped to her wilted blue-and-white-checked bodice, then lower, in an assessment as blatant as any she'd ever received. Amelia tried to stand straighter, wishing she could appear more ladylike before him. A borrowed, too-large, unfashionable gingham dress would hardly inspire tender feelings in a man, she figured.

"Didn't anyone ever warn you about letting a man kiss you?" he finally asked, frowning.

"Warn me?" He wasn't going to kiss her again, she realized. Her hopes sank like pebbles tossed in the water.

He squinted at her, rubbing his palm over his jaw where his whiskers used to be. "You can't mean—?"

"Mean what?"

"Your mother, a sister . . . no one talked to you about letting a man kiss you? Warned you what might happen?"

Mutely, Amelia shook her head. "My mother died shortly after I was born, and I haven't any sisters." She thought about it some more. "I suppose my brothers and father were too well mannered to bring up such an . . . er, personal subject."

"Well mannered." Mason stared at her, his expression disbelieving.

Amelia shrugged. Her family loved her, but she had no illusions about her prospects, and neither did they. She wasn't "marriageable," and never had been. She was too short, too plain, and too lacking in wealth—given her father's propensity for investing every dime into the business instead of his daughter's dowry—to expect many suitors. Her father had explained it all to her many times. She was fortunate her family needed her, he'd said, and Amelia had agreed.

Surely she was the last lady to require a lecture on letting men kiss her, and obviously her father and brothers had known that.

"They're gentlemen," she said loyally.

"That's no excuse."

Amelia narrowed her eyes. "Are you casting aspersions upon my family?"

"Your family? Hell, no." Mason caught her chin in his callused fingertips and lifted her face to his. "I've got the utmost respect for gentlemen."

"Even though you're not one?" she teased, hoping to lighten his mood. He was so close, even close enough to fulfill her wish and kiss her. She imagined his lips descending to meet hers as they had yesterday, and shivered a little.

He frowned, absently tracing his thumb over Amelia's chin. "I don't feel like one. Not now." His gaze swept over her face, then lower. Abruptly, he dropped his hand and stepped backward.

"The next time a man tries to kiss you like I did," he told her, his expression fierce, "you'd better—"

"Better what?"

What was Mason lecturing her for, anyway? He was the one who'd started all the kissing in the first place. He was the one who'd gotten her interested in it.

She'd only been trying to hug him yesterday after their escape. Was it her fault the situation had developed into something more? Her fault for responding to him?

No, it wasn't, Amelia decided, doing her best to stare him down. In this, at least, perhaps she could have the upper hand.

Looking frustrated, Mason broke eye contact first. It felt like a victory—a small one, but hers all the same.

"Scream."

"What?"

"Scream your head off. I know you've got it in you."

Grumbling beneath his breath, he climbed into the wagon again and started rummaging through the supplies with jerky, impatient movements.

"And then what?" she inquired.

"That ought to be enough," he answered sourly, pulling a worn brown men's hat from a peg set into the curved frame that supported the canvas. He turned it over, examining it, then plunked it on his head and came out again.

He stopped in front of Amelia, giving her a hard look. "No more talk about kissing," he warned. "It's not going to happen."

"But I don't see what's wrong with it," she persisted, trying not to feel hurt by his rejection. "I know you care a little about me."

She touched Mason's sleeve when he would've turned away. "You rescued me, you called me Amy . . . you touched me with such gentleness that I—"

"That you decided to give yourself over to an outlaw?" His lips twisted with something akin to disgust as he shrugged free of her grasp. "Don't be a fool, Amelia. When we get to Tucson, just walk away. Get on that stage and forget about me. It's the only way."

He left her and headed toward the front of the wagon.

"But it was only a kiss!" Amelia called after him. "I—"

Mason stopped, half-turned. He held himself rigidly, as though forcing himself to remain where he stood. "It wouldn't end there," he said quietly. "If I touch you again, I won't be able to stop."

She gaped at him, stricken by the intensity of his expression, the haunted vulnerability in his eyes. He meant every word, Amelia realized. And it was more than a kiss they were speaking of. More than intimacy between a man and woman.

It was love.

Thirteen

"I have an idea," Amy announced the next day, a short while before sunset.

They'd traveled all through the previous night, stopping to sleep and rest the oxen shortly before dawn. By Mason's estimation, he and Amelia were thirty-odd miles nearer to Tucson.

And still far too many miles from retrieving Ben.

But the risk of being followed limited their traveling to night-time, when darkness kept their movements hidden. There was only so much he could demand of the oxen, too. Mason didn't dare push them harder, but the waiting grated on him, all the same.

"It's a really good idea," Amy said, a little louder.

Mason groaned. The last thing he needed was Amelia with an idea in her head. Judging by the enthusiasm with which she said it—she was fair bouncing in her lady's lace-up shoes—it was going to be a humdinger. But he didn't have the heart to say so.

"What's your idea?" he asked instead, passing her as he carried the freshly washed tin plates back to the wagon. He was so stuffed with the beans and cornbread she'd made for dinner that all Mason felt tempted to do was lie down inside and sleep. There was a lot to be said for a good, woman-cooked meal.

"Well," Amy said, handing him the clean spider with both

hands, "I've been thinking about how we're going to make it into Tucson without being discovered."

"I'll take care of it."

"But Mason—" She dogged him all the way to the wagon, hard on his heels. "We'll have to sneak in. Or else disguise ourselves somehow."

"Disguise?"

She smiled, shrugging with affected girlish modesty. "That's my idea."

"No. No, no, no." Mason waved his hand. "I don't even want to know what you mean by that."

"I mean, look at you! Anyone could recognize you, and in a heartbeat, too. You're a very distinctive-looking man."

Facing him, she boosted herself onto the wagon tongue and sat there, her legs kicking to and fro beneath her skirts. He glimpsed a hole in her black cotton stockings, just behind her ankle, and looked the other way. Aside from one of her hare-brained schemes, the *other* last thing he needed was more thoughts about Amy's legs . . . or the rest of her.

Sleeping next to Amelia the past two nights had been straight torture. Not that Mason had done much sleeping. Knowing she was there, wrapped naked in a quilt only a few feet away, had kept him in a near-constant state of arousal. It had been damned frustrating. He couldn't see any reason to let himself in for more of the same now by sneaking glances at her legs.

He looked at her face instead. It shone with enthusiasm for her disguise plan. Recalling what she'd said, he asked, "You think I'm distinctive-looking?"

She laughed. "Don't look so wary. I mean it as a compliment."

He shrugged, telling himself he didn't care what she thought of his looks anyway. He wasn't some damned peacock, strutting around for a female. Scowling, Mason dug a cheroot from his coat pocket and propped the thin cigar between his lips while he went back to the campfire for a twig to light it with. As he'd expected, Amelia jumped down from her perch and followed him.

"Distinctive sounds like some namby-pamby mama's boy dressed in a purple waistcoat and britches," he muttered around the cheroot. Lifting a burning branch, he lit the cigar. Tobacco-scented smoke spiraled upward, joining the mesquite smoke from the campfire.

"I mean distinctive as in memorable," Twirly Curls explained. She propped her chin in her hand and stepped backward a pace, studying him. "Take those all-black clothes, for instance—"

"These are poet bandit clothes," Mason interrupted. "They were good enough to convince *you* of who I was."

"Exactly. Now you'll either be mistaken for the poet bandit—an outlaw—or yourself—an outlaw. We've got to come up with something that'll blend in a bit more." Chin still in hand, she circled him slowly. "What were you before you became an outlaw?"

He hated to admit it, but she had a point. If the sheriff's wanted posters had reached Tucson already, he'd be hard pressed to walk down the street without risking capture by some bounty-hunting knuck. If that happened, he'd likely never reach Ben in time. What were the chances he could escape from two jails in a row?

"I'll bet you were a . . . soldier," Amy mused, looking him up and down. "You've got that soldier's bearing, like you could take the weight of the whole world on your shoulders and still stand up straight."

She smiled, as though taken with the image of him as Atlas, balancing a globe on his shoulders.

Mason laughed. "You've got an eye for those things, Amelia. I was stationed at Fort Lowell until a few years ago."

"And then?"

He squinted at her, deliberating, then admitted, "I had a farm a little ways from here." Scanning the landscape around them, he added, "Up north, just off the Gila River."

"It's near here?" Amy asked, her gaze following his pointing finger. "Why didn't you say so? We could just go there, instead of sleeping in a wagon bed."

Mason looked toward the Gila, toward the farm where he hadn't even been able to lay in spring seed before he'd been set on the run—looked toward his past—and remained silent. For all he knew, the Territorial government had taken over his land until the coroner's jury made their decision about Ellen's death.

He hadn't had time to wait for their verdict. Not if he wanted to see his son again.

He shook his head. "No. I'm going to Tucson. I have people to meet."

"Who?"

He said nothing. Amy crossed her arms primly over her chest and frowned. "Mason Kincaid, you've got to be the most stubborn man I've ever met," she said. "Why won't you trust me? Maybe I can help you somehow."

"I shouldn't have told you as much as I did," he said, turning away from the expectation he saw in her face. He'd been a fool to trust her, even with that much of his past. "I've got to get things ready. We're heading out again after sunset."

She stared at him for a long moment, measuring him. Then, as though she'd reached some sort of decision, Amelia blew out a great gusty sigh.

"All right. But if you won't confide in me, will you at least consider my disguise idea?"

Mason tossed down his cheroot stub, grinding it into the soil with his boot heel. He squinted at her from beneath his hat brim. "Nope."

"Mason! It's a good idea," she protested.

Digging the toe of her shoe into the ground, Amy gazed out

toward the distant mountains. The sun had nearly reached their peaks.

"I want to help," she went on, not looking at him. "It's—it's partly my fault you got caught and locked up at Maricopa Wells. I didn't want to admit it before, but if not for me I think you would've gotten away from the stagecoach. Even away from that man who was shooting at you."

"Amy—"

She turned to him and laid both hands flat against his shirt-front. Her face tilted upward toward his. "Please let me help, Mason. I . . . I know I've been a bother to you, held you back from whatever you've got to get in Tucson. I swear I'll do better." Her hands fisted in the fabric of his shirt, and her chin took on a determined angle. "I *know* I can do it."

Gently, he untwisted her hands from his shirt. Something told him he was going to regret agreeing with her, but Mason did it anyway. Anything to get Amelia to quit touching him. Just being near her got him heated up enough, without her touching him, too.

"All right. What's your damned idea?"

She brightened. Before he knew what she intended, Amy swept his borrowed hat from his head. "A haircut!" she announced, dangling his hat from her fingertips behind her back as she surveyed his head. "I'm very talented with a pair of scissors."

Mason fought the urge to run his fingers through his shoulder-length brown hair. He wasn't about to primp for her. Hell, no.

"It'll change your appearance completely," she went on, standing on tiptoes to brush his hair back from his face with her fingertips.

"What's wrong with the way I look?" he demanded.

"Nothing," Amy assured him with a hasty glance. Her fingertips glided over his temples, then wavered as she lost her balance. Rising on tiptoe again, she added, "It'll just be different, is all. A good beginning to your disguise."

Her breasts brushed against his chest as she swayed, trying to reach the back of his head. Mason automatically reached to steady her, then froze just as his hands reached her hips.

Being this close was a bad idea.

A very bad idea.

He stepped backward and snatched his hat from her hand. "Let's get it over with then."

Twenty minutes later, Mason sat on a rock beside their covered wagon. Amy, shears and comb taken from the wagon in hand, circled him. Finally she stopped, her eyes narrowed in concentration.

"At this rate you won't get done 'til midnight," he grumbled, looking up at her, feeling exposed and foolish under her eagle-eyed scrutiny.

"Hush," she said, smiling. "I'm making a decision. You're just afraid I'll cut crooked and make you look all funny."

He snorted. "Nothing could make me look funny."

"Want to bet?"

She moved closer, coming to stand between his legs where she could reach his head better, and raised the comb.

Mason's hand clamped onto her wrist. "Just make sure it's longer than my whiskers were yesterday," he ordered.

Amy nodded. "Yes, sir," she said, giving him a mock salute with the comb. "Anything else?"

Don't stand so close, he thought. But that was idiotic—she had to be close to him to cut his hair. He'd just have to ignore the inviting sway of her breasts practically in his face, the womanly curve of her hip near his hand, the warm softness of her skin, only inches away.

This haircut was going to kill him.

"No, nothing else," Mason said, gritting his teeth. He

clenched his hands over his knees, his arms arrow-straight. "Go ahead and do it."

"This won't hurt a bit," Amy said as she leaned closer. Her fingers delved into his hair, dug into his scalp, massaged. He felt the comb slide along the top of his head as she made a part; then the comb's hard tortoiseshell teeth swept his hair away from his face.

Her fingertips moved across his head with gentle, deliberate precision, deftly arranging his hair to suit her. Mason wanted to close his eyes, to surrender to her care, to let himself enjoy the feel of her hands on him. Instead, he gritted his teeth harder. What kind of man was he, to be moved by a touch as simple as this?

Sighing, Amy paused and lowered her palms to his shoulders. The movement made her breasts sway gently, right at eye level. The poorly fit bodice of her latest borrowed dress gaped open slightly, revealing the smooth hollow between her breasts, hinting at the round, sensitive softness beneath her dress.

Closing his eyes briefly, Mason tried to think of something, anything, except how much he wanted to fill his hands with her softness. Anything except how much he wanted to undo each of those tiny pearl buttons, to see her bared before him. His blood raced, pulsing with heat.

He swallowed hard and turned his head away, feeling his self-control retreat further with every moment that passed. How long did a damn haircut take, anyway? How much longer was he supposed to endure this?

Dimly, he became aware that Amy had stopped combing. She frowned down at him, the long scissors' blades resting casually on her shoulder.

"I really can do this, Mason. Please relax. You're stiff as a board."

He grunted and clamped his hands tighter onto his knees.

Part of him was stiff as a board, and it sure as hell wasn't his hair.

Pursing her lips, Amy moved from between his legs to stand behind him. Her skirts trailed over his knee, leaving behind the scent of soap and flowers and woman. She started combing again, her hands sliding and tugging slowly through the hair at the back of his head. Wisps of cut hair drifted down, gathering at his feet. Mason shifted atop his rock, trying for a more comfortable position.

Only one comfortable position came to mind. Him, with Amelia pulled down on that rock. Touching her the way he longed to do, making her *need* the way he needed now. Thrusting into her sweetness until they were both spent and breathless. Making love to her, haircut be damned.

Hell. Mason stared blankly toward a cholla bush in the distance, waiting for his head to clear. Behind him, Amy still stroked and combed, oblivious to all he'd been thinking. The *snick-snick* of the scissors sounded in his ear as she worked, underlaid by the low-pitched melody of the song she was humming.

She was innocent. Inexperienced. And she was leaving him behind as soon as they reached Tucson.

He was a wanted man. An outlaw without a future. And she'd be better off without him.

Mason still wanted her.

He cleared his throat. "Almost done?"

She laughed. "I've just gotten started! You do want it to look nice, don't you? That takes a little time."

More time than Mason had, if the state he was in now was any indication. His pants felt two sizes too small. He squirmed atop the rock, trying in vain to relieve some of the pressure.

Amy snipped a bit more, then stopped. Resting her forearms on his shoulders, she leaned over him from behind to get a glimpse of his face. Her hair swept across his cheek, followed closely by the warm fullness of her breast against the top of his shoulder blade. Mason groaned.

"Why, Mason, I swear a person would think I'm torturing you, the way you're behaving!" she said, staring at him curiously.

Torturing him. Amelia couldn't possibly know how right she was. It might've been enough to make him laugh, except for the desire that kept him nearly rigid with the effort of keeping it in check.

Instead Mason stared straight ahead. "I'm fine."

A muscle in his jaw ticked with fatigue, worn out from keeping his teeth clenched. Opening his mouth wide, he stretched his jaw to relieve the tension, then clamped it shut again.

"No, you're not." Amy's brows furrowed. "You think I can't do this, don't you?" she asked, her voice quavering.

"No."

"It's true! Do you think I haven't noticed you scooting away from the scissors every time I come near?"

He was too dumbstruck at the depth of her misreckoning to say anything more at first, and so she just went right on talking. Each carefully pronounced syllable was like a knife, carving the hurt she felt deeper into Mason.

"Do you think I haven't seen you making those pain-filled faces when you think I'm not looking?" she asked, waving the scissors. "That I haven't seen—"

"Amelia, no. I—" How could he tell her the truth? Tell her how he wanted her, wanted to make love to her, wanted to keep her with him and make her his own—despite his better judgment?

He couldn't. He never spoken such things aloud in his life, not to any woman. And even if he could have, it was plain Amy didn't feel the same yearning, the same need, that he did. Plain that he'd hurt her without knowing it, and he didn't know how to set it right.

Take advantage of this offer to enjoy Zebra's newest line of historical romance novels....Splendor Romances (formerly Lovegrams Historical Romances)- Take our introductory shipment of 4 romance novels -Absolutely Free! (a $19.96 value)

Now you'll be able to savor today's best romance novels without even leaving your home with our convenient and inexpensive home subscription service. Here's what you get for joining:

- 4 BRAND NEW bestselling Splendor Romances delivered to your doorstep every month

- 20% off every title (or almost $4.00 off) with your home subscription

- FREE home delivery

- A FREE monthly newsletter, *Zebra/Pinnacle Romance News* filled with author interviews, member benefits, book previews and more!

- No risks or obligations...you're free to cancel whenever you wish...no questions asked

To get started with your own home subscription, simply complete and return the card provided. You'll receive your FREE introductory shipment of 4 Splendor Romances and then you'll begin to receive monthly shipments of new Zebra Splendor titles. Each shipment will be yours to examine for 10 days and then if you decide to keep the books, you'll pay the preferred home subscriber's price of just $4.00 per title. That's $16 for all 4 books with FREE home delivery! And if you want us to stop sending books, just say the word...it's that simple.

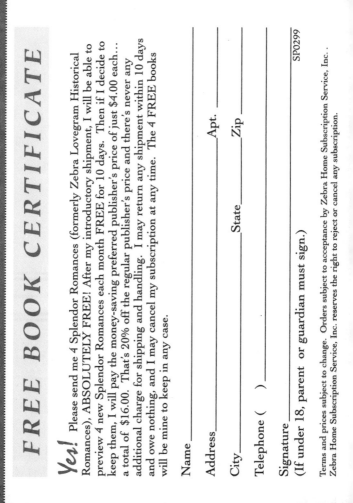

4 Free BOOKS are waiting for you!
Just mail in the certificate below!

If the certificate is missing below, write to: Splendor Romances, Zebra Home Subscription Service, Inc., P.O. Box 5214, Clifton, New Jersey 07015-5214

FREE BOOK CERTIFICATE

Yes! Please send me 4 Splendor Romances (formerly Zebra Lovegram Historical Romances), ABSOLUTELY FREE! After my introductory shipment, I will be able to preview 4 new Splendor Romances each month FREE for 10 days. Then if I decide to keep them, I will pay the money-saving preferred publisher's price of just $4.00 each… a total of $16.00. That's 20% off the regular publisher's price and there's never any additional charge for shipping and handling. I may return any shipment within 10 days and owe nothing, and I may cancel my subscription at any time. The 4 FREE books will be mine to keep in any case.

Name _____

Address _____ Apt. _____

City _____ State_____ Zip _____

Telephone ( ) _____

Signature _____ SP0299
(If under 18, parent or guardian must sign.)

Terms and prices subject to change. Orders subject to acceptance by Zebra Home Subscription Service, Inc. . Zebra Home Subscription Service, Inc. reserves the right to reject or cancel any subscription.

"It's not your fault," Mason began, groping for the words to explain away at least part of what she'd so sorely misunderstood. "It's just that you . . . that I—"

"I know, I know." She pushed herself upright again, using his shoulder for leverage. Gripping the scissors tightly, she leveled him with a look that held more hard-won knowledge than he'd imagined she'd have reason to keep. It sent her hurt twisting straight into his soul, gave him a glimpse of her life before. Mason didn't like what he saw.

"I can't help being the way I am," she told him, the words sounding oft repeated. "It's not my fault you don't have faith in me. Isn't that what you were going to say?"

She started combing again, snipping faster this time. Hearing tears in her voice, Mason started to turn his head to tell her she was wrong. Her hands clamped tight over his ears, holding him still with a strength he never would've guessed Amelia possessed.

"I've heard it before," Amy said. "You don't have to tell me again."

Regret choked him. Was it her father who'd put these notions into her head? Her brothers who'd told her how they lacked faith in her? Mason wished he could wring all their damned gentlemanly necks for hurting her.

If only he were better with words, but all his explanations only made things worse. He'd never been much for talking. Until now, he hadn't cared.

"But you agreed to my disguise plan," Amy went on, combing and cutting with a vengeance, her voice a bit stronger now, "and I intend to hold you to your word."

She moved in front of him again, then paused to peer critically at the front of his hair. Her gaze studiously fixed on the task at hand, Amy lifted a long hank that hung across his eyebrow and snipped it.

Mason caught her hand and slipped the comb from it. As it

fell into his lap, he twined his fingers with hers and pulled their joined hands against his chest, forcing her to look at him.

"I want you to do it."

Flushing, she tried to tug her hand away. "You don't—"

Mason held fast. "I want you to do it," he said again. "I believe you'll do a good job."

She stared at him, her eyes blue and wide and suspicious.

He caressed her hand, felt his heart beating faster beneath her touch, and added, "Hurry up before I change my mind and haul you down here for a kiss, instead."

Fourteen

"You're bluffing," Amelia said, the scissors going slack in her hand. Of all the things Mason might have said to her, this was the very last one she'd expected.

She wanted to believe him. Wanted to believe he truly had faith in her—or at least in her ability to give him a decent haircut or cook a palatable meal. More than ever before, it seemed so important that he find her capable. If only for a little while, Amelia wanted to feel trusted. Needed.

But could she trust Mason, an outlaw and a man she'd only known for days, however familiar he seemed to her now?

He squeezed her hand, making her doubly aware of the work-roughened strength of his grasp. Mason could pull her down for a kiss, and would if he took a mind to, she realized. The proof was there in the cocky angle of his half-shorn head, the hot glimmer in his eyes, the quickening of his heartbeat beneath their joined hands.

And she wouldn't be able to stop him.

"Do I look like I'm bluffing?" Mason asked, stroking his fingers lightly over her knuckles.

The heat of his body seared through his shirt, warming her far more than the waning sunlight did.

"You—you look like a hungry cat contemplating a goldfish bowl," Amelia stammered, trying to pull her hand away again.

He confused her so much! One minute he looked as though

he'd just as soon have left her at the roadside waiting for the stagecoach that had abandoned her. The next, he seemed as though she'd hurt him somehow. And the next, he was laughing at her. She wished mightily Mason would just make up his mind how he felt about her and have done with it, once and for all.

He gave her a lazy smile. "I guess that makes you the prize goldfish."

"And you the tomcat," she said, feeling her mood lighten a little. "On the prowl after a poor, defenseless little creature." She made a tsk-tsk sound, teasing him.

Unsmiling, Mason slid his hand down her wrist in a slow caress. The subtle friction of his palm over the tender hollows of her wrist and along the underside of her forearm set every inch of skin he touched atingle. She stared at his sun-browned hand, amazed that such sensation could be engendered by so simple a touch.

To her surprise, he released her hand. But his attention remained solely, compellingly, on her. Slowly his gaze roved over her hair, her dress, her body, and finally came to rest on her face.

It was, she realized, another caress. Amelia wanted to gasp at the intimacy, the heat, of it. Her belly tightened with anticipation and her knees felt quivery, just standing there. Even though Mason hadn't so much as leaned toward her, the look he gave her put Amelia in mind of the times he'd kissed her.

It made her want him to kiss her again.

Now.

"A beautiful creature, that prized goldfish," Mason said, his eyes never leaving hers. His lips quirked upward, just faintly, leaving no doubt what he meant by his words. "Not defenseless at all."

"Oh?" she asked, trying to sound more casual than she felt standing there between his legs, close enough to feel his body heat warm her skirts.

Suddenly she had a greater understanding of how that gold-fish might feel beneath a tomcat's patient, predatory scrutiny.

Afraid her trembling hands might betray her feelings, Amelia folded her arms tightly across her chest, letting the scissors poke out beneath her elbow.

"And what defense, pray tell," she asked, "does a tiny gold-fish have against a tomcat?"

Mason's smile widened. But it was the yearning in his eyes that made her heart lodge in her throat. She knew she should move, should get on with her work and retreat from whatever this was awakening between them. It felt dangerous, seductive.

And far too compelling to turn away from unexplored. Amelia could no more step away at that moment than she could turn the desert green with a simple wave of her hand.

"The goldfish lures that tomcat," he said, his voice low. "Whether it means to or not."

Mason clamped his hands roughly on his knees, flexing his fingers as though seeking purchase on something more ephemeral than flesh and bone. "He can't help but want something so tempting."

"Mason . . ."

He raised his gaze to hers. "Even knowing it's not his to take."

She couldn't move, couldn't think. Mason . . . wanted her? Could that really be what he meant? Stricken, Amelia could only stare at him at first.

"Mason, I—"

"It's nearly sunset," he broke in, frowning up at the sky. Straightening his arms again, his spine rigid, Mason said, "You'd better finish up."

"Finish up . . . ?"

He smiled, but somehow the easy intimacy between them had evaporated like so much morning dew in the heat of day.

"With my hair. We've got to get moving, Amelia."

Disappointment made Amelia's hand waver as she raised the shears again. Trying not to think of all he'd said, she sifted her hands through the thick, coffee-colored strands beneath her fingers. Just a few more snips around his ears and . . .

And it was no use trying not to think about it. Mason wanted her! Why, then, had he refused her invitation for a kiss only yesterday? Nibbling her lower lip thoughtfully, Amelia went on combing and cutting, but her thoughts were on the man sitting stoically on the rock in front of her.

She chanced a look at his face. Familiar, yet changed without its shadow of beard stubble, it wore as impassive an expression as ever. It was impossible to guess what Mason was feeling. He possessed the finest poker face she'd ever seen, much to her frustration.

Sighing, Amelia moved closer to snip the fine dark hairs at his temples. She combed a lock of hair and held it between her fingers, then slid the scissors upward to cut. They wobbled in her shaky hand and conked him in the temple instead.

Nothing moved except Mason's eyes; then his eyebrows raised. He looked at the scissors, then at her. "Didn't mean to get you all riled up," he said, "with all that talking."

He frowned, as though talking were the vilest of activities.

"I'm not riled," Amelia lied, wishing she could use both hands to hold the scissors. Maybe then she could cut steadily. But she figured such obvious maneuvering would hardly inspire confidence in her abilities. "You're wiggling."

His lips turned up at one corner. "So you decided to bash me in the head for it? Remind me not to make you really wrathy, Amelia."

"I'm not wrathy," she protested, backing up a bit. Her skirts brushed his legs. "It's just . . . just . . ."

Just the fact that Mason had piqued her curiosity with all his kissing and talk of wanting. Amelia could hardly stand to be left wondering. She wanted more of that quivery, thrilling feeling, more low-pitched words of beauty and temptation. If the determined set of his shoulders was anything to judge by, she reckoned Mason wasn't going to give it to her.

"It's just nothing," she said curtly. "Turn your head so I can cut the other side."

"Of my hair," he reminded, obediently looking toward the mountains. "I like my ears where they are."

Amelia made a face. "And I like a little more quiet while I work, please," she said, ignoring the smile he gave her in return.

She needed to focus her attention on finishing his haircut. To that end, she leaned forward, unthinkingly propping her knee slightly on top of Mason's thigh for balance. Instantly, his hands came around her leg, wrapping just above her knee to steady her. The heat of his palms burned through the layers of her skirts and petticoat, all the way to her skin beneath. Suddenly, she became aware of the granite-hard feel of his thigh, muscular and warm beneath her. Amelia's breath caught.

Their eyes met.

The pressure of his hands on her thigh increased, became a gentle kneading that moved steadily higher, bunching her skirts. She shivered, caught up in the sensation, unable to take her eyes from Mason's. His eyes darkened as he watched her, almost as though their senses were one, almost as though he experienced every feeling as Amelia did.

Blindly she reached for him, felt his shoulders bunch beneath her hands as she held onto him. His hands roamed higher, spanned the width of her waist, pulled her closer. The comb and scissors fell from her hands; dimly Amelia heard the implements thud behind them onto the barely moist soil. Mason's hands slowed, his movements sensual and dreamlike . . . but her pulse beat faster, keeping time with her breath.

Exhilaration filled her. This was what she wanted, what she needed. Twining her fingers in his shirt, she lay her cheek across the top of Mason's head, felt the soft, uneven ends of his hair tickle her skin. His arms flexed, holding her tighter. His thumbs swept upward, making tender circles beneath her ribs.

Amelia gasped, feeling like squirming, like rubbing against him, like holding him tighter, all at once. Wavering, she squeezed his shoulders for balance. Incoherent whimpers rose in her throat, only to fade beneath a new onslaught of sensation as Mason's head came forward, his face buried in the neckline of her dress. He moaned, and his hands slid up her back, flattening against her shoulder blades.

He pushed her closer, trapping her between his hands behind her and his face at her bosom. His jaw, roughened by the beginnings of a beard she hadn't noticed before, rubbed slowly over the swell of her breasts, awakening her skin with each tiny prickle of movement. He nuzzled her collarbone, inhaling hoarsely as though he, too, felt breathless as Amelia did.

"Mmmm, so soft," Mason murmured, kissing the hollow of her throat. His lips glided to just above the lace-edged neckline of her dress, leaving a row of hot kisses along her skin.

"So soft, so . . ." His fingers flexed at her back and his body quivered with barely suppressed emotion. "Ahhh, Amy. I'm just a man. I can't—"

"Please," she cried, digging her fingers into his hair to hold him to her. "Please, Mason."

Her breasts ached, fairly throbbing with the need for his touch. Surely he could ease the inexplicable longing that rose within her, surely he couldn't bring her this far, only to leave her wanting . . . wanting.

"I need . . . Oh, I think I'll die if you stop touching me, I—" Amelia's words ended on a strangled plea, wrenched from her lips as his hands slid from her shoulder blades down to the small of her back, then away. Releasing her?

Driven by the need to reach him, to make him understand how she felt, Amelia clutched at his head, leaned down to him. A kiss could change his mind. With her heart pounding in her chest, her fingers trembling, she tilted her head to reach Mason's lips. She closed her eyes. Before her courage could desert her, she lurched forward to press her lips to his.

Her nose bashed into Mason's.

Pained tears sprang to her eyes. She opened them to see him only inches away. Horribly, he was frowning at her.

"Amelia," he started to say, leaning slightly away, "I can't—"

He was trying to stop her. No, no—she could do this. Frowning with renewed determination, Amelia puckered her lips and forced his head to tilt sideways too, then tried again.

Their lips met. She kissed harder, and for the first time in her life it occurred to her to resent the inexperience that made her so clumsy. It filled her with frustration. Amelia tried to mimic the way Mason had kissed her, skimming her tongue gently over his lips, teasing his mouth open.

It wasn't working, she thought miserably. She didn't know what to do, how to touch him, how to share the remarkable feelings he stirred within her. Screwing her eyelids more tightly shut, Amelia flicked her tongue in tiny lapping motions over his lips.

With a tortured groan, Mason threaded his hands in her hair and cradled her to him. Their mouths melded into hot, unending sweetness as he took charge of the kiss, hungrily tasting her lips, teasing her tongue with his own, making her wild for more . . . more. It felt like surrender and joining at once, like a union she'd waited for all her life without knowing it.

Amelia couldn't think, could only feel as the kiss deepened and went on. Mason's hands covered her breasts, possessing her, and her body responded with all the eagerness her heart had kept hidden. Her nipples tightened, yearning for his touch. His palms skimmed over their delicate peaks, then he cupped her fullness in his hands. He squeezed, ever so gently, and Amelia cried out, the sound muffled against his mouth.

His shuddering moan wrested from her whatever hesitation

still remained. Nothing had ever felt so heavenly as Mason's hands caressing her, his lips kissing her—his heart, reaching out to her. Joyously, she kissed him back with all the passion that swelled within her, holding him close.

No sooner had she done so than Mason ended the kiss. With a roar of frustration, he clamped his hands onto her upper arms and pushed Amelia away.

"No," he gritted out, holding her at arm's length. He stared at the shadowed ground, his expression ominous, breathing as heavily as if he'd just run all the way from Maricopa Wells.

Without Mason's heat to warm her, goose bumps prickled along her arms. Sundown had come and gone without her noticing, Amelia realized. Suddenly everything seemed colder.

"We're leaving," he said. He rose from the rock slowly, as though the movement pained him, then released her. "Get your things and get in the wagon."

"Now?"

"Now."

She could only stare at him, her body still tingling with all the wondrous new sensations he—he!—had aroused. Amelia reached out to catch hold of Mason's sleeve.

He shrugged off her hand and stalked toward the front of the wagon. She followed him, struggling to catch her breath after all that had just passed between them. How could he turn away from her now, of all times?

"Mason, wait! Can't we just—?"

"Just what?"

He rounded on her, teeth bared. She retreated a pace, but he was already upon her. Mason towered over her, silhouetted by the sunset's dusky, red-streaked skies behind him.

"Just lie together here, on a rock, for God and any passing *mejicanos* to see?" He rubbed his whiskers, frustration evident in every jerky movement.

Amelia tried to speak, but no words came out. Hand on her throat, she stared up at him.

"You want me to strip you naked and take you right here?" he went on, louder now. "You wanted to give yourself to an outlaw? Well, you damn near did."

She gasped. Mason only glared down at her, still breathing heavily. He looked as though he'd like to shake her silly. As though he might even enjoy doing it.

"No!" she cried, anger and tears swirling together to make her voice crack on the word. "No, I didn't want—"

"I did."

His gaze held her, searing her with the knowledge, the desire, it contained. Images of her and Mason engaged in the kind of brazen, carnal coupling he spoke of rose in her mind and called a heated flush to her cheeks. Was that what had begun between them? What she wanted?

Something akin to disgust curled his lip. Swearing beneath his breath, Mason whipped his hat from the rock he'd been sitting on and jammed it on his head.

"Wait!" Amelia cried when he turned. "How . . . ?"

Her voice cracked again, wavering, but she refused to weep. Not here, not now. She balled her hands into fists at her sides to keep from disgracing herself by reaching again for a man who thought so little of her. She couldn't as easily keep herself from asking the question that burned in her heart.

"After all that's happened," she asked, "how can you turn away from me now?"

Mason stopped. All she saw was the determined set of his shoulders, the hard denial of his stance, and her hopes sank. He wasn't going to tell her anything more. She'd have to wonder, and wonder . . .

Anger and helplessness loosed her lips. "Is it because you don't know how to love? Don't know how to care without making it into some cheap, vulgar"—tears squeezed her throat tight, making it nearly impossible to speak—"animal thing! Some kind of cruel—"

His hand closed on her shoulder, and even in the dusky light Amelia could see the anguish that tore through Mason.

"Don't," he said. *"Don't."* His thumb stroked over her lips, silencing her. His eyes begged her to obey.

An instant later, his unspoken plea had vanished beneath a layer of gritty resolve as unchangeable as the desert sky overhead. His hands left her—and left her confused and yearning.

"It wouldn't be that way between us," he said.

"Then why—?"

He shook his head. "I'm just a man, Amy. There's only so much tempting I can take. Enough of it, and I won't be able to turn away."

"Then don't!" Amelia grabbed his arm. "Don't turn away from me, Mason." Somehow, he needed her. She was sure of it. Something within him called out to her, and she could no more deny it than stop breathing.

His eyes turned dark and regretful. "You don't know what you're saying."

"Yes, I do." She bit her lip, desperate for something to convince him. Only one thing came to mind. Love. "I do know, and I tried to tell you before, but you wouldn't listen."

"I still won't. We're leaving."

His rejection smacked at her pride. It knocked the wind from her as surely as hitting the ground after falling from the heavy, swaying branches of the old maple tree back home did. Why wouldn't he listen?

Mason walked away from her into the darkness gathering near the head of the covered wagon, leaving Amelia with only one argument left.

"You can't walk away forever, Mason," she called. "I'll still be here. And I'll still be falling in love with you."

Time skidded to a stop. Mason did, too. Around her, Amelia

became aware of crickets chirping nearby, of water rushing along the banks of the creek they'd stopped beside, of the sage-scented breeze that tossed her skirts against her ankles. Of the utter stillness of the man only a few feet away from her.

It might as well have been a few hundred miles.

"Love is pretty words and hoping," he finally said, his voice gravelly. "It doesn't last."

Half-turned, Mason looked at her over his shoulder, his back straight and determined. He was too far away and dusk was gathering too quickly for her to make out his expression.

"Neither will you, if you keep on believing in it."

"Mason—"

"Let's go," he said quietly, and Amelia had no choice but to follow him into the darkness. Filled with frustration, she climbed into the wagon for the journey that would take her that much closer to Tucson and, when it was finished, away from Mason forever.

Fifteen

Amelia spotted Picacho Peak when they were still miles from the stage station that was their destination for the night. Amidst the low rolling saguaro-studded hills, the mountain rose, isolated and strangely luring in the moonlight.

Not quite as large as the mountains she'd spent her first night with Mason in, Picacho Peak looked almost like a rocky funnel set upside down in the desert, almost like a volcano, except it wasn't open at the top. There, the peak split momentarily into two, as though a gigantic finger had pressed into the center.

"It's enchanting," Amelia said to Mason, bumping along beside him on the hard plank driver's bench. "Is there really a stage station there?"

"Yep," he replied. "Hard to miss a landmark like that."

They were the first words he'd said to her since they'd left their campsite beside the creek bed. Shrouded by darkness, they drove along the road in silence. Even accustomed as she was becoming to Mason's ways—he'd never been talkative, Amelia had to admit—she couldn't help feeling wounded now by his silence. It seemed personal, as though he didn't want to speak with her in particular.

It made her doubt the wisdom of staying to help him, however much he needed her. In whatever way. You couldn't force a person to accept help—or caring, for that matter. Maybe she'd been deluding herself all this time, just because she needed Mason to help her get to Tucson safely.

By the time she spied the faint lantern lights of the Picacho Peak station in the distance, Amelia still hadn't reached a decision. Trying to put her troubles aside for the moment, she watched the low, long adobe station building as they neared it.

It appeared not half as well traveled as Maricopa Wells. Only two rigs were parked in front, plain buckboard wagons both, and less than a dozen horses roamed placidly in the corral alongside the station. A lighted kerosene lantern hanging on a hook by the front door cast a glowing circle of welcome toward passing travelers, though. And good smells of spicy meat and baking cornbread rose from the chimney along with wood smoke, sharpening her appetite.

Suddenly, Amelia found herself quite anxious to get inside.

A moment later, she realized Mason was guiding the oxen and wagon in a wide arc around the stage station. He was passing it by!

She grabbed his arm. Some part of her registered the heat of his skin, the well-used strength of his muscles, and the rest of her just wanted to get inside for dinner.

"Where are you going?" she cried. "The station's right over there. Aren't we stopping?"

"Outlaws don't drive up to the front door, pretty as you please," Mason said, not looking at her.

Now that they'd left the road, such as it was, he kept his attention focused on controlling the animals.

"We're going around back. With luck, anybody who hears us will reckon we're station hands and won't come round to check."

He guided the animals carefully through the darkened desert undergrowth, raising crickets and scaring long-eared jackrabbits from their hiding places. Amelia gazed longingly toward the station, listening to the sounds of voices and of pots banging as work went on inside.

"I hope they'll talk to us," she muttered forlornly, thinking of all the conversations she'd been deprived of since being left behind by the stagecoach. In all her life Amelia hadn't gone so long without visiting with people. It just wasn't natural to do without a nice chat.

"They won't turn us away," Mason assured her, stopping the wagon. He scanned the stage station and yard, then the moonlit desert behind them. Apparently satisfied, he set the brake and turned to Amelia.

"Follow me," he said, rising.

Amelia stood, then jumped down from the wagon beside him. He caught her, steadied her atop the marshy soil—it must have rained here, recently, too—and then released her as fast as he would have a burning tumbleweed.

"And keep your mouth shut," he added, giving her a stern look. "I'll do the talking."

"Are you sure you know how?" Amelia muttered, straightening her skirts.

"What?"

"I said, sure, I'll start right now." She smiled sweetly at him. Thankfully, Amelia was certain the cool darkness hid her blushing cheeks.

Mason stared suspiciously at her for a moment, then started toward the stage station. She tromped along behind him, devilishly pleased over her little bit of rebelliousness. At times, being with an outlaw like Mason made her want to abandon every ounce of proper behavior she'd ever learned.

A few yards from the wood plank door set into the rear of the low-slung stage-station building, he stopped. "Stay here. I'll be right back."

From the corner of her eye, Amelia spotted a muscular, dark-haired man rounding the corner of the station.

"Wait!" she hissed to Mason.

Too late. He'd already stepped into view. The man would spot him, probably raise an alarm. They'd both be hung for outlaws now, she thought with a panicky shiver. What could she do?

Her stomach twisted as the man spotted Mason. The stranger's eyes widened and his hand went to his gun belt. Then, to Amelia's amazement, he started laughing.

She stared as he stretched his hand forward in greeting to Mason. Both men shook hands, clapping each other on the back. A torrent of rapid speech followed—Spanish, she thought, but couldn't be sure. The man's voice sounded like that of the station hand at Maricopa Wells.

Mason sounded like he always did. Brief. He motioned toward the station building, said a few words in Spanish, and then the stranger disappeared inside.

Amelia was about to step into the yard to join Mason when the leather thong holding the back door closed wiggled, then the door swung open. She stepped back into the shadows, holding her breath. Would this be a friend, too? There had to be some reason he'd ordered her to stay behind in the shadows.

The reason he'd ordered her to stay behind emerged. She had long, beautiful black hair, a white, happy smile, and graceful, mostly bare arms that wrapped around Mason's neck and hugged him tight. A woman. Amelia squinted harder, trying to see her better.

She was beautiful. Dressed in a simple white gown with colorful embroidery, her hair unbound, the woman looked like an exotic goddess. A hot flare of emotion like she'd never experienced flooded through Amelia, making her hands clench into fists.

Jealousy, she realized, and ashamed as she was to recognize that was what it must be, she felt powerless to stop it. Watching the woman hang with obvious affection all over Mason, watching the scoundrel's delighted grin as she did so made her blood boil.

No wonder he'd wanted to keep her in the shadows. All the better to greet the woman he *truly* cared about.

They were still hugging and talking in rapid-fire Spanish when Amelia smoothed down her tattered borrowed dress, gritted her teeth, and stepped forward into the yard.

"I don't believe we've been introduced," she said, stepping toward Mason and the woman with a false smile plastered on her lips. For once she felt grateful for the years of deportment she'd been subjected to at Briarwood Young Ladies' Seminary. At least she wouldn't embarrass herself socially, however rude Mason acted.

She extended her hand to the woman. "I am Miss Amelia O'Malley, a visitor from the States," she said, doing her best to ignore the glare she was sure Mason had aimed in her direction for daring to disobey his instructions. "I'm so pleased to make your acquaintance."

After a quick, private glance toward Mason, the woman stopped hanging on him long enough to accept Amelia's hand. Mason only stood there, crossing his arms over his chest and watching them both with an aggravatingly bemused expression on his face.

The woman was truly breathtaking, Amelia realized with a sinking feeling. Up close, her caramel-colored skin and dark eyes acted beautifully to set off her hair. Hair that, she was somewhat dismayed to notice, flowed straight and smooth down her back, something Amelia would never in a million years achieve with her fine, unruly curls. Several uncharitable thoughts crossed her mind, most involving the scissors stowed away in the wagon.

The woman said something to Mason—a question, from the sound of it—in Spanish. He answered in kind, and they both laughed. Amelia narrowed her eyes and withdrew her hand, trying to achieve a poised, carefree pose.

"Doña Juana," Mason said to the woman, sweeping his arm

toward Amelia with a gallantry she'd never witnessed from him, "meet Miss Hoity-Toity O'Malley."

"Mason!" Amelia stared at him, aghast.

"Please, call me Juana," said the woman with a warm smile. Her melodious voice made her words sound like poetry.

"I think you may have misunderstood what you saw of my greeting, Miss O'Malley," she went on gently. "I am an old friend of Mason's, but that is all." Juana cast him a chiding glance. "However this rascal *gringo* might wish it to seem to you."

Mason looked at the dirt, grinning like a schoolboy caught pinning his desk mate's braids to her chair. Unrepentant, but resigned to being discovered sooner or later.

Amelia felt like kicking him. "Of course it makes no difference to me how Mr. Kincaid greets his friends," she lied.

Mason raised his eyebrows. "Mr. Kincaid?"

He was enjoying this, the rat!

"I'm happy to know he still has some friends," Amelia added, narrowing her eyes at him.

"I am also," Juana said. She smiled and moved closer to take Amelia's arm. "These days, with all this trouble, he needs them."

They walked arm in arm toward the open doorway. There, Juana stopped, eyeing Amelia carefully. Her voice held an edge when she spoke again.

"You are a friend, aren't you, Miss O'Malley?"

Her hand tightened in the crook of Amelia's elbow, and with some surprise she realized she couldn't move forward without a struggle.

Mason saw it, too. "Put your claws away, *tigresa*," he said. "I trust her."

He strode past them into the station. Releasing her, Juana followed him, but Amelia could only stand there for a moment, plumb certain she'd misheard the words Mason had uttered so matter-of-factly.

I trust her.

"Manuel told me what happened at Maricopa Wells," Juana said, her voice carrying from within the station's back room. "A rider came through this morning looking for you. And your lady outlaw."

She looked for Amelia—the lady outlaw she spoke of, unfortunately—and spotted her still standing in the doorway.

"Please come in, Miss O'Malley. You must be tired after your journey, and hungry. And"—she slanted a mischievous glance at Mason, her eyes sparkling—"if I know Mason, hungry for some conversation, too."

"I'm a man, not a gossipy old woman," he muttered, pinching his fingers into a pot on the stove behind Juana.

He withdrew something—a bite of meat, Amelia surmised from the looks of it—and popped it into his mouth. Licking his lips, he went back for more, for all appearances not caring at all whether she joined them inside or not.

"Talking to him is as enlightening as talking to the base of Picacho Peak," Juana said, drawing Amelia forward. "Just like my James."

Amelia stepped inside. The room she found herself in was narrow but long, with tan adobe walls, a white muslin-covered ceiling, and a hard-packed dirt floor that soothed her feet with its evenness after so many days in the desert. A scarred rectangular table squatted near the stove, with a wash basin and cupboards beyond.

In the absence of windows, lanterns brightened the room from hooks set into the walls at evenly spaced intervals. At the other end of the room, a battered-looking upright piano, several straight-backed chairs, a rocking chair, and a vividly colored rag rug defined the space as a sitting area.

"This is cozy," Amelia said, smiling. "Thank you."

The warmth inside made her skin tingle, and her stomach rumbled at the savory smells of roast meat and bread. On the huge cast-iron stove beside Mason, coffee perked, adding its rich aroma to the air, too.

"Manuel told me James is at Fort Lowell," Mason said.

"He left yesterday," Juana said, nodding her head. She showed Amelia to a bow-backed chair at the table, then went to the stove. "But he should be returning late tonight."

Spying Mason still at the stove-top pot, she picked up a wooden spoon lying nearby and whacked his hand with it. "Wash before grubbing around in my pots," she scolded.

Amelia laughed. He paused, another bite of beef halfway to his mouth, and gave Juana a wolfish grin. Then he ate the meat.

"Your *chalupas* smell as good as ever, Doña Juana," he said. "But I think you've turned ornerier. Time was, you'd never turn a starving man from your table."

"Starving man?" Amelia asked, arching an eyebrow. Leveling him a what-about-my-cornbread-and-beans look, she crossed her legs and clasped her hands at her knee. She waited for his answer, her top leg kicking back and forth.

"Ornerier?" asked Juana, hands on her hips.

Mason glanced from one woman to the next, then grimaced.

"You want sweet-talking, ask Manuel," he finally said, eyeing a stack of flat, pale pancakes on the table near Amelia's elbow.

"You just make these?" he asked, heading for the plate—and away from the long reach of Juana's wooden spoon.

She sighed, but without rancor. Amelia recognized the sound. It was the same one she used on her brothers back home, filled with affection, tolerance, and a good measure of resignation.

"The *tortillas* are fresh and so are you, Mason Kincaid," Juana said, turning her back to him while she stirred the contents of the pot. "You can leave my brother out of this."

On his way to the *tortillas*—Amelia could see now how Mason had learned to speak Spanish, with so much of it being used in the Territory—he paused beside her chair. His hand dropped to the nape of her neck, his fingers absently kneading the taut muscles there as he listened to Juana talk about happenings at the stage station.

Amelia felt like sighing. Between Mason's soothing touch, the warmth of the room, and the relief of being in friendly surroundings at last, she thought she might finally be able to relax.

Juana, her hands wrapped protectively in her apron, carried the steaming pot of meat from the stove. Her gaze flicked to Mason's hand on Amelia's neck, then away. Pursing her lips thoughtfully, she set the pot in the middle of the table. With a studied casualness Amelia could detect, even embodied in Spanish words as it was, Juana asked Mason a question.

His hand stilled. Slid away. "No."

Juana shrugged. "It looks like it," she said.

Scowling, Mason pulled out a chair across the table from Amelia and sat in it. She felt his withdrawal from her as plainly as if he'd slapped her first, then turned away. As it was, it didn't help that they faced each other across the table. That only meant she had a better, if unwelcome, view of his granite-jawed face.

Squaring her shoulders, Juana smiled at Amelia. "Please help yourself," she told her, nodding toward the meat and *tortillas* on the table. "I have other work to attend to"—her gaze slanted toward Mason, dark with a meaning Amelia couldn't decipher, then back again—"but I'll return once you've eaten."

"Thank you," Amelia said, "for everything. Thank you very much."

Juana nodded gravely. *"Bienvenida.* You're welcome," she replied, and then she was gone.

Sixteen

While they were finishing dinner, James Fergus arrived. Juana's wiry, redheaded husband burst into the room with two mongrel hounds yapping at his heels and Manuel at his side, calling out a greeting to Mason in a thick Scottish brogue.

"Mason Kincaid, ye old rascal," he exclaimed, slapping his friend on the shoulder. "How do ye fare, with a price on your head and all?"

His keen, blue-eyed gaze fell on Amelia. "Fare well, with a lassie like this by your side," he went on before Mason could reply. His smile charmed a blush to Amelia's cheeks as he bent to grasp her hand. "She's a beauty, just like your Ellen was."

Ellen? Mason's wife, Amelia realized. The woman whose death had sent him on the run. Her hand remained in James's, but her gaze went straight to Mason.

He stared at the tabletop, appearing lost in thought. If not for the tapping of his fingertip against his coffee cup, she might have believed he wasn't even listening to their conversation. With Mason, even such a small gesture as that rubbing, rhythmic fingertip was telling. Was he remembering the woman he'd loved? The one he loved still?

"God rest her soul," James added, his sympathetic gaze flicking briefly toward his friend before settling again on Amelia. Had he guessed already how she felt about Mason?

She longed to ask him what he knew about Mason's life before, about his wife and her passing. But how could she, with Mason only a few feet away and obviously unwilling to talk about it?

James squeezed her hand. His fingers were chill with having just come in from outside, and he carried a breath of that cold night air with him on his plain workman's clothes. But his touch was caring, and his manner made Amelia feel as at home as Juana's invitation to dinner had.

For her hosts' sake, Amelia put her thoughts of Mason's past aside until later.

"Thank you," she said, bowing her head slightly. "Mason, if all your friends are like Juana and Mr. Fergus, I'll remember my time as a lady outlaw fondly."

"Och, call me James, lassie," he commanded, releasing her hand. "And what's this I hear about remembering? Are ye leaving us so soon, then?"

He winked at Mason, and the mood in the room lightened with his gesture. "Losing your way with the ladies, are ye? I never thought I'd see the day."

"He still has a way with your woman," Manuel put in from his place near the stove. He handed a cup of steaming coffee to James, then poured one for himself. "If he'd held my sister any tighter, he'd have broken her ribs."

He ambled toward the table, then paused beside Mason's chair. Both hounds sat at Mason's knee, their massive tawny bodies alert as they watched eagerly for a bite of fallen meat.

"What happened to your hair, *amigo?*" Manuel asked, squinting at Mason's hatless head. "Did that crazy *barbero* in Tucson cut your hair while he was drunk again?"

He clucked his tongue, shaking his head with pity.

Calmly, Mason finished chewing his last bite of *tortilla;* then he picked up his coffee cup. "Amelia cut it," he said.

"Oh, lassie." James gave her a mournful look.

Amelia felt like sinking straight into her chair. Mason's hair *did* look awful, she realized upon closer inspection. She hadn't noticed before, since he'd kept his hat on until they'd begun eating. After that she'd been too engrossed in Juana's wonderful, spicy food to notice.

"He didn't let me finish," she explained. At the memory of the reason why the haircut had ended so abruptly, the memory of the intimacies they'd shared atop that desert rock, a renewed flush climbed her cheeks. "He just stuck his hat on and drove us straight here instead."

Manuel nodded. "I can see why," he told Mason. "Maybe Juana can fix it for you before you go."

He frowned doubtfully toward the jagged spikes of hair sticking up on the left side of Mason's head. "Or maybe just shave you bald and start over."

"Then the pretty ladies would leave you alone, to be sure," put in James.

They all laughed, Mason included. Here, he was like a different man—more lighthearted, more at ease. More like the man he must have been, before he'd been set on the run as an outlaw. Amelia wished she could have known him then, known the man everyone at Picacho Peak seemed to remember. The man they treated him as, still.

If she'd had any doubts about his innocence, seeing his friends' faith in him would have laid them to rest. There'd been no guardedness in Manuel's laughing greeting earlier, no hesitancy in Juana's embrace. They all believed in him. Perhaps Amelia could trust in Mason, too, no matter how he pushed her away at times.

Mason's gaze touched her, and she saw that he was still smiling. "It's not Amy's fault," he said in her defense. "I was in a hurry to get here for some of Juana's good cooking."

"And you should have been," said Juana, entering the room with an armload of soiled stoneware plates. She stacked them on a cupboard beside the washtub, then wiped her hands on her apron, turning to scrutinize Mason.

"You need to get some meat on those sorry skinny bones," she said, twisting her mouth. "Couldn't heft a frying pan to feed yourself, eh? No wonder you left home."

Skinny? Mason? Amelia looked at him, wondering how Juana could think a man so strong needed fattening up. For an instant, she saw what Juana saw—a man with a face a shade too gaunt for his big build, eyes too shadowed—and then the impression faded. He was just Mason again. Her Mason.

His eyes darkened. "You know why I left," he said quietly.

His gaze captured each person's at the table in turn, save Amelia's. Each one looked downward.

"I am sorry," Juana whispered, adding something more in softly spoken Spanish. She patted his shoulder, then went to stand behind her husband.

"The rider who came brought us wanted posters, too, lad," James said, capturing Juana's hand and clasping it loosely near his shoulder. "I burned the blasted lot of them."

Mason's lips tightened. He stared into his coffee cup, his finger again stroking the plain stoneware mug. Was he worried about the wanted posters? Surely he'd known they'd be issued.

"Have you had news of Ben?" Juana asked. "We—"

Mason's head snapped up. *"Luego."*

His terse command silenced Juana before she could say more. Clearly he didn't want to talk about Ben, whoever that was. Across from him, Amelia cursed the all-but-useless Latin she'd learned at the young ladies' seminary. An education in Spanish suddenly seemed much more useful.

"Ben?" she asked, raising her eyebrows hopefully toward Mason.

Utter, conspicuous silence descended upon the table.

Mason's fingers clenched tighter on his coffee cup. Unsmiling, he shoved his chair backward and stood. With mounting dismay, Amelia watched him set his coffee cup atop the stack of unwashed plates. He remained there, gripping the cupboard's edge, his back to them.

Juana delicately cleared her throat. "James, didn't you have something to discuss with Mason?" she asked.

Her husband's head jerked like that of a man caught napping and startled awake. He nodded.

"Amelia, you would perhaps help me clean up? We haven't many travelers in the front room, but the ones we have are messy," Juana said, nodding toward the stack of plates she'd carried in. "It has been a long time since I have had a lady's company."

How had the mood in the room changed so quickly? Amelia, confused and troubled, tore her gaze from Mason's back long enough to mumble that she'd help wash up. Scooping up her plate and Mason's, she stacked them and stood.

Something was wrong. Something to do with Ben, she guessed. Hesitating beside the table, Amelia saw a shudder pass through Mason. His knuckles showed white on the dark wooden cupboard's edge.

"Mason?" She started toward him, her free hand outstretched, drawn by the need to comfort him. His rigid shoulders, his bowed head made her heart twist. He looked so vulnerable.

So alone.

Juana stopped her before Amelia reached him. Wrapping her arms around Amelia's shoulders, she guided her to the washtub.

"Sometimes there is nothing we can do," she murmured, her dark eyes compassionate and knowing. "Sometimes we must let them struggle alone."

Tears and frustration crowded Amelia's throat. Her gaze flew to Mason as though called to him.

"I can't!" she whispered. Behind Juana, Mason straightened and followed the other men out the back door. "I—"

"You must," said Juana, reaching for the serviceable black

pump handle set near the washtub. "He will turn to you when he's able. Not before."

Amelia swiped the back of her hand across her burning eyelids. "What if he's never ready?" she asked, her voice cracking shamefully on the words. "What then?"

"Then he will remain alone, *pequeña.*"

Juana worked the pump handle slowly, filling the washtub with water. It splashed inside the silvery zinc tub, spotting them both with droplets. When it was filled, she turned to Amelia again, her manner businesslike.

"Will you help me carry this to the stove?"

Dumbly, Amelia nodded and took up the narrow handle nearest her. Holding her breath, she managed to get the tub to the stove and heft it on top.

"Mason is your friend," Amelia said once the job was accomplished. "Don't you care that he's hurting?"

"*Sí,*" Juana snapped, cracking a match across the stove top with far more force than necessary. "Of course I care. He is my friend. But more than that, he is a man. He will not accept my help."

Her forehead creased with worry, she leaned in front of Amelia and lifted the glass chimney of the lantern that hung there. She handed it to Amelia, turned up the wick, and lit the lamp. Satisfied, she took back the chimney and replaced it.

"I have to do something," Amelia said. "Mason says I can't help him, but I owe him so much. And I . . . I . . ."

Juana smiled gently and squeezed Amelia's arm. "You love him."

"Does it show?" she asked miserably. The thought that everyone at the table had likely known her feelings—and had witnessed Mason's indifference—filled her with mortification. Juana had known her mere hours before guessing.

"A woman knows," said Juana. Pursing her lips, she gazed up at the brass studs that fastened the white muslin at the ceiling.

Then, she smiled. "I am always closest to my James at night, when we're alone. At night he can hear my heart. He listens."

Her expression turned wistful. "Perhaps you can help Mason then."

"He's grouchy at night," Amelia protested. "I don't think he gets any sleep."

"Ahhh," murmured Juana, one slender fingertip poised at her lips. "I know just the remedy for that," she said. She leaned closer. "Tonight when he cannot sleep, you must kiss him, well and often."

"That's all?" Amelia asked, feeling skeptical. After her experiences this afternoon during Mason's haircut, she had her doubts he'd be receptive to such a tactic. It might even make him madder.

"The rest will take care of itself," Juana assured her, stirring soap into the washtub water. "If you want to reach a man, kissing is the best way to make him start listening."

Encouraged, Amelia nodded. Anything was worth a try at this point, she figured. She didn't have much time to lose; he'd told her they'd reach Tucson tomorrow evening. After that, he'd try to send her away. He'd all but promised it.

She'd have to act tonight.

Mason waited as long as he could before coming inside. By the time he did the stage station was dark, lit only by the lamp Juana had told him she'd leave in the room he was to sleep in. He saw its glow through the partly opened door and staggered toward it.

By now, Amy would be asleep in whatever room Juana had bedded her down in. Only one more night, Mason thought as he neared the door, reaching to drag his suspenders from one shoulder, then the other. Only one more night and he could leave Amy in Tucson, his conscience clear, and get on with what needed to be done. Get on with finding his son.

Bleary-eyed, he shouldered the bedroom door open and went inside, nudging it closed again behind him with his foot. His suspenders flopped around his thighs as he crossed the room, pulling off his shirt.

"Mason?"

He froze. Stared toward the bed, his shirt still bunched in his hands.

Amy.

He threw his shirt onto a chair, too weary to hurl it with any force. "I told Juana I'd sleep outside before sharing a room with you," he said bluntly.

Holding the thick patchwork quilt against her chest, Amy blinked at him sleepily. Her bare shoulders gleamed pale above the quilt, betraying how little she had on beneath it. The low lamplight shone on her hair, turning it golden, and Mason's fingers itched to smooth it from her face.

"I know. You're supposed to be sleeping on a pallet out there," she said, nodding toward the station's back room. "Juana told me."

Juana. He'd been duped, Mason realized. A noose tightening around his neck couldn't have made it plainer. *I'll leave a lamp burning for you,* she'd told him. *Come in whenever you're ready.*

He snatched his shirt from the chair.

"Wait! Where are you going?"

"Anywhere but here."

Lack of sleep made his head spin as Mason turned toward the door. Damned matchmaking Juana. His fingers touched the latch.

"Mason, who's Ben? Who's Ellen?"

He stopped, leaned his forehead against the cool smoothness of the fitted-plank door.

"Was she your wife?"

Mason traced a whorl embedded in the wood of the door, trying not to hear the plaintive note in her voice. It called to mind their places in the kitchen earlier . . . he with his hand unthinkingly, protectively, on Amy. She, accepting his care without question.

And then Juana's soft-spoken Spanish question had made him remember.

Have you found another Eastern woman?

No, he'd said. No. Thinking that Amelia and Ellen were not the same. Eastern ladies both, but different inside. Was it true? Or did he only want it to be?

Hell.

"I asked Juana," Amy said behind him, "but she wouldn't tell me."

"Good."

Mason wrenched open the door, felt the rush of cool air as it swept inward. An instant later, the bedsprings creaked. Before he could step outside, Amy was there.

She touched his arm. "Please don't go."

Teeth gritted, Mason held his ground.

"This is our last night together," she said quietly. "Won't you let me help you?"

Outside, two cats snarled and hissed. Fighting? Or mating? Mason couldn't tell which. His hand wavered on the planed edge of the door.

"You can't help me."

"Then let me comfort you." Her hair, silky and loose, brushed across his shoulder. Her scent enveloped him, lured him.

"No."

He couldn't, couldn't . . . but between the bone-weariness that numbed his thoughts, the quiet of the night, and the temptation of the woman behind him, he couldn't remember why. She trailed her hand down his arm, following the curves of muscle, sinew, and bone all the way to the inside of his wrist. He felt his blood pulse against her fingertips. The room closed in, squeezing them together.

Her breath fluttered against his shoulder. "Close the door, Mason. Now that you're here, stay with me."

"I'm leaving." But his feet stayed as though nailed to the floor.

"I love you," she whispered, her voice breaking.

And he remembered why he had to leave. His fingers groped for the doorjamb, caught it. Mason levered himself outward like a man leaping across a chasm ten feet wide, breathing hard. Blinded by the sudden darkness, he lurched toward the back door.

He heard feet padding hard across the floor before he made it halfway there. Amy's small, soft body slammed into him from behind, her arms going wide around him. Her hands groped his chest, his belly, his arms, as she tried to get her bearings in the dark.

Breathing his name again and again, she clamped her hands on his shoulders and writhed around to his front. Lace and thin fabric scraped Mason's skin. Somewhere, she'd abandoned the quilt.

"I won't let you go," she gasped, scrabbling upward like a kitten trying to climb his chest. Her kisses landed on the side of his chest, his shoulder . . . his mouth.

Her breasts pushed against his chest, rubbing hard with her movements. Heat seared between his bare skin and whatever flimsy thing she had on. He ached to rip it away, to cup her breasts in his hands. To taste her. His shaft tightened, hardened, strained beneath his clothes. Her soft, smooth thighs gripped his hip as Amy tried to keep from falling sideways.

The days of denial, of wanting her, melded into a single hard edge of need. Mason groaned, near witless with wanting to take her. His hands found the warm roundness of her buttocks and squeezed them.

Cupping her in both hands, he held Amy high against him. The tender, womanly feel of her drove the last of his resistance from his mind like leaves scattered before an autumn wind. All he knew was the need to keep her close, to satisfy the hunger he'd denied for so long.

A low purr of feminine need rippled from her throat. The erotic sound of it sent an uncontrollable shudder coursing through Mason. She needed, she wanted, too. *Wanted him.*

Eagerly she kissed him faster, harder, anywhere she could reach. Amy's hands found the nape of his neck and she pulled him to her, kissing all along his jaw. Her thighs tightened, seeking purchase.

"Careful," he murmured, his hands still cupping her, holding her high enough to protect himself from her squeezing knees. "Easy, now."

"I won't leave you," she whispered fiercely, clutching his shoulders. "You can't make me go again. Not tonight."

In a stray shaft of moonlight he glimpsed her face, small and determined beneath her tangle of blond hair. She jutted her chin forward. Her gaze, luminous with passion, challenged his.

Mason couldn't have left her if the station burned down all around them. In his chest, some tightness, some ache he'd only been half-aware of, eased.

"Yes, I can," he rumbled. "I can make you do whatever I want."

"No." Her arms tightened stubbornly around his neck, her legs around his hips. His body pulsed in response.

"Watch me," Mason said.

He wrapped his arms all the way around her, swept Amy up fully against him, and strode back toward the bedroom. Inside, he kicked the door closed, then looked down at her. The barest smile lifted his lips.

"Kiss me," he told her, "and I'll show you how."

Her eyes registered the challenge in his words. Her woman's smile answered it. Cradling his neck in her hand, Amy pursed her lips and made ready to kiss him.

"But if you do," he warned, stopping her with her lips only inches from his, "there's no going back. I won't be able to stop."

Mason breathed deeply, holding her gaze with his. He needed to know she understood, needed Amy to know what would happen before she chose. But everything within him urged him to take her and let the consequences be damned.

"I'll make you mine, Amy," he said hoarsely. "Is that what you want?"

"Yes," she whispered against his mouth, and the next thing he knew was the heat of her kiss. *"Yes."*

Seventeen

Mason laid Amy atop the rumpled bedclothes as tenderly as the fire in his blood allowed, eager as a man about to bed his virgin bride for the first time. She unwound her arms from his neck, then, shyly, scooted sideways in the narrow bed to make room for him, too. The wobbly smile she gave him was like a glimpse into her heart, beautiful and innocent at once. Its warmth humbled him. For her, he'd make this night special.

Stepping away from her, Mason reached to turn up the lamp.

"I want to see you," he murmured, turning the wick key in fingers suddenly gone thick and fumbling. His mouth felt dry. His heart pounded, crowding his throat as he turned back toward the bed and the woman he'd waited so long for.

Golden light flared and trembled. So did Amy. Bolstered by the pillows heaped at the carved wood bedstead, she lay waiting . . . waiting for him.

Waiting for the man she thought he was, the man she thought she knew.

Mason frowned, suddenly unable to move closer. This was wrong. False. Making love to Amy now would be a lie. As sure as the soil beneath his feet, to make her his now would be a betrayal.

She held her arms out to him, and the lamplight cast her body into revealing shadows beneath her delicate white gown. The sight made his gut clench and his shaft throb with urgency. Amy wanted him. Wanted to care for him. Now, now there was nothing he wanted more.

"Mason?" she whispered. "Is something wrong?"

He shook his head, eager to cast his doubts aside. She was a grown woman. He'd warned her enough. Warned her to get away from him when she could, warned her there was only so much tempting a man could take.

He was, after all, only a man—a man who needed like any other. A man who wanted to taste a woman's loving, feel a woman's soft, welcoming body next to him in the night. It was more than he deserved, Mason knew. But that didn't make him yearn for her any less.

He set his knee on the edge of the bed, felt the mattress dip beneath his weight. Amy's hands settled on his bare upper arms, reaching to guide him to her. She kept her eyes open, taking in his appearance with undisguised curiosity. Undisguised interest.

Mason felt no hesitancy in her touch, saw no grim forbearance in the curve of her lips. He hadn't known a giving woman in so long it seemed as though he'd only dreamed it in his past. Yet here was Amy, willing, wanting, to love him.

He bent his head and kissed her, trying to smother the doubts that bedeviled him. She tasted sweet, warm. Her arms twined around his neck, holding him to her as she pressed her generous, womanly body upward to meet him. Mason groaned, flexing his fingers on her waist, bunching her gown higher, fighting for control against the overwhelming pleasure of touching her. Of being touched by her . . . with love.

Love he didn't have the future to satisfy. Love that could never be, between two people as different as he and Amy were. Mason bent his head, pressing his forehead to her shoulder, trying to catch his breath. Amy's breath panted past his ear, and her body quivered beneath him.

He raised his head, calling himself a million kinds of fool for what he was about to do.

Something in his movements must have betrayed his thoughts, because she stilled, then sagged slightly into the quilts. Her eyes looked enormous, searching his face with a questioning, vivid blue intensity.

"Mason? What's wrong?"

Straightening, he set her back gently amongst the pillows. His hands shook as he settled himself in the middle of the bed, already feeling the loss of her that would come next.

Mason clamped his hands together savagely to stop their damned telltale trembling. "There's something you've got to know."

"Know? Now?" Amy leaned forward, her hand outstretched to touch his knee. "I know all I need to. I know that I lo—"

"About me," he interrupted, staring toward the lamp without seeing it. Anything, anything but look at her and see the horror on her face when he revealed the kind of man he really was. "You have to know everything."

And once she did, it would be all she would see. No more warnings would be needed to keep her away.

"I already know," she protested. "You already told me about the sheriff and your escape, and what they said about your wife." Amy's hand settled on his knee, stroking. "It was Ellen, wasn't it? Oh, Mason, I know you'll set it right. You—"

"No." He growled the word, forcing it past his constricted throat. "It's true."

"But—"

He wrenched his leg out of reach. Better to refuse her touch now than to be denied it later.

"My wife is dead because of me," Mason said. His gaze bored the truth of his words into Amy, kept her denials at bay. "Sure as if I'd poured the poison down her throat myself."

Amy flinched, and his voice broke. He sucked in a gulp of air, forcing himself to go on before he lost the will to do what needed to be done. To tell the truth. To destroy her belief in him.

"It wasn't always like that between us," he said quietly, staring toward the lamp again. "We . . . I met her back in the States, in Pennsylvania. When I was in the Army. Ellen was . . . she was different from the other women I knew. More refined, but more . . . flirtatious, too."

She'd sent him on a merry chase. Rounds of parties and balls, all in the hopes of seeing Ellen, of stealing a kiss on a veranda corner. Of persuading her to come home with him to the Territory. At the time, it had seemed what she wanted—what they both wanted.

"After we got married," Mason went on, "we came back here to live. To the farm on the Gila."

He glanced at Amy. She nodded without meeting his eyes, frowning at a spot just over his shoulder. At some point she'd grabbed the quilt again. She held it to her chest like a shield.

"The Army was no life for a lady," Mason said, rubbing his palms along his thighs. "I thought we'd be happier on the farm. I figured I could make a good living, selling grain to the express stations and military posts nearby."

"I built a home for us"—he flexed his fingers as though still feeling the gritty adobe bricks in his hands—"and before two harvests had come, Ben was born."

Amy's head turned. Tears glittered in her eyes. "You have a son?"

He nodded, his throat tightening at the thought of his boy. Where was he now? Did Ben believe his father wasn't coming for him, that he didn't care about him? Frustration roughened his words. "He's six years old. I—"

"Where is he now?"

Unblinking, barely breathing, she waited for his answer, watching him with eyes gone wide and horror-filled. Did she think he'd hurt his own child?

"Tucson," Mason ground out, pushing away from the bed.
Away from her.

He strode across the small room, his footfalls noiseless
against the packed-dirt floor. "What did you think I was going
to Tucson for? I risked hanging to leave Maricopa Wells. I've
been hunted and shot at since the day I went on the run from
the sheriff. I risked everything to get there."

He leveled a hard look at Amelia. "What the hell did you
think I wanted?"

Her mouth opened, but no sound emerged. Clutching the quilt
closer, she tried again. "T-treasure," she stammered. "Or—or,
revenge against somebody." Her voice rose, beseeching him.
"You're an outlaw! What was I supposed to think?"

"Not that I'd endanger you for the sake of money," he told
her. "Or revenge."

Mason rubbed his jaw, trying to staunch the sense of betrayal
her words engendered. He'd been relying on her faith in him
more than he'd known. Believed in it more than he'd wanted to.

"I didn't see it at first," he said woodenly, "but Ellen wasn't
the kind of woman for life out here. She was. . . . lonely." The
word choked him, now that he knew the depth of her sadness,
now that he knew what it led to. "Lonely without her friends
and city life. She wanted to leave."

"Leave you?" Amy whispered.

Pacing, Mason paused beside the bureau, turned down the
lamp. Shadows deepened in the corners of the bedroom. "Leave
me, leave the Territory."

"But she had . . . had a child. Ben. Why—"

"It wasn't enough." Mason's fingers dug into the scarred bureau top. "I couldn't give Ellen more children, the children she
wanted. Couldn't give . . . give her the life she wanted." He
gulped for air, starved for breath; his chest squeezed, hurting
him.

He couldn't face Amy, couldn't bear to see her face when she learned the truth. His throat felt gravelly, aching. "I promised to take care of her. Promised to give her all I could. And she . . . she believed me."

"Mason, I—"

"When Ellen died, part of me was relieved. Relieved!" He whirled to face her at last, unable to stop the choked sound that came from his throat. Damn, but it felt weak to say the words. "And the rest of me knew I could have stopped her."

Mason slammed his hand into the bureau, welcoming the fresh pain that roiled through him. At least this was pain he understood, action and reaction that made sense. Ellen's death was a waste, a sickening waste, and the knowledge that he might have prevented it ate at him.

"How?" Amy asked quietly, her eyes clear now and her posture straight and motionless atop the mattress.

Her composure baffled him. Mason stared at her, hardly able to believe she hadn't shrunk into the corner already, hefted a gun from his gun belt to protect herself with, screamed for Manuel and James to help her.

"How, Mason? Stopped her from doing what?"

He stared, groping for words. Images of Ellen rose in his mind—Ellen pleading with him to move to the city, to go back East, to find out why, month after month, another child never came to them. And then, after enough years had passed, begging him to leave her alone.

And eventually, he had. Anything to escape her sighs, her accusing looks, her mouth pinched with disappointment. Nothing short of a good horn of whiskey had fortified him enough to risk trying to make love to her again. Nights of reaching for Ellen, only to feel her shrink away, turn her face to the wall.

"She was my wife," he said, pacing again. "I promised to take care of her." He stopped and glanced at Amy. "I didn't."

"It's not your fault she wasn't suited for this life. She must have known before you were married that your life was here, in the Territory."

"She told me she was unhappy. I . . . thought it would pass. I promised to move as far as Tucson, once I'd made something of the farm. To me, it was over with then."

He raked his hand through his hair, only half-feeling the jaggedly shorn strands run through his fingers. "But not to Ellen. Not long after, she stopped waiting. She . . . swallowed a vial of laudanum she got from a drummer passing through, and by the next morning she was gone."

Ben had run through the fields to fetch him, his little legs pumping as fast as they were able. His eyes had been so scared in that round, babyish face.

"Mama's sleeping! She won't wake up today," he'd cried, trying to drag Mason home again. Looking half-sure he was in trouble for bothering his papa at work in the fields, but too afraid for his mama not to try, Ben had been the only one with Ellen at the end.

Mason pushed the heel of his palm against his closed eyelids, hiding the damned shameful tears that burned at the memory.

"I should've seen the laudanum. Should've listened to her more. Moved to the city sooner. Dammit, I could have done something to help her." His voice broke, wavered. "She trusted me."

From behind, Amy's arms came around his waist. She leaned against him, holding him tightly. He didn't know when she'd moved to comfort him. More, Mason couldn't imagine why.

Roughly, he wrenched her arms from around him and stepped out of reach. Keeping his back to her, he took a deep, shuddering breath.

"I drank my way through the morning Ellen died, and I didn't quit all through her funeral. At her wake, the whole house smelled like whiskey. Ben wouldn't even come near me."

He remembered his son's wrinkled nose, his red, tear-blotched face turning away from him, and he ached at the loss.

"Mason—" Amy whispered, but this time she didn't come near. This time she held herself rigidly apart from him. The span of earthen floor and rag rug might as well have been a valley a thousand miles wide. And Mason knew, at last, that he'd driven her away, too.

"God help me, but by then I don't even know if I loved her anymore," he said, his fists clenching uncontrollably at his sides. "I didn't want her to die, but I swear I don't know if I mourned her true at the end, and at least she deserved that." A sob tore from his throat, and fresh grief shuddered to life within him, too much to be contained.

"Mason, dear God . . ." Amy grabbed him, hurled herself at his chest, and the hot wetness of her tears burned his skin. "You can't go on like this," she cried. "Please, please—"

"No—" He tried to push her away, tried to hold her apart from him. But somehow his arms wouldn't obey his mind, and his heart stayed there with Amy. Convulsively, Mason's hands buried in her hair, holding her closer instead.

"Don't you see?" Amy cried, the words muffled and tear-choked. "Ellen didn't trust you too much." She raised her face to his, her eyes begging him to listen. "She believed in you too little."

"No!" It was an anguished cry, a denial of something Mason couldn't believe. Beneath his hands Amy moved closer and closer, and everything in him knew he should push her away.

"You gave her so much," she said, squeezing his shoulders as she tried to make him hear her. "A home, a child to love. . . . your love. How could you have known she'd leave all that behind?"

Her hands roved higher, stroking his jaw, his cheek. Mason closed his eyes against her touch, tried to steel himself against believing her.

"You couldn't have known," she went on. "You couldn't."

He swallowed hard, dared to open his eyes and meet her gaze. It shimmered with tears, wavered and leapt—or did his own tears only make it seem that way? His weakness shamed him. The last thing he wanted was her pity.

"I should have known," he said, clenching his jaw as he stared past her. "All the signs were there, after—"

"After!" Amy cried, her fingers gouging into his shoulders. "Afterward you knew, but who could have known before?"

"The laudanum—"

"Every household keeps it on hand. I did, back home."

Through her tears, she smiled faintly at him. "Forgive yourself, Mason. For your own sake. For your son's. This is tearing you apart, and I—"

"It cost me my son." His eyes burned. Mason swallowed hard, but the ache in his throat wouldn't quit. If he never did anything else, he'd get Ben back. This time, he'd keep him safe. Keep him loved.

"You'll find him," Amy said.

Her arms hugged his neck, and she touched her forehead to his. He wanted to close his eyes again, to hide his damned weak tears. Something in the way she looked at him wouldn't let him.

"You found me, didn't you?" she asked. "If not for you, who knows what would've happened to me after the stagecoach drove away?" She smiled, softly. "You saved me, Mason. Over and over again. I know you can save Ben, too."

"But Ellen—"

"It wasn't your fault," Amy said, stroking his hair back from his temples.

Her touch felt warm. Good.

"How anyone could think so is more than I can understand. You weren't even home when it happened."

She straightened, smoothed her hands down his chest. Her

fingertips whispered over the wiry, dark hairs there, then fluttered across his rib cage to wrap around his waist.

"Poor little Ben," she murmured, frowning as she laid her cheek against his chest. "I was so young when I lost my mother, I only barely remember her. But this— oh, Mason, it must've been so sad for him . . ."

Her words whispered away, lost in the darkness cast around them by the barely lit lantern. She hugged him tighter, fiercely, as if she could push her belief in him straight through his chest and force him to listen. More than anything she'd said, Amy's willingness to hold him close spoke truly. Mason's breath eased, and the tightness in his chest slowly lessened. Her trust in him was like a balm for his soul, no matter how he tried to resist it.

She wavered against him and blinked. Too weary, he supposed, to stand any longer. Still, her arms around his middle didn't loosen.

"Amy," he murmured, steadying her, "you've been too long on the road and too long without sleep for all this."

"I want to help you."

She scooted closer. Her underclothes brushed his pants legs, and the frilly lace edge of her borrowed white underdrawers reminded Mason of exactly how little she had on.

"I want to help you find Ben."

"Tomorrow."

Mason hefted her into his arms. No complaints about letting her walk came from her lips, no squeals of protest or panted demands amidst her struggles, that she put him down. Instead, Amy laid her head on his shoulder and smiled as he carried her to the bed.

"I hope he likes me," she said as he laid her onto the rumpled quilts.

"Ben?" An image of his boy's face, round and sun-browned beneath stubborn dark hair, rose in his mind. Damn, but missing him hurt.

"Yes." Amy slid across the sheets, then sat up and pulled the quilts hip-high, bunching the thick patchwork fabric in her lap. "Is he like you?"

Wiping tears from his eyes for the last time, Mason smiled and willed himself to give her something easy to sleep on. His troubles with Ellen and Ben and the Sharpe brothers were just that—his. Not hers. Once he'd gotten Ben and headed for the Mexican border as he'd planned, Amy's life would go on without them.

"Except for the haircut," he said, rubbing the rough-shorn hairs sticking up from his scalp.

She smiled, sniffling. "You should've let me finish."

Finish . . . finish tempting him, finish testing every bit of damned resolve he had in his body. At the memory of their closeness on the rock at sunset, Mason's mood sobered. The way he wanted this woman was a danger to them both.

"No." He turned, fists clenched, making ready to leave her for the night. Maybe tomorrow he'd ask Manuel to take her to Tucson himself. Without an outlaw by her side, Miss Twirly Curls would probably be safer, anyway.

"Mason—"

"I asked Manuel to return the wagon we took from Maricopa Wells," he said. "And explain to the station master that I forced you to come with me. The gun and the way I dragged you out of there ought to be proof enough of that."

He winced, remembering the bruises he'd left on her throat, then made himself go on. "The only reason they locked you up in the first place was because you were with me. Manuel's already left, hours ago. He'll set it straight and you'll have your life back again."

Amy rose on her knees, and the quilts fell away. "You're not leaving now, are you? After all we've said, I—"

"All the more reason to leave."

Mason squinted toward her, wishing he could remember her

this way. Just a pretty woman who wanted his company for the night. Hell, if he was better at pretending, in that moment he could've convinced himself they might really be together. Convinced himself he could love someone again—be loved in return.

Damned fool dreams. Pretty words and hoping, that's what love had turned out to be. Bitter in the end.

Confessing it all left him raw and exposed. Surely something begun like this would have to end bad. Frowning, Mason scooped up his shirt from the chair and slid it over his shoulders.

"It won't take long to get to Tucson tomorrow," he said. "I asked Juana to wire ahead, find out if that damned stagecoach took your bags of books all the way to the Wells Fargo station in the city. She ought to know by morning."

Amy blinked at him. "I guess you've got this all planned," she whispered. She stared down at the quilt, her fingers plucking at the edges of a dark calico square. "How to get rid of me, I mean."

Her voice held an edge that spoke of pain, but her bearing was one hundred percent proud lady. Whatever pain she felt, Amelia O'Malley was too proud to show it to the man who'd caused it. Even half-sunken into the soft feather mattress and blankets, she somehow managed to keep her spine straight and her chin lifted.

Hell. Why did she always turn gritty on him just when he least expected it?

Rubbing his sandpapery jaw, Mason stepped closer. "Amy—"

"It's all right." She raised her overbright gaze to his and squared her jaw. "I have work to do, anyway. Books to be delivered. I almost forgot, what with everything that's been happening. But my father and brothers are counting on me."

Counting on her to get back to the States and work her fingers to the bone caring for them, Mason thought, taking a step closer to the bed. If all she'd told him about her family was true, he doubted they'd rely on her to conduct business. But it was too late to argue, and in a few days her book orders wouldn't matter to him anyway. More, he didn't want to hurt her by pointing out any of that.

"The future of J. G. O'Malley and Sons rests on my shoulders," Amy was saying. She lifted them higher, as though to resume her duty, and her face took on a determined cast. "It's high time I paid attention to a matter I can do something about," she added, giving him a meaningful glance.

Her chin wobbled crazily for an instant; then her lower lip trembled. She bit down on it, trying to hide its unsteadiness. "Instead of a stubborn, set-in-his-ways man who wouldn't know how to accept help if it sat on his head like a two-ton ostrich and refused to b-budge."

She flopped onto the mattress, searched rapidly for the corner of the quilt, and then yanked it over her head. Beneath it, Mason saw her turn onto her side. The inviting curve of her backside and hip rounded the quilt into the most alluring gown he'd ever seen.

"Good night," she muttered from beneath the heavy covers.

He sighed, biting back a smile. This woman exasperated him, pestered him—demanded things Mason had no intention of ever handing over. Like trust. Like agreeing to let her "help" him in whatever harebrained, naive manner she had in mind.

Yet still she drew him.

He stepped closer. "What you're saying, then," he drawled, keeping his eyes on the bumpy shape in the middle of the bed, "is that help is really a two-ton ostrich?"

She didn't move. The quilt rose and lowered slightly with her breathing, but that was the only sound. Mason stepped closer, and his heart lightened with every inch he came nearer to her.

"No wonder I never recognized it."

He shucked his boots, dropping them onto the rag rug that covered the clean-swept, packed earth floor. He'd told her everything about his past, Mason realized as he paused beside the bed. Everything. And still she hadn't turned away from him.

Forgive yourself, Mason. For your own sake. For your son's.

Her words had made her forgiveness understood.

Hope niggled at him, pestered him. He hadn't felt so blamed confused since the night Ben was born—half of him despairing it would be the end of his wife, the other half overjoyed at the arrival of his child.

Mason bent his knee onto the mattress and lifted a corner of the quilt covering her. "You don't look like a two-ton ostrich to me," he told Amy as he peered beneath at her shadowy figure, "but you sure as hell refuse to budge. Move over."

Eighteen

Amelia, half-suffocated beneath the heavy quilts, listened in amazement. When she could remain silent no longer, she folded them back at the top and stuck her head out. Cooler air rushed at her, tasting unbelievably fresh.

"Are you actually making a joke?" she demanded of Mason, staring at him suspiciously.

His weight made the mattress yawn to her left like a boat sinking underwater. She rolled over to get a better look at him and just kept right on rolling until his knee stopped her descent. It pressed against her hip, pinning her in place with nowhere to look except up at Mason.

So she did. Beginning at his bent knee, Amelia's gaze traveled the length of his trouser-clad thigh, skimmed over the wrinkled creases leading to his pants buttons, and wound up at the place where his chest hair tapered and disappeared beneath those buttons. Feeling her cheeks heat, she boldly followed that brown sprinkling of hair upward to where it swirled across the broad, flat muscles of his chest, just barely visible between the opened ends of his shirt.

He was a beautifully made man. Whatever work he did all day on his farm near the Gila River certainly had benefited him, Amelia thought, letting her gaze wander across his shoulders and then down the lengths of his arms. She remembered the cherished feeling of being held in those arms, and knew that however piqued he might make her, Mason was the man she truly loved. No one had ever made her feel more special, more desired.

"Yes," he said, and even though she wasn't looking at his face, Amelia heard the smile in his voice.

Yes what? she thought, trying desperately to remember the course of their conversation. No one had ever made her feel more scatterbrained, either.

"But a two-ton ostrich begs for a joke the same way your lips beg for a kiss," he added, propping his hand just to the left of her head atop the lofty goose-down pillow. "I couldn't resist."

He meant her remark about how he didn't ever want help. Feeling justified in her comment after having practically ambushed him with kisses just to get him to talk to her, Amelia said nothing. Undaunted, he only nudged her sideways a bit with his knee and settled farther onto the bed.

The motion brought him closer, close enough that his chest almost brushed hers. Suddenly, the quilt between them felt like an absolute necessity. Amelia clutched the top edge of it, feeling the smooth-stitched fabric soothe her fingertips. If only it soothed her breathing as well. Her breath came subtly faster the nearer Mason came, and there wasn't the least thing she could do about it.

"Amy," he said, brushing his free hand across the tops of her knuckles along the quilt edge, "I need your help."

Back and forth, back and forth, his palm gently brushed over her knuckles. The rhythmic motion stole her attention, made answering him twice as difficult.

"Wh-why should you want my help now? You've tol-told me enough times that I can't help you with anything," she finally managed to say, and it was hard, so hard, to keep the hurt out of her voice.

It was true enough. She'd offered to help him at every turn, to comfort him at least. Only a little while ago, he'd refused her at the very moment he'd needed her most.

His fingers lifted to her cheek, followed its curve warmly upward to the hollow of her temple. The care in his touch made her heart lurch, then beat faster.

"This is something only you can help me with," Mason said. With no warning at all, he raised his knee, braced his hand on the mattress beside her, and an instant later he was straddling her.

"Mason!" Shocked and surely red-faced, Amelia slapped her hands onto the mattress and tried to push herself back and away from him. She only succeeded in raising her torso partway—the rest of her still trapped beneath Mason's strong, solid thighs.

Although it didn't hurt, she was well and truly pinned beneath him, and his body sent warmth searing straight through the quilt as easily as if it were nothing at all. She balanced herself on her elbows and stared up at him.

As though she'd never spoken, he went on: "Seems to me we were in just about this same position a little while ago." His gaze darted to each of her elbows, then higher. "Except I'm pretty sure your hands weren't plastered down there before."

He frowned, as though he were trying to remember and couldn't. Amelia recalled their earlier, intimate position well enough that her heart started beating faster at the memory alone. Did she dare risk herself again, though? Mason Kincaid was a hard man to know and an even harder man to help. Maybe there really was nothing she could do for him.

"I do recall you saying something about comfort," he murmured.

His hands touched her bare shoulders, smoothed lower to stroke her upper arms in a wordless urging that she begin again what had started between them before. His work-roughened palms rasped faintly over her skin, reminding her of all that was different between them . . . of all that might still be.

"Please," Mason whispered hoarsely, and his eyes echoed his plea in their soft shadowed brown depths.

He wanted her still, Amelia realized. But the decision to take things further between them was hers to make.

She could no more refuse him than she could leave him alone in his pain. The past had been cruel to Mason, had taken away the people he cared about and the life he'd known before. It was more than a good man should be made to suffer. Especially alone.

Especially when he was the man she loved.

Amelia raised her arms and pushed down the quilt separating them, smiling as she opened herself to him. "Yes," she whispered, closing her eyes as she drew him closer. "Yes."

His lips touched hers, and it was like a homecoming. Mason kissed her, and her whole body trembled at their union. Deftly, he opened her mouth to him, teasing, touching, slipping his tongue inside to meld with hers. Joyously, she accepted his kiss and gave all she could in return, arching to meet him, pulling him closer.

Inexplicable tears prickled beneath Amelia's closed eyelids, joining with a rush of new sensation as Mason kissed her anew. Slowly, softly, his lips touched hers and then retreated, slid luxuriously from one corner of her mouth to the next, only to leave her crying out for more when next he kissed her jaw and neck instead.

This was what loving meant. This caring, so new to her, and this joining, so right between them. Tongue-sweet and thrilling, his kisses went on and on, now returning to her mouth, now gently nipping the side of her neck. Amelia clutched his head in her hands, trying to guide him where she needed him, and still he tortured her with slow kisses she yearned for but could never predict.

Rising slightly, Mason pushed the quilt away completely, then straddled her again. Before she could react to their renewed closeness, he swept her hair from her forehead, gazing at her, and any thoughts of protest she might have entertained flew straight out of her head as though coaxed from it by his skillful, loving fingers.

"Thank you," he whispered, and his smile was the most endearing she'd ever beheld.

"Thank you for what?"

"For knowing when not to listen to me."

His lips curved into hers, still smiling as he kissed her, and she wanted to smile, too, both at his jest and at the new lightness in his bearing. Mason's shoulders moved against the dark with an ease she'd never sensed in him, as though a great weight had been magically lifted away. Had she truly helped him, after all?

"Thank God for stubborn women," he added, pressing kisses to her temple, her cheek . . . her mouth. Distracting her.

She cupped her palms around his shoulders and held him slightly away. "Stubborn? Stubborn women?"

"Mmmm." He swirled his tongue in a gentle arc along her lower lip, then suckled it. His eyes closed, and so did Amelia's—for a moment.

She'd never have guessed it would be so hard to kiss and have a conversation at the same time. His touch made her wits fairly scatter.

"Have you known so many stubborn women, then?"

"None so stubborn as you," Mason replied, his gaze still on her lips. "And none I wanted like this. God, I need you, Amy."

His hands slid warmly to her shoulders. His fingers slipped beneath her chemise strap, stroked the skin it hid, then hooked it away from her shoulder. He pressed his lips into the curve of her neck, setting her skin atingle.

"Mmmm . . . so beautiful."

"Mason . . ."

"Shhh."

Frowning slightly, he traced a reverent path from her shoulder to her upper arm, then lifted her chemise strap and slid it in place again. Disappointment made Amelia twist beneath him, silently urging him to go on touching her.

His hands cupped her jaw, and his fingers delved into her hair. "I'll give you everything you need," he promised with a kiss. "Everything. Everything . . ."

The rest of his words were lost in the heat and weight of his long, hard body pressed lovingly on hers, in the feel of his hands scooping between Amelia and the mattress to flatten against her shoulder blades and hold her closer. His taut muscles pressed against the sides of her bosom, evidence of the masculine strength Mason kept so firmly in check, but his arms supported her effortlessly.

Amelia writhed against him, loving the feel of their bodies together, loving the differences between them. She cupped the stubble-roughened stretch of his jaw as he kissed her, inhaled the musky, male scent of his skin, and knew that lying with him would forever transform her. How could she not love him more, after sharing so much?

Moaning, Mason lifted her higher against the pillows, then paused to spread her hair across their cotton softness. His fingers combed through her curly unbound strands, his knuckles trembling slightly as they brushed her cheeks. He raised his gaze to hers, and the tenderness she saw there whisked the breath from Amelia's lips.

"There'll be no rushing this," he warned, and though his voice sounded harsh with the effort his restraint cost him, his eyes were gentle. "Not when I've wanted you for so long."

"But we've only known each other for days," she whispered.

"It feels like forever."

His thumb stroked across her cheekbone, then lowered to her mouth. Softly, she felt it sweep the fullness of her bottom lip.

She kissed it, savoring the sound of his indrawn breath. Emboldened by the knowledge that her touch could affect him, too,

Amelia bit down gently, testing her teeth against the pad of his thumb. He moaned and she captured his hand in hers.

"Love me," she whispered, tugging his hand toward her shoulder. "Show me how to love you."

Anticipation swirled in her belly, tightening into an aching need to feel his hands stroking her again. His eyes darkened and Mason complied, slipping her chemise strap aside. The gentle rasp of its lace edge felt a hundred times more intense than usual against her skin, his caressing fingertips a thousand times more arousing.

Amelia closed her eyes as his fingers fluttered across her shoulder, dipping low enough to brush her collarbone. His shirtsleeve, then the warm inside of his wrist, touched the upper swell of her breasts, awakening every inch of sensitive skin. Mindlessly, she leaned forward, seeking more.

"Ahhh, so soft . . ." he said, turning his hand to skim his knuckles along the lace-trimmed edge of her chemise.

She opened her eyes and just glimpsed his large, tawny-skinned hand as it glided over the paler, softer slope of her breasts. The erotic sight only made her breath come faster and her yearning increase as, with his other hand, Mason stroked his thumb past the wild pulse in her throat.

As though he'd commanded it, her heartbeat quickened.

Longing for his hands to move lower, Amelia bit her lip and tossed her head. "Please," she moaned, hardly recognizing the breathless, ragged voice she heard as her own.

Mason recognized it. Answered it. With a fierce, possessive smile he tightened his hand on her neck and drew her to him. His lips descended on hers with a bruising force she welcomed.

Kissing, licking, biting, he mastered her mouth and set her senses burning with need. Beneath her questing hands his big body shuddered, then his hips thrust into the cradle of her thighs. Heat emanated from him, searing through the thin fabric of her chemise and pantalets, and the rigid proof of his desire made Amelia gasp.

At the sound, Mason stilled. Breathing hard, he shifted atop her so they barely touched, his hair dark and pillow-tossed, his eyes closed. Alongside his thighs, his fists clenched. Confused, she touched his chest, palmed his soft swirls of hair, whispered his name.

He threw his head back, exposing the lean line of his throat. He swallowed hard. "Don't be afraid," he murmured, spreading his fingers apart to relax his fists. "I need . . ."

". . . you. This."

His voice ground away beneath a moan. The bed springs creaked as Mason settled back on his heels, then finally opened his eyes.

They were filled with love.

Filled with love and longing—a longing belied when he slid her chemise strap up again. Amelia bit her lip, wanting to scream as Mason's fingers outlined the thin strap, smoothing heat into her shoulder.

Slowly, he lowered it. "It's hard to wait for you, Amy," he said, kissing the heated line he'd drawn.

"But I want this to last." He raised it again. Tremors raced across her shoulders and tingled down her arms, making her seize the ends of his opened shirt for support. He was going to drive her crazy, crazy with wondering and needing and the dizziness that swamped her every time he caressed her.

"Easy," he murmured, squeezing her arms, and the leisurely movements of his big hands felt as frustrating as they did soothing. He slid his hands upward to her shoulders, this time slipping away both chemise straps at once.

Her chemise drooped, letting cooler air wash over the tops of her breasts. Automatically, Amelia held it up with one hand. The motion pushed her bosom higher, and Mason's hungry gaze went straight there, lingering on the bare skin he'd revealed. He lowered his head and reached for her, and she held her breath, already feeling the glide of his fingertips against her skin, the pressure of his hands on her shoulders.

Instead, he tipped her head back and kissed her. His hands tangled in her hair as the hungry demands of his mouth increased and his tongue slipped inside to stroke hers.

This was no tender, easy kiss, yet an answering need swelled within her, amazing in its ferocity. Amelia dug her fingers into the knotted strength of his shoulders and held on, opening her mouth wide to receive his kiss, pressing hard against him. As if of their own accord, her hands spread apart his shirt. Eagerly, she tugged it over Mason's shoulders.

The kiss ended and she sank into the piled-up pillows, her lips swollen and wonderfully tingling. His shirt dropped from her fingers. Looking up, she saw that the low-lit lamp glowed just enough to reveal Mason's broad shoulders, his lean-muscled middle . . . his wicked smile.

"Oh!" Amelia cried, embarrassed at being caught watching him, yet too curious to stop. She lay her palm flat against his chest, where his heart beat wildly as her own, and felt an answering smile quirk her own lips.

She licked them, trying to regain a shade of composure, and failed. "You're . . . you're beautiful," she whispered. "So strong and beautiful and—"

"So are you."

Mason stared, his intensity confusing her until she felt his warm hands cup her breasts and realized her chemise had drifted to her waist while they kissed. Her nipples rose against his palms and she hardly dared breathe, lest he stop touching her. Nothing had ever felt so wonderful. His hands traced her, shaped her, gently squeezed, and the heated glide of his skin on hers drove all else from her mind.

He moaned and Amelia arched higher, baring herself to him. Nothing mattered more than the pleasure of his touch, the feel of his hard, gentle body against hers. His thigh settled between her legs, sending warmth clean through his heavy twill pants and her pantalets to her skin beneath. Mindlessly she tightened her thighs around the granite length of his thigh, tilting her hips higher to ease the pressure building within.

Mason cupped her cheek, stroked the curve of her ear, kissed her as though he were a drowning man and she the air he needed to breathe. Again and again his lips met hers, his mouth devouring, his hands caressing her face, her neck, stroking back her tousled hair. More and more emboldened, Amelia swept her hands across his back, traced his spine . . . returned his kiss with a passion she'd never known herself capable of.

Love, love whirled between them, sweetening every touch. When he cradled her breasts in his hand, he held more than her body—he held her heart. And even without flowery words of love, his care for her sounded in every sigh, every moan—made itself known with every shared look. There could never be enough of such union between them, and the knowledge soared through her soul, transforming her . . . imparting the courage to give back all the pleasure she received.

Amelia caressed his shoulders, buried her fingers in the softness of his hair until it tickled beneath her nails and its soapy washed scent filled her nose. She urged his head closer and Mason came eagerly, pressing her breasts beneath his chest as he lowered his mouth to her neck and suckled. His tender nip just beneath her ear sent fresh shudders through her.

"You taste like spring," he murmured against her earlobe.

His teeth nibbled at its sensitive flesh, sending a jolt of pleasure from her head to her belly and lower. She held him tighter, gasping. Her response was rewarded with the soft swirl of his tongue tracing the outer edge of her ear, then by the return of his hands to her breasts.

"Yes," Amelia cried, twisting to push herself more fully into his hands. Mason watched her, his eyes glittering with barely leashed need. He plucked his fingers gently from the curved slope of her breasts to their taut peaks, ending each stroke with a delicacy that made her quiver.

His loving went on, and she nearly wept his name, consumed with the wanting of something she couldn't describe, let alone ask for. Filled with frustration, she ran her hands from his chest downward, holding, stroking until she reached his belly and then moving lower to grip his steely thighs.

A moan rumbled from her throat, shocking her, but Amelia was beyond caring. The next sensuous stroke of his hands on her breasts set her trembling helplessly. Her fingers kneaded his thighs and the squeezing relieved the pressure, but not enough. Never enough.

Yet somehow, somehow, Mason understood. Briefly, all too briefly, his hands cradled her breasts completely, and his mouth found hers in a searing kiss. Sucking slowly, nibbling, he gentled their contact until nothing remained between them but leisurely kisses and, to Amelia's profound dismay, her chemise as he covered her with it again.

She felt like ripping the garment aside. She managed nothing more than a sigh as Mason's hands came to rest on her knees, then slid upward, stealing her attention afresh. Her thighs tensed and drew slightly together, automatically shielding her femininity from him. He stilled . . . but his hands remained where they were.

"Amy?" Mason leaned down, kissed her. His breathing sounded at least as labored as her own. "Only if you want this."

He closed his eyes briefly, then opened them. In the lantern's half-light he looked a stranger suddenly—one intent and drawn tightly with a need she instinctively recognized.

"But tell me now," he said, wrapping his hands fully around her knees as though prepared to wrench her legs apart, to take her then and there. *"Tell me."*

Everything womanly inside her urged Amelia to go forward.

Biting her lip, willing herself to trust enough to open to the man she loved, she arched her neck into the coolness of the pillows.

"Yes."

Her smile felt tremulous. His was fierce, male, triumphant. Still Mason's hands remained on her knees, unmoving as slowly, shyly, she relaxed against the mattress. She wanted this, wanted to know him fully. Wanted so much to experience every part of love.

Before long, she wanted nothing more than for his hands to go on caressing her. She mimicked his motions, hesitantly squeezing his thighs as he straddled her . . . and still he waited. When at last his hands moved, they stroked languidly toward the apex of her thighs and back again, at once exciting and frustrating her anew. Digging her thumbs into his pants legs, Amelia ground her teeth.

Mason saw, and smiled. "You touch me," he murmured, inching his fingers higher, "and I burn."

His expression turned serious, yearning . . . and inexplicably determined. Beneath his palms, even her kneecaps tickled, teased into a sensitivity she'd never imagined. Between her legs, a slow ache began, merging into her heartbeat and quickening with every moment he delayed.

His thumbs brushed the insides of her knees. "You're beautiful," he said, his eyes following the path she hoped his hands would make next, "so beautiful, and *mine.*"

His hands tightened, then began moving. His breath broke, then quickened. "I touch you—and I'm alive again."

Helplessly, Amelia nodded, transfixed by the rugged sweep of his voice and the meltingly slow crawl of his fingers on her thighs. Higher, higher, they traveled, and beneath them she felt her bones turn to warm honey, useless to support her.

"Yours, yours—please," she begged. Through half-closed

eyes she glimpsed his loving smile, and knew he'd meant every word of his warning to her.

There'll be no rushing this.

The throbbing deepened between her legs, became a demand that consumed her. Quivering, pinned beneath his hands and the intensity of his gaze, she waited for his stroke to ease the ache inside her. Mason's fingertips branded through her thin cotton pantalets, slid higher . . . brushed past her woman's mound to capture her hips and squeeze them in his powerful hands.

Her whole body responded to his possessive grasp. Unthinking, she thrust upward and the pressure within increased, spiraling from the juncture of her thighs to her hips and further. She gasped, loving him, loving his hands that kept her safe, grounded her, led her upward again with the hard length of his thigh for support. Tremors shook her, leaving her breathless.

"Easy," Mason whispered, ducking his head to kiss her, "easy, it's all right."

His hands slid over her ribs, covered her breasts, and even through her chemise she felt her nipples tighten to meet his palms. "Ahhh, you feel so good, so good . . ."

He rubbed slow, sensuous circles over her breasts, and the gentle abrasion of her chemise against her overheated skin heightened every motion. Amelia writhed closer, let her hands rove from his thighs upward. His stomach contracted when she touched him there, and each feathery stroke of her fingertips made him suck in his breath.

She had that effect on Mason . . . maybe even made him feel as good as he did her. The thought burst forth in a surge of wholly feminine pride, then vanished beneath the increasing urgency his hands on her breasts created. She wanted her chemise gone, wanted to feel his chest bare on hers . . . *wanted.*

With a growl of need he wrenched her chemise to her waist, baring her completely, and she . . . wanted. He cupped her breasts, lowered his head, and drew one taut peak into the soft, wet warmth of his mouth, and she wanted . . . wanted *this*. Wanted his mouth on her, wanted to bury her fingers in his hair and hold him to her so he'd never stop.

His tongue licked velvety against her nipple, then his mouth slid to her other breast, trailing warm, sweet breath and ripples of delicate sensation. He sucked, and Amelia half-flew from the mattress, lost in the tug of his lips, the drag of his tongue, the piercing need that arrowed from her breast to her heels and everywhere in between. She moaned, and his thumb stroked across her other nipple, drawing it to stiff attention.

More, more than she'd imagined and yet they still weren't close enough. She clutched Mason's head, gasping as he loved her, aroused even by the gentle rasp of his shadowed beard against her skin. Her breasts felt heavy, tingling . . . needing, and he gave willingly, eagerly . . . expertly. She'd have given anything to stay forever beneath his hands and mouth, and as his loving went on, she knew what it meant to surrender completely.

Trembling, Amelia savored his mouth on her breasts, his hands stroking long, curved pathways from her shoulders to her ankles and leaving no part of her untouched. Mason kissed her, holding her to him with one big hand splayed across the back of her head, holding her captive for the mastery of his lips, his tongue, his heated gaze. He saw her and loved her, and if she hadn't heard the words from him, she knew in her heart that he felt them.

He loved her.

She knew it and rejoiced in it, and the knowledge freed her to return his kiss, to respond fully . . . to show him how much she wanted him, too. Amelia clawed at her pantalets' drawstring. Her fingers tangled, clumsy without her full attention to their task. His next kiss turned them nerveless, and a moment later the plucking softness of his hands at her breasts curled her fingers into desperate fists.

Mason's hands covered hers, squeezed her fists, and a satisfied sound rumbled from his throat. "Let me," he murmured, drawing her clenched fists to rest alongside her hips.

He held them there, pressing her wrists into the timeworn quilts beneath them. His gaze roamed over her with an intensity that made her want to squirm, to cover herself . . . to stop the involuntary tightening of her nipples and the quickening of her breath.

"Beautiful," he whispered, releasing her wrists. His fingers trailed up her hip, across her belly toward the drawstring.

Now—now he'd pull the narrow fabric strip that hid her from him. Now he'd ease her pantalets away, let them join his shirt on the floor beside the bed, look at her nakedness with the hot appreciation the rest of her had already earned. Now he'd touch her where she needed his loving most. The spiral inside her wound tighter, throbbed more with each heartbeat. Anticipation made her bite her lips as his hand neared the drawstring.

Nineteen

Mason made his hand move slowly, easing toward Amy's waist. She felt small, warm, wonderfully curved beneath him. Sweat beaded on his forehead, wrung from him by the need to move faster, surer. The need to take her . . . now.

She panted and twisted below him, and he slid one hand to her hip to hold her steady, afraid he'd accidentally hurt her if she kept on so wild. Watching her, he grasped the drawstring on her underclothes and pulled. She came up off the bed along with it, shivering, arching toward him. Gently, he eased her back down . . . and cupped her woman's mound in his hand.

Sweet heat seared his palm; through her clothes he felt her delicate curls prickle his skin. His shaft throbbed in response, hurting him, stealing his breath and pulsing against his too-tight pants. Mason ground his teeth, fought for control. Damn, he'd been a fool to start this between them, when all he wanted was to make love to her hard and fast and forever.

His promise to Amy echoed in his ears, underlaid by her throaty whimpers and urgent, breathless pleas. She whispered his name and Mason bent his head to her breast.

"Mason, ohhh . . ."

She bucked beneath him, wild and trembling, and her heart pounded beneath his cheek. He sucked harder, set his teeth gently against her skin, nipped slow, faint circles over her breast, and all the while Amy's warmth pulsed around him, lured him.

God, he needed this. Needed her. So good . . .

"It's all right," he whispered to her, calming them both with the words. "Mmmmm, so sweet . . ."

His hand curved over her, covering her completely through her underclothes, his fingers sweeping lower into the heat between her thighs. Stroking upward again, Mason coaxed her legs wider. She opened herself to him, gave herself to him, and the enormity of her gift humbled him.

She trusted, loved, wanted him. No gift could have meant more.

Steeling himself to go slowly, he went on stroking her, urged forward by her hands on his arms, his back, his belly, compelled by the bite of her nails against his skin. Her lips touched his shoulder, then her teeth.

Amy's kisses, her delicate bites and shuddering sighs, inflamed him. He trailed his tongue from her nipple to the smooth roundness of her breast, moving lower, kissing toward the alluring curve of her belly. She quivered, clutched him harder. The moist musky scent of her feminine arousal rose from between her thighs, tantalizing him more than any perfume . . . tempting him as much as her softness did.

He had to feel her, love her . . . touch her.

Her legs and belly tensed as Mason moved to her waist and bunched her wadded-up chemise in his hands. Guiding Amy upward, he slid the garment past her hips, down her legs to the floor. She drifted back to the mattress, her lower lip caught between her teeth, her eyes wide and beautiful beneath the pillow-tangled mass of her hair. She reached for him, and her welcome made his heart pound faster.

Caressing her breast, her hip, he lowered himself until his chin nearly touched her stomach. She thrust her fingers into his hair and whimpered as he drew his cheek across her middle, then repeated the motion, coming ever closer to her pantalets' drawstring and the secrets her clothes hid from him. Catching the waistband in his teeth, Mason tugged hard, too savage with need to tease either of them much longer.

Slowly, too slowly, Amy's underclothes eased past the smooth curves and scented secrets of her hips and thighs. Moaning, he clawed with both hands at her waistband, dragged it lower, buried his face in the lush curls of her woman's mound. The slick, perfumed moistness there drove him wild, made him gasp and shake to possess her. Her curls tickled his jaw as he eased lower, impatiently pushing her pantalets past her knees, past her ankles to the floor.

"Ahhh," he murmured, caressing her luxuriant hips in both hands, holding her tight against him. His heart felt near bursting from his chest . . . his shaft ached and pulsed, heavy with need. "Ahhh, Amy, I can't . . . can't wait. Oh, God, I—"

Convulsively his fingers tightened. Gasping, he reared over her, slid the length of her body to capture her mouth with his. She met him eagerly, moaning low in her throat as their tongues met and mated with a ferocity he'd soon make their bodies match. Closer and closer he held her, his mind ablaze with the pleasure of feeling her next to him, of making her his, of the knowledge that she wanted him, too.

Amy arched, opening her legs wide to receive him. Her knees brushed his pants legs, rubbed against the fabric, and suddenly Mason needed the rest of his clothes to be gone. He grabbed at his pants buttons, clumsy with just one hand but needing the other to hold her. Panting, he undid the first button. The second. Amy kissed him, cried out for him, and Mason managed the remaining buttons in a fevered rush.

He tore himself from her body, rose from the bed wrenching open the waistband of his pants. She moaned, tossing her head against the pillows, watching him through half-closed eyes that glittered with desire.

"Mason, Mason . . ."

He wanted to swear, wanted to rip the clothes from his body

and feel her naked against him. His heavy arousal demanded more caution. Carefully, quickly, he shed his pants and drawers, leaving them to puddle beside the massive bedstead along with everything else they'd worn. He looked up at her . . . and the wonder in her expression rooted his feet to the rug.

"Oh, Mason . . ." Easing upward in bed, Amy reached her trembling hand toward him, her mouth a circle of surprise and shyness.

Swallowing hard, he closed his eyes, readying himself for the silken feel of her hand. He opened them just as her fingers sheathed him, making him throb and surge high against her palm. Need raked him, drawing shudders that swept from heels to head as he fought not to shove her down on the bed, not to take her then as he longed to do.

Tentatively, she stroked him, raising her other hand to fondle him with an innocent joy that melted into his heart even as it made him grind his teeth with torturous need. Finally Mason wrapped his hand around hers, slowing her maddening strokes and silencing her confused protest with a kiss, leaving them both breathless. Cradling her, he lowered himself to the bed, unable to stop touching her . . . touching her everywhere.

Quivering, Amy opened herself to him, wrapped her arms around his waist . . . sighed as he came to her. Nothing had ever felt so good, so right, as their bodies touching, skin on skin. Mason held her tighter, closing his eyes. Slowly his hand slid down the warmth of her side and hip, lower to the softness between her legs. Slowly he stroked her there, felt her tremble beneath him as his fingertips found every tender, private place that had been hidden to him before.

Leisurely he caressed her, urged on by her muted cries and the secret shuddering within her. He lay his head on her shoulder and cradled her with his other hand, keeping her close enough to feel every tremor that passed through her, every quickening of her heartbeat, every panted cry.

"Mmmm . . . you feel so good." Mason slowed his fingers' motions, savoring their glide over her slick, sensitive flesh. Amy clutched his arm, grabbed fistfuls of bunched-up quilt, arched higher against his hand, and every movement made need burn hotter inside him.

"Mason, ohhh . . ."

"It's all right," he murmured, biting back a moan as he gently slipped his finger within her softness, felt her heat convulse around him. "It's all right, Amy . . . Let it come."

Incoherent, velvety cries rose from her throat. Wildly, she bucked against him, nearly sending him over the edge as her hips thrust again and again . . . then stilled as her fulfillment peaked, leaving her breathless. Gasping, she sank onto the bed, pulling him down along with her, trembling anew with every contact their bodies made.

Mason lay his head on the pillow just over her shoulder and watched her, his arm across her chest holding her, feeling her breasts rise and fall as her breathing gradually slowed. Gently, he stroked her cheek, turned her face toward him.

"Beautiful," he whispered, kissing her damp, flushed cheek. Nothing in the world could have stopped the smile that rose to his lips. "So beautiful."

Smiling too, Amy opened her eyes. Sleepy satisfaction filled her gaze, turning her eyes a darker blue. Then, slowly, her eyes widened, her gaze reflecting a growing dismay as she realized all that had happened between them. Her hand clapped over her mouth, stifling a gasp.

"Oh, my goodness!" The blush of her cheeks spread lower, dappled her neck and bare bosom with mottled pink. Frowning slightly, she craned her neck back into the pillow to peer at him and stammered, "M-Mason, I—"

He quieted her, drew her hand away, kissing each long, slender finger in turn. Amy squirmed and tossed her head on the pillow beside him, her gaze traveling from the nubbly adobe wall to the oil lamp to the shadows on the ceiling—anyplace but at him.

She rolled all the way onto her back, her other arm flung over her closed eyelids to hide her expression. Propping himself on his elbow, still holding her hand, Mason looked down at her. As though she sensed his attention, her blush swept lower, drawing his gaze to her barely shimmying breasts and their pink tips.

Smiling his pleasure at the sight, anticipating the loving still to come, he moved over her, settled himself on his haunches between her thighs. Oblivious, Amy kept on talking, her voice quavering more than he liked to hear. Especially when it was his woman talking.

His woman.

"Oh, Mason, I'm sorry!" she cried, halfheartedly trying to twist her fingers from his grasp. "I don't know what came over me, but I—"

"Shhh." Threading his fingers with hers, Mason pressed their hands into the jumbled quilts and lowered his mouth to hers, easing them both into the pillows beneath. Sweetness filled his heart even as he felt her stir beneath him.

The moment the kiss ended, she drew a quick, and to his pleasure, a chest-expanding breath. "But you must think— Oh, I'm not sure how I can ever look at you again, after—"

"Quiet." Mason slid lower, cupped her breasts in both hands and felt her nipples bud beneath his palms. He groaned, settling himself firmly between her thighs. "We'll talk later."

"But—"

"Later." He kissed her again, moved aside her arm and kissed her closed eyelids, caressed the smooth roundness of her breasts and felt her shudder beneath his hands. Amy moaned, brought her hands to his shoulders, held him closer. Her stroking hands urged him, welcomed him. His breath held as he nestled himself between her thighs, felt her warmth and wetness caress him . . .

a tremor shook him as the head of his shaft nudged deeper, nearly joining with her.

He stroked himself intimately against her, almost overcome with the pleasure of touching her. Ahhh, but he had to wait, wait until she was ready . . . Frantically, Mason held her head in his hands and kissed her, his hips tilting to stroke again and again, arousing them both.

As the kiss ended she gasped, arching higher, trembling. He gritted his teeth, savage with the need to take her. "Amy . . . Ahhh . . ."

She clutched him, pulled him tighter, and her response drove the last of his control from him. Groaning, shaking with the effort to go slowly for her sake, he entered her inch by inch. Her body pulsed around him, sending pleasure coursing through him, and all of it was nothing compared with the pleasure of raising his head and seeing her eyes open to meet his gaze.

Love, and loving desire, flowed between them. Her face glowed with it, and her body spoke of it with every touch, every arch to meet him, every sensuous meeting of skin against skin. Mason gazed at her, stroked her cheek, and in that moment he was lost.

"Are you ready?" he whispered, and some part of him knew it was more than lovemaking he spoke of, even as he shuddered and slowly entered her a little further, even as he felt her tremble in response.

Her eyes widened briefly. "There's more?"

Ahhh, true Amelia. The thought glimmered through him, smiled into his heart, then vanished beneath a fresh, urgent desire to possess her.

"Yes," was all he could manage aloud, his mind and body urging him toward completion. *Love her, love her . . .*

She smiled, writhed beneath him, and at her whispered, *"Yes,"* Mason made their union complete. His first smooth thrust ended their isolation, joined them in heat and blind pleasure and the snug, perfect fitting of their bodies together. Pleasure shafted through him, increasing quickly as he searched Amy's face for signs he'd hurt her and found none. Instead she lay still for only a moment, wonder filling her eyes, then instinctively rose to meet him.

Wanting her, needing her, he slipped his hands to her bottom and squeezed. He cupped her, lifted her to him, thrusting again and again. Again. Their cries of pleasure mingled, Mason's hoarse with a need too long denied. Loving her was all he'd ever wanted, ever needed, and he abandoned himself to the sheer pleasure of it with each loving stroke.

Each thrust joined them more fully, sent him nearer and nearer to the edge of fulfillment . . . and, finally, beyond. He clutched her as each spasm took him, wrung his body of anything beyond his release, leaving only warmth and their joining behind.

Breathing hard, Mason cradled Amy to his chest. His heart pounded, his ears rung, and the cool night air against his damp skin raised goose bumps all along his backside . . . but he'd never felt better in his life. A wide grin rose to his lips, too powerful to be denied, as he buried his head in the crook of her neck and kissed her shoulder.

"Oh, Mason," she whispered, her hands roving over his back, his shoulders. "Oh . . . oh, my!"

She giggled, and he felt her legs and toes wriggle next to his along the length of the quilt beneath them.

"Not funny," he growled, nipping her neck.

"Oh, I'm sorry, but I—" She stroked him, craned her neck back to peer at his face again, and stretched like a cat beneath him. "I just never imagined a person could feel so good," she said, blushing again. "I just . . ."

She cupped his cheek in her hand and gave him a serious look. "Mason, I just love you so much."

Love. Loved him.

She'd said it before, but now—now it seared deeper within him, called forth a response that . . .

That Mason wasn't free to give her.

Hell. Closing his eyes, he lifted himself and rolled over to lie beside her. Yawning, Amy snuggled against his chest, bringing one worn edge of the quilt with her and tucking her head atop his shoulder with a trust he didn't deserve.

A trust he wanted all the more, just the same.

Uneasiness stole over him, moving as stealthily as the roving moonlight that snaked in between the shutter slats at the window. Beside him her breathing evened, fluttering across his chest as she eased into sleep.

Love.

That wasn't what he felt. Lust, hunger . . . but not love.

Not love, no matter how near it his heart felt.

With a muttered curse Mason rolled from the bed, sending the rope springs creaking. His toes curled into the rag rug as he crossed it, then padded across the smoothness of the cool earth floor to stand beside the lamp. He paused beside it, waiting for Amy's breathing to deepen again. Waiting until she wouldn't know he'd gone.

"Mason?" Her throaty whisper came toward him from the pile of blankets, then grew louder as she turned her head on the pillow. "What's wrong?"

Nothing. Everything.

"I just need to turn out the lamp."

"Hurry and come back to bed," she mumbled, and he heard the smiling invitation in her voice. "It's cold without you."

Mason turned the key, casting the room into darkness except for the shadow of the shutters on the far wall. Casting his heart into the light one last time as he lifted the blankets and crawled into the warmth beside Amy. She nestled against him, all sweet-smelling, smooth woman, and it was so good to find her waiting for him.

Amy pressed her cheek against his heart and drifted asleep, and just those simple acts awakened all the yearning he'd hidden for so long. What would it be like to find such warmth waiting for him, night after night? What would it be like to come inside her, to pleasure her, night after night? To love her?

His chest squeezed, hurting him. Aching, Mason reached over her shoulder and pressed his palm hard against the adobe until its hard-textured bite cleared his head. Then he turned onto his side, faced away from Amy and the life that could never be his.

And hoped it would make it that much easier to turn away from her tomorrow, when he took Ben across the border and left her forever.

Twenty

The crash of wood on adobe jerked Amelia awake. Heart pounding, she lurched upright in bed, only to find herself alone and squinting against the bright shafts of early morning sunlight streaming in between the shutter slats.

A man loomed in the doorway. Manuel. He came inside, frowning, boot heels thunking solidly on the floor with every stride. He glanced first toward the window, then toward the bed.

Stifling a shriek, Amelia raised the quilts higher. Dimly, she registered Manuel's frown and the opened door in his wake, now creaking slowly away from the adobe wall it had crashed into. Sunlight divided him into stripes of brightness and shade, and fresh air swept in along with him, telling her he'd been outside until only moments earlier.

Where was Mason? She scooted nearer to the wall that bordered the bed, horribly conscious of her nakedness beneath the blankets—and of being alone with a man she barely knew.

"Stay there, Amy."

Mason's voice sent relief sweeping through her. Amelia looked for him and found him beside the oil lamp, kicking his way into his wrinkled trousers. Straightening, he buttoned them and gave her a look that warned her to obey.

She did, realizing that now that Manuel had discovered them together, all of Mason's friends would know what had happened between them last night. They'd likely think poorly of her because of it, too. With reason. Whatever had possessed her, to give herself so wantonly to a man she'd known mere days? Even the love between them didn't excuse such behavior. A shamed blush heated Amelia's face, climbing nearly to the roots of her hair.

Mason saw, and frowned. "Let's take this outside," he said, shouldering past Manuel without looking at him.

Juana's brother raised his hand to hold him there—a hand that Mason shrugged off as he wheeled around again. Ire sparked between both men, its expression in Manuel underlaid by worry. Something was wrong.

Manuel's sun-browned, dirt-smudged face looked solemn beneath his thick black hair and dark brows. His *sombrero* hung by its rawhide ties down his back. Its disarray, along with his sweat-dampened clothes, served as chilling evidence of his haste in reaching them.

"You are being followed, *compadre*," he said to Mason. "A posse was stopped, watering their horses at Maricopa Wells when I returned the wagon."

He glanced at Amelia. "I'm sorry, *señorita*. They could be here any minute."

Mason swore and reached toward the chair beside the lamp. Picking up his shirt, he slid it over both shoulders, not bothering to button it before hefting his gun belt, too. He lowered his head to check the ammunition, rapidly scanning each shell pocket.

"The station master must have pointed me out to them, after I told him about the wagon. *Entremetido!*" Manuel raked his hand through his hair, making it stand on end. "I think I threw them off the trail, *amigo*, but they will be behind me soon."

Mason nodded, then raised his gun belt to his hips and fastened it.

A posse, after Mason? The notion of a sheriff in pursuit had been bad enough. She'd known he was an outlaw, but since their escape from Maricopa Wells, that fact had become easier and easier to deny.

Now here it was again, embodied in a posse that would capture, hurt, kill him if they could. Amelia shrank into the pillows, unable to do more than watch him until Juana stuck her head through the doorway.

"What's happened?" she asked, wiping her hands on her long apron as she entered the room. She frowned toward Manuel, taking in his rumpled clothes and sweat-shiny face, and then turned her worried gaze upward at Mason. Whatever she saw in his face made her frown deepen.

From the corner of her eye she glimpsed Amelia, still in the bed. After a moment's startled pause, Juana propped both hands on her slender hips.

"Whatever this is," she said quietly, raking both men with a stern gaze, "it had better be important for you to have awakened Amelia and invaded her room like this."

Manuel stared back at her. "But she—"

"She is a *lady* who doesn't need a couple of knucks like you arguing nonsense in her room," Juana insisted firmly.

She was defending her, Amelia realized, making sure no harm would come to her reputation because of what Manuel had seen. The warning to him was plain in her voice, and the sound of it left Amelia humbled with gratitude.

"Now either clear out," Juana went on, "or tell me what's happened."

"The sheriff's posse's caught up with me," Mason gritted out.

He nodded toward Manuel. "How far?"

"Five, six miles, maybe more." Manuel ducked his head, checked his ammunition, too, then looked up again. "I outran them when I hit the rises near the Gila."

"Good." Mason turned, reached for his flat-brimmed black hat, and jammed it on his head.

Leaving. He was leaving because of the posse.

"I'll have one of the hands saddle a horse for you," Juana offered quietly, turning to leave. "Keep it as long as you need."

Manuel stopped her. "I already did. I'm going with him."

He held his sister's gaze, his head held high. His unwavering stance beside Mason said much, bespoke a long-standing friendship between them. Amelia realized she'd been correct last night. Everyone at Picacho station trusted Mason, trusted him enough even to take his side against the law.

Juana watched them, her arms crossed over her chest. After a minute, she sighed. "I don't see where you have much choice," she agreed. "Be careful, both of you. I won't have my good horses returned with bullet holes in them—or my friends, either."

Mason nodded his thanks to her. He paused, clapped his hand on Manuel's shoulder, then turned and headed toward the door.

"Mason, wait!" Amelia cried, stuck beneath the quilts where she couldn't go to him.

He looked back at her, but his gaze went through her toward something else, something in his thoughts alone. Then Mason turned his attention toward Manuel instead, and her heart sank as even that small contact ended. Every part of him was focused on the problem at hand. The posse.

"Which direction?"

"Del norte."

A muscle in Mason's jaw ticked. All traces of sleep had vanished from his expression, leaving nothing behind except a dark, dangerous-looking man. An outlaw.

He pinned Juana beneath his darkened gaze. "Can I leave Amy here with you? They won't be looking for—"

"Leave me here?" Shock propelled Amelia from the bed. Frantically she snatched for a quilt to cover herself with, wrapping it around her torso with both hands.

"I'm not a . . . a *parcel* to be passed from hand to hand at your will, Mason Kincaid," she said, marching toward him with the ends of the quilt slipping from the bed and trailing behind her. "I'm going with you."

"The hell you are."

He looked down at her, all hard, unrelenting man. His hat brim shadowed his face, and between that darkness and his day's growth of beard, suddenly Mason looked a stranger to her. Not the man who'd held her so tenderly last night. Not the man in whose eyes she'd glimpsed a love she'd never expected to find.

Not the man she wanted facing a posse's drawn guns and promises of frontier justice.

"Then . . . then why can't you just hide from them?" she cried, waving her hand that wasn't holding up the blanket. She stepped nearer, frustration and fear coiling in her stomach. "Why do you have to go? Why?"

Her voice broke on the words, threatened tears Amelia didn't want to shed. Weeping wouldn't change his mind. Not when it was this Mason, this cold, determined Mason, who stood before her.

"Surely James and Juana can hide you here!" she cried, her voice muffled as she scooped up her chemise and pantalets from the floor and threw them onto the bed. She was going with him no matter what he said—or else hiding with him wherever they could.

She snatched her dress from the ladder-backed straight chair and threw it down, too. "They're your friends, they'll want to help—"

"Enough." His jaw tightened, as did his hand on her arm, stopping her from getting dressed. With Amelia's cooperation assured for the moment, he glanced over his shoulder at Juana. An unspoken question passed between them.

She nodded. "We'll watch over her until you return," she said. She tried to smile at Amelia, and failed.

"Godspeed, Mason." Sniffling, Juana buried her hands in her apron and left, her shoulders squared for the task ahead of her.

He couldn't separate them now, Amelia vowed. She meant to stay with him, and she would. What kind of woman would desert the man she loved when he needed her?

She sat on the bed and hastily pulled her pantalets on, shielded from view behind the blanket. Raising it higher, she struggled to get her chemise over her head without uncovering herself completely.

"I'll wait for you outside, *amigo*," said Manuel.

She heard his long, impatient strides toward the door, and popped her head out from beneath the blanket just as he paused with one hand on the thick door frame.

"You'll be needing somebody to cover your back against those *bastardos*," he said with a wolfish grin. "I'll go with you for as long as it takes."

"Thank you," Mason said, nodding his assent as he watched Manuel leave.

His expression revealed nothing of his thoughts, and Amelia couldn't stop to guess at them, not if she meant to leave with him.

Mason moved toward her, stopped her flustered attempts to fasten the chemise he'd torn from her last night, and pulled her upright against him.

He captured her face in both hands and tilted it upward to meet his gaze. "Amy, I have to go."

She lifted her chin higher. "I'll go with you. I'm almost dress—"

"No." He stopped her when she tried to turn in his arms and pick up her dress from the bed. "You have to stay here."

With a sound of frustration Amelia pressed her hands to his chest, wanting more than anything to make him stay. She searched her mind for something that might convince him, yet beneath her palms Mason's body quivered like a tightly strung wire. Eager. He was eager to be gone, even if it might separate them forever. Her hopes sank.

"Please don't go!" she cried, past caring if anyone heard her—past caring that she was begging him not to leave her. She clenched a fistful of his shirt and buried her face in the warm curve just beneath his collarbone, trying to swallow past the tightening in her throat. Why wouldn't he listen to her?

"Just hide!" she said. "Or—or surrender. You're not responsible for what happened to your wife. Just tell them, and I'm sure—"

"No." His arms swept to her waist, held her. "Men like that don't want explanations. They want the bounty for bringing in an outlaw, plain and simple."

"But—"

"And if I stop to explain, I won't reach Ben in time."

Ben. *His son.* Amelia slumped against his chest as defeat seeped through her, cold enough that she might never feel warm again. How could she ask him to stay, when it might cost him the person who mattered to him most?

She couldn't.

Mason raised his hands to her neck, and his touch felt so familiar, so strong and warm she thought she might weep from wanting it. Her throat ached with unshed tears. She hardly dared raise her head to look at him, lest he see them shining in her eyes, too. How could he be leaving now, when they'd shared so much?

"Kiss me goodbye," he whispered, his thumbs stroking beneath her chin to urge her face upward. Tears spilled onto her cheeks, and Amelia felt them slide cold and wet toward her ears. She sniffled.

"No," she croaked. Her fingers tightened on his shirtfront as she shook her head. "No, I won't say goodbye."

His mouth tensed. Mason's hands stilled, then moved away from her face. Brushed past her neck. After a moment's pause, he lowered them to his sides, not touching her at all. The loss of him sharpened the ache inside her, and foretold every day's loss from this instant on.

"Goodbye," he whispered hoarsely.

"No!" Amelia lurched toward him, wrapped both arms around his middle, not caring when her chemise gaped open and her blanket dropped to the floor. Anything, anything to keep him with her. She looked up at him, at his dark eyes and stern-set jaw and his arms still not around her, and felt her heart splinter at the proof of how easily Mason could leave her behind.

"Please, don't go," she whispered, unable to force anything more past her constricted throat. *"Please* don't—"

"Every moment I stay, everyone here is in greater danger," he said harshly. "In danger because of me."

Raising both hands to her temples, he swept her hair back, digging his knuckles into her scalp. He forced her head up to meet his gaze, and she could no sooner look away than she could stop loving him.

"Every moment I stay, *you're* in greater danger," Mason said, giving each word painful emphasis as his hold tightened on her hair. A tremor passed through him, making the muscles in his throat knot and release.

His eyes closed. "I'm leaving."

He released her, opening his eyes again. Resignation had turned them bleak, colder than she'd ever seen them. She truly couldn't stop him. Desperate, Amelia raised herself on tiptoe and smashed her mouth against his.

He responded with the kiss she'd longed for, a kiss that echoed all they'd shared. Leaving, leaving . . . the knowledge that this kiss might well be their last sweetened it nearly past bearing, made her tremble as Mason's arms swept around her and held her tightly. His tongue stroked hers, delving deeper, and the pressure of his mouth on hers was everything she hungered for. He tasted of tears, her tears, and just as she began to believe she'd convinced him to stay, Mason ended the kiss and stepped away from her.

She wanted to grab him, to make him admit he cared—or at least that he regretted leaving, that he'd be back for her. His steely posture and distant eyes told her his leave-taking had already begun. Pride stiffened Amelia's spine even as she swiped away tears, blinking to hide the new ones that followed. A painful lump rose in her throat, making speech difficult.

"Be safe, Mason." Even her lips wobbled with the words, and she endeavored to sound brave to him. Clearing her throat for the task, she let her gaze wander to his eyes again, and regretted it when she glimpsed the impatience there. "I—I'll wait for you."

His fingers touched her lips. The ghost of a smile touched his. "Don't worry, Amelia. I'm too mean to be captured for long," he said.

"Amigo!" Manuel's voice, muffled by its journey inside through the thick adobe walls.

Mason closed his eyes and swallowed hard. *"Minuto!"*

He turned, his hands going by rote to his gun belt. In the doorway he paused. In his eyes she saw the weight of the man he'd become, of the outlaw's destiny he'd been cast into, and the knowledge of all he'd suffered softened her heart.

"I love you," Amelia whispered.

He looked at her a long moment, his expression inscrutable. "That's why I'm leaving," Mason finally answered.

Before she could reply, he was gone.

Twenty-one

"He will return for you, you know."

Juana's words, so confidently given, made hope flare inside Amelia like a newly lit candle. The doubt that had plagued her since Mason's leaving doused it just as quickly. She plunged her hands into the bread dough she was kneading for Juana and gave it a vigorous push.

"Unless he . . . he . . ." Struggling over the words, she flipped the dough and sent white puffs of flour drifting over the tabletop. Her stomach knotted with unspoken worries.

Unless he can't.

Unless he's captured.

Killed.

She couldn't say her fears aloud without redoubling them, without fearing she might inadvertently make them come true. Some superstitious part of her wished mightily to pretend Mason was invulnerable, however impossible a wish that was. The rest of her knew exactly how precarious one life was—his wife's death was proof enough of that.

Innocent or not, in the West a man accused was only as safe as the marksmanship of the posse chasing him was poor.

With every hour that passed without the clatter of Mason's horse in the stage station's courtyard, Amelia's fears grew. Her ears strained at every hoofbeat, every noisy stagecoach arrival. Her heart thrilled to the sound of every male voice that drifted through the loosely latched shutters—until she realized the voice wasn't Mason's.

"If anything happens, we will know of it soon enough," Juana said. "James went to Tucson as soon as he heard. If I know my husband, he's giving the lawmen there a 'bleeding earful,' right now. He'd ride back to tell us if they brought Mason in."

She rolled her dark eyes and added a handful of the onion she'd chopped to the pork stew simmering on the stove top, then wiped her hands clean. "Besides, you know as well as I do, that man is too ornery to be locked up. The sheriff might set him free just to spare himself the trouble."

Amelia smiled faintly at that, imagining Mason hulking into the Tucson jail, all bared teeth and bad temper. *She* wouldn't like to be the one to try and lock up Mason Kincaid. He'd already escaped from one sheriff's pursuit and another's jail cell—but could he manage it a third time?

"Everyone in these parts knows Mason," Juana went on in her melodious, Spanish-accented voice. Her gaze traveled a competent, practiced arc from the bubbling, chile-scented stew to the floury dough beneath Amelia's hands to the woodpile beside the stove. "This will all get straightened out, one way or the other."

She stooped to add more wood to the stove fire, keeping busy as she'd seemed prone to do since Manuel had returned with news of the posse that morning. But Amelia quit kneading, staring at the mound of dough without really seeing it. She wished she had Juana's faith, and her ability to work steadily amidst troubles rather than flounder beneath them. More than that, she wished she had Juana's knowledge of all that had happened in Mason's life before.

Now she might never have the chance to hear it from him.

The bread dough blurred into the plank tabletop beneath it as her eyes suddenly brimmed with tears. Blaming them on the

fresh onions, Amelia sniffed them away, then blinked and resumed kneading.

Maybe if she found out *how* he came to be a wanted man,
she could still help Mason somehow. It seemed every new en-
lightenment that arose only sparked a new question.

"If everyone knows Mason, knows he couldn't have been
responsible for his wife's death," she asked slowly, "then how
was he ever accused? How did he lose his son?"

She flipped over the springy, yeasty-smelling dough and went
on kneading, mindful of Juana's speculative glance her way.

And determined not to let her see how much the explanation
might mean.

"You want to know if I believe he is guilty."

Juana's blunt statement stripped Amelia of her assumed nonchalance. Her fingers sank mindlessly into the bread dough.
"No! No, that's not what I meant at all!"

She darted a glance at Juana and found her standing with
both arms crossed over her chest, eyeing Amelia with something
that came very near hostility.

"Do *you* believe he's guilty?" Juana asked.

"I believe he feels responsible." She turned the dough and
pushed the floury heels of her hands into it, thinking about it
some more. "And responsible for the loss of his son."

"Ha!" Juana frowned, hefted a split mesquite branch, and
shoved it into the stove fire with far more force than seemed
necessary. "That's what those brothers of Ellen's wanted him
to believe. They came out here, all fancy men from the States,
and snatched poor Ben away before Mason could even sober
up from Ellen's funeral."

She looked at Amelia and shook her head. "Any man would
have taken to the bottle, facing all he did with her. Especially
at the end."

"His wife's *brothers* took Ben?"

Juana waved away Amelia's surprise. *"Bastardos.* Selfish

men," she muttered, her Spanish accent growing stronger. "They thought their nephew belonged in a civilized place, not here in the Territory with a drunken papa and no mother."

"But he's the boy's father!" Amelia cried. "Surely Ben would have been happier at home with him."

An image of a little boy, dragged away crying by the uncles he barely knew, filled her mind. After losing his mother, Ben would have needed his father all the more. Couldn't his relatives see that?

"Ah, but *they* were happier having their revenge on Mason," Juana said. "I don't think they ever liked him, ever thought he should have married Ellen and brought her West with him. They are cruel men. I saw it myself at her funeral."

She shuddered, and her mouth turned down at the corners. "They called Mason every vile name I've ever heard, and some I haven't." She smiled wryly. "They said he drove Ellen to what she did."

Amelia stared at her, stunned by the idea of men who would strike out in such a way at the funeral of a man's wife. Men so vindictive they'd risk hurting their own small nephew in the name of revenge.

"But they were Mason's relatives, too, Juana. By marriage, at least. Maybe you misunderstood, maybe—"

"No." Juana shook her head, her voice firm. "No. They accused him. Accused him of killing their sister." She picked up the bread dough from Amelia's table, ripped it in half, and began rounding one portion into a smooth-topped bread loaf. "The lawmen were duty-bound to take Mason in and find out the truth."

"And that's when he escaped? When the posse started after him?" Amelia guessed.

"Not at first," Juana said, frowning as she shook away the flour clinging to the bread dough. "Sheriff Shibell came out alone to talk to Mason at first. He knew him, just like everybody else. He didn't believe what those *bastardo* brothers of Ellen's said." She cast Amelia a sharp glance. "None of us did."

She muttered something below her breath and shook her head. "But by then those Sharpes had taken Ben away, and Mason went after them."

"So when the sheriff got there," Amelia said, thinking aloud, "and found Mason gone, he assumed he'd run because he was guilty."

"Yes." Juana's lips tightened. "And set the posse after him, then and there. *Tonto.*"

Amelia sighed. "I don't understand any of this," she said. "If Mason was trying to get to Tucson to find his son, what was he doing robbing stagecoaches in the meantime?"

Juana shrugged. "Not robbing. Trying to ask about where those *bastardo* Sharpe brothers had taken his son without being caught, I'd say. A clever one, that Kincaid."

"I don't think I ever saw him take any money," Amelia reflected, thinking back on the stagecoach robberies she'd witnessed since embarking on her Arizona Territory mission. "And it did turn out to be a very effective disguise."

It had certainly fooled her. She nearly blushed to recall how convinced she'd been that she was meeting the famous poet bandit. So much had happened since then, those convictions seemed far away indeed.

"But he never talked to me about it," Juana went on. "Maybe James or Manuel. Mason is not a man to confide in others."

Amelia remembered his pain when he'd described to her the loss of his wife, his freedom . . . his son. That Mason had trusted her enough to reveal himself to her humbled her. And she—she had convinced herself this morning that she meant little to him, if he could leave her so easily. Sorrow slowed her hands as she scraped dough from the tabletop and threw the scraps away.

She had to find a way to clear his name, to restore his freedom if she could. She loved him. And she owed Mason at least that much for the many times he'd saved her since her arrival in the Territory.

Amelia's eyes narrowed. Her father was an influential man back home—perhaps if he sent a wire to the sheriff in Tucson? Arranged a work furlough? She could easily imagine the sheriff agreeing to such a plan, especially if J. G. O'Malley vouched for Mason.

Except Mason would never agree. He'd think it indentured servitude, she was almost certain. And he'd be partly right. Amelia bit her lip, trying to think of another plan. Surely there was something she could do to help. Mason was an innocent man.

Juana plunked the unbaked loaf into a pan and started shaping the next, frowning to herself over the story she'd been telling. "Those Sharpes were right about one thing, though. Mason did not belong with her."

Surprised at the venom in Juana's tone, Amelia paused in the act of wiping up flour from the tabletop. "You didn't like Ellen?"

Juana plunked the second loaf into a pan with an unladylike snort. "Like her?" She wiped her hands and looked at Amelia. "Tell me. What is to like about a woman who cares only for herself?"

"But surely she loved her husband, her son—"

"Ellen was cold, *pequeña*. I think Mason did not see it at first, because she was so beautiful. After time . . . after time he could no longer ignore it."

Juana lifted a crate of crockery bowls and battered cutlery, balancing its weight against her hips as she headed for the stage station's front room. Amelia followed her into the long, low room, thoughts of Mason's wife—and of her acknowledged beauty—slowing her movements as she followed Juana along the rough-hewn tables, laying bowls at each place setting.

Suddenly she felt too messy, too poorly dressed and too pitifully groomed to ever hope to hold Mason's interest. Not like his beautiful wife, the mother of his child. Glumly, Amelia gathered a handful of spoons and knives to add to the place settings, ashamed at her shallow concerns and yet wholly unable to put them aside.

Mason's leaving made every doubtful thought she'd ever entertained about herself leap straight into her mind and set up housekeeping again.

"I thought you were the same," Juana said with a small laugh, going to light the lamps hung at even intervals along the adobe walls. Evening was nearly upon them, deepening the shadows where the farthest oil lamps hung. "Another fancy Eastern lady, come to hurt my friend."

The words struck Amelia like a careless blow, made her heart thump hollowly in her chest as she clutched the tableware still to be set. Was that how she truly appeared? No wonder Mason had seemed so unfriendly at first, so unwilling to view her as anything more than a burden to be disposed of as quickly as possible.

He'd had other priorities. His freedom. His son. And she'd distracted him from them all. Regret tightened inside her like a fist. Numbly she watched Juana replace the chimney on the last lamp and blow out the lighted taper she'd used.

"I—I never meant to hurt him," Amelia said, staring just past Juana's shoulder. No wonder Juana and Mason got along so well—neither had the slightest fear of speaking their truths, however bluntly. She rubbed the smooth silver in her hands, trying to summon the courage to go on. "I didn't even mean for him to rescue me. I never—"

"Oh, Amelia!" Juana exclaimed, touching her shoulder lightly. "I know that! You needn't look so worried. I changed my mind when I—"

Hoofbeats entering the courtyard stilled her voice. A horse whinnied, then blew. An instant later, the door swung open.

Manuel.

Alone.

Yet he'd vowed to stay with Mason for as long as he was needed.

Amelia's spoons and knives fell from her nerveless grip, clattering to the floor in a shower of dull silver.

"Where's Mason?" she cried, rushing toward him. If Manuel had returned alone, did that mean the posse had captured Mason?

Manuel raised his hands, palms upward. *"Señorita,* he—"

No. She couldn't listen.

Mason had to be outside. Nothing had happened. He was fine. Fine. Maybe even waiting for her, and she was wasting time talking with Manuel. She pushed past him and entered the courtyard, her head swiveling for any sign of Mason.

The sun had nearly set, casting the boxy, mesquite-bordered area into long, cool shadows. The breeze ruffled her hair, lifting tendrils from her chignon to stream across her face. Brushing them impatiently aside, Amelia looked toward the hitching post. Manuel's horse stood tethered there, its sides lathered and heaving.

Manuel's horse only.

Her heartbeat quickening, she scanned the rest of the courtyard. Station hands at work, wagons being repaired at the blacksmith's shop, and high rounded creosote bushes crowded her vision. No tall, broad-shouldered man rode in toward the station. No Mason.

"No, no," Amelia whispered, wheeling blindly toward the opened stage station door. Warmth hit her when she stumbled inside, seeking Manuel.

He stood beside Juana, his broad-brimmed *sombrero* gone, looking as though he'd climbed on his hands and knees the whole way up Picacho Peak. Dried mud caked his shirt to his chest, and his trousers were ripped at the knees. His face, when he looked at her, was lined with fatigue, dirt-smudged and haggard.

She couldn't move any farther. Dread rooted her to the spot.

Juana tugged a chair from the table, scraping its legs across the hard-packed earth floor. She nodded toward it, motioning Amelia into it with a subtle inclination of her head. New sorrow pulled at the corners of her mouth. Bad. The news Manuel brought was bad.

"No." Amelia backed up, the room swimming. Even in the low lamplight, everything looked different—brighter, blurrier, farther away. Small sounds reached her—the horse shifting outside, the stew bubbling in the back room, a bird crying near the window—but whatever Juana was saying was lost to her.

Her fingers felt numb. She tasted denial, breathed it in the air, and whatever the news Manuel had brought, she didn't want it.

"No." She backed up farther. Her hip bumped against something, then a chair and wash basin toppled, crashing into the adobe wall behind. The sound galvanized her, sent her feet into motion with only the need to get away guiding her.

Tables, more chairs blocked her path. Blindly she pushed them aside, her throat tightening with tears that wouldn't come. Manuel's message was false. Mason was strong, he knew how to survive in the desert and beyond. He'd never—

Warm fingers closed on her upper arm. "Señorita, I must tell you." Manuel's voice in the darkness swirling around her. "I promised I would tell you—"

Fury swept through Amelia with such force it made her shake. She spun, wrenching his hand from her arm. "You left him!" she spat out. "You promised to stay with him! How can you speak to me of promises when you—you—"

Rage choked her, made it impossible to go on. Instead she

glared at Manuel, seeing only the man who'd failed to help
Mason. The man who'd brought everything upon their heads
with his carelessness in returning the wagon to Maricopa Wells,
the man who'd all but led the posse straight to Mason, and she
knew what it was to hate someone in an instant.

"Amelia." Juana's tone sounded gentle, like that of a mother
to a grieving child. *"Pequeña,* sit down. Listen to him." Her
hand touched Amelia's shoulder. "Manuel is only keeping his
word. He came to—"

"No! If not for him, Mason would never have been found.
The posse would still be searching. And Ben would have a father
now, not—"

A sob rippled through her. Manuel's roar of anger made it
stick in her throat, unvoiced.

"If not for *you,* he would have been with his son days ago!"
he yelled, his Spanish accent thickening as he advanced toward
her. "Instead he stayed here to lie with you, and put us all at
risk. *Puta!* Do not raise your voice to me."

He looked ready to strike her, his eyes blazing against his
dirt-smudged skin. His hand shot forward, clamped around her
wrist, and Amelia shrank before him, shocked from her rage by
the bitterness in his face. Manuel wrenched her wrist to waist
height. He pressed his thumb into the fragile bones at its center,
forcing her hand to open.

"Manuel, no!" cried Juana. "Not like this!"

"This one deserves no better." His eyes met Amelia's, and
for an instant she thought she glimpsed pity there. It vanished
just as quickly. "She is as bad as that bitch wife of his."

He pushed his fist into her palm, forcing something into her
hand—something light yet familiar. She felt its fine-honed edge
bite into her skin, but couldn't look closer to see what it was.

"Mason asked me to give you this," Manuel said, releasing
her wrist with a cruel snap of his arm.

"And to say goodbye."

He spat into the ground at her feet. With one final, scathing look he strode away, leaving Amelia wavering. Goodbye? *Goodbye?* Hysteria pushed at her, unraveling her thoughts as quickly as they came. She stared at Juana, unable to move or speak.

Suddenly, Juana's image wavered and blurred, and as though noticing the fact from a great distance, Amelia realized she was crying. Tears streamed down her cheeks, running into her mouth, her ears, tasting of salt and disbelief.

"Goodbye?" she croaked. It couldn't be, he couldn't be gone. *Mason, Mason* . . .

"Ahhh, *pequeña,*" Juana murmured. "I did not think it would come to this. I had hoped there would be another way. Another way for Mason, too."

"Another way?" Amelia unfolded her clenched fist, feeling a dull sense of relief as the object she'd held so tightly stopped pressing against her skin.

"He needs you," Juana said. "I do not know why he would choose this, after all that has happened."

"Choose? Choose what? Oh, Juana, I . . ."

Her voice cracked, blunted by confusion and pain, and Amelia looked down instead of speaking. Her satchel key winked up at her, resting within the reddened impression it had created in her palm. She'd forgotten Mason still had it.

A tear ran down the bridge of her nose and splashed onto her hand, wetting her already dampened skin. Why this, why now? The last thing she wanted was her satchels. The last thing she cared about was working on her book orders again, when Mason . . . when Mason was gone.

A fresh sob wrenched through her. Bent with the pain, Amelia closed her fist around the satchel key. She wrapped her arms around her middle, trying to ease the ache.

"*Pequeña.* Little one." Juana hugged her, stroking her back gently. "I know this is hard," she murmured. "I know, I know. But at least he is safe. At least he—"

"What?" Amelia's head snapped up. She sniffed, trying to clear her stuffy head, all her attention centered on Juana's face. Dear heaven, had she heard her aright? "What did you say?"

"Mason is safe, he got away."

Juana looked at her quizzically; then understanding showed in her dark eyes. Smiling, she put both hands to Amelia's face and used her thumbs to wipe the tears from her cheeks.

"You did not hear me before," she said quietly. "Did not hear Manuel when he first arrived."

"I thought—I thought . . ." Oh, but she wanted to scream aloud as the realization struck her that Mason was safe. Safe. "I thought he was captured, ki—"

"No. No, he is safe."

"Then why—" Amelia opened her fist, looked down at the satchel key. "Why did he give Manuel this? Where has he gone?"

Juana's hands settled on her shoulders. "To Tucson. He's gone to get Ben. He's not . . ."

She paused, as though reconsidering her words. "I thought you wept because Mason did not return for you," she said gently.

Amelia stared at her. Her thoughts were jumbled, too confused to be sorted out. Mason wasn't coming for her? He was safe, but not coming back for her?

"He . . . he promised," she whispered. "That's why I agreed to stay, to wait for him."

I love you.

That's why I'm leaving.

Pain twisted, reborn within her. He'd told her then, straight out, what he meant to do—and why. He didn't want her love. Didn't want her. I'll wait for you, she'd said.

And Mason had said goodbye.

Like a fool she'd chosen not to listen, chosen to ignore the words her heart didn't want to hear. Now her same foolish heart ached more with every moment that passed. Once again she'd loved someone who didn't want her . . . cared for someone who didn't care back.

Why had she expected more? She'd been nothing more than an obligation to Mason—an obligation he'd gratefully gotten rid of as soon as they'd reached Picacho Peak.

You can't help me. He'd told her time and again, pushing her away each time. You can't, you can't . . .

Just like her father. No matter how worthy she tried to be, it never seemed to be enough. Maybe would never be enough.

Juana touched her arm, and the compassion in her gaze brought new tears to Amelia's eyes. "Mason promised?" she asked softly, her eyebrows raised. "Then maybe Manuel misunderstood. Maybe he's—"

"No. *I* misunderstood."

"Pequeña—"

Amelia shrugged off her gentle hug, stepped back and tried to wave away Juana's concern, as well. "Mason told me. I didn't believe him then. Now"—she drew a deep, shuddering breath— "now I guess I have to."

Sniffling, she swiped her eyes with the back of her hand. Someday the hurt would go away. Until then, she'd have to manage as best she could.

"Will there be a stage for Tucson tonight?" she asked, staring numbly through the still-open doorway. Hard as it was to imagine herself leaving without Mason, it seemed she'd have to. She'd have to get her books, get on with her book-order deliveries—get on with her life back home when she'd finished.

"Not for you," Juana said firmly. "Not after this."

Taking Amelia by the elbow, she steered her between tables and chairs toward the stage station's back room. "No matter how big a fool Mason chooses to be, that does not mean you must leave us, too."

Halfway to the back room, Amelia dug in her heels. "No," she said, shaking her head. "I have another life to lead, Juana.

I can't stay here with you. What would James say? And Manuel?"

Manuel hated her now, she'd seen it in his eyes. After all she'd accused him of, she could hardly blame him. Grief had made her thoughts run amuck, made her seize upon the first opportunity to lay blame on someone, however undeserving.

"Bah! Who do you think runs this place? The men are always gone, off to Tucson or Fort Lowell or riding half-wild across the Territory with one excuse or another."

Amelia laughed, surprising herself.

"I can use your help," Juana went on. "And your company. A lady friend is hard to come by here."

"Oh, Juana." Cocking her head, Amelia smiled at her. "Thank you, but I—"

Juana held up her hand. "Manuel is angry now, yes. But not at you only," she said, giving Amelia a determined look. "He did not want Mason to go into Tucson alone. He thought it too dangerous, and now he's loosed his venom on you."

She stared toward the doorway leading to the stage station's back room, shaking her head slightly. "It was cruelly done, Amelia. I am sorry."

"I'm sorry, too." Amelia glanced at her, twisted her hands within the folds of the calico dress she'd borrowed from Juana. "Do you think he would accept an apology? I don't want to leave without making amends. What I said to Manuel was horrible."

"Still this talk of leaving?"

"I have to go," Amelia told her, wishing in that moment it wasn't true. Something told her she and Juana might have been good friends, given different circumstances.

A rumbling sounded outside, reaching her through the still-open front door of the stage station. Distant at first, then louder, Amelia recognized it as the creaks and hoofbeats of a stagecoach and team drawing up the winding Picacho Peak road.

"The passengers we expected for supper," Juana said, going to the door to look outside. She closed it against the clouds of gritty dust stirred up by the stagecoach's arrival, then turned to face Amelia again.

"Mason warned me about this part of you," she said, folding her arms and smiling at Amelia. "When he asked me to wire Tucson and find out if your books were at the station there. He knew you'd want them."

Of course he did, he knew he wasn't returning for me, Amelia thought. But she could hardly say such a thing aloud.

"He did?" she asked instead.

"Yes." Juana swept past her, heading for the back room to collect the stew and serving utensils and leaving Amelia to follow.

"In fact," she said, pausing in the act of stirring the thick, meaty stew, "he said he figured you'd sell every last book in those bags, once you got them back."

"Really?" Amelia asked, brightening a bit. At least Mason had thought her competent in one area. That was certainly more acknowledgment than she'd ever received from her father or brothers back home.

Juana nodded. "He said he'd never met a more determined person in his life, man or woman." She stuck her hand on her hip, her wooden spoon jutting out sideways. "Of them all, he said you were the dog-stubbornest."

Amelia frowned. "He said that?"

"Sí." Steam rising from the stew wreathed Juana's face—her smiling face—as she lifted the heavy cast-iron pot from the stove top. She nodded toward the pinto beans simmering in another pot, motioning for Amelia to carry it into the front room. "That is what he said."

Hefting the bean pot in both hands, Amelia followed her through the doorway. There she stopped, surprised at the quantity—and variety—of stagecoach passengers shuffling inside the station.

Juana glanced over her shoulder. "That is when I knew you and Mason belonged together," she said, reexamining Amelia with narrowed eyes. She smiled wider. "Only a dog-stubborn woman could keep up with a man like that. When you get to Tucson—"

"Juana, I—"

"When you get to Tucson," she interrupted, raising her voice to be heard over the din of people filing inside, scraping chairs away from the tables, and paying for their meals, "you find Mason. Find him and make him listen to you, *pequeña*. You and Mason belong together."

Twenty-two

George Hand's saloon in Tucson was dark and cramped, but since it was tucked into the corner of Meyer and Mesilla streets a good two miles from the courthouse and jail, it suited Mason just fine.

Although the whiskey was rotgut and the *mescal* was even meaner, the saloon still found its share of patrons. Men who found the teakwood bar and faro tables of Brown's Congress Hall Saloon too rich for their blood usually wound up at Hand's, where the cards fell straight and the soiled doves of Maiden Lane were only stumbling distance away.

If luck were with Mason, so were the Sharpe brothers.

Anticipation, predatory and too long denied, made Mason's fingers tighten on the drink in front of him. A day of searching for them had whetted his appetite, not blunted it. He meant to find the Sharpes, get Ben, and get the hell out of Tucson and on the road to Mexico, with his boy and his life his own again. No matter what it took. Grimacing, he drained his drink, then slapped the glass onto the plain bar counter, motioning for another.

The bar owner nodded, holding up a hand for Mason to wait while he finished with the saloon's only other customer, a soiled dove named Cruz. Stroking his wiry, collar-length beard, George Hand leaned over the bar toward her, pouring whiskey

into her glass. He was nothing if not solicitous toward Cruz—
and all the business she brought into his house.

Mason watched them, his fingers idly stroking the other glass
on the bar counter. His second drink, ordered along with the
first and still untouched. He pushed it away, then drew it nearer,
drawn from their conversation to the amber depths of the liquor
his glass held.

Whiskey. How long since he'd drunk it? He tried to remember, thought of the time in the wagon with Amy outside Maricopa Wells, and snatched his fingers from the glass. They came
away slick and cold with condensation, cold as Mason felt inside with leaving her.

"Any luck today?" asked Hand, whisking away Mason's
empty glass. He dunked it into the *olla* in the corner, swished
it around in the pottery jar's contents, and pulled it out again.
Wiping it dry, he set it onto the bar counter beside the whiskey
glass.

"No." Mason absently lined up both glasses, then took a swig
from one. It cooled his throat, slid into his empty belly and
reminded him he'd never stopped to eat. "I went clear from
Levin's over to the old *plaza* where Camp Lowell used to be.
Not a damned sign of them."

He slammed down his glass, clanking it against its partner
on the bar top. Cruz glanced at him from two stools over, all
low-cut dress and too-sweet flowery perfume, and winked.

"Feeling tense, sugar? I can help you out with that, if you
want. Make you feel real fine."

Mason bared his teeth at her.

"Not now, Cruz," Hand said, shaking his head.

She shrugged and finished her drink, then wiped her mouth
neatly. "Mason and I, we've got an understanding," she said,
tossing her dark hair over her shoulder. "I just thought we might
expand it a little."

Hand raised his eyebrows at Mason.

"She's keeping an eye out for the Sharpes for me," Mason muttered. "I spent part of the day over on Maiden Lane. If I've got those bastards pegged right, one or all of them will be visiting the cribs before they head East. If they do, I'll know about it."

"Good idea." Hand reached below the bar counter, raised a whiskey bottle, and started to refill Mason's second drink. He paused, frowning down at the paired glasses in front of him.

"What in blazes is the matter with you, Kincaid?" he asked, thumping the bottle onto the bar. "You ordered that whiskey— you gonna drink it or look at it for another hour?"

Mason stared at the glasses, one filled with whiskey and the other beside it filled with water, and raised the water. He drained it in one gulp, then saluted the *olla* with the empty glass.

"Look at it," he growled. "While you fill this one again."

"Dammit, I make my money off'n whiskey," Hand grumbled, yanking the glass from the bar and stomping toward the water jar. "At this rate I'll be havin' the water vendor in here twice a damned month, and goin' busted after that."

"Good thing you've got boarders."

"Just you, and you ain't payin' me none," Hand said, slopping a fresh water glass in front of Mason. "At least help me out an' take a tumble with old Cruz here. *Her* I make money off of."

Cruz smiled. "Lots of money," she said, smoothing her hand over her ruffly red dress. "What do you say, sugar? I ain't seen you since Fort Lowell days. Almost forgot what it's like to entertain a—"

"No."

Mason stroked his whiskey glass, looking down into it instead of at Cruz. Maybe one drink wouldn't hurt. One horn of whiskey to wipe out all the damned things he couldn't forget, couldn't put behind him even with miles of separation. He dipped his finger into the whiskey, tracing moisture round and round the glass rim.

Hand leaned over the bar. "You ain't gonna find those fellas you're looking for tonight," he said. "It's clear past midnight already. I ought to just close up anyhow." He jerked his head toward Cruz. "Go on with Cruz and forget about it for a while."

Forget. Damn, but he wanted to forget everything. Ellen, the Sharpes, Ben. All of it hurt like hell to think about.

And it was nothing compared with the pain that seared him every time he pictured Amy beside him, loving him.

Being left behind.

Hell.

Mason raised his whiskey, liking its warm weight in his hand. He could taste it, feel the bitter peace it would bring. He inhaled deeply, filling his nostrils with the liquor's tangy scent. Just one little drink . . .

"A little comfort never hurt nobody," Cruz said, sliding down from her barstool. Mason sensed her coming nearer, smelled her perfume and the clove-sweet scent of the laudanum she drank throughout the day, and lowered his head.

"No, Cruz."

"Why not? You find yourself another fancy Eastern lady, sugar?" She touched his arm, wrapping her fingers around it to pull herself up against his shoulder. "I reckon that ain't never stopped none of my other gentleman callers."

"I said no."

Mason hurled his whiskey glass. It shattered against the saloon's whitewashed wall in a spray of liquor and glass shards.

The motion only fueled the anger already inside him. He wanted to break something. Hurt something. Teeth clenched, he slammed his hand onto the bar top. Pain surged up his arm as he shoved himself from the stool and straightened to his full height.

"Don't ask again," he snarled.

Cruz jumped backward, staring at him with eyes gone wide. She nodded. "Sorry, sugar. I—I'll let you know if I see them

Sharpe fellas who took your boy." She cast a hasty glance at
Hand, busy gathering up broken glass behind the bar. "See you
at the *fiesta* tomorrow, George."

" 'Night, Cruz."

She shoved open the saloon doors, letting in cooler night air
and the sounds of dogs barking in the distance. A mule brayed
nearby, and tinny music drifted over from the Gem saloon down
the street. Mason kept his head down, not looking as he heard
the doors swish closed again behind Cruz's departing back.

Hand straightened behind the bar, holding the cloth he'd used
to wipe up Mason's whiskey.

"What the hell's the matter with you?" he asked, shaking the
glass fragments from it into the trash. "You ain't never been
one to be mean like that, not even to a whore. You known Cruz
a long time."

Mason glared down at him. Another man would have shut
up. George Hand, only chest-high to Mason, didn't.

"What kind of damn help you think her and them painted
ladies are going to give you now, since you went all wrathy on
Cruz?"

Looking disgusted, he shook his head, then wadded up the
cloth and threw it behind the bar. "I dunno what's deviling you,
Mason, but this ain't like you."

Mason grabbed the full whiskey bottle Hand had left on the
bar. The liquor sloshed inside, a siren's call compared with what
he'd been hearing from himself every hour since leaving Amy
back at Picacho Peak.

He'd taken the coward's way out, sending Manuel back with
that key.

Tell her goodbye, he'd told Manuel. Tell her . . . And then
he'd stopped. Tell her what? That he loved her? Love meant
promises Mason couldn't keep. Lying words said over a Bible
that would only haunt them both later. Tell her to be happy? To
be safe? She would be both.

If he stayed away.

Amy deserved better. Better than a life lived amongst strangers in Mexico, better than life as an outlaw's woman. Better than him.

Just tell her goodbye, he'd finally said. And Manuel had ridden away to keep his promise, leaving Mason to live with the consequences.

"It just ain't like you," Hand said again, spreading his palms along the bar. He looked pointedly at the whiskey. "It ain't."

Mason looked at it too, raising the bottle to the lamplight. "It is now," he said.

He headed toward the saloon doors, the whiskey dangling from his fingertips.

"Much obliged for the drink, Hand," Mason told him. "But you can keep your damned opinions to yourself. At least until I'm drunk enough to forget them in the morning."

Tucson was, Amelia decided, quite possibly the noisiest town she'd ever encountered. Horses trotted past and mule-drawn freight wagons rumbled by at a dangerously rapid pace, music seemed to spill from the saloons night and day, and overhead the windmills creaked incessantly. Conversations in English, Spanish, and sometimes, unfamiliar-sounding Chinese, swirled around her and added to the confusion.

Passersby filled what little space remained in the streets. Farmers and ranchers ducked past Indian women carrying enormous pottery jars on their heads, and tipped their hats to ladies paying calls. Water, wood, and vegetable vendors plied their goods from handmade carts set between the shops, making up tunes to entice buyers. These remained in Amelia's head far longer than she wished.

Children smiled shyly up at her from their parents' sides as she passed, and each one of them made her think of little Ben. Had Mason found him? Were they all right? She found herself looking closely into each young face, watching for resemblances to Mason. Every glimpse of a dark-haired, brown-eyed boy made her look twice as closely, her heart pounding fiercely.

It was silly, really, Amelia told herself. As fruitless as her thoughts of Mason were. She had little chance of finding Ben herself. Mason had never described the boy to her. He could have blond hair, or red; blue eyes instead of brown. For all she knew, Ben resembled his mother. Amelia hadn't the slightest notion what Ellen had looked like.

Aside from impossibly beautiful, she amended.

Dabbing her damp forehead with the handkerchief Juana had given her before she'd boarded the stage yesterday, Amelia squinted up at the broiling sun overhead. Not even noon yet, and already her dress, chemise, petticoats, and corset felt like a cambric-and-calico prison. She sighed and stepped into the shade of a restaurant's overhanging *ramada* to catch her breath, plunking down her satchels on the ground beside her.

There were no raised board sidewalks here. Mud and manure abounded, making careful attention to where she stepped a necessity. But there were plenty of book buyers in Tucson, and Amelia had visited nearly everyone in her J. G. O'Malley & Sons order book, making deliveries and taking new orders wherever she could.

She opened it, thumbing past the pages of new orders she'd taken from the soldiers at Fort Lowell, where, upon James's suggestion, she'd stopped before continuing into Tucson. Evidently Jacob had bypassed the fort during his last order-gathering trip into the Territory, and Amelia had found an eager audience for her wares.

The officers and enlisted men—and their wives—had pored over her J. G. O'Malley & Sons catalogue and had listened to her sales talk long into the afternoon, placing order after order to fill her book. Seated beneath the shady cottonwood trees of

Fort Lowell's "officer's row," she'd penciled in orders until her hand cramped.

She'd been successful. Fulfilled her plan to return home with enough book orders to dazzle her father and brothers. With such evident success to her credit, surely they'd be forced to admit Amelia could help with J. G. O'Malley & Sons, too. She'd proven herself a good book agent and a reliable helper, just as she'd set out to do.

Then why did the accomplishment leave her feeling so empty?

Tightening her lips, Amelia hummed a low-keyed hymn, pocketed her handkerchief, and tried to think of something else. She looked around her for distraction's sake, seeing the flat-roofed adobe shops silhouetted against the hot blue sky, the people and wagons streaming by . . . and cared nothing for any of it.

All she cared for was Mason. Thoughts of him were never far from her, however she tried to push them away. With him, she'd found something far greater than a log filled with orders and the book agent's position she'd coveted. She'd found caring. Appreciation.

Love.

Amelia saw again the respect on Mason's face when she'd gotten them released from their cell in Maricopa Wells, when she'd driven them away and made good their escape, and she knew that no one else had ever seen in her the good things Mason did.

Or had, before he'd left her.

A fresh prickle of tears blurred the page in her hands. Blinking rapidly to force them back, Amelia flipped past the last of the soldiers' orders and scanned the order book for the location of her next delivery. Better to go forward. Better to get on with what she could salvage, rather than look back at all she'd lost.

Drawing a deep breath, Amelia scanned the street, then

picked up both her satchels and trudged on. Eventually she'd be able to feel happy again. Truly, it couldn't be possible to die of a broken heart like the poets said—no matter how hers hurt now.

Perhaps Juana was right. Perhaps she should try to find Mason, try to find out why he hadn't returned for her and set it right again. But if he could elude a posse and the Tucson lawmen alike, surely he could remain hidden from her, too. Tucson was a big place, the largest city in the Territory. She hadn't the slightest notion how to find him.

Or what she would say to him if she did.

I love you?

That hadn't mattered enough to make him return for her. Humming a little louder, Amelia tried to push the thought away as she continued down the edge of the street. In front of her, a gentleman helped his wife, large with child, down from their carriage. Amelia paused in the cooling shade of a meat market's *ramada* to let them pass, watched the man open the shop door and smile down at his wife before escorting her inside, and her heart sank a little lower at the sight.

It had been one thing to expect never to marry, to believe her father and brothers when they'd told her that her only future was to care for them and the home she'd grown up in. It was something else altogether to taste the future she might have shared with Mason, only to have it snatched away again.

Frowning, Amelia quickened her step, crossing Mesilla Street in a few short strides. If she gave in to many more thoughts like these, she'd be tempted to retreat to the safety and solitude of her room at the Palace Hotel, where she could just lie down and bawl her eyes out with no one seeing. Her next customer was only a little ways ahead. Better to focus on that, else she'd never find the strength to go on.

She reached the street corner and glanced around. The business she was looking for ought to be right here. Setting down her satchels again, Amelia opened her order book and double-checked the address. She looked up at the small, hand-lettered sign on the cramped-looking adobe building closest to her, and sighed.

A saloon. Her next customer operated a saloon.

Well, that needn't stop her, Amelia resolved. It wasn't as though the place was teeming with ruffians about to rush outside and accost her. The establishment appeared a bit run-down, but that in itself wasn't a crime.

Straightening her spine as courageously as she could, Amelia raised her chin and attempted a worldly air. She stepped closer just as the nearby church bells of San Agustin tolled, loud as a sign from the Almighty Himself. Startled, Amelia skittered backward. Heavens above! She couldn't enter a saloon alone, book order or no. Who'd have thought the owner of such an establishment would be interested in literature, anyway?

Cautiously, she shaded her eyes with her hands and peered into the saloon's gloomy interior. George Hand, whoever he was, obviously preferred his establishment's customers to do their imbibing in the dark. She couldn't see a blessed thing.

"Errr . . . hello?" she squeaked, wavering on tiptoe as she tried to catch a glimpse of the book customer she'd come in search of. "Excuse me, but—"

The saloon doors swung, then stilled, propped in place by the man peering over them. His chest-length dark beard, prominent cheekbones, and shadowed eyes put Amelia in mind of Abraham Lincoln, except this man was at least a foot shorter.

"Ma'am?" he asked politely. "George Hand, here. What can I do for you?"

His voice sounded gravelly, but kind. Shuffling her satchels and order book, Amelia noticed a few passersby staring curiously in her direction and felt a blush heat her cheeks. "Oh, I, ah . . ."

"Ma'am"—he lowered his voice conspiratorially—"you ain't lost track of your husband, have you? I don't—"

"Oh, no!" Her blush deepened, feeling as though it fairly blazed toward her throat and chest. Amelia put a hand to her throat, welcoming its coolness. "It's not that at all."

"If it is, you can step inside and ask in private," he went on, his eyes like those of an old basset hound beneath his busy dark brows. "Don't no lady have a thing to fear from George Hand."

He thumped his hand on his chest, letting the saloon doors swing open, then held one open for her.

Amelia glanced backward. "No, thank you. Honestly, I haven't lost my husband."

He pursed his lips, looking skeptical.

"I mean I'm not married."

His eyebrows raised.

"I'm a book agent," she almost shouted, scrabbling for her order book. Tucking it beneath her elbow, Amelia put her hand forward and assumed her best book-agent demeanor. "I'm Miss Amelia O'Malley, representing the J. G. O'Malley and Sons book company, at your service, Mr. Hand. I believe you ordered a volume of poetry from one of our agents some months ago?"

This time it was Mr. Hand's turn to blush.

"Uh, why don't you come inside, ma'am?" he said, stammering a bit as he shook her hand. "There's folks 'round here might find the notion of George Hand reading poems and such mighty amusing. I'd rather not hand out more ammunition for the fire than I got to, if you follow my meaning, ma'am."

Amelia glanced around. "I'm not sure I ought to," she began, noticing yet another pair of ladies pointing in her direction. At this rate, she'd ruin the good name of J. G. O'Malley & Sons. "I've never entered a . . . an establishment such as yours, and I—"

He saw who she was looking at, and nodded toward the two ladies. "Them old biddies wouldn't even see you in here. 'Sides,

I'm about to close up anyway, head out to the big *fiesta* down at Levin's Park this afternoon."

Wavering, Amelia peered over his shoulders toward the saloon's interior. She couldn't see any customers, but that didn't mean the saloon was empty. There might be a man drinking at the bar right now, and she'd never know it from where she stood.

He raised his hand, palm facing. "Word of honor, ma'am. No harm'll come to you in George Hand's place."

Just this one delivery, Amelia promised herself. Then I'll go back to my room and rest for a while.

She imagined the high double bed back at the Palace, a nice wash at the fancy porcelain basin and a good long restorative nap, and made up her mind.

"Very well, Mr. Hand," she said, stepping between the swinging doors into the saloon's cool interior. Everything looked black, dimmed as her eyes adjusted to the lack of sunlight. The place smelled of sour whiskey and, oddly enough, stale lavender perfume.

Amelia turned to her host. "I'm sure you must be eager to have your volume of poetry," she said, "and I—"

"Let's just keep this poetry business 'tween ourselves, ma'am," he interrupted as he hurried in behind her, his forehead wrinkled into a sheepish look. "Or I won't never hear the end of it from my friends."

He darted a glance toward a door set into the saloon's rear wall, then lowered his voice. "I got one boardin' with me right now, won't never let me live down being a po-e-try reader."

Smiling, Amelia set her satchels atop a scarred round tabletop and opened one to withdraw his book. "That's perfectly fine with me," she told him, squinting to see within her satchel. "Although if your friend likes books, perhaps he'd like to see my book catalogue. J. G. O'Malley and Sons has an excellent variety of reading material for all tastes and—"

"Oh, no, ma'am!" Mr. Hand interrupted, looking plainly horrified. "He, ahhh—he don't see many folks these days."

He snapped his mouth closed, his gaze wandering toward the back door again. Amelia could see well enough now to realize there were no other customers in the saloon, and the tightness in her shoulders eased a bit.

"I see," she said, pulling out the slim volume of romantic poems Mr. Hand had ordered. "That's too bad."

"Ain't that right," he muttered, shaking his head. "And that ain't even the half of it, ma'am," he added, his face brightening as he accepted the book. "My friend, he's had a bad turn of luck lately. Wife passed on not too long ago."

"I'm sorry to hear that," Amelia said, watching as Mr. Hand licked his fingertips and began turning pages in the book. If his expression of delight was anything to go by, the rest of her afternoon could be quite profitable, indeed.

"Would you like to view our latest catalogue?" she offered, drawing it from her satchel and extending it toward him. At least talking with Mr. Hand would keep her mind from her other troubles. If only for a little while, it was a respite she needed.

Twenty-three

Damn, it was hot.

Sunlight pushed at his eyelids, making Mason's head throb painfully. Even his scalp felt like a poker growing ever hotter in the fire—especially in the places where Amelia had cut his hair short.

Scowling himself awake at the thought of her, he cracked open his eyes. Whitewashed adobe and tilting blue sky filled his vision; then the stench of fresh manure hit him. Swearing, Mason shut his eyes again. The glimpse he'd had—and the smell—was enough to remind him of every sorry detail of last night.

The alley beside Hand's saloon was a hell of a place to sleep.

Gradually he became aware of the prickly adobe wall at his back biting through his shirt, the sounds of horses plodding and wagons clanking on the streets nearby, and the bells of San Agustin tolling what sounded like a funeral dirge. It clanged through his head, setting his teeth on edge.

Grimacing, Mason opened his eyes and pushed his hands into the rocky soil to lever himself farther upright. In his lap, the whiskey bottle tilted and then rolled sideways, the last reminder he needed of the night he'd just spent. He grabbed it, scowling at the liquor sloshing inside, and something inside him got even madder than before.

He'd come out here last night meaning to forget everything.

Meaning to drain that whiskey until oblivion took him. He'd held the full bottle in his hands and stared it down, daring himself to take the first drink.

Now Mason turned it, raised it to the light, and gazed through it into a world turned amber. Whiskey brought no peace. No peace that lasted anyway. And still he kept it always nearby.

He'd kept a flask in his coat pocket until Maricopa Wells and a bottle in the wagon since then, and had spent a night watching James and Manuel drink while he'd sat by thirsting. Not a drop had passed his lips since they'd taken Ben away. Still Mason kept the whiskey nearby, ready to take the ease it promised and the forgetfulness he tortured himself with.

Not anymore.

Still holding the bottle, he hauled himself to his feet, blinking at the blinding sunlight overhead. What the hell time was it, anyway? He needed to get busy looking for Ben. Looking for the Sharpe brothers. Looking for vengeance.

He'd been too long grieving over losing Amy. It had been his own damned choice to leave her behind, the only choice he'd had. No use crying over it now, Mason told himself, propping the whiskey bottle atop an old beer barrel from Levin's. A woman like Amelia O'Malley didn't belong in the West, especially not in Mexico. She didn't belong with him. As many times as he'd told her they'd go their separate ways once they reached Tucson, she'd never said a contrary word.

A man could only conclude Amelia had wanted to be clear of him, had wanted to get on with her own life.

Stepping back a few paces, Mason drew his Colt and leveled it. He'd only hastened the inevitable with leaving her behind in Picacho Peak. Never mind the pain of losing her, he told himself, squinting toward the whiskey bottle. Never mind loving her.

It was over. He had to move on.

He cocked the hammer. Sunlight glinted off the whiskey bottle, hurting his eyes. Squinting, he sighted it again.

"I win," Mason said, and pulled the trigger.

The red brick, square-faced Palace Hotel was the most welcome sight Amelia had seen all day. Shadows had already begun lengthening across the street when she headed toward it, looking forward to the clean lobby and the temporary haven of her room after a day spent slogging through the muck-filled Tucson streets and talking with one customer after another.

Now the streets were nearly deserted, except for the occasional horse tethered in front of a shop or saloon. The vendors had retreated—for *siestas,* Mr. Hand had informed her—and the ladies had apparently finished their calls and gone home. Stepping beneath the Palace Hotel's porch, Amelia carried her much lighter J. G. O'Malley & Sons satchels easily, now that nearly all of her books had been delivered.

She entered the lobby, breathing deeply of the roast beef-scented air wafting from the hotel's kitchens. The success of her book-agent ventures today was almost more than she'd dared hope for. Capped off with Mr. Hand's generous order, Amelia's order book fairly bulged at the seams with order-filled pages.

"Miss O'Malley!" called a masculine voice from someplace beside her.

She glanced up to see the hotel's fat-jowled, bewhiskered proprietor at the lobby desk, waving an envelope in her direction.

"Oh, Miss O'Malley!" he cried again, leaning across his gleaming polished-wood counter without a care for its condition. "A wire's come for you, delivered only a few minutes ago."

A wire? It could only be from Jacob, Amelia thought, her stomach sinking with dread. No one else knew she'd come West. No one else knew she'd booked a room at the Palace over a week ago, before setting out on her ill-fated stagecoach journey from the railroad's terminus at Gila Bend to deliver her book orders to Tucson. No one except Jacob, who'd instructed her in all those things before his planned elopement with Melissa.

The news couldn't be good. Amelia dragged her feet across the carpet. Fingers trembling, she accepted the telegram from the proprietor.

Thanking him in a voice turned whispery with apprehension, she glanced down at the envelope. The wire was addressed to her, all right. There'd be no escape via that route. Crunching it in her fist, Amelia turned down the hall leading to her room, her heart thumping. Either her scheme to act as a book agent had been discovered, or something even more awful had happened.

Either way, Amelia didn't want to open the wire and find out.

By the time she got inside her room, it seemed less a sanctuary than she'd hoped. She sank onto the ivory coverlet-covered bed, staring sightlessly at the telegram. What reason could Jacob have had to contact her—and why now, when she was due to return to Big Pike Lake in little more than a week?

Her stomach flip-flopped as she ripped open the telegram and slowly unfolded it. Addressed to her from her father—*her father?*—the message was only a few lines long. Barely able to breathe, Amelia scanned the text.

"Have learned all from Jacob," it read. "More gumption than I expected from you."

Sighing, Amelia let the telegram, still in hand, drift to her lap. A small part of her felt pleased at her father's acknowledgment, however backhanded and grudgingly given. The rest of her ached at the knowledge of how little he must have thought her capable of, to have said such a thing.

More gumption than I expected from you.

As an admission of admiration for his daughter's qualities, it lacked much. But as an expression of her father's disappointment, it was wholly typical—and far more familiar than she wished. Fingers trembling, Amelia raised the telegram again.

"Come home immediately," she read further, feeling her heart sink as she imagined her red-faced, infuriated father bellowing those words to the poor telegraph clerk. "I shall have your commissions waiting. Regards, your father, J. G. O'Malley."

Her commissions? Amelia sat up straighter, quickly rereading the message. Yes, that's what it said—her commissions. Stunned into stillness for an instant, she could only stare at the telegram. A forgery? she wondered suddenly, flipping it over to examine it. As quickly as she had, Amelia turned it right side up again. No, not that. The message bore the unmistakable imprint of her father's impatient nature. The message had to be genuine.

I shall have your commissions waiting. Why, that meant he'd . . . that meant he was offering her the commissions from Jacob's sales!

Clutching the telegram, Amelia leapt from the bed feeling as though she might soar through her open hotel-room window at the news. She jigged over to the glass-topped bureau, grinning at her own exuberance, and propped the telegram behind a perfume bottle. Then she skipped back a few paces to admire it.

She'd done it! There, in print, was the proof she'd longed for, the proof that meant her father would allow her to join J. G. O'Malley & Sons officially. The proof that meant he believed she could do the job as well as her brothers did—maybe better! After all, she was the one with *gumption*.

Amelia hugged herself, leaning closer to reread the telegram. Things would be different when she returned home. J. G. O'Malley & Sons employed book agents all over the United States and its territories. She'd have accounts of her own, an income of her own—maybe her father would even turn over Jacob's book accounts in the Arizona Territory to her.

The customers she'd dealt with already had treated her with

nothing but kindness and respect. The Territory itself was beautiful and wild, so unlike everything back home. Amelia could easily imagine herself setting up housekeeping in Tucson or nearby, maybe opening a small bookshop of her own. Skipping back toward the bureau, she rummaged inside for clean clothes, tossing undergarments onto the bed behind her as she located them.

She thought of the shops she'd seen since arriving in Tucson, and decided a book and news depot might do quite nicely. Her father would likely finance the venture, too. She'd persuaded him to appoint her an official book agent, after all. It seemed quite likely, now, that she could persuade him to help her with other things, too. Smiling, Amelia took her nicest pale blue baize gown from its peg in the wardrobe and shook it out. Such grand plans called for a celebration.

Luckily for her, such a celebration was about to begin. With her books almost entirely delivered, and her agent's position and her father's respect assured, Amelia was in exactly the mood to join in it.

Grabbing the flowered-porcelain pitcher atop the bureau, she filled the matching basin with water, dipped a cloth inside, and began scrubbing her face and neck clean. That done, Amelia stripped off her wrinkled, muddy-hemmed dress and, humming, scrutinized her appearance in the mirror. Exactly what, she wondered, was the appropriate hair style for a *fiesta?*

Mason sat on a rock in the shade of a gnarled old mesquite tree at Levin's Park, a mug of tepid water in his hands, and cursed whoever had decided to host a *fiesta* right in the middle of his search for Ben and the Sharpes. From the looks of it, the whole town had turned out for music, dancing, beer, and whiskey—including the sheriff and his posse. He'd already spotted several of them wending through the crowds, weapons holstered but at the ready.

Hell.

If he were smart, he'd leave. Take his chances with finding his son tomorrow, or the next day. Eventually he'd find him. He didn't intend to quit until he did. But without knowing exactly when the Sharpe brothers planned to leave Tucson and take Ben back East with them, Mason didn't dare wait. He'd lay odds they were at the *fiesta,* right along with the rest of the town, and he meant to find them.

Beside him, George Hand swallowed the last of his third mug of Levin's ale, then swiped the foam from his mustache and squinted at Mason.

"I still dunno why you had ta shoot up my bottle of Old Orchard," he complained, shaking his head. "Perfectly good whiskey"—he mimed aiming a pistol and shooting it—"blam! All shot to hell."

"I paid you for it."

In preparation for his escape to Mexico with Ben, James had brought him all the money Mason had saved from his farmhouse near the Gila—along with the news that Amelia was in Tucson, too. "Ye'll be sorry if ye let that lassie get away," he'd said. "Take her with ye to Mexico."

Damned interfering friends. Frowning, Mason yanked his hat lower to hide his face, then scanned the crowd. He wasn't likely to be spotted here, on the edge of the *plaza*—but he wasn't likely to find Ben or the Sharpes from there, either. He'd have to get on the move again soon.

"That ain't the point," Hand went on, pushing up from the rock with his beer mug held close against his scrawny chest. He staggered sideways, straightened, then pointed his mug at Mason. "That was perfectly good whiskey in that bottle."

"It's over with," Mason said. Over with in more ways than George Hand could ever have guessed at. He stood, too, leaving his water on the rock behind him.

"So's your good relations with Cruz and her gals," Hand

muttered, weaving beside him as they walked past the *cantina* toward the *plaza's* center. Raising his voice to be heard above the guitars playing a Spanish melody, he said, "You had to go an' bust up her place, didn't ya?"

Mason frowned. "It's not busted up, I—"

"Ya just scared away half her customers," Hand interrupted, "tearing through there like a damned berserker after them Sharpes is all." Grinning, he elbowed him in the ribs. "I heard some of them ladies was runnin' 'round half-naked, trying to call their fellas back."

"I didn't notice," Mason said. He'd been too busy chasing one of Ellen's no-good, sanctimonious brothers down the hallways in Cruz's house. The coward had ducked out a back window in the end, leaving Mason staring after his retreating backside with an eye toward revenge and a gaggle of perfumed, pissed-off whores clustered around him so tight he could barely breathe.

Hell.

At least he knew the Sharpes were still in Tucson. The hell of it was, after the scene at Cruz's, they knew *he* was on the loose, too. Mason had no doubt they'd alert the posse and redouble their efforts to get Ben out of town. Time was running out.

He and Hand skirted past a noisy cock fight going on amid a circle of yelling, half-drunk men down the alley, and headed toward the center of the *plaza.* There the music was even louder, and the close-packed bodies of dancers and drinkers generated even more heat. The combined smells of sweat, liquor, *tamales,* and chile-roasted pork were nearly overpowering. Overhead, early fireworks sizzled and sparked the sky with brilliant blues and greens and oranges.

Mason kept his head low and his eyes moving, seeking out any sign of the posse or the Sharpes. Townspeople flowed past, none of them paying any mind to either him or Hand. They pushed between dancing couples and shouting children waving confetti-filled *cascarónes*—children who caught his eye, made him pause and look closer.

But none of them had Ben's dark hair, his always-ready smile, his freckled, sun-browned face. None of them was his son.

Mason's gut tightened. He needed to find him. Soon. It would be full dark before long; the only remaining natural light shafted between the buildings from the setting sun, golden-hued and streaked with blood red. Already women bearing lighted oil lamps were making their way along the fringes of the crowd, setting lanterns atop squat adobe walls and hanging them from low tree branches at Levin's Park.

"Maybe I'll jist go an' smooth things over for ya with Cruz and the ladies," Hand offered with a grin. He stumbled over a rock, then righted himself. "G'night, my friend," he slurred, "an' good luck."

Mason nodded him off, watching Hand bob through the crowd. Good luck was exactly what he needed. Either that or a miracle.

Too bad he wasn't damned likely to get either one.

Twenty-four

Smiling and nodding at the townspeople she recognized, many of them J. G. O'Malley & Sons book customers whom she'd already met, Amelia made her way toward the open-air *cantina* at Levin's Park. According to the proprietor at the Palace Hotel, Levin's hosted the finest *fiesta* in the Territory, and she meant to get a feel for the community that might be hers if all went according to her book-agent plans.

Tall cottonwood and mesquite trees bordered Levin's Park, hedged by tidy white picket fences. Branches stirred overhead as Amelia left the close-packed street and stepped into their late-afternoon shade. Smiling, she stroked her fingertips along the rough tree bark, surprised to find so many trees growing so well in a place like Tucson. It was like having a little piece of Big Pike Lake, right there at the end of Pennington Street.

At the *cantina,* customers sat on benches beneath the shade of its *ramada,* balancing plates of spicy Mexican food on their laps and talking while they ate. Chiles, pork, and roasted corn perfumed the air.

Amelia sniffed appreciatively, her stomach rumbling its complaints over the meager lunch she'd had at the hotel kitchen earlier. Nudging past two ladies with parasols and all-white dresses—the prevailing fashion in the Territory, it seemed—Amelia ordered a drink and a plate of *enchiladas,* then stepped back to wait for her food.

Music swelled toward her from the bandstand at the far edge of the *plaza,* mingling with the variously accented voices of passersby. Tapping her toes—clad, at last, in a new pair of balmorals—she gazed out in the direction of the music.

Dancing couples swirled past in time with the fiddles and guitars, kicking up puffs of dust in their wake. Amelia watched the laughing, chattering women and the men holding them closely, and her stomach tightened with envious longing. Would Mason have held her, have danced that way with her, if he were here?

She closed her eyes and imagined Mason's hand clasping hers for the dance, his other hand holding her warm and steady at the waist. Humming with the music. she pictured the two of them sweeping along together, close enough to come together for a kiss, and nearly sighed aloud. Dear heavens, but she missed him. How would she ever be happy again, without Mason?

Several pairs of boots, some with jangling spurs, thumped nearby and came closer. Men, circling her? Amelia opened her eyes, and found herself staring straight at the star badge pinned to the vest front of the man standing in front of her. Sucking in a quick, startled breath, she raised her chin to confirm her suspicions.

The sheriff.

He stood less than an arm's length away from her, a lean-built man with piercing blue eyes and a neatly trimmed beard and mustache. Amelia's knees quivered, blessedly hidden beneath her pale blue baize skirt. She clenched it in both hands, trying to appear more composed than she felt.

Four or five men, uniformly dusty, stone-faced, and heavily armed, stood behind him. The posse. Dizziness swamped her, leaving her dry-mouthed, trembling harder.

The sheriff stepped closer, his gaze fixed straight on her. He must have discovered her association with Mason, Amelia realized. And now he'd come to question her—maybe to haul her off to jail!

"Pardon me, ma'am," he said.

Heart hammering, she fought the urge to run. Running had only served to deepen Mason's troubles in the past.

"Sh-sheriff," she stammered, plastering a frozen smile on her lips.

Run, run! her instincts urged. But the shaking in her knees had spread, and she doubted her legs were strong enough to carry her anyplace.

"Wh-what can I do for you?"

He tipped his hat. "Would you mind stepping this way, ma'am?" he asked, indicating a place just to the left of the *cantina's* kitchens.

Amelia shuffled woodenly sideways, her gazed glued to the sheriff. Would he draw his gun when he took her to jail, or simply order her to go? Should she just tell him she didn't know where Mason was, or wait for him to ask? Feeling light-headed enough to float clean out of her balmorals, she shoved her hands into the folds of her dress to hide their telltale trembling.

An unexpected smile creased the sheriff's leathery face, brightening his eyes as he touched his hat brim again. "Thank you kindly," he said, moving past her toward the *cantina's* counter. "I believe these are my *tamales,* right here."

He slid a tin plate overflowing with spicy-scented food from the counter into his hands, then, still holding it, edged past Amelia. "Never stand between a man and his food, ma'am," he said with a wink. "A lady could get hurt sorely that way."

Relief rushed through her, threatening to buckle Amelia's knees right there in front of the sheriff and everyone. Her answering smile felt ghastly, patently false compared with his jovial one. Giving him a stiff little laugh, she nodded and turned to leave.

Run, run! Everything inside her urged her to flee. Instead

Amelia made herself walk sedately, head held high, past the *cantina's* kitchens to the right as though she were headed toward the *plaza* for dancing.

"*Señora!*" yelled a male voice behind her. "*Señora!*"

Her breath left her. Amelia stopped, hardly daring to turn around. The voice had sounded Spanish-accented, not like the sheriff's gravelly tone, but perhaps one of the posse . . . ?

Her heart hammered, sounding loud in her ears. It made the music from the band in the *plaza* sound muddled, as though they played through cotton-stuffed instruments. Turning slowly, she looked behind her.

At one of the *cantina's* cooks, who held a plate of steaming food and a tin cup toward her.

He held it higher, jerking his head at Amelia. "You want this, or no?" he called, frowning.

As anyone would, she figured, considering how peculiar her behavior must seem. Breathing in a big, fortifying breath, she nodded. Calm down! she ordered herself. If Mason *had* been there, she'd likely have called the sheriff's attention to them both with her nervousness. With trembling fingers, Amelia opened her reticule for the money to pay for her meal.

That task accomplished, juggling the hot tinware and cup, she darted a glance at the sheriff and his men. The waning sunlight fading into the adobe shops and trees bordering the *plaza* made it difficult to see clearly, but she could still make them out, seated at the two outermost *cantina* benches. Some ate from heaped-full plates, and several of them appeared to be speaking intently about something. From such a distance—and with all the revelry of the *fiesta* going on around her—it was impossible to tell what.

Amelia bit her lip, debating the wisdom of edging closer to listen. If she knew what the posse planned, then perhaps she could find Mason and warn him.

Warn him. It was a wonderful plan, to be sure, except for the size of the city and the impossibility of locating a man who chose to remain hidden within it. Mason had been on her mind all day as she'd traveled the length and breadth of Tucson delivering books. She'd thought of trying to locate him time and again, and had been forced to admit defeat before even beginning. How did one go about finding an outlaw, even if she were his ally?

Even if she were the woman who loved him.

No, it was hopeless. And yet . . . Providence had seen fit to hand her the opportunity to find out more about Mason's pursuers. Maybe she'd be equally lucky later and find him before the posse did. Deciding it couldn't hurt to try to learn whatever she could, Amelia held her meal as though searching for a place to sit, and edged closer.

". . . ain't gonna find him nohow," one of the men in the posse was saying.

The music swelled, drowning out the sheriff's response. Concentrating harder, Amelia moved as near as she dared, then stopped beside a gnarled old tree at the edge of the *cantina's ramada*. A rock jutted up from within the tree's meager canopy of leaves, forming a perfect seat for listening to the posse's conversation. Someone had already used it, she saw, judging by the tin cup of water still atop it.

Whoever it was, they'd have to find another seat. Moving slowly, trying her best not to call attention to herself, Amelia sat beside the abandoned water cup and spread her skirts neatly around her. She propped her plate on her lap, her drink on the ground beside her, and assumed what she hoped was a nonchalant expression, then listened.

". . . after what them Easterners said"—it was one of the posse members, his voice muffled by what sounded like a mouthful of food—"I don't reckon he would."

They had to be speaking of Mason! Excitement thrumming through her, Amelia leaned slightly sideways.

". . . neither," came another voice. "But that ain't—" The guitars played louder, drowning out his next few words ". . . chase out there."

A stooped, white-haired woman passed by Amelia's rock, carrying several lighted lanterns hanging from their handles on a thick pole. Stopping a few feet away, she slid one from the pole and hung it from a tree branch instead, illuminating the area beside the *cantina* where the cottonwoods grew closer together. A group of children played amongst them, blinking up at the lantern light like moths drawn to a bright window.

Move on, Amelia pleaded silently to the woman, afraid she would draw the lawmen's attention toward her listening post. Hunching her shoulders, she nibbled at her *enchiladas* without tasting them, waiting for the woman to carry her too-revealing lanterns elsewhere.

One of the children yelled something. Amelia's gaze snapped from her plate to the sheriff. He looked toward the sound, frowned, then resumed his conversation. Craning her neck slightly, she peered toward the children—who now seemed to be playing a game of tag—trying to see them through the sheriff's eyes.

He couldn't see them from his place at the *cantina* bench, she realized; none of the posse could. Her shoulders eased with relief. At least the shouts of the children wouldn't call undue attention to her. Pushing her food around on her plate in an attempt to seem preoccupied, Amelia waited for the lantern woman to move on.

Finally, she did. Feeling slightly more well concealed without a whole string of lighted lanterns gleaming a few feet away, Amelia peeked from beneath her bangs in the lawmen's direction.

". . . find him," came the sheriff's voice. It wavered in and out, at times overwhelmed by the music and at others coming to her more clearly. "Don't want . . . owe it to . . . tonight."

A hoarse shout from within the cottonwood trees at her back overrode his next sentence. The children, still playing. She glanced back to see them circled together, leaning over something in the center of their group. She wished they'd play their game a bit more quietly, however impossible a wish that might be.

Under the guise of setting down her tin plate, Amelia leaned forward on her rock to catch the next statement, made by one of the burliest members of the posse.

"Ain't them no good son of a—"

Another yell from the children drowned out whatever else he said. Amelia frowned and swiveled on her rock, intending to quiet the rowdies with a schoolmarmish frown or a few quick-spoken words. Instead she stared at the group, shocked into stillness.

This was no game at all. The group of perhaps six or seven children she'd seen had clustered around another child—one nearly a head smaller than they were. Now that she heard them aright, the shouts were jeers, obvious from the cruel tones used to deliver them. While she watched, a young boy kicked hard into the center of the circle, and the yelling grew louder.

Amelia glanced quickly at the sheriff. He went on talking, not looking toward the stand of cottonwood trees at all, obviously unaware of what was going on only a little ways away. Then she remembered he couldn't see the group from his place beneath the *ramada,* and looked back toward the children again.

Another boy on the edge of the circle scooped up something from the dirt and held it overhead. A rock, she guessed, peering closer. Seconds later, more children scrabbled in the dirt, looking for rocks of their own. Abandoning her plate and cup, Amelia stood, torn between listening further to the sheriff's plans in the hope of helping Mason somehow, and putting an end to the children's taunting. Surely one of their parents was nearby, surely they or a neighbor would . . .

The first rock flew into the circle's center.

Amelia's temper flared. No more rocks would fly toward that smaller, outnumbered child. Lips pressed tight together, she marched straight toward the taunting group with all the authority she could summon. Their faces grew more distinct as she approached, and she realized none of them could be more than nine or ten years old. Mostly boys, wearing farm clothes and the occasional child-sized *sombrero* that shielded their features from her. So young, and already so cruel?

"You there!" she called. "Stop that at once!"

Oblivious to her, they pushed together as a group, kicking toward the center of the circle. Muffled cries rose from within it, then the awful sound of pounding fists. Her blood racing, Amelia ducked a poorly aimed rock and grabbed the nearest bony-shouldered boy she could reach. She dragged him from the group, creating an opening to wedge herself into.

"Stop it, all of you!" she cried, hauling another child—a pink-ribboned, jeering girl—away from the circle. The girl stumbled backward, wide-eyed at adult intervention, Amelia supposed, and ran toward the *plaza*.

"Stop it!" Coughing from the dust their scuffles had raised, Amelia pried a rock from the hand of the next youngster she saw and shoved herself farther into the circle. Almost as one, the group stepped back as they became aware of her presence. Still yelling insults, two more ran through the cottonwood trees.

Two remained, both boys. One stood almost as tall as Amelia, albeit stockier and meaner looking. Recognizing him as the first rock thrower, she grabbed his shoulder just as the smaller boy landed a punch in his belly.

She caught only air. The boy struck doubled over, yelling, between gasps, a stream of profanities such as she'd never expected to hear from a youth.

Furious, she grabbed his ear and pulled as hard as she could. The tactic worked as well for her as it always had for Miss

Fitzsimmons back at Briarwood. The boy yelped and immediately straightened, his lips compressed with pain.

"You ought to be ashamed of yourself!" Amelia scolded, feeling for all the world like pushing the ruffian into the dirt where he belonged. Picking on younger, smaller children, indeed!

"Where are your parents? I've half a mind to turn you over to the sheriff. Perhaps you didn't realize he's right over there," she threatened, nodding in the direction of the *cantina*.

With the instigator in hand, Amelia looked past him to see if the younger boy had been badly hurt. At the sight of him, though, whatever else she'd meant to say dropped straight from her mind.

The poor child stood panting, staring at the dirt, one leg bent as though he favored it. Was that where they'd kicked him? Fresh anger surged through her. The boy was surely hurt, and quite likely scared as well. He kept his head down, swiping blood from his lip with his torn sleeve. Would he allow her to help him?

The youth she held used the moment's distraction to wrench himself free from Amelia's grasp. He made a horrible sound in his throat, like a person choking, then spat heavily, straight toward the hurt boy. Turning, with one last bold look at Amelia, he ran from the cottonwood trees, his parting words echoing behind him.

"At least my pa ain't no murderer!"

"Neither is mine!" shouted the younger boy, coming up from wiping his lip with his fists doubled, angling his whole small body into a fighter's stance. "I'll kill anybody who says he is!"

Left alone with the boy, Amelia held her breath, careful to remain motionless. She felt almost afraid to approach him, lest she scare him away. Ignoring her, the child stared at the older boy's retreating back. Only his profile was visible to her, but determination and defensiveness fairly vibrated in the air around him.

His dark hair stood on end, ruffled during the fight. His face was blackened with dirt all along the side facing her, as though someone had rubbed his cheek into the ground. From a rip in his pants his bony knee showed through, making him seem fragile somehow despite the angry stance he showed to the world. He couldn't have been more than seven or eight years old.

"Let me help you," Amelia whispered, carefully stepping closer. "It looks as though you've been hurt, and I—"

He jumped back a pace, everything about him screaming wariness. His eyes met hers, dark in the light of the lamp swinging from the tree branch, and within them she glimpsed fear.

"I won't hurt you," she said, holding out her hand to touch him. The way he stood, so proud but alone, made her heart want to shatter. Ducking his head, he brushed his fingertips over his eyelids, smearing a streak of dampened dirt over his brow.

He was crying, Amelia realized. "Please, I—"

The boy raised his head and met her gaze full-on, despite the tear smudges on his freckled cheeks. His hair, his eyes, his demeanor . . . something about them was powerfully familiar. Almost as though she'd seen the boy before, although she knew she hadn't, and . . . and then she knew.

Amelia gasped, her fingers trembling just inches from his slender, straight-held shoulders. She wanted to weep at the sight of that small, lost face. The face so like his father's. So like Mason's.

"B-Ben?" she whispered. "Ben, is that really you?"

Twenty-five

Mason wove through the *fiesta* crowd, careful to avoid the hanging lanterns that might reveal his presence to the sheriff or one of the men in his posse. With George Hand long gone to Cruz's house, none of the Sharpes in sight, and night falling quickly, his chances of finding Ben looked bleak. His last hope was the group of children he'd glimpsed playing beneath the cottonwood trees near the *cantina.* Maybe Ben was with them.

Leaving the *plaza,* he approached the *cantina's ramada*—and saw the sheriff sitting at a bench beneath it. Mason swore beneath his breath and ducked behind one of the *ramada's* support poles, then headed around the kitchens instead. Rounding the back corner, he nearly slammed into two boys running full-out from the cottonwood grove.

"Whoa, boys," he said, holding out both hands to stop them. His palms touched their shoulders, and both boys looked up . . . and up . . . until their gazes reached Mason's face. "Watch where you're going, there."

Their eyes bulged wide. "Ahhh!" Screaming, they scrambled from beneath his hands. Feet pounding hard, they ran past him down the alley as though the devil himself were chasing them.

Frowning, Mason watched until they disappeared into the *fiesta* crowd. If those boys were any indication, the children's games he'd seen were already finished. Even if Ben had been among them, he'd likely be gone, too, by now.

Instead of checking within the cottonwood grove, maybe he ought to go search the crowd in the *plaza* one more time, before it got any darker. Turning, Mason headed back down the alley.

Footsteps pounded up behind him. Another child ran past, this time a girl with long, pink ribbon-bound pigtails streaming out behind her. Her dress billowed, kicked up by her long strides toward the *plaza*. She vanished into the crowd, just as the two boys had.

Mason's steps slowed. What the hell had made them run like that? He stopped and looked over his shoulder. Nothing but empty, deep-shadowed alley and the surrounding adobe buildings met his gaze.

Curious now, he turned and headed back around the corner of the *cantina's* kitchen. Maybe fifty yards away, the cottonwood trees rose into the sky, backlit by intermittent fireworks. At least two people still stood within the trees, but Mason was too far away to make out their features. The smaller of the two was almost certainly a child. The other looked tall enough to be an adult. The same person who'd set those first children running like their feet were on fire?

Hand on his gun belt, he moved closer, keeping to the *cantina's* back wall to remain hidden as well as he could. Their voices, too low to make out the words, reached him as he stepped away from the wall. Snaking into the deeper shadows beneath an overgrown mesquite, Mason climbed over the picket fence separating Levin's Park from the rest of the town. He hunkered down to listen, squinting into the darkness toward the pair ahead.

Muffled words came toward him, borne on a warm breeze between the cottonwoods. The sound mingled with the farther-off music in the *plaza,* making it nearly impossible to hear clearly. Mason shifted impatiently, edging closer. The child was a boy, he saw, a boy with dark hair. He kept his face turned away, talking intently with his companion.

He reminded Mason of Ben.

But so had many others. He couldn't just charge out into the grove without knowing for sure. All the same, his fingers flexed on the butt of his Colt with excitement. His pulse sped up, his heartbeat roaring in his ears. Mason looked toward the person talking with the boy—a woman, he saw as he neared the tree they stood beneath—and his breath stopped.

Amy.

She crouched on one knee before the boy, her skirts spread on the dirt all around her. Her hair was upswept into the same fussy, fancy curled style she'd worn when he'd first rescued her from beside the road. In the light shining over her and the boy from the lantern a few feet away, she looked like an angel. A spanking-new, stylish one without a care in the world beyond hair ribbons and dresses.

She looked, Mason realized, exactly as though she'd never met him. Never spent days on the run. Never come close to drowning herself in an *arroyo,* never busted them both out of jail, never thrown herself into his outlaw's arms.

Never loved him.

His heart ached at the sight of her. He yearned to go to her, to touch her and assure himself she was really there. To soak up the love she'd given so freely, the love Mason knew now he'd needed all along. To explain why he'd left her behind.

Yet something held him back. He gritted his teeth, fighting the urge to race into the cottonwoods and take her in his arms, knowing it wasn't right.

Knowing it would only make her unhappy in the end. Unhappy like Ellen. Unhappy in Mexico with him and Ben.

Digging his heels into the soft soil beneath him, Mason watched a moment longer. Amy had made it to Tucson, then. If her fancy dress and geegaws were anything to go by, she'd retrieved her book satchels and her money, and was getting along just fine.

Without him.

He couldn't go to her. Wouldn't. But the pain inside him only sharpened, honed by the sight of Amy and the knowledge that his love for her had only gathered strength while they'd been apart. He'd been a fool to believe anything else. And however torturous it was to have Amy so near and yet so far out of reach, Mason knew he'd stay and watch her as long as he could.

He couldn't turn away. She would never know, would never be hurt. And he . . . he would be hurting forever, with only the memories of her to warm him.

Amy's hands touched the boy's shoulders. Gently, she smoothed back a lock of hair from his forehead. Even considering the several inches of space remaining between them, the gesture put Mason in mind of a hug.

The boy sniffled, then nodded, his profile nearly turned toward Mason. His relaxed posture, the easy set of his sharp, small-boy's shoulders, all conveyed his comfort in Amy's presence. But what child, here in Tucson, could Amelia know intimately enough to hold that way?

Only one.

Ben.

Mason's feet were moving even before he'd fully decided to act. His boots crunched over tangled branches and fallen dried mesquite pods. He ran full-out toward his son.

He could almost believe he'd imagined him. Believe that he'd conjured him up somehow, just from wanting to find him for so long. Yet there he was, all elbows and knees and messy hair and solemn little face, just as Mason remembered him. *Ben.*

Amy spotted him before his son did. She looked up over Ben's shoulder, and her face went white with shock. Whispering something to the boy, she nodded and then stepped back.

Mason had no time for anything more. For in the next instant, Ben turned at Amy's direction, and saw him.

His face lit up like it did on Christmas morning—maybe

bigger. "Pa! Pa!" he yelled, running with his skinny arms outstretched.

Mason glimpsed his son's huge grin as it broadened his freckled cheeks, saw that his clothes were wrecked and unfamiliar.
And then sixty pounds of wriggling boy slammed into his middle, and Ben's arms came around his waist, and he couldn't see
anything at all for the tears that blurred his vision. He squeezed
his son, and nothing in the world had ever felt so good as holding him again.

Burying his face in Ben's dark mussed hair, Mason tightened
his hold on him, breathing deeply of castile soap and dirt and
hay, and all the mixed-up scents that always surrounded his
into-everything boy. He kissed the top of Ben's head, almost
afraid to let him go and risk losing him again.

"Pa!" Ben cried, the sound half-buried in Mason's shirtfront.
"Pa!"

Right then, Mason decided that was the sweetest sound he'd
ever heard. Grinning like a fool, heedless of the tears on his
cheeks, he hugged Ben tighter and pressed his lips to his boy's
hair. His heart swelled with love, with gratitude . . . with relief
at having found him at last.

Before long, Ben started squirming to be free. He sucked in
the huge breath that always foretold a barrage of questions and
stories and comments, and Mason let him go so he could listen.

"What took you so long?" Ben asked, sounding breathless.
His gaze, quick and eager and filled with sudden happiness,
met his father's. "I knew you'd come after me. I told everybody
so. Everybody."

Mason put his hands on the sides of Ben's head, tilting the
boy's face upward to the meager lantern light. More tears tightened his throat and made his words feel choked when they came.

"You did, eh?" he asked, hoping Ben wouldn't hear the qua-
ver in his voice.

He *had* believed his father would come for him. The realization shook Mason to his soul, lightened his spirits, made him doubly determined to create a good life for them in Mexico.

"Uh-huh. Uh-huh," Ben said, nodding vigorously. "I even told Uncle Nathan and . . ." He went on, the words pouring over themselves, and Mason listened as Ben explained how he'd told his uncles his pa would be coming for him, and they'd better watch out when he did.

He'd been hurt, Mason realized. His lip was swollen, smudged with dried blood at the corner. His face was covered with filth on one side, although it looked as though someone had, recently, at least attempted to clean some of it away. His clothes looked like he'd wallowed around in that same mud, and he kept one leg bent at the knee as though afraid to put his whole weight on it. Darkness slanted over Mason. Whoever had hurt him would pay.

"And then she said she was your friend," Ben was saying, his voice cracking with his urgency to get everything out, and Mason realized his son was speaking of Amy. Shoving back his anger over Ben's injuries, he looked for Amy and found her standing a few feet away.

"And so," Ben went on, "I reckoned it was all right to talk to her. You're not mad, are you, Pa?"

"No, son," Mason said slowly. "I'm not mad."

"Good." Satisfied with that, Ben nudged closer against Mason's middle. His head pressed into his belly, and his skinny arms came around to hold tight to his father.

"I'm tired of visiting," the boy said, his voice muffled. "All my uncles are *old.* I want to go home. Can we go home tonight? Where's old Candy?"

Rearing back, Ben looked past the cottonwood grove toward the street, as though fully expecting to find the old nag he spoke of—his favorite mount—saddled and ready for them.

"Our horse is at home," Mason said, stroking Ben's hair from his forehead until he leaned against him again.

Lord, but he hated this. Hated the mean-spirited accusations that had sent him on the run and made taking his son back home impossible.

"I borrowed another one from James and Juana," he said. "Do you remember them?"

Ben nodded, his hair rubbing soft on Mason's shirt.

"I borrowed a fine horse from them—"

"Not as fine as Candy."

"Not that fine," Mason agreed, "but a good one, and it's saddled up around back at my friend George's place. Just waiting for us."

Waiting for them to ride clear out of town, away from everything familiar Ben had ever known. His throat aching, Mason breathed deeply and hugged his son's shoulders.

"Can we go get it, Pa?" Ben asked, stepping back with his hand still clasping Mason's shirt. His eyes shone in the moonlight. "I don't want to wait for Uncle Nathan and the rest of them. They can just go back to the States without me. It's all right. I don't think they'll mind a bit. And I—"

He paused for breath, and Mason spoke instead. Always Ben talked so quickly, the words practically blurred together.

"We're not waiting for your uncles," he said.

"Good. All they ever wanted to talk about was Mama, and how sad it was she ended up *here*, like this was some horrible kind of place, and I—"

"We're going to visit somebody else," Mason interrupted gently. "Some family of Juana and Manuel. They say we can stay with them for a while, just until—"

"In Mexico?" Ben's eyes brightened. "We're going all the way to Mexico, Pa?"

Mason nodded. Later he'd tell him more, tell him Mexico was no grand adventure, but their new life. Maybe by then, Ben would welcome the news. For now, he couldn't bear the thought of disappointing him with the truth.

"All the way to Mexico," Mason said. "But first"—he glanced toward Amelia—"I have to thank Miss O'Malley for helping you."

Ben's face reddened. Looking shamefaced, he stared toward the ground, digging up puffs of dirt with his toe. "I forgot," he mumbled.

Mason leaned down, waited until Ben glanced up at him— and then winked. "I'll take care of it," he whispered.

Amy remained where he'd first seen her, only a few feet away. She kept her back to them, probably trying to allow them whatever privacy she could. Her shoulders slumped and her head stayed down, exposing the fragile-looking nape of her neck beneath all that fussy hair. Something about the way she held herself told Mason she was weeping, and the pain in his gut redoubled.

He'd hurt her already, with leaving her, he realized. And he'd have hurt her still more if he'd stayed. There was no way around it, no way through it. As far as Mason could tell, their being together could only cause Amy more pain.

"You should've seen her, Pa," Ben said, looking toward Amy too. "She scared the daylights out of those bullies that were picking on me. Sent 'em clean out of here, yelling like they'd been whupped." He grinned, plainly delighted. "She was meaner than a *schoolmarm*. And all 'cause of me."

Mason thought of the screaming children running past him down the alley, and stared at Amy. *"Miss O'Malley* did that?"

"Only I held my own," Ben interrupted quickly. "It wasn't like I needed to be rescued by a *girl,* or anything," he assured his father, his stance reflecting perfect six-year-old swagger.

Ruffling his hair, Mason smiled down at him. "I know, son. You're mean as a wildcat with a stepped-on tail."

The boy puffed out his chest. "Did you hear that, Miss O'Malley?" he called. "I'm mean as a wildcat!"

"I've never met a braver boy," Amy said, turning to face them.

Tears shimmered in her eyes, but her voice sounded nearly carefree—except to Mason. He heard the sorrow hidden behind her encouragement for Ben, and knew that he was mostly to blame for it.

Regret knifed through him. Love and need made him walk toward her, with Ben trailing at his heels. The boy kept his fingers clenched on his father's shirtsleeve as though afraid to release him, and Mason's heart twisted further. How could he have found what he wanted, only to still need so much more?

He stopped beside Amy and gently nudged her chin upward with his knuckles. "I never figured you for a meaner-than-a-schoolmarm bully chaser," Mason said, looking down at her.

Her lips quivered on a smile, but at the same time, a tear slid a curved path down her cheek. Amy blinked as his hand slid higher to sweep it away, blinked harder as he caressed her cheek. Her smooth, soft skin felt like heaven beneath his fingertips.

"I-I didn't know it was Ben, until . . . until—"

Her voice cracked, then stopped. She swallowed hard, ducking her head. Tears fell harder, dampening Mason's wrist.

"I'm sorry," she mumbled, wrenching from his grasp. "I thought I could—"

"Amy—" Pain seared through him, ripping away whatever else he'd thought to say. God, he needed her like nothing he'd ever known, needed her love and her smile to light his mornings and her body beside him at night. Needed *her*. At that moment he'd have taken her to Mexico or anyplace else, just as long as they could be together, but the impossibility of it all stilled his tongue.

"Pa, you're making her cry."

Ben's voice sounded affronted. Releasing Mason's shirtsleeve with a massive frown, he went to stand beside Amy. He patted her upper arm, clearly mimicking her earlier care of him, Mason felt sure. He glared at his father.

"Amy . . ." Mason swept his thumb across her cheekbone,

encouraging her to look up at him. She did, her eyes wondrous and blue and filled with a love he knew echoed his own.

"Amy, I'm sorry. I never meant to hurt you."

He felt like he'd never breathe again, never know the forgiveness he sought. Never deserve it. Still he searched for the words to explain. "Oh, God, I'm sorry, and I—"

Her fingers covered his mouth, tender against his lips. "Don't, Mason. You can't help—can't help—"

A sob stole the rest of her words, and Amy looked past him as though trying to summon the will to go on. He felt her body quiver beside him, and everything within Mason told him to hold her, to ease her . . . to love her. He moved to pull her into his arms—and she stepped back.

"Let's just say goodbye," she whispered. "You need to get Ben safely to Mexico like you said, and I . . . I—"

Her face crumpled, and her hands fisted at her sides. Amy rubbed her eyes with the heel of her hand, her fingers trembling, then blinked up at him.

"You need to get away," she said, her composure returning. Her posture stiffened, even though her chin still wobbled with holding in a sob. "And I won't be the one to stop you."

"Amy—"

"Go," she croaked, "before it's too late."

Too late. It was already too late. Too far past a time when they might have been together.

Blindly Mason grabbed her, hauling her into his arms even as he cursed the fate that had made him an outlaw. Because of it he was a wanted man. Because of it, he'd become the worst possible man for a woman like Amy to love.

And the only man forced to return her love in silence. How could he begin to tell her what was in his heart, when it could only hurt her more?

He couldn't.

Mason held her closer, and Amy leaned against him, at least for the moment.

"I never wanted this," he murmured against her hair, and anguish tore through each bitter word. "Never wanted to hurt you. That's what it would be if I—"

"No!"

She shook her head, her denial vigorous. Instantaneous. And, Mason was sure, ill considered.

"That's what it would be," he went on, overriding her, "if I forced you into a life on the run. I'm an outlaw, Amy. I—"

"But we can fix that, Mason!" She raised her head, gazed up at him with hope bigger than the moon in her eyes. "I can help. I've thought of little else for days. If we—"

"No."

Her lips pressed together, plainly holding in a sharp reply. She stared past him, looking over his shoulder as he went on.

"Life with an outlaw is no life for you," Mason said, raising his hand to her cheek. He caressed her, trying to urge her to meet his eyes. At least then she might know the truth of his regret.

The truth of his love.

"Mexico isn't—"

Her fingers tightened hard on his shoulder. Her eyes widened, her face going even paler than it had when Amy had first seen him behind Ben, and Mason quit talking to look over his shoulder at whatever it was that had her so upset.

At exactly the same time, a group of men stepped beyond the *cantina's ramada* over the picket fence and into Levin's Park.

The sheriff and posse. Only a few yards away—and coming straight for them.

Twenty-six

"They're coming this way!" Amelia cried, digging her fingers into Mason's arm.

Oh, Lord, why this, why now? Hadn't things already been awful enough, with Mason barely able to look at her? Every time he had, he'd seemed as though he wanted nothing more than to run in the opposite direction.

Was he angry at her? Ashamed at having left her behind? Amelia didn't know—and didn't care. Joy had filled her at first sight of him. Even though her thoughts were muddled with the shock of finding Ben, of coming face-to-face with Mason again, the only thing Amelia wanted was to be with him, wherever and however she could.

Except Mason was going to Mexico with Ben. No matter what she said, he wouldn't take her with him. His blunt refusal to even listen to her had cut Amelia to the quick.

Life with an outlaw is no life for you.

How could she argue with that, especially with the posse nearly close enough to hear their conversation?

Beside her, Ben quit patting her arm to stare at the sheriff and his men, now clustered beneath a tall cottonwood at the edge of Levin's Park. His eyes grew big.

"Are they still after you, Pa?" he asked, looking up at his father. "Why don't you just tell them you didn't do anything wrong?"

"I can't, son." Mason faced them again, his expression hard and determined in the moonlight. "Come on."

Catching hold of Amelia with one hand and Ben with the other, he hauled them at a run toward a bushy mesquite tree in the distance.

Fear of his capture made Amelia's strides clumsy. She stumbled over rocks and gullies, and reached the tree panting with exertion. Mason shoved her and Ben into the dried leaves and curly mesquite pods beneath it, then crouched at the edge, watching the posse advance.

"But you always say tell the truth, and you won't get into trouble," Ben insisted in a small, confused voice. "That's what you always say, Pa."

"This is different," Mason whispered.

His whole body strained forward, half-hidden by tree branches, every muscle taut with readiness. Amelia sensed the hard strength in him, the determination that drove him, and knew that no matter what, Mason would not give up until he got Ben to a safer place.

"Now shush," Mason told the boy. "Stay back there, and don't make a sound."

"All right, Pa."

Amelia put her arm around Ben, drawing his little, shivering body close. "Are you scared?" she whispered. "Everything's going to be all right, I'm sure of it."

"I know," he whispered back, big with bravado. "Nobody can beat my Pa. He's the very meanest of the mean wildcats."

"I think so, too," she said, realizing it was excitement that set Ben shivering, not fear. At least that would be one less trouble for Mason to worry over. Spreading her fingers amongst the strong-smelling dirt and leaves beneath the tree for balance, Amelia leaned forward and looked toward the posse.

Their conversation drifted toward her, snatches of it between music from the *plaza* and fireworks popping in the distance.

"You sure she's the one, Sheriff?" asked one. "I ain't missing the *fiesta* just 'cause you want to meet a pretty girl."

Throaty masculine laughter met that remark, echoing among the group. Leaves and twigs broke beneath their slowly advancing footsteps. More conversation followed, then came the sheriff's voice.

"Hell, no," he said, his voice a bit slurred. Intoxicated? she wondered. The *cantina* had served whiskey and other drinks, as well as *enchiladas*. "I ain't sure," he went on. "But if it means we find Kincaid, I'm game to try just about anything by now. I want this damned thing finished."

Amelia gasped. Lightning-fast, Mason's hand covered her mouth. He lowered his head until their eyebrows almost touched.

"Quiet," he whispered.

His warning gaze shifted to Ben, too, and the boy nodded. Then Mason's focus returned to Amelia, and she wanted to tremble at its razor-edged intensity. Dear heaven, she'd never seen him this way. His determination to protect his son—at all costs, she was sure—nearly scared her witless.

"Amy, I need your help," he said.

She nodded mutely, stealing a glance at the sheriff and his men. They'd stopped for the moment, talking about something.

"You take Ben"—his nod toward the boy made it plain he expected his obedience—"and head 'round behind the *cantina*. I'll make sure no one follows you, and catch up with you later."

Ben watched them both, his eyes shining with adoration at his father. He said nothing, but plainly the boy had no worries about Mason's safety.

Amelia, on the other hand, had many. They doubled when Mason drew his pistol from his gun belt and checked its ammunition. Images of him crouched behind that mesquite, desperately holding back the posse with nothing but one gun and luck on his side, filled her mind. Outnumbered so sorely—and in the dark, no less—he'd be hurt or killed for certain. Captured, at the least.

"No! You can't stay here alone," she whispered harshly, covering his hand with her own. Beneath their joined fingers, Amelia felt the cold barrel of his gun, and her fear increased. "Come with us! We can still sneak away, and not be found—all of us."

"No." With one eye on the sheriff and his men, Mason shook his head. "But if they're busy with me, they can't get to Ben. Or you." He moved his hand from beneath hers, readying himself. "I'll meet you at San Agustin church. Do you know it?"

Miserably, Amelia thought back on her travels through Tucson and remembered the church bells tolling, remembered passing by San Agustin's elegant, white-stuccoed face as she'd walked toward the newspaper office to deliver a book order. "I know it. But I still think—"

"It's the only way." Lowering his weapon, Mason faced her. He spoke rapidly, intently, his gaze focused on Amelia as though to make sure she understood. "If I'm not there before sunrise, take Ben to James and Juana. They'll know why."

"Pa!" Ben's small voice whispered through the dark. "I don't want to go to Picacho Peak. I want to go to Mexico with you!"

Mason swallowed hard. Putting one hand to Ben's shoulder, he squeezed gently and said, "You will, son. Now go with Miss O'Malley. Do whatever she tells you and be a good boy, understand?"

Ben hung his head, seeming reluctant, but not afraid. "Yes, Pa," he muttered.

With one final squeeze and a kiss on his head, Mason released him. The boy scooted back within the mesquite's sheltering branches to wait, quick as a mouse and at least as silent.

Somewhere nearby, a bottle smashed. Breaking twigs and voices coming nearer foretold the posse's continued approach.

Amelia realized she'd been holding her breath, and released

it with a whoosh. Her heart hammered so loudly it seemed she could hear nothing else. "Mason, I don't think—"

"Will you do it, or not?" he whispered harshly. His eyes, darker than the night, bored into hers. Amelia wanted to help him, wanted to make sure he and Ben got away safely, but was this truly the only way?

She could think of no others.

She nodded, and was rewarded by the flash of gratitude that lit Mason's face. "Thank you," he said.

Tears gathered in her throat. The knowledge that she might never see him again made her soul ache. Amelia looked at him. "Be careful," she whispered. "Ben needs you, and . . . and so do I."

His gaze softened. Despite everything, Mason looked—for the moment—happier than she'd ever known him. "Amy, I—"

"Wellll," came a slurred, unfamiliar voice behind them. "Now ain't this touching?"

Amelia jerked her head up, gripped with shock. A gray-haired man garbed in a sloppy suit towered behind Mason's crouched form. He smirked down at them.

"Uncle Nathan!" gasped Ben.

Nathan. *Uncle* Nathan—one of the Sharpes who'd taken Ben away. Almost without thinking, Amelia moved to shelter the boy.

"So there you are, you little prick," the man said meanly.

He narrowed his eyes to peer beneath the mesquite, and Amelia knew whatever protection she could offer Ben would never be enough against a man so filled with hate. Despair ripped through her. The sheriff and his posse on one side, this cruel Sharpe brother on the other—what more could possibly go wrong?

"I knew I'd find you sooner or later," the man went on, sneering. "And right here with your no-good liar of a father, too."

His gaze shifted to Mason. His body tottered right along with it, forcing him to sidestep drunkenly to regain his balance. Whiskey fumes poured from him, as though he'd bathed in the stuff sometime in the past. No wonder Ben had been able to get away—his uncle had probably been too drunk on *fiesta* liquor to notice his absence at first.

The Sharpe brother shuffled from foot to foot. "Came out here for a piss, and look what I see," he said, eyes narrowed. "The man every bounty hunter in town is hot to find."

He smiled. "I been looking all over for you, Kincaid."

"Congratulations, you bastard," Mason said through gritted teeth. "You saved me the trouble of hunting you down myself."

He leveled his gun and took aim. *"Get away from my son."*

Amelia's body quaked, shivering with fear. Sharp mesquite branches dug into her back, scratched her arms as she pushed Ben farther behind her. Dear Lord, would Mason shoot the man right here, in front of everyone?

Then he truly would be an outlaw, separated from the son who needed him forever.

"Mason, no!" she whispered harshly. "He—he's not worth it! He—"

"Quiet," Mason snarled, not looking at her.

His hand holding the gun looked rock-steady. He kept the weapon leveled straight at the Sharpe brother's heart. Glancing over his shoulder, Mason looked toward the advancing posse, then back at the man beneath his gun. In a terrible instant, Amelia knew what he planned. Her whole body went cold.

"Take Ben and go," he gritted out. "Remember what I said."

The Sharpe brother sniffed down at them. "Really, Kincaid. You won't shoot me right here, in cold blood. Not in front of your boy."

"No!" Amelia cried again. Mason's face looked a mask of determination, of vengeance impatient to be satisfied. It left no doubt he'd do what he said. He straightened slowly to his full height, his gun never wavering from its target.

"That's why he's leaving," Mason said quietly. "Go," he told Amelia.

Trembling, she gathered Ben's hand in her own. "Please don't," she whispered, making ready to run. "Think of Ben. Think of Ellen," Amelia said urgently. "Don't make them right about you, Mason."

"Go!" he said, cocking his weapon. He jerked his head toward the *cantina*. "Go."

Nathan Sharpe raised his hand. "Oh, Sheriff!" he yelled, waving furiously. "Sheriff, over here!"

Dumbstruck, Amelia stared toward the posse. So did everyone else. She saw the sheriff's face swing toward them, immediately alert. His hand snapped to his gun belt.

She had to act now. In an instant, a way to do so struck her.

"Mason!" she yelled. He turned, startled, Amelia thought, since she was no longer whispering. With the moment's surprise it gained her, she thrust Ben's hand into his father's. "Take Ben and be safe," she urged.

Before he could react, Amelia gathered all her strength and threw herself shrieking toward the Sharpe brother. He staggered beneath her weight, then toppled in a whiskey-soured heap to the ground. She grunted, the breath knocked from her with the impact.

Beneath her, Nathan Sharpe lay momentarily still. Dazed, she guessed, if the look on his face was anything to go by. So was she. Amelia looked for Mason and Ben, and saw only stars.

Finally she spotted them, hand in hand just behind her at the edge of the lantern light. Mason's expression spun through a kaleidoscope of emotions—first astonishment, then understanding, then wretched indecision. He shifted his weight forward and back, frowning toward her.

"Go," she hissed. "Ben's safer with you."

He lowered his weapon, holstered it. And then she had no more time to look. The Sharpe brother flailed beneath her, rolling to get free. Shrieking for all she was worth, Amelia let him roll her into the dirt. She beat her fists against his bony chest.

"Help! Help!"

"Shut up, you bitch!" he ground out, gasping. She lurched atop him instead.

"Get off me!"

He shoved her aside, sending her scraping amongst the fallen leaves on her backside. Determined, Amelia launched herself toward him again, still screaming for help. His elbow gouged into her stomach. Panting, Amelia whacked his arm away.

"Help! Help, he's attacking me!"

Choking dust puffed up around them. Amelia coughed and yelled louder. Thank heaven for drunken, clumsy men. Thank heaven for the darkness that would muddle their struggle—and send the sounds of it that much more clearly toward the sheriff and his men.

Blessing her good fortune, she dropped backside-first onto the Sharpe brother's chest, kicking her feet into the air like her brothers always did when they wrestled with each other back home. Then she dug her balmorals into the dirt and bounced again, teetering madly.

Thank heaven for brothers.

"Ooof!" He reared up, suddenly strong with fury and liquor, and sent her flying into the dirt. Swearing, he tackled her. His body weight crushed away her breath. Amelia kicked wildly, the edges of her vision growing dark.

Where was the sheriff? Surely he hadn't been that far away. Groaning with the effort, she twisted her neck to look toward the *cantina*.

And saw Mason and Ben melt into the shadows behind it. *Safe.*

"Ma'am? Ma'am!" Masculine voices and lantern light surrounded her. The weight of Nathan Sharpe vanished as one of the posse hauled him from atop her. More dust rose around

Amelia, stirred up by the sheriff and his men. Coughing, she lowered her cheek to the ground, trying to catch her breath.

She just wanted to rest. Ignoring for the moment the Sharpe brother's slurred protests and the lawmen's gentle inquiries about her safety, Amelia found herself staring toward the *cantina*. She scanned the empty alleyway behind it, and smiled.

They were safe.

She'd managed to rescue Mason after all, just as she'd promised.

Rescued him straight out of my life, Amelia thought. Crushing sadness replaced her relief at their safety. And then the world went black.

Twenty-seven

One week later
Hermosillo, Mexico

The house looked larger than Amelia had expected, especially tucked as it was beside a field greening with new crops, a half-mile or so distant from the main Ruiz farmhouse. Made of adobe with two small glass windows and a broad *ramada* sheltering the porch and entryway, it looked comfortable and serene.

Exactly the opposite of the way she felt.

Breathing deeply, Amelia fought the urge to fuss with her hair yet again and smoothed down her skirts, instead.

Her fingers trembled within the pale pink folds of her new gown, chosen with particular care for the occasion. When she'd taken it from the box to show Juana before leaving Picacho Peak, her friend had exclaimed over its fineness, its fashionable cut, and its becoming color. At the time, Amelia had agreed. Now, on the brink of the biggest risk she'd ever dared take, worrying over something like a dress seemed trivial, indeed.

Would Mason be happy to see her? Would he speak to her at all, or would she only anger him by arriving in Mexico unexpectedly? Since the night of the *fiesta,* she'd turned those questions round and round in her mind, seeking some way to make a decision.

Only two things remained constant. The first, that she loved

Mason Kincaid with all her heart, wherever he chose to live. The second, that Amelia would be unable to forgive herself if she didn't at least try, one last time, to be with him.

"Are you scared, *señorita?*"

Manuel Ruiz, seated beside her as he drove the wagon up the lane to the house, tossed out the question with all the nonchalance of someone with nothing to lose. To her surprise, when she'd returned to Picacho Peak after Mason and Ben's escape, Manuel had been the first to offer to help her. Over Juana's good *chalupas* and coffee, he'd told her all he knew about where Mason had gone.

And then he'd offered to take her there.

"A little scared," Amelia admitted, glancing over at him. Ahead, the house drew nearer and nearer in the warm morning sunlight. She wiped her damp palms on her skirt. "He never said he wanted me here, Manuel."

"He would be *loco* not to," he said. "I was wrong about you. Mason will see that he was, too."

Rapping the horses sharply with the reins, Manuel urged them into a trot. Amelia slid and bumped across the seat, trying to catch hold of the edge for balance. Finally she succeeded, and the ride became a little less tooth-jarring.

"I hope you're right," she whispered.

A little ways from the house's front door, Manuel pulled the team to a stop. Dust churned from beneath the horses' hooves as they slowed and then stopped, snorting and tossing their heads. Setting the brake with his foot, Manuel looked at her.

"Do you want me to go in with you?"

What Amelia wanted was to have the deed already done, to have this uncertainty ended. But that was something no one else could give her. Manuel was kind to offer, but this was something she would have to do alone.

"Thank you," she said, "but I think I can do it."

She rose, smoothing her dress with all the meticulous care

her trembling fingers could manage. At least a full minute later, she raised a hand to pat down her hair, too.

Manuel's fingers closed gently on her wrist before she could. "You look *bella,*" he said gruffly. "Beautiful." He nodded toward the house, which remained undisturbed despite their arrival. "Go. If you need me, the main house is only a short walk away."

"All right." Amelia stared toward the porch and *ramada,* trying to imagine herself walking bravely up to that door. Knocking. Seeing her whole life change in an instant.

Impulsively, she leaned over and kissed Manuel's dusty, bristly cheek. "Thank you," she said. "For everything."

What she needed, she decided, was determination. Amelia summoned all she could, breathed deeply, then climbed from the wagon in a flurry of pink and lace. Heart pounding, she straightened and held up her hands for her baggage.

Manuel frowned. "Are you sure, *señorita?"* he asked. "I can always return with your things later."

"No," she replied, trying to smile. "If I'm to do this, I might as well do it fully."

She pulled down the nearest rubber cloth satchel herself, then Manuel handed her the rest of the pieces one by one. A hatbox. Her J. G. O'Malley & Sons satchels. Another hatbox. And several fine leather suitcases she'd borrowed from her brothers for her trip to the West. Before long, a small pile of assorted baggage rested at her feet.

"I hope Mason knows all he is getting," Manuel said with a grin. "You travel with more things than my *burro* does."

Amelia laughed, hefting a suitcase in each hand. "I just hope he still wants all of it," she said. *Especially me.*

Glancing over her shoulder toward the house, her expression sobered. "Thank you, Manuel. I'll come to the main house later and tell you know how everything turns out."

He raised his *sombrero.* "Good luck," he said, and then he

spurred on the horses and was gone in a trail of dust, leaving Amelia standing alone beside her pile of baggage.

Gripping her suitcase handles tightly, Amelia turned toward the house. Dear heaven, let Mason still want me, she prayed. Otherwise, she'd truly gotten herself into a fix this time.

The knock on the door came just as Mason was setting the noon meal on the table for Ben. He carried the plate, still steaming, to the table and set it down beside the glass of milk already there.

The boy wrinkled his nose. "Scrambled eggs again?" he complained. Picking up his fork with a resigned air, Ben poked a curdy bit of yellow egg. Then he squashed it beneath his fork tines.

Mason sensed what was coming next, but was powerless to stop it. For what had to be the millionth time this week, his son propped his head forlornly in his hands and said, "I'll bet Miss O'Malley cooks real fine, Pa. Can't we ask her to visit for a spell? Please? Please—please—please—please—"

The knock had saved him. Mason abandoned his own plate of eggs, swiveling his head toward the sound. He stood. "Those eggs are good for you," he said, speaking sternly as he crossed the big room that housed the kitchen and living area alike. "Eat."

Mason stopped at the door, his hand on the latch. His heart hammered. Even knowing that no one would pursue him and Ben all the way to Mexico, even knowing that no lawman could bring him in from Sonora, he still felt the same way every time an unexpected knock came at the door.

Trapped.

Frowning, he yanked open the door. Air rushed in, someone stepped forward—and rapped him sharply on the nose.

"Oh!" Amelia O'Malley shrieked, retreating a pace. "I meant to knock on the door."

Mason stared, feeling befuddled. Surely he'd gone round the bend. Amy couldn't be there, standing on his doorstep. She was in Tucson—or Big Trout Pond by now, for all he knew. He was in Mexico with Ben. He'd have sworn he was imagining her, except the bridge of his nose still stung.

"Surprise!" she squeaked, rising on tiptoe.

Her cheeks colored dusky pink, bright with what he figured was nervousness. Or insanity. She'd have to be half-loony to have followed him all the way to a country where she couldn't speak the language and didn't know a soul.

Except him and Ben.

Maybe they were both crazy.

"I-I . . ." Her lips trembled, a sign Mason recognized well enough as impending tears. "I hope you aren't mad."

"Mad?" Mason repeated, feeling dazed. She was really, really there. Amy had really come for him. Outlaw or no, she loved him well enough to follow him all the way to Mexico, even believing, as she likely did after all he'd said, that he didn't want her there.

She dropped two suitcases on the porch at her feet. A mountain more lay piled on the path behind her. She looked up at him, and determination showed plain on her face.

Dog-stubborn determination.

Opening the purse swinging from her wrist, Amy withdrew a folded paper and held it toward him. "At least hear me out," she said.

"Hear you out?" Fully aware that he probably sounded a lack-wit, and caring not in the least, Mason looked from the paper to Amy's face.

Lord, she was beautiful. Just as he'd dreamed so many nights over this past week. And now she was here.

"Yes." She frowned, waggling the paper. "Mason, you're a free man. The Sharpe brothers dropped their charges. They went back East the day after the *fiesta*."

He moved nearer and raised his hands to her arms, stroked the smooth warmth of her skin. Mason looked into her eyes, and all he saw there was love. Love for him.

"All that time," Amy went on doggedly, speaking quickly as though afraid he'd stop her, "the sheriff was looking for you to tell you so. They know you're innocent."

She frowned slightly, looking confused. "Aren't you listening? You're a free man." She shook the paper in her hand. "It's all in this letter."

"To hell with the letter."

Mason pulled her close, crushing the paper between them. When he lowered his mouth to hers, it was the sweetest kiss they'd ever shared. Cradling her head in his hands, Mason held the woman he loved, and kissed her as thoroughly as he knew how. Their mouths met, hot and eager and seeking, and with Amy beside him, he knew what it was to finally be loved.

When the kiss ended she leaned back, her body trembling in his arms. Her cheeks reddened even further, and Mason knew this time it was passion, not nervousness, that caused her to blush. Amy's gaze, blue and wary, met his.

"James is watching over your farm at the Gila River," she said hurriedly. "And he's rounded up a bunch of the station hands to—"

Mason kissed her again, quickly.

"—to start the planting there before it's too late. And all the wanted posters are gone, and the sheriff even put an announcement in the newspaper to—"

Mason kissed her again, more slowly this time. Eyes closed, he sought the letter in her hand—and tossed it to the floor.

"You're not listening!" Amy protested, her brows wrinkled with worry. "That's the proof of your freedom. It's important."

"Not as important as this," Mason murmured, bringing his lips down on hers again. Finally her arms came around his neck. Gradually she kissed him back, and by the time he raised his head again, Amy leaned limply against him. Her fingers stroked the nape of his neck, tickling the fine hairs there.

"Does this mean you're not mad?"

He kissed her neck, loving the warm, soft feel of her body pressed against him. So familiar. So needed. So beloved.

"I'm not mad."

"Are you sure?"

"Quit talking." Mason squeezed her close and kissed her again, trying to impart everything he felt for her with that one moment's union. Amy threaded her fingers through the uneven strands of his hair, murmuring, between kisses, something about haircuts.

"You're not listening," he said, cradling her face in his hands. Mason brought his face close to hers, smiling. "I said, quit talking."

She gave him a saucy grin that astonished him. "Or you'll go on kissing me?" she asked. Amy frowned, pretending to consider those consequences. "I don't know, Mason—"

"Or you'll miss it when I tell you I love you," he said. He stroked back her soft curly hair, delighting in the answering love in her eyes, and said it again. "I love you, Amelia."

Her eyes shimmered with tears—this time tears of happiness, Mason hoped.

"That's all I needed to know," Amy whispered. "I love you, too, Mason."

Behind them, a little boy's whoop rang into the air, startling them both.

"Yippee!" Ben yelled. "No more scrambled eggs!"

Mason laughed, and an instant later, Amy joined in. Between the laughter all around him, the woman at his side, and the boy dancing a jig in the kitchen, Mason found all he'd ever dreamed of.

A life like this was guaranteed to please.

And he meant, every moment, to make sure it did.

Dear Reader,

I hope you enjoyed Amelia and Mason's story! Writing it was great fun for me, as was researching all the different aspects of life in territorial Arizona. I love to spend a few hours (or days!) poking around ghost towns and museums, deserts and historical sites, all in search of those fascinating details I hope will make my characters' worlds as real as possible for you.

Amelia and Mason loved deeply enough to bring out the very best in each other. To me, that's the essence of true love. It's something I enjoy writing about more than anything else, and in any format—short contemporary romances like my first two Kensington books *Surrender* and *The Honeymoon Hoax,* time-travel short stories like my novella in the upcoming Zebra anthology *Timeless Spring,* and Western historicals like *Outlaw.* I feel lucky to have the greatest job on earth: creating stories I hope will touch your heart, spark your imagination, and tickle your funny bone, too.

I'd love to hear from you! Please write to me at P.O. Box 7105, Chandler, AZ 85246-7105. Send e-mail to *lplumley@home.com,* or visit me on the internet at *http://members.home.com*

Very best wishes, and happy reading!
Lisa Plumley